...Me

Grace Lowrie

Published by Accent Press Ltd 2017

www.accentpress.co.uk

ISBN 9781786155368
eISBN 9781786155351

Printed and bound in Great Britain by Clays, St Ives Ltd

'None can have a healthy love for flowers unless he loves the wild ones'

Forbes Watson

Acknowledgements

I'd like to say a massive thank you to the team at Accent Press, for taking a chance on an unknown author like me. I am hugely grateful for all the wonderful work you do to get my books out there. If it weren't for you, my stories would just be words locked inside a laptop. Writing can be a lonely process at times, so it is immensely uplifting to have the reassurance, experience and support of Accent Press, and their many successful authors, just a facebook post away.

Special heartfelt thanks go out to my fabulous best friend and fellow author, Alice Raine, for reading and believing in my writing, inspiring me to continue, and regularly making me cry with laughter. I'll never be able to thank you enough.

My sincerest gratitude to my other friends (you know who you are), for not saying I was crazy when I wanted to quit a career in garden design, to write romance. Your willingness to answer random, practical questions – on everything from bicycles and underpants to rugby – is always appreciated. Any errors are my own.

And last, but not least, to my phenomenal family – thank you for always being there, cheering me on, tolerating my reclusive tendencies and giving me a kick up the bum when I need it. I love you more than I can express.

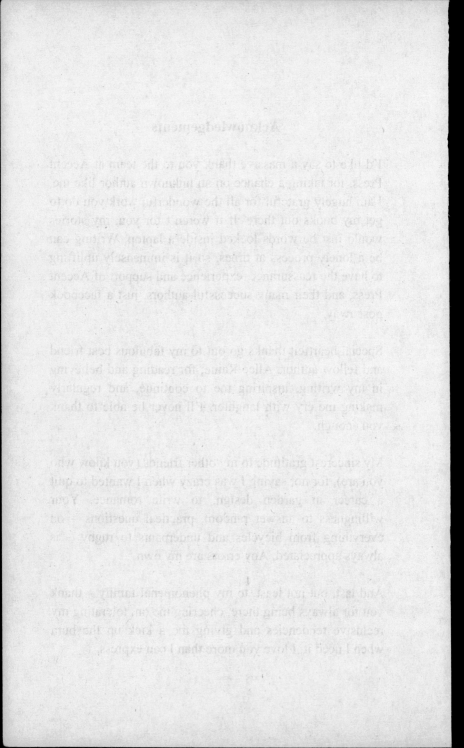

Chapter One

As I woke up so did the pain. It stabbed into my consciousness with steely determination, causing a thick wave of nausea to roll through me. Even with my eyes shut I could tell I was lying on the living room floor: the floorboards hard under my arm, hip, and knee, and the grain rough beneath my cheek. An icy draft chilled my calves where my nightshirt had ridden up. For several seconds I waited and listened to the wheezy snoring coming from the bedroom to be sure my husband was asleep. Once unconscious it was a fairly safe bet that Vic would remain so, at least until midday.

The flat was dark when I opened my eyes, and all was quiet in the cafe below, but outside in the street the market traders were busy reversing their vehicles, unloading their goods, and setting out their wares. They shouted, joked and laughed with each other in loud voices, combating the unsociably early hour, the raw weather, and the monotony of their work with bold and colourful banter.

I began to move but only gradually and in stages, gently testing my stiff limbs and joints for pain before risking sitting up. As the blood returned to my arm it brought prickly pins and needles with it, but that discomfort was nothing compared to the searing throb at the back of my head, the place where I'd connected with the edge of the coffee table. A tentative probe with my fingertips located the lump and a small amount of blood matted in my hair. Not life-threatening then.

Staggering to my feet I glanced at the clock, recognising that I was late and wouldn't have time for a shower. Knocking back some bitter-tasting paracetamol, I stripped off my nightshirt and washed quickly in the bathroom sink before creeping into the bedroom. In the oppressive murk I pulled on clean clothes, perching carefully on the corner of the bed to put on socks, and studiously ignoring the slumbering body sprawled diagonally across it. Getting a sweatshirt on over my head was awkward, my hands were still shaking and my head pounding, but I managed. To hide the blood, I tied a red scarf around my hair and paused to check my reflection, using the dim light of the street lamp peeking through the curtains and a cracked hand mirror. I looked tired and as pale as usual – my complexion that of a woman who has spent most of her thirty-five years stuck indoors – but there was no bruising evident on my face, nothing to provoke comment or draw unwelcome attention. And that was some relief. How has your life come to this, Rina? I silently asked the woman in the glass. But she stared back at me, resigned.

Vic wasn't always so violent. He'd gradually become more aggressive over time, little by little, step by step. Back when we were first married his temper would result in nothing more than a warning glare, a tightening grip on my arm or a cruel pinch of my thigh. But over the years, with time and increasing amounts of vodka, the violence had escalated, had become a part of our relationship. I had married out of necessity and there was no going back, no way of escaping – not that I could see anyway.

Before leaving the flat I did a quick sweep of the space

– it wouldn't do to leave it in a mess – straightening the coffee table and wiping away a crimson smear from the edge with a tissue. Collecting up the used mug, plate and cutlery, I deposited them in the sink, noting that my husband had eaten most of his dinner after all, despite his vicious outburst about it being burnt.

On the landing I gently tugged the door to the flat closed and tiptoed down the stairs in my plimsolls, keeping to the outer edges of each tread to minimise any creaking. At the bottom I checked that the customer toilet was stocked with soap and paper before stepping into Vic's Cafe. With a brief scan of the seating area, to confirm that the tables and chairs were as tidy as I'd left them, I moved into the kitchenette behind the counter. I swept through on autopilot; tying on my apron and flipping switches for the strip lights, the radio, the coffee machine, the oven and the deep fat fryer. Half-listening to the headline news, I unloaded the dishwasher and then the larder and the fridge, dragging out the usual ingredients: bread, baked beans, eggs, sausages, bacon, milk and margarine. Once I'd loaded up the toaster I approached the plate glass windows at the front of the cafe, raised the frayed, floor-to-ceiling, heavy-duty roller blinds and unlocked the door, swivelling the 'closed' sign around to 'open'.

Beyond the mildew-edged glass, the street lamps barely penetrated the muddy January gloom. A northerly wind snapped and billowed at the tarps and awnings, while men and women, bundled up in numerous layers of clothing, toiled away in earnest. I recognised all the usual suspects: Melvin and his pimply teenage son on the

3

hardware stall; Jo the greengrocer; Mags selling antiques and Gary the florist with his buckets of season-defiant blooms.

Jo, her arms laden with sacks of potatoes, grinned at me and I raised my hand in a wave. Exchanging the sacks for a plastic crate of goods, she staggered in my direction and I opened the door for her, marvelling at her robust strength.

'Mornin' Rina,' she said, depositing the crate in the doorway, where years of foot traffic had worn away the lino.

'Thanks, Jo.' Suppressing a shiver I eyed the motley selection of past-their-best vegetables at my feet. Vic had worked out a deal with Jo to save himself money but it was me who had to peel and prepare the battered carrots, lettuce, cucumbers and tomatoes to disguise their bumps and bruises. Of course I had to hide my own bumps and bruises too but Vic usually only injured parts of my body I could conceal with clothing and most people, like Jo, simply didn't see what they didn't want to. 'How's Teddy doing?'

'He's gettin' there,' she said, burying her fists in her pockets. 'Vet says the antibiotics have kicked in; he'll be back to barking at postmen before long.'

'That's great; such a relief.'

'Yeah, it's not been the same on the stall without him – too quiet by half. Anyway, must finish setting up but I'll be in for me breakfast later,' she said, hunching against the cold and turning away.

'Yeah, see you later.'

Working in the greasy spoon had been stressful for

4

me at first. It wasn't so much the routine – juggling the cooking, serving and cleaning for long hours every day – it was the physical contact with other people that I struggled with. It made me uncomfortable. Having grown up in care, I found it hard to trust people. In the past I had avoided them if I could, stayed out of range, and maintained a distance. But that wasn't always an option in Vic's Cafe. I did what I could – kept the counter between myself and the customers most of the time, called them over to collect their orders if possible and carefully navigated my way around the tables when necessary. But I still had to receive cash. I'd rather they just placed their money on the counter for me but most people held it out in their fingers or, worse, in the open palm of their hand. Even now after eighteen years of working here, I had to fight the impulse to flinch at every touch.

And yet it was these regular characters – market traders wearing fingerless gloves; builders armed with hard hats, high-vis vests, and dusty boots; paint-spattered decorators; lone parents treating their offspring; OAPs riding mobility scooters; and students buried in revision notes – it was these folk who kept me sane from one day to the next with their daily greetings, gossip and grumblings which they shared, offloaded or simply chatted away, while I took their orders and fed them. And I was content to listen, patiently absorbing the ins and outs, ups and downs, and dramas of their lives, while my own life slipped by. No, despite the challenges of my job I was grateful for it – it was preferable to the alternative. Bending down I lifted the heavy crate from the floor and let the door swing shut behind me, as I turned back to the kitchen to start frying.

Chapter Two

I was hiding. I was a thirty-year-old man, hiding in his dad's bathroom.

I'd heard that grief could express itself in strange ways, as if it was a living, breathing monster. But it wasn't my grief that I was hiding from; it was the people downstairs in the lounge. And that wasn't like me; I was usually comfortable in a crowd, good at saying innocuous things to put people at their ease. Jasmine, my girlfriend, said that I reminded her of a British Ashton Kutcher – my looks and mannerisms in particular – and that it was that that made people warm to me. Whether that was true or not, I liked people and they liked me. And these were good, kind country folk; they were just trying to be supportive.

But all the overt attention was stifling. People had been stealing glances at me all day: throughout the service; at the cemetery; even squinting through the tinted car windows as we crawled through town, watching with a careful air of sympathetic curiosity – waiting to see James Southwood's monster express itself.

Because Dad was dead – a heart attack just a few weeks into the New Year. Reg Southwood – town stalwart and all-round good guy – was gone, just like that and I felt numb. Jasmine kept reminding me how 'lucky' it was that he had died so quickly. I knew what she meant – I wouldn't wish a painful, lingering death on anyone – but I still wished she'd stop saying it. It didn't *feel* lucky. I would have liked to have said goodbye, or at the very least, thank you. Thank you for rescuing me from care and adopting me when I was just a scrawny seven-year-old and thank you for not sending me straight back when your wife (the only mother I have any memory of) died, just three years later.

Gazing at the faded paisley curtains framing the bathroom window I listened to the murmur of dignified voices in the room below: friends and neighbours from all over Wildham, many of whom I should know better than I did. The names and faces were recognisable but I'd been away a long time, first at university and then working in London, so I had trouble putting them together. The city wasn't far away geographically but it sometimes felt like another planet, and since Jasmine didn't like venturing beyond the M25 we'd barely visited Dad in the two years and five months we'd been together. We were supposed to have come up and seen him on Boxing Day but Jasmine had been laid up with a hangover, following our two-day stay with her own highly strung family so Dad had driven down to call on us instead.

Mum made them herself – these curtains – I vaguely recalled her sitting at the dinner table one weekend when I was nine, guiding the fabric through the Singer machine with her fingertips, her slippered foot coaxing the pedal, the pace. Dad had hung them up for her and I could tell she was pleased with the result. We all pretended not to notice that one curtain stopped an inch short of the windowsill. She had died not long after that.

The door handle jiggled, making me jump.

'Just a minute,' I called through the door.

8

'It's Liam. You all right mate?'

Despite his casual tone, I recognised his concern. 'I'm good mate, thanks. I'll be out in a sec.'

He didn't reply and his tread was heavy on the stairs as he retreated.

Liam Hunt had been my best mate since school. We hadn't seen much of each other over the last few years but then our friendship had been built on a shared passion for rugby – that and the fact that we were both motherless, though that wasn't something we ever discussed. Liam was here to pay his respects to my dad but he also had my back – and that meant a lot.

Washing my hands in the sink, accompanied by the familiar clank and hiss of the cistern re-filling, I glanced out the condensation-fogged window. Through the dying January light I could just make out the plant nursery and garden centre below. Soon everything would need 'tidying in readiness for spring' (Dad's standard phrase) – the spent foliage of each plant trimmed back; the roots top dressed with fresh compost; and every pot labelled with species, variety and price.

But who would organise that this year? Dad's Will seemed relatively straightforward and to the point. Since he had no other close relatives or partners in the business, and I had no siblings, everything belonged to me now: house, garden centre, nursery, the lot – he had even made me sole executor of the business so that it could be kept running during probate. But he had never meant for me to run the business myself surely? My parents had loved it, built it up from nothing, but they had always wanted more for me. That's why Dad had packed me off to university;

that's why I worked in insurance, climbed the corporate ladder, paid into a pension and drove a company car. I'd not worked on the nursery since I was a teenager. The notion that it was now mine made my head swim.

With growing unease I noticed the rickety lean of the timber storage sheds; the ripped and greying plastic sheeting of the polytunnels; the tower of empty wooden pallets that usually held neat stacks of compost bags; and the raised benches bereft of stock. Clumps of straggly weeds had pushed up through the uneven rubble paths and were now collapsing under the choking weight of rotting sycamore leaves. Even allowing for the time of year, the family business was looking shabbier than it should. The grounds and buildings needed attention and new stock would need to be ordered in time for spring. Why had Dad let things slide like this? Had it become too much for him recently? He'd never mentioned anything over the phone – but then we never talked, not really.

Downstairs someone barked with restrained laughter, interrupting my mounting worries. Time was up. Taking a cursory glance at my reflection and straightening my tie, I unlocked the door and headed back to my guests.

Liam stood hunched in a corner near the front door with his girlfriend, Cally. They nursed their drinks – a pint of orange juice and small glass of wine respectively – while they listened to another of our mates blithely relaying one of his notoriously far-fetched stories. Liam and I nodded to each other, a discreet look of understanding passing between us, and Cally smiled at me, her eyes misting with sympathetic tears, but I didn't stop to chat.

The lounge felt unnaturally stuffy, as if the peeling wallpaper, sagging upholstery and threadbare rugs were creeping closer, but at least somebody had cleared away the last of the Christmas decorations. In the centre of the room Jasmine oozed chic in her little black dress, her bottle-blonde curls swept up behind her head, her eyes sparkling. She gesticulated expressively as she talked, her voice distinctively high-pitched and girly against the more sombre tones. There was no denying she held the attention of almost everyone present, as usual, but for once I was grateful because it took the focus off me.

'*There* you are, James,' she said with a glossy smile, squeezing my arm as I reached her side. Jasmine was often affectionate with me in public as if practising for a new part in a play, or auditioning for the role of 'girlfriend'. 'Your guests were starting to wonder where you'd got to!'

The ice cubes in her glass chinked as she tottered slightly in her six-inch heels. With a downward glance I noted, with relief, that she had managed to scrape the worst of the mud from the cemetery off her designer shoes. From the indignant look she'd given me at the time – while sinking – I knew she blamed me personally for the boggy state of Dad's graveside but hopefully I'd now been forgiven.

'Sorry I was just taking a call, is everyone alright?' I said, smiling at the faces around me. 'Has everyone had something to eat and drink?' With my free arm I gestured towards the sideboard which was crammed with a seemingly infinite supply of donated triangular sandwiches, cocktail sausages and mini scotch eggs, most of which, as a vegetarian, I couldn't eat. There was a general murmur of assent and a teary-eyed woman nodded and patted my arm reassuringly. It took me a moment to realise it was Barb, a woman who had been a close friend of my mother's and an employee at the garden centre. Barb would be in her seventies now; was she still working for my dad when he died? Glancing around I spotted a few other faces I recognised as being staff members and it dawned on me that the future of their jobs now lay in my hands. Mine wasn't the only life that Dad had left a hole in.

'It's been a long time, Barb, how are you?' I said placing my hand over hers.

'Oh I'm fine, dear, never fear,' she said, smiling and dabbing her nose with a hankie.

'Were you, I mean, do you still work in the garden centre?'

'Oh yes, just part-time you know; helping out in the plant area; keeping the customers happy – that sort of thing.'

'Well, look, I don't want you to worry. I don't know what I'm going to do with the business just yet but whatever happens you and the rest of the staff will be looked after. Dad had a really strong life insurance policy – I made sure of that – and if there are any wages owing I'll make certain they are paid.'

'Oh, James, don't trouble yourself with any of that just now.' Tears spilled from her eyes and she hastily wiped them away.

'I just wanted you to know,' I said.

Jasmine interrupted by leaning in. 'The people from up the road are waiting to say goodbye before they leave – they're in the kitchen.' Her expensive perfume didn't quite mask the tell-tale scent of cigarette smoke caught in her hair. She was supposed to have given up but I pretended not to notice as I thanked her, excused myself and headed into the room next door.

By the time I'd spoken to everyone, at least briefly, and the last of the neighbours had left, Tupperware and soggy hankies in hand, it was dark outside. With a dazed weariness I closed the front door to my dad's cottage and leaned back against it. Jasmine was touching up her lipstick in the hall mirror, her faux fur coat already on and her handbag suspended from her elbow.

'Ready to go, James?'

'Go?'

'Traffic should have died down by now and I have a nine o'clock audition tomorrow – I need my beauty sleep.'

'I should probably stay here for a bit.'

Turning she stared at me, one hand raised to her neat hairdo. 'Stay? Here?'

'Yes. My boss has given me some time off and there are things I need to –'

'How long are you staying for?'

'Well I, I don't know, maybe a week or so.'

'A week?' Jasmine glared at me impatiently, frown lines bunching between her carefully crafted eyebrows.

There was a growing list of things to sort out and look into and I felt no desire to rush back to my job: all worst-case scenarios, better-safe-than-sorrys and stats-based pessimism. Perversely Jasmine's impatience to leave only made me want to stay longer. I shrugged, mutely apologetic. Pressing her lips together, her nose flaring,

Jasmine yanked on her leather gloves, marched out of the house and wordlessly stalked across the gravel, to where her convertible was parked nose to nose with my hatchback.

As I watched her drive off into the darkness, vaguely hoping she would stick to the speed limit, it dawned on me that one of my own worst-case scenarios had been realised – my last remaining family was dead. I was no longer a child but still – it felt like I'd been abandoned, orphaned, all over again.

Chapter Three

'Wake up you stupid bitch,' he spat, grabbing a handful of my hair and yanking me sharply out of bed and onto the floor.

The bedside clock read 2:45 and I hadn't heard Vic come in but I was awake now – wide awake. What had I done this time? The wound on the back of my head had only just healed and now this. My fingers clutched futilely at his hand in a desperate attempt to relieve the burning in my scalp as my bare feet scrabbled for purchase on the floorboards.

'Where is it?' he demanded, shoving me through the living room doorway, the chipped skirting board grazing my knee.

'What?' I gasped, blinking in the glare of the overhead light as he released me. Through the archway the contents of the pedal bin had been emptied all over the kitchen floor.

'My fucking newspaper – where is it?'

Vic liked to study the sports pages of the paper and make cryptic notes in the margin before placing his bets. It was an old-fashioned way of doing things but he was superstitious about the process and took his gambling seriously. Gripping the edge of the couch I hauled myself to my feet, quickly scanning the room and trying to think, all the while keeping his balled fists in my peripheral vision as they trembled with rage. Carefully I lifted his heavy denim jacket off the coffee table where he had flung it, the sour stench of booze, cigarettes, and sweat rising with the garment and revealing a neatly folded newspaper underneath.

Vic snatched the paper up. 'How many fucking times have I told you not to touch my stuff?'

I physically bit back the retort that sprang to my lips. If I'd left the paper on the floor where he'd dropped it he would have complained about my not tidying up. I couldn't win and I'd long since learned not to argue; arguing just made him more likely to hit me.

Ripping his jacket out of my hand Vic shrugged into it and helped himself to a six-pack of beer from the fridge. 'Clear this up,' he said, indicating the leaking heap of rubbish with his foot on his way to the front door.

I stared after him in mute defiance, not taking my eyes off him despite the warm trickle of blood making its way down my shin. I never let him see he'd hurt me if I could help it. As he slammed and stomped his way out of the building I listened, aurally following his progress. Only once I was sure he wasn't coming back did I let the tension seep out of my muscles. I'd have to be up in a couple of hours' time and I'd never get back to sleep now. Resigned to a weary day ahead I cleaned and dressed the gash on my knee, wrapped myself in a dressing gown and righted the kitchen. With Vic gone I could afford to treat myself to some comfort. Carefully I extracted the small fish-finger box from the bottom drawer of the freezer, made myself a coffee and settled in the corner of the couch with a twenty-four-hour news channel, on low, for company.

There weren't any fish fingers in the box. It just made for a good hiding place – Vic only ever ventured into the freezer for vodka or ice cubes. I tipped the cold, meagre, plastic-wrapped contents out into my lap: a wad of five pound notes and some change; a clear plastic hospital bracelet; a tightly folded sheet of A4 lined paper and a faded, dog-eared colour photograph.

I started by counting the cash: just seventy quid and forty-six pence in total but every penny hard earned. It was all the wealth I had in the world. Vic kept a tight rein on his finances and I didn't even have a bank account. I was only ever given enough currency to buy what Vic wanted me to buy and he checked every receipt so that each and every penny was accounted for. He claimed that as his wife I shouldn't need funds of my own but really it was his way of making sure I couldn't leave him. I had scraped together this cash by deviously smuggling tips away in my bra, tiny amounts of coinage at a time so that Vic wouldn't know, and then cautiously changing the coins into notes when I accumulated enough. I thought of it as my rainy-day fund but what that rainy day might entail I wasn't sure. I suppose I hoped that if I left one day without stealing a chunk of Vic's money directly from the till he might be less inclined to come after me to retrieve it. But it was a vain hope – my husband considered me his property and was too well connected; wherever I went he would find me.

Escape would not be an option until he was dead – and who knew when that might be. Anyway, where would I go? Dreary as my life was it had a routine familiarity now and was infinitely preferable to selling my body or living on the street.

I set aside the hospital admission bracelet, unwilling to face what it represented, reluctant to go there in my mind and rip open that particular wound. Instead I took a large gulp of coffee and turned my attention to the piece of paper, carefully unfolding it until I could read the familiar words written there:

The dog ran with the ball.

I smiled at the bold letters, painstakingly transcribed in blue biro at double height and, above them, his name:

Jamie.

Picking up the photo I scrutinised the grainy image of the small boy I once knew: wide chestnut eyes gazing out from beneath a matching mop of shaggy fringe, a lopsided grin that revealed missing front teeth. He had his hands thrust into the pockets of his dungarees as he leaned affectionately into my left side. He was tucked under my arm; the only person I'd ever allowed to rest there. He was five years old at the time and I was ten. To the right of me stood three other foster kids but I no longer remembered their names, only Jamie's.

He had been a smart, vivacious kid, a fast learner and eager to please. But his small size made him an easy target – that and the fact that he rarely spoke. Rather than talk to anybody directly he preferred to stand on tiptoe and whisper into my ear so that I could speak for him, as if he was afraid of his own voice. I was the only person he trusted to be his spokesperson, which wound the adults up no end, but I didn't mind at all.

During weekends and holidays I built dens under furniture for him to hide in and made up games for us to play. And at night, when he was afraid of the dark, afraid to be alone, he would crawl into bed with me and I would spell out words by tracing them on his back with my finger; usually something reassuring like 'Y-O-U A-R-E S-A-F-E W-I-T-H M-E.' He'd be asleep before I had finished.

I'd have done anything for that little boy. I loved him unconditionally as if he were my real brother. And he had needed me, really needed me, like no one else ever had, before or since. Of course I tried to be happy for Jamie when he was adopted – it was what we foster kids all yearned for, to have proper parents, a real family, a normal life ... but it was as if Jamie had taken a vital part of me away with him and left me hollow inside.

At first, I'd had more to remember him by, various other belongings he'd left behind: books, a toy car, a blue mitten ... but over the years, as I'd stumbled in and out of various homes and hostels and doorways, they'd all been stolen from me. Nothing was sacred when you lived on the state or on the street.

In the relative silence of the night I stared unseeing at the scrap of handwriting practice in my hand as all the usual questions floated through my mind: Where was Jamie now? Was he happy? Healthy? Rich and successful? Was he a husband? A father?

I would never know the answers. So why couldn't I just let him go?

Chapter Four

It was only when my mobile abruptly vibrated on my desk that I became aware I'd been staring vacantly out of the window for the best part of an hour. I'd found myself doing that a lot recently – ever since Dad's funeral my mind had a tendency to wander, especially at work. On this occasion I'd been considering the view from my office. A window was a distinct luxury to someone working in a cubicle in the artificially lit, open-plan office on the floor below. I had worked hard to achieve my promotion and this small room, with its view of a brick wall and concrete stairwell, was my reward. But recently, after a spell in the countryside, I sorely missed green open space.

Of course, if I pushed back far enough in my fully adjustable, ergonomically correct swivel chair and craned my neck, I could just about see beyond the building next door and catch the very tips of the tree out on the pavement. But it wasn't enough. At the moment the tree was leafless anyway; the bare branches like spidery cracks against a grey sky, barely alleviating the monochrome pallor of this corner of the city. I couldn't immediately recall which variety of tree it was, which bothered me, but after much deliberation I decided it was almost certainly a London Plane. Picking up my mobile I yawned and made a mental note to check the tree the next time I passed by. The message was a text from Jasmine:

Out with friends 2nite, C U tomoro x

I texted back '*OK x*', just remembering to add the kiss at the last moment. Jasmine's messages always ended in a kiss, regardless of whether they were sent to me or to the window cleaner. The kisses didn't mean anything and yet she got irrationally offended if I accidentally sent her a message without one. All of my previous girlfriends had placed great importance on similar minor details – the correct timing and use of a pet name, the financial value of a gift, the position of a toilet seat – as if the success or failure of our relationship hinged on them. Maybe it did – how would I know? Either way I'd always tried my best to adhere to my girlfriends' myriad rules and preferences and the relationships were doomed to failure regardless.

Returning my gaze to the brickwork outside the window, a procession of pretty faces floated through my mind. Some I remembered more than others: Cecily the half-Brazilian model with an addiction to grapefruit, the tarter the better; Jessica who worked in PR, talked too fast and always wore lipstick to bed; and Dionne the Australian aromatherapist who left various rocks and crystals on every available surface, even inside my briefcase. She was convinced they would improve our relationship, or more specifically improve me, but if they did help it was too subtle an effect for me to detect. All the women I'd dated over the years were attractive, lively and ambitious in one way or another and all inevitably disappointed in me by the end. Jasmine and I had been together almost two and a half years now – a record for me – but I suspected the end was nigh.

The truth was I just wasn't good at love. It wasn't something I usually dwelled on or analysed; on the contrary I avoided thinking about it completely. But it was there inside me – a cavity, a void, an absence of something that everyone else had and took for granted. I'd once seen a TV programme about sociopaths and some of the signs were disconcertingly familiar: I often employed charm to conceal the emptiness I felt inside and regularly felt alone despite rarely ever being single – I'd been hopping from one failed romantic relationship to another, ever since I was a teenager.

But no matter how much I wanted it, I just wasn't good at getting close to someone – or letting them get close to me. Jasmine was a case in point: my Dad had just died. Shouldn't I be sharing that with her in some way? Shouldn't I *want* to share my grief with my girlfriend and allow her to comfort me? The very idea was terrifying but why? Was my aversion to getting attached to someone a result of my own biological mother abandoning me as a toddler? Surely not – it had happened when I was too young to have any memory of it and I rarely even thought about her. And yet, since Dad's death, I'd been pondering all sorts of things.

My parents and I had never talked much about my adoption, or my life before it, and I was never one to daydream about who my birth parents might be – there was never any point since the official records clearly stated that their identities were unknown. I was a foundling, abandoned in a church hall and raised in the custody of foster parents until my adoption by the Southwoods aged seven. My life with them was as happy as any child could hope for (up until Mum died at least) so I had almost no reason to dwell on my time before then.

Almost. There was one reason; one person, whom I'd never been able to forget; her name was Kitkat.

She was older than me by about five years – a tall, skinny, tomboy of a girl with mousy hair and badly chewed fingernails. Smart, fierce and intimidating she had been residing with the Plumleys for some time when I came along, a naive three-year-old and small for my age. But, as soon as the other foster kids started to pick on me, Kitkat had stepped in to defend me, outsmarting them and twisting their words (and sometimes their arms) until they gave up. She caused no end of trouble for herself in the process but for some reason she took me under her wing and I'd been grateful to her ever since.

For the four years Kitkat and I were together we were very close. The Plumleys had an old dog called Mungo, who we were fond of, but otherwise it was just her and me. I was frightened of everything and everyone, horribly insecure, and had trouble expressing myself. Sometimes I would go days or weeks without speaking. On those occasions Kitkat would act as my mouthpiece; I would whisper my words into her ear and she would safely communicate them to the rest of the world for me. She was the nearest thing I had to a sibling, a sister. She was my family.

I was thrilled to be adopted by the Southwoods – of course I was – but after the initial euphoria wore off it took quite some time to admit, even to myself, how much I missed Kitkat. I wanted to completely forget all about my time in care but, try as I might, there was no forgetting her. Eventually, when I was ten, after Mum died, I asked my dad to go back for Kitkat. I pestered, begged and guilt-tripped him until, against his better judgement, he took me back to the foster home to see her. But the Plumleys were long gone; the house was divided into flats and the neighbours were alien and disobliging. Kitkat had been absorbed into the confidential anonymity of the care system and that was that. And yet my loss of Kitkat was an ache that never went away. Perhaps it wasn't surprising that I had intimacy issues after all.

Slouching in my seat, I turned back to my computer screen and the report I was supposed to be compiling but it wasn't particularly pressing and the only meeting I'd had scheduled for the afternoon had been postponed. Since returning from compassionate leave, I was struggling to get back into the daily grind.

The days following the funeral hadn't been much fun. The weather was typically cold, damp and miserable; my dad's absence was unnervingly palpable and my list of 'to do' jobs increased daily. Each evening I called Jasmine on her mobile, to hear her news and reassure myself that I still had someone in my life who cared about me, but it often felt like she was speaking to me from a different planet. Being back in Wildham and my childhood home had stirred up a whole host of memories that I'd long forgotten or simply buried. It was disorientating, like stumbling about in a dream, everything familiar but slightly off-key.

Picking up my pen, I spun it a few times between my fingers and doodled on my jotter. I'd spent hours just sorting through and boxing up my dad's possessions. Some things I'd thrown out, some I'd donated to the local charity shop and some I'd boxed up and brought back to London with me. But all the furniture I'd just left in situ. I was reluctant to clear the house completely because there was still the family business to get to grips with and I didn't fancy staying in an empty house while I did that.

Thankfully the cottage itself hadn't required too much attention: the two-up two-down was a little tired and the decor needed some updating but it was structurally sound. I'd given it a thorough clean from top to bottom, brightened up the kitchen and bedrooms with a few fresh coats of paint, had the chimney swept, and repaired the guttering. From an estate agent's point of view Southwood Cottage was characterful, comfortable and situated in an attractive rural location, just minutes from the small town of Wildham and the A1. If necessary it could be marketed as a doer-upper and sold entirely separately from the business. It would be snapped up by a developer easily enough. The nursery and garden centre, on the other hand, might take longer to sort out.

Despite the picturesque setting, Southwood's was an inhospitable place in which to work out of season. Ever since Dad's death the team of permanent staff, zipped up in layers of thermal and waterproof clothing, had continued to risk chapped lips, chilblains, and frostbite on a daily basis to keep the place running – even as their employment prospects hung in the balance. With the help of Dad's life insurance money I was managing to keep paying their wages, for now. But probate could take several more weeks and getting the place ready for sale would be another matter.

I glanced at the clock on the wall above the door. Two more hours to go and the working week would be over. Tomorrow was Valentine's Day but Jasmine didn't seem fussed about celebrating it this year. Obviously I'd bought her the handbag she wanted – she'd helpfully emailed me the link so I could order it online and have it delivered straight to her – but I had no idea what, if anything, she might get me in return. A tie maybe? Picking up my mobile again I re-read her text. It wasn't unusual for her to be off doing her own thing with her friends on a Friday night but it used to be that I would be out having a few drinks with my colleagues at the same time. When had that fizzled out?

My fingers hovered over my contacts list as I considered texting a couple of workmates and suggesting a post-work pint but there was no point. They were both family men now – they preferred to be home in time to read bedtime stories to their kids and help their wives make dinner. I briefly contemplated taking a walk down to the floor below and asking some of the juniors if they were free but instinct stopped me; I'd been promoted and they hadn't. I was confident there were no hard feelings between us – I'd been careful not to rub their faces in it – but I was effectively their superior now and, in this corporation at least, you didn't socialise with your boss unless you absolutely had to. In fact, not one of my friends or colleagues from the city had attended my dad's funeral or sent so much as a condolence card. But I guess that was OK – I can't honestly say I'd missed them at the time. Relinquishing my phone I sighed. Maybe I would just get in the car and drive straight into the countryside; get a head start on the weekend – Valentine's Day be damned. I'd arranged a meeting with the nursery and garden centre staff for tomorrow morning and, if possible, I wanted to make a good impression. I wasn't sure if their loyalty to my father would extend to me for much longer but I needed to find out because, if I was going to get the place smartened up and sold off, I definitely needed the staff onside to help make it happen.

An emotion I couldn't quite identify intensified in my

gut and I turned back to the window, once again craning my neck for a reassuring glimpse of tree without understanding why.

Chapter Five

'What can I get you Mags?' I said, raising my voice above the general cacophony of sound.

'I'll have a baked spud please, love; I'm trying to be healthy – lose a few pounds before the big day.'

'Of course! The wedding's at the end of this month isn't it?'

'February twenty eighth – just two weeks now!' Mags helped herself to cutlery from the pot-full on the counter, while I tapped her order into the till. 'I was gonna skip lunch entirely but I'm starvin' and it's bloody perishin' out there.' I glanced through the condensation-streaked windows at all the people bustling past, heads down and chins tucked in as they negotiated sleety puddles. 'And Sal says I oughta wear a hat since I'm mother of the bride an' all but I ask you, Rina, can you see *me* in a hat?' I smiled as I tried to picture short, stocky Mags in anything other than the jeans and the grey fleecy body warmer she routinely wore. 'I mean it's only a registry office after all and she's already got me wearing this hideous pinky-beige colour that she swears is all the rage. With a hat I'll look like a sodding mushroom!' Her face creasing like worn leather and her eyes sparkling, her throaty laugh temporarily triumphed over the hiss of frying food, the roar of the coffee machine and the chattering of the radio and my other customers.

'You'll look bloody gorgeous and you know it – just

make sure you don't upstage your own daughter,' I said.

She chuckled. 'Fat chance! Anyway, my future son-in-law is taking her out for a romantic dinner tonight – y'know for Valentine's – so at least that should stop her fussing for a bit.'

I smiled. I was aware it was Valentine's Day but only because they kept mentioning it on the radio. It didn't mean anything to me personally – it never had. 'Do you want beans on your potato?'

'Bless you, love, yes please. And plenty of cheese and real butter if you've got it – none of that bland, spreadable crap.'

'No problem. Anything to drink?' Along the counter a guy in a baseball cap was banging a salt shaker on the counter top to dislodge a blockage in the nozzle. I slid another one towards him and he accepted it with a grunt of approval before sprinkling salt liberally onto his meal.

'A Coke. But better make it a Diet,' Mags added.

Travis, Vic's right-hand man, cut in over her shoulder. 'All right, Rina, Vic around?'

'Yeah, he should be down soon,' I said, glancing at the digital clock on the microwave and mentally bracing myself for whatever frame of mind he might be in today.

Vic ran a small empire in this corner of London. Aside from owning the cafe and part-managing the minicab firm near the station, he also loaned money to people and recruited muscle-bound security for pubs and clubs – he had a nicotine-stained finger in every pie. But Vic most liked to think of himself as a 'Business Facilitator', taking advantage of various 'opportunities' as and when they arose – by connecting the right people. He was popular and, most crucially, *trusted*, in local circles, wielding a certain amount of power and respect. I was never made privy to any details but over the years he'd introduced thieves to buyers, drug dealers to suppliers and prostitutes to pimps – always securing a cut of the dirty profits without any serious risk to himself.

Having emptied a can of beans into a saucepan on the hob, I served another customer two teas and a ham sandwich while Mags's jacket potato was cooking in the microwave. Once the large spud had softened up I rubbed it with a little salt and oil before transferring it to the oven to crisp up the skin. I was busy grating cheese with my back to the cafe when Vic, whistling cheerfully, made his entrance. Without turning around I listened intently for any change in his mood as he greeted the regulars by name and casually helped himself to coffee – and cash from the till. It was only as he disappeared upstairs again, with Travis in tow, that I realised, with a start, that I had been grating my own fingers and bleeding into the cheese. Hastily scraping it all into the bin, I wrapped my sore fingertips in blue plasters, cleaned the grater and the chopping board and started again.

Of course I knew Vic was no angel when I married him at eighteen. I was desperate at the time and flattered by Vic's attention. He wasn't particularly good-looking – he'd always been a bit short with a lean, hard, wiry sort of body and ginger hair which he bleached white and spiky on top. But he had charisma – a swagger to his step, a twinkle in his eye, and tough-guy confidence with the tattoos to match. Marrying him would provide me with the safety and security I longed for, or so I'd thought at the time. In reality I'd

31

swapped one nightmare for another – trading a perilous life on the street for a prison of a marriage.

Retrieving the potato from the oven I set it on a plate, slashed it open in the shape of a cross, slathered the insides with butter, ladled baked beans inside and deposited a generous handful of cheese on top. Mags was at the counter before I could call to her, cutlery in hand.

'Thanks, love,' she said as I set a can of Diet Coke next to her plate.

'Would you like a glass?'

'No thanks, this is great.' Tucking the can into her armpit, she picked up her lunch and set off towards the table she'd secured.

'What can I get you?' I said, smiling at the next customer as I washed my hands.

For the next two hours I tried to forget about the men in the flat upstairs, and whatever business they might be conducting, and simply focused on feeding customers. It was busy, with several orders for cooked breakfasts, toasted sandwiches and hot chips – fuel to stave off the cold outside. But the lunchtime rush had eased by the time Cherry turned up, wearing a thin jacket over a plunging top, a short, gold lamé skirt and very high heels.

'Ta, Rina,' she said distractedly as I poured her a cup of tea. Cherry rarely ate at the cafe but often drank copious amounts of tea in between clients. She was currently flicking through a newspaper colour supplement, only glancing at each page long enough to check out the pictures. 'Hey, you heard about that local actress? Jasmine Reed? Says here she might be doing a movie.'

'Oh yeah?' I said. I had no idea who she was talking about. I watched some TV from time to time and leafed through the magazines that customers occasionally left lying around but the entertainment industry, in fact the rest of the world as a whole, seemed so far removed from my own experience that mostly I let it all wash over me. Books though – books were another matter entirely. I hadn't many – just four dog-eared paperbacks that had been left behind over the years and not reclaimed by their owners – but I'd read each one countless times. In a book I could really lose myself, be someone else for a while – escape. Leaving Cherry to her celebrity gossip I rinsed a cloth out in the sink and started clearing tables.

'You've missed a bit, Rina,' Vic said behind me, a menacing edge to his voice.

I stiffened and my blood cooled, the cloth in my hand suspended over the table I was wiping. I'd been half listening to the radio and hadn't heard him and Travis come back downstairs. I was fairly confident Vic wouldn't cause trouble in front of customers but I couldn't help being on my guard. The men having a late lunch at the next table glanced up with interest and Cherry gave half a laugh over by the counter. Her false nails tapped out a tune on her mug of tea as I straightened and turned towards him.

He chuckled. 'For fuck's sake *smile*, babe – it's just a joke. It's a wonder you ain't scared all the customers away with a face like that,' Vic added, his teeth bared in a grin.

'You made me jump,' I said, relaxing my shoulders and smiling.

'Yeah, I got you good din't I?' Vic winked playfully at two women sitting in the window, who blushed and smiled in response. Travis disappeared out of the door with a nod goodbye as Vic picked up a discarded newspaper and sauntered back towards the counter. 'I'll have another coffee and a bacon butty when you're ready, babe.'

Despite Vic's good mood I knew better than to keep him waiting. While I poured his coffee, Cherry relinquished her seat, slithering off the stool and squeezing her feet back into her shiny high heels. She always sat there – in Vic's favourite spot – as if she was keeping it warm for him. I set his coffee before him and Cherry smiled and rolled her eyes at me in token camaraderie. The bacon spat and sizzled in the frying pan and I buttered some white bread while Vic calmly perused the sports section. Cherry, now settled on the stool next to him, crossed her legs deliberately revealing more thigh from beneath her skirt but he didn't seem to notice.

I was well aware my husband fucked Cherry occasionally – they weren't exactly discreet – but it was an arrangement that worked for all three of us. Vic wasn't one of her paying customers; on the contrary *she* usually owed *him* money and, from my point of view, as long as Cherry kept my husband satisfied, it meant I didn't have to. It wasn't that Vic had a big sexual appetite – the amount of booze he consumed flattened his libido anyway – but I simply loathed sex. Based on experiences in the past I found it painful and humiliating so I was grateful to Cherry for removing the necessity – so much so that she and I were almost friends, up to a point.

'Do you have a busy afternoon planned?' Cherry asked, smiling up at Vic through thick eyelashes.

'Yes,' Vic said, without elaboration.

I set his sandwich down before him, sliced into two neat triangles the way he liked it, and accompanied by a bottle of tomato sauce. Setting his paper aside and eyeing his plate, he picked up the bottle and gave it a shake.

Cherry, realising that Vic wasn't about to offer any distraction, paid for her tea and tottered out the door with a wave goodbye – which I returned and Vic ignored.

Having messily wolfed down his bacon butty, Vic abruptly switched off the radio, drove the last stragglers out into the market, flipped the sign to 'closed' and locked the door. As I commenced my usual clean up routine, Vic quietly attended to the contents of the till, his head bowed and eyes narrowed, the sinews in his forearms twisting under his tattoos as he counted. I suppose to a casual passer-by it looked like he was helping, by cashing up the day's takings, but it was only because he enjoyed fingering his money and scrutinising the till roll for discrepancies. I rarely made a mistake nowadays. Any shortfall not covered by the tips dish I would have to pay for in bruises.

By the time I'd wiped down the Formica tables, laminated menus and moulded plastic chairs, refilled the condiment jars and sauce dispensers, and swept the linoleum floor, most of the market stallholders had packed up and left for the day. Vic had gone too, disappearing out through the back door without farewell or comment.

Allowing myself a brief moment to relax I put the radio back on before tackling the kitchen. Tidying the food away, I loaded and started up the dishwasher, cleaned the kitchen surfaces, scrubbed the grease from the wall tiles, de-scaled the sink, and mopped the floors. Finally I carried two sacks of rubbish out to the large bin by the back door and cleaned the downstairs toilet with bleach before heading upstairs to make Vic's dinner. He was unlikely to be back before midnight and he usually ate out but he liked to have a meal waiting for him just in case he did turn up hungry. Sometimes Vic disappeared for days at a time without warning or explanation, like an alley cat, but there was always the threat of his return.

Having thrown together a spaghetti carbonara, using a packet of sauce, I plated up Vic's portion and settled myself on the couch to eat alone. But I only picked half-heartedly at the meal before giving up and retreating into the shower. Does Jamie, wherever he is, like spaghetti carbonara? The random thought popped into my head out of nowhere, as so many thoughts of Jamie did. Even after all this time he was never far from my mind. In a futile attempt to expel the fried sausage smell from my skin and hair, I scoured myself with soap before pulling on my threadbare nightshirt. Then, too weary to think, I crawled into my side of the bed to sleep, while trying to keep a cautious ear out for my husband.

Chapter Six

Hugging the slow lane of the motorway, I coasted along at just 65 mph behind an elderly man in a vintage Mini Cooper. I was in no hurry; the closer I got to London the heavier the traffic grew, along with my mood. I'd really clocked up the miles in the past month, dividing my time between the city and the country in an effort to prepare my dad's estate for sale, while also keeping my boss happy. February had been bitterly cold and grey throughout and, frankly, I was glad to see the back of it.

The majority of my energy had been spent sorting out the family business. It was a nursery really, specialising in the growing and selling of popular garden plants through the modest little garden centre attached, rather than offering anything as grand as giftware or furniture. The seven permanent members of staff that my dad had employed – Frank, Lil, Leah, Barb, Jenny, Priya and Max – were eminently capable and had been wonderfully patient with me, despite being anxious about losing their jobs. Between us we'd managed to keep the business running. I'd planted, pruned and re-potted stock; weeded and swept paths; scrubbed walls and benches; and shovelled several times my own weight in compost and horse muck – I had blisters to prove it (much to Jasmine's horror) but they gave me a certain sense of satisfaction. Much of the work was familiar to me from my teenage years; the names of plants, pests and diseases sprang up in my mind as if eager to be put to good use and the staff had given me refresher lessons in driving the forklift, fixing the emergency generator and operating the tills.

With the aid of some particularly helpful guidance

notes from Dad's bookkeeper, I'd spent many evenings studying the company accounts in an attempt to get a handle on them: the seasonal variations, the average running costs and the predicted profits. I now had a sound overview of the family business and, as I'd suspected, it was in urgent need of financial investment if it was to make a profit this year. My father's stubborn refusal to take out a business loan, no matter how small, was almost certainly to blame. But, on the other hand, his reluctance to rely on credit meant that he had virtually no debts, no outstanding mortgage and no money owing to suppliers. There would be inheritance tax to pay once probate was finalised but, with the garden centre's existing loyal customer base and no significant competition nearby, there was plenty of scope for growth, expansion and considerable profitability. The untapped potential in Southwood's Nursery made it ripe for sale.

Now, navigating the streets of London on a Sunday evening – expletives from the people-choked pavement mixing with the determined subwoofer bass beat of the car behind and a police car screaming past, its pulsing lights temporarily blinding me – I knew I was going to miss the peaceful serenity of the only place that had ever felt like home.

As soon as I unlocked the front door to my flat I could tell Jasmine wasn't there; it was too quiet. Struggling up the stairs with my suitcase, I was irked by the usual jumble of gloves, mugs, scarves and shoes that cluttered the edges of each step. Jasmine had moved in with me just six months into our relationship – it was her suggestion and I was grateful for the company. She had wasted no time encouraging me to redecorate, putting her stamp on the place and making herself at home, but unfortunately she had a childish habit of dropping things as soon as she finished with them and I was forever clearing up after her. So I was surprised when I stepped into the living room to find it tidy; the minimalist modular grey furniture that Jasmine favoured was conspicuously clutter-free. She must have had guests. I pulled the handle of the coat cupboard and an avalanche of clothes, magazines, tea towels, empty food packets and unopened post tumbled out onto the floor at my feet. I sighed.

Having hung up my coat, I moved around the apartment drawing the blinds in an attempt to cosy the place up a bit. Somehow the warm original character of the building – the coving, the timber-framed sash windows and the generous floorboards that I had worked so hard to save when I first bought the place – were lost in my girlfriend's cool urban interior styling. The white walls and stainless steel surfaces almost gave me goosebumps, despite the central heating.

By the time I had tidied up, put the bins out, opened my post, poured myself a glass of Pinot Grigio and dealt with the most urgent paperwork, it was nearly midnight. I tried not to feel apprehensive as Jasmine burst through the front door and clattered up the stairs in her heels and a hum of cigarette smoke and aftershave.

'Oh, you're back,' she said.

'Hello, Jasmine.'

'I wasn't expecting you back until tomorrow.' She was flushed and rattled and I wondered if it was because of the pair of boxer shorts I'd spotted lying in the doorway to the master bedroom. They weren't mine. Had she been sleeping with someone else or only left the pants there to provoke me? Either way I didn't feel up to confronting her tonight.

'I told you on the phone I needed some paperwork for my meeting tomorrow.'

'Oh, I thought you'd pick it up on your way to work in the morning,' she said, removing her faux fur coat and letting it slide to the floor by the cupboard door. 'Just as well you're back – the bins need emptying.' I refrained from pointing out that I'd already done so and suppressed a familiar twinge of irritation as she kicked off her shoes, padded off to the master bedroom in her stockinged feet, and closed the door behind her without so much as a 'goodnight'. Our relationship was falling apart and, despite Jasmine's increasingly callous attitude, it was probably more my fault than hers.

Twenty-nine-year-old Jasmine Reed, with her expensive, girly blonde curls, bow-shaped mouth and long-lashed blue eyes, was a rising star in the acting world. She could sing, dance, giggle, pout and cry on command, and with the energy she poured into her stage performances she even gave twenty-year-olds a run for their money. Men wanted her and women wanted to be her so when she'd singled me out two and a half years ago and set her mind to seducing me, I'd let her – I was the envy of most guys we knew. But I'd always known we wouldn't last.

Draining the last of the wine from my glass, I rinsed it out in the kitchen sink and set it neatly on the draining board. We'd never had much in common with each other but Jasmine had insisted that was a good thing. "Opposites attract!" she used to say. She liked that I *wasn't* an actor; that I had a secure, nine to five job; that I was available on evenings and weekends to escort her to events and parties where I said the right things, put people at their ease and looked good on her arm.

But lately, in the last couple of months, everything Jasmine once liked about me grated on her. She considered my job to be boring; my laid-back demeanour, irritating; and my popularity, nauseating. I was no longer invited along to parties or introduced to her friends. She said I was emotionally closed off – that I lacked passion and ambition. And maybe she was right – since the funeral I'd felt neither passion nor enthusiasm for my work. It didn't help that I'd never told Jasmine that I loved her. But then I'd never told anyone I loved them.

Putting the chain on the front door, I switched off the overhead lights and took my files and papers into the spare room, my bedroom. Jasmine had suggested I sleep there so that she could have a few nights' undisturbed sleep; she claimed I breathed too loudly. But that was back in January and she hadn't asked me to return. Perhaps I should have requested re-admittance to the master bedroom but if she'd said no we'd be forced to acknowledge the increasing distance and the complete lack of affection between us.

Of course I was also worried Jasmine might say yes; that she'd invite me back into bed with open arms. For any other guy that would be a dream come true but my libido was currently at an all-time low. I was no longer aroused by my pretty, vivacious girlfriend the way everyone else seemed to be and if we shared a bed again it would be obvious. It was always the same with every girlfriend I'd ever had – as soon as the initial attraction wore off I struggled to get it up. Jasmine would take it very personally. For now it was easier to stay put in the spare room, especially if she might be cheating on me. I couldn't let her go on walking all over me indefinitely but I didn't want her to leave yet. I couldn't face a break-up right now – I didn't want to be alone.

While undressing I knocked the stack of files with my elbow and dislodged a flurry of paperwork. It mostly comprised those documents necessary for probate –

copies of Dad's Will, death certificate, insurance policies, property deeds, bank statements etc. But they were not the only legal documents I'd salvaged during my search of Southwood Cottage. As I collected up the scattered papers the certificate of my adoption caught my eye.

It was strange seeing the proof of my origins set out in black and white and immediately I found myself thinking of Kitkat. Back then she was always there for me – I could tell her anything and she always knew what to say or do to cheer me up. If only I'd never lost touch with her we might still be friends – she might be here right now...

Climbing into bed, I lay down and stared at the ceiling. I felt very alone. Was it time to try and find Kitkat again? A friend from my university days, Brian, worked as a private investigator in London. I had given him free insurance advice over the years – should I ask him to return the favour by tracking her down? On second thoughts the idea of divulging the sad truth of my origins to anyone, even a friend, did not appeal. Perhaps with the aid of the Internet and all its far-reaching social media, it might be possible to find Kitkat myself. The trouble was I'd never known her real name.

My nickname for her stemmed from the ceremonial way she would share her chocolate-covered biscuits with me; the ones she managed to 'obtain' from the newsagents. I still recalled the way she would carefully ease the paper wrapper off sideways without breaking it; gently run her thumb nail through the foil, snapping the two fingers of biscuit apart, before handing one to me with intense satisfaction. She claimed that the biscuits were designed especially for sharing; it was only when I started school that I discovered that other kids did not agree. I would proudly wear one of Kitkat's paper wrappers around my wrist for days, like a badge of friendship, until it inevitably tore and fell away. Everyone else at the time – other kids, foster parents, teachers and social workers – had all referred to her as Kat but that was presumably a nickname too.

No, after twenty-three years it wouldn't be easy tracking her down but I had to try – she was the closest thing to family I had left and, unlike both my mothers and all my ex-girlfriends, Kitkat had never left me – it was *me* who had abandoned *her*.

43

Chapter Seven

Cherry leaned into the counter and I noticed dried toothpaste at the corner of her mouth. 'So then I said to him, "If you're so rich and powerful why don't you have a girlfriend?" and he said, "Who says I don't?" The cheeky bastard!' Cherry cackled, her bosom heaving.

As the pensioners in the corner waved goodbye and slipped out of the door my stomach tightened with tension. The man opened up an umbrella and his wife took his arm as they set off together in the rain. With them gone there were just the three of us left in the cafe – no witnesses if Vic lost it.

It was two in the afternoon and my husband had been drinking. I could smell it on his breath. Not beer but vodka. He was angry about something and spoiling for a fight. He hid it well behind a mask of impassive neutrality and a deceptive smile but I knew when he was fuming; there was an eerie stillness about him, the calm before the storm. And right now Vic was set to blow.

Cherry was clearly not as attuned to Vic's moods as I was or she would have known to stop talking long before now. She was describing her session with a rich city banker she'd picked up the night before in extensive, lurid detail. It wasn't Cherry's occupation that riled Vic – he couldn't care less how many men she screwed – it was the particulars of this John's lifestyle that irked him: his top of the range Ferrari, the size of his hotel suite, the fact he could spend a ton on champagne and not drink it. Vic resented those things because he secretly wanted them for himself. Usually he took his frustrations out on me but right now Cherry was unwittingly in the firing line and, with no other customers around, I was beginning to fear for her safety.

I'd already interrupted Cherry and tried to change the subject, more than once, but she was pleased with her night's exploits, caught up in some sort of *Pretty Woman* fantasy, and wouldn't be diverted.

'I nearly ripped his shirt when I tried to get it off 'cause he had these chunky cufflinks – solid gold they were!' Her eyes widened for emphasis.

Vic's jaw tightened and I stepped out from behind the counter grabbing a broom. 'Cherry, I don't suppose you could do me a favour and clear that table by the door, while I sweep the floor?' Cherry looked at me blankly; I never asked her for help.

But before she could reply Vic said in a steady voice, 'You think that makes him something special? Flashing some bling? He can't be all that fucking clever if he wastes his dough on the likes of you.'

A spasm of hurt flickered across Cherry's face before her features hardened. 'At least he fucking paid for it,' she retorted.

And that was it – Vic snapped. His arm shot out like lightning, his hand closing around Cherry's windpipe as he forced her back against the counter. Her eyes bulged in terror and I launched my body between them, my face just centimetres from Vic's, my head blocking his view of Cherry, the broom handle gripped tightly in my hands.

'Don't, Vic, please,' I gasped, staring into his eyes. They were unnervingly icy, as he glared back at me with loathing. 'Someone might see,' I added.

'Move,' he snarled.

'Please,' I whispered again, adrenalin pounding in my ears. 'Hit me if you have to but let her go, please.'

The door opened with a familiar click and sweep and Vic automatically released Cherry and stepped back. We turned in unison to see Travis frozen mid-step in the doorway. 'Shit, should I come back later?'

Vic stalked towards Travis. 'Get out of my fucking way,' he growled as he pushed past him and stormed out.

Once I was sure he had gone I turned back to Cherry. 'You OK?' Her hand shook as she touched her painted fingertips to the flushed skin of her throat but her expression was already settling into a mask of neutrality.

'I'm fine,' she muttered, sinking back onto a stool. I could see that she wasn't but I knew she wouldn't want me to make a fuss in front of Travis. Sex worker or not, Cherry had her pride and hated appearing weak. How many times had she been roughed up by men over the years? Clearly she hadn't been expecting that kind of treatment from Vic though. Perhaps she had always assumed, like I had, that his wife-beating was reserved for his wife. Returning to the kitchen, I set aside the broom and reached for the teapot.

'What's eating him?' Travis said. He'd sauntered up to the counter, leaving a trail of rainwater across the floor.

'Who knows,' I muttered, pouring Cherry a fresh beverage and sliding it over to her. She had her head down as she rummaged about in her handbag for her fags. 'What can I get you Travis?'

Travis glanced from me to Cherry and then back again,

the curiosity plain on his face, but he knew better than to poke his nose into Vic Leech's business.

'Just a Coke thanks, Rina,' he said, fumbling in the pocket of his jeans for some change.

Cherry stood up as I retrieved a can from the fridge. 'Just nipping out for a fag,' she mumbled, already on her way to the door as two more customers walked in. I made a mental note to make her eat something when she came back – something sweet for the shock. Thank god Travis had arrived when he did. In gratitude for his timely arrival, and in anticipation of his discretion, I slid a king-sized Mars bar across the counter along with his Coke.

'On the house,' I said, watching Cherry on the pavement outside as she attempted to light up in the rain, one trembling hand cupped around a disposable lighter.

'Wow, thanks,' Travis said cheerfully.

'My pleasure.' Vic would notice the shortfall the next time he did a stock check but, right now, I didn't care.

Chapter Eight

By the time I'd finished loading up the van ready for market the rain had stopped and the sun was peeking out from behind the clouds. Shaking out my shoulders I looked around in satisfaction. The first half of March had been relentlessly cold and drizzly but now, at last, spring was finally asserting itself. It was evident in the fresh green buds bursting into leaf, the frothy candy pink cherry blossom and the cheery yellow primroses and narcissi jostling for space in the hedgerows. The surrounding hills basked in sunshine as a clear blue sky spread out above, completing the near-idyllic scene. I found myself taking a deep lungful of fresh air and savouring the sound of birds singing and the warmth on my skin. How could anyone viewing this place now not be tempted to buy it? Surely the estate agent would be ringing with a serious offer soon? With probate completed I'd put both the cottage and the business straight on the market. It had only been a week but so far all the 'offers' had been well below the asking price and from developers who simply wanted to flatten the place. I was reluctant to surrender my family legacy under such circumstances – it just felt wrong.

With Easter just over two weeks away and in a last minute bid to increase revenue, I had found a market stallholder in the city willing to trial our seasonal, hand-planted pots and hanging baskets. Gary, a flower seller by trade, sold to the London crowd and was consequently prepared to offer me a better price for the stock than it would sell for in Wildham. I figured it was worth a try because, if all went well and the planters proved popular, it could become a regular revenue stream – which would look great on the books.

No matter how long it took to find a decent buyer for Southwood's though, one thing was for sure: I couldn't go on living in two places at once; it was killing me. Flexing my back, I raised my arms and stretched – tipping my head from side to side to release the tension in my neck. This week, by re-arranging several appointments, I'd managed to wrangle a bit of time away from my day job – escaping to Wildham yesterday at lunchtime. But I would have to be back in the office in time for a company forecasting meeting tomorrow afternoon and in-between I wanted to deliver this planted stock to market while it was fresh. It had been a long day of physical labour and my muscles still ached from my exertions the night before. My mate Liam was lock forward for the local rugby squad – the Wildham Warriors – and had invited me along to Tuesday night rugby practice. I'd relished the opportunity to be part of the team, throwing myself back into the game and discarding my troubles at the side of the pitch. But I hadn't played since university and my body was paying for it now.

Rugby aside, trying to keep a hand in both businesses – a foot in both worlds – was exhausting and, as patient and understanding as my boss was, if I carried on this way for much longer, I was going to get myself fired.

Dusting the compost from my hands, I locked the van and said goodbye to Lil, thanking her for all her help. She had more than forty years of experience in planting up pots and hanging baskets and made it look easy. As with every aspect of running the nursery, I found I still had plenty to learn.

On my way back to the cottage, I experienced a wave of sadness on seeing the mass of tulip buds that were forcing their way up through the ground, either side of the back door. The bulbs that Dad planted every autumn in Mum's memory were still going to provide a spectacular display of colour, regardless of the fact that Dad would not witness it this year.

By the time I'd showered and changed, swapped my contact lenses for my glasses, and packed everything ready for my return to London in the morning, I was ravenous but the day wasn't over yet. Re-heating some vegetable soup and buttering myself some bread, I settled at the kitchen table in front of my laptop to put in a few hours of insurance work. It was after eleven when, having proofread and emailed a last policy report to my boss, I was finally free to check my personal inbox for messages – or, as I liked to think of them, Kitkat clues.

Given the confidential nature of the fostering service and that my search was not for a blood relative I had inevitably hit a brick wall as far as official channels were concerned. But I'd been surprised by the number of open websites, chat rooms and forums dedicated to finding those who were missing, lost or estranged.

It was hard not getting bogged down in the raw, heart-wrenching detail of thousands of other posts; my own futile search (for someone half-remembered, who may not remember me) was time consuming enough, without getting sidetracked by the desperate plight of others. But

I'd uploaded what little I knew: the name and address of our foster parents at the time; the dates we were there; a brief physical description of Kitkat; and her approximate age, then and now. In the absence of her real name I'd suggested other alternatives: Katherine, Kate, Katie, Kaitlyn, Kathy or Kathleen – but I was just stabbing in the dark.

My stomach tensed with nervous excitement at the sight of two new emails in my inbox but it was short-lived. Rather than information relevant to my search, they turned out to be words of comrade-like encouragement from other ex-foster kids. As kind as the messages were, I couldn't help feeling deflated. Half-heartedly I keyword-searched the various sites for posts with the names Kat and James (just on the off-chance she was actually looking for me) but came up empty as ever. Sighing, I shut down the laptop, took off my glasses and rubbed the bridge of my nose. What if she simply didn't want to be found?

Chapter Nine

Feeling typically frazzled for ten o'clock on a Thursday morning I turned the fryer down to a low heat, rested my elbows on the counter and gazed out at the market with envy. I had a clear view of Jo's stall – a multicoloured array of fruit and vegetables held aloft on emerald carpets of artificial grass: bunches of smiling yellow bananas, stacks of glossy red tomatoes and bulbous sweet peppers, as vibrant as traffic lights. It was a warm, sunny, spring day outside and I longed to go for a walk, to feel the sun on my skin, the breeze in my hair – but of course I would do no such thing.

Vic didn't like me leaving the building without his prior permission and even then I was only allowed as far as the market. In much the same way as we got discounted fruit and veg from Jo, Vic had similar deals set up with the butcher, the fishmonger and the bakery round the corner. In the first few years of our marriage I'd taught myself to cook by watching TV shows and following recipes from magazines. Vic would take me to the local supermarket once a month so I could stock up on the ingredients he couldn't scrounge from stallholders or bulk-buy from the cash and carry. But my culinary efforts were wasted on him and he resented spending the extra money. Now we ate at the cafe during the day, our evening meals were plain and simple and the trips to the supermarket had long since dried up. The only other place I'd ventured to in the past eighteen years was the hospital.

The way Vic controlled and confined me with his set of 'rules' and the constant threat of violence was wrong, I knew that. I no longer found his possessiveness flattering; I'd long ago recognised him for the bully he was. A private part of me – the daring girl I used to be – silently railed against my husband like a feral cat trapped in a cage: all bared teeth and sharp claws. But in reality it was not worth fighting. With my aversion to physical contact and crowded places Vic's restrictions on my movements had, over time, become easy to adhere to and were now strangely comforting. The irony was not lost on me. It was only on days as beautiful as this one that I was really conscious of how confined my life had become. I sighed. Today I couldn't even roll up my sleeves because Vic had carried out an impromptu stock check the day before and noticed a few things missing – a Mars bar for one. He had grabbed my arm in order to berate me about it, painfully twisting my wrist and giving me fresh bruises that would invite difficult questions if seen.

From where I stood it seemed Gary the flower seller had some beautiful new blooms in: buckets bursting with lilies, carnations and roses and – were those freesias? They must smell fantastic.

A glance around the cafe confirmed that every customer was seated with food or a newspaper; no one needed me or was even looking in my direction. Recklessly grabbing a handful of paper napkins, I walked over to the front door and wedged it open, quietly revelling in the noisy, fragranced air that assailed my senses. Standing on tiptoe and craning my neck to discover what else Gary might have on his stall, I clocked a tall, attractive, young man. He was unloading a colourful selection of planted pots, troughs and hanging baskets from the back of a small van. I'd never seen him before and something about the way he laughed politely, presumably at one of Gary's bad jokes, drew my attention.

Straight away I could tell he wasn't from around here – it wasn't just his good looks: we sometimes got stray city types cutting through the market, lost or on their way to somewhere more important. And it wasn't just the way he was dressed – in trendy jeans and a smart rugby shirt that implied better taste and breeding than was the local norm. It was his energy – an air of wholesome health and vitality, a light in his eyes that spoke of optimism and fresh possibilities. In these parts that was rare indeed.

I was too far away to hear what they were talking about but I unconsciously leaned into the door frame as the young man finished unloading the last of his wares, his broad shoulders and back muscles flexing and moving with practised ease, his thigh and butt muscles filling out his jeans with each smooth crouch and squat. He was locking up his van when Gary suddenly jabbed a finger towards Vic's greasy spoon.

Blinking in alarm, I abruptly snapped out of the strange trance I had drifted into as the stranger began to turn in my direction. Embarrassed, I pivoted on my heel and returned to the counter before he could catch me staring at him like a lunatic. What the hell had got into me? I wasn't the sort of woman who lusted after men – especially not twenty-something boys who were too young for me and completely out of my league. Picking up a cloth I wiped down the already clean counter top, holding my breath as the tall, dark figure sauntered in through the open doorway.

Chapter Ten

Shaking Gary's hand on our agreement I thanked him before strolling over to the cafe he'd recommended for a late breakfast. He was impressed with our Easter planters and that was a weight off my mind. I was confident that the stock was top quality and Lil had made a professional job of the planting but it was a relief even so – a regular weekly order was just the sort of custom the nursery needed and would look promising to a potential investor.

The woman working in Vic's Cafe captured my attention even at a distance – something about the way she moved. She was not conventionally pretty like Jasmine. She was tall, pale and slender almost to the point of gauntness, with eyes slightly too large for her face, a long nose and a sharp chin. Not my usual type at all. But there was something about her, a quiet dignity and grace which was somehow incongruous in a modest greasy spoon, and which distracted from the noise, the heat and the odorous smell of fried meat.

I found myself taking a stool at the counter just to be near her, as if we were two friends in a room full of strangers. She blushed slightly as I caught her eye. I was staring but I couldn't help it.

'What can I get you?' Her voice was steady but gentle.

'Oh, um, I'm not sure,' I said, picking up a menu and glancing at it blindly. 'Just some coffee and toast would be great.'

'Brown or white?' With her fingertip she entered my order into the till.

'Brown, please.'

She nodded and poured my coffee. 'Help yourself to milk and sugar.' With her chin she indicated further along the counter, her eyes briefly connecting with mine.

'Thanks.' As I smiled at her she turned away, her cheeks reheating. I was used to girls blushing around me. Jasmine had once said that my good looks were deceptive and gave women the mistaken impression I'd be good in bed. She'd been mad at me at the time. Lately she was mad at me *all* the time but, with my constant driving back and forth to Wildham, we'd become like ships in the night. Despite what my girlfriend might think I got the feeling that *this* woman did not blush often or easily and I was pleased to have had an effect on her.

Mesmerised, I watched as she moved about the small kitchen area. I guessed she was a few years older than me. Her coffee-coloured hair wasn't thick like mine but as delicate as finely spun silk, the undersides subtly streaked with silver where it had been hastily pulled back in an elastic band. Several long strands had escaped and hung down obscuring her face and my fingers itched to reach out and hook the tendrils back behind her ear.

Most of her body was hidden under ill-fitting clothes: a man's long-sleeved, khaki T-shirt and jeans that hung from her hips, the denim frayed and worn thin. Though too big at the waist they were short in the leg, revealing tantalising glimpses of elegantly boned ankles. Now and again she smoothed her hands down over the apron which was tied tightly at her slender waist and hinted at feminine curves, concealed from view. She set two slices of buttered toast down before me and I felt oddly crushed by the sight of a simple wedding band on her left hand. She wore no other jewellery as far as I could tell.

'Can I get you anything else?'

She met my eyes again and I saw that her irises were a soft grey-green, imbued with a rare iridescence and framed by long, fine lashes; requiring no make-up whatsoever. But there was a subtle guardedness there – as if she had already seen more than her fair share of bad things.

'This is great, thanks.' I wanted to say more; to keep her there with me; to find out something, anything, about her. But for once I couldn't summon a single word; all the small talk I usually deployed had deserted me. She let slip a perfect, fleeting smile as she moved away to clear some tables.

Stirring milk into my coffee I glanced around at the cheap moulded-plastic furnishings, the outdated tiled walls and the worn lino beneath my feet. I even perused the sticky, laminated menu but my attention was inevitably, repeatedly, drawn back to the woman who'd served me, while she chatted cheerfully to other customers. She spoke plainly, her language peppered with London colloquialisms, but she was not as coarse as some of those she was conversing with and her voice was seductively warm and gentle.

I took a gulp of coffee and it scalded my tongue, despite the milk. The waitress returned to the other side of the counter to serve a new customer and her sudden smile somehow reached right inside my chest and winded me.

Unnerved I looked down at my plate and took a large bite of toast, though my appetite had vanished completely. Who was this unknown woman? And why did she have me tongue-tied and completely turned on?

It was 10 p.m. by the time I'd finished at the office, driven back to the flat and let myself in. The forecasting meeting had gone well and I'd managed to identify some interesting trends amid the reams of dry analysis reports, despite my mind's continual attempts to wander. I was shattered but, rather than sleep, what I was most looking forward to was a good hard wank. I hadn't been able to stop thinking about the woman from the cafe this morning. Every time I closed my eyes those hypnotic grey-green eyes flooded my mind and I recalled the sound of her voice, her fleeting smile and the way she moved. For the first time in months I had a boner – in fact I'd been getting them all day, ever since I'd laid eyes on her. I wasn't entirely sure why she had provoked such a strong reaction in me – she was a complete stranger after all and we'd barely exchanged more than a few words – but it was a relief to know my equipment still worked. I was aching for release.

'You're back late,' Jasmine observed as I entered the living room. She'd spent the last three days in Manchester auditioning for various parts in a TV show but it would be at least a week before she found out if she'd been successful. Now she was draped across the settee, wearing a silk dressing gown but still fully made up, her fuchsia-pink fingernails clutching a cigarette. Apparently she'd given up all pretence of quitting.

'I hope they're paying you well for all this overtime.'

I didn't comment; it wasn't overtime; I was making up all the hours I'd missed. Jasmine and I had spoken by phone while she was away but she was unaware that, in her absence, I'd snuck off to Wildham to help get the garden centre ready for the spring rush. Admitting that now would just provoke an argument. Depositing my briefcase and jacket at the end of the settee I realised too late that the bulge in my trousers was now obvious.

Jasmine sprang to her feet before me, a devious smile on her face 'Did you miss me, James?' She kissed me and I tried not to grimace at the taste of tobacco on her lips as she cupped me with her hand. With a dazzling smile and a flutter of her eyelashes she took a step back, stubbed her cigarette out in an ashtray on the coffee table and then shrugged out of her gown. It drifted to her feet to reveal a transparent, black baby-doll outfit, decorated with bright pink bows.

I laughed. 'What on earth are you wearing?'

'I just bought it; do you like it?' She looked up at me through her lashes while posing with a hand on her hip.

'Oh my god, are those crotchless pants?' With undisguised curiosity I bent to get a better look.

'Yes.' She giggled slightly and I wondered how much she'd had to drink. As I straightened up, she stepped closer and started to unzip my fly. 'Can I help you with this, big boy? It's been a while…'

'Jas, you don't have to do that,' I started to protest – I was uncomfortably aware that my state of arousal had been induced by someone else entirely. And yet, for the first time in weeks, Jasmine was happy with me – smiling at me; wanting me; reminding me of how things were when we first got together. If I refused her now she'd feel rejected and I was tired of hurting her; sick of feeling like a failure. Under the circumstances it was easier to go with it and give my girlfriend what she wanted, even if she was disconcertingly dolled up like a porn star.

We had sex right there on the sectional settee and, although I made sure she was satisfied, before I found my own release, it wasn't enough to stop me from feeling ashamed afterwards. Sleeping with my girlfriend, while thinking about another woman, was wrong on every level and I hated myself for it. Could I sink any lower?

Climbing off her I staggered to my feet, awkwardly pulling my trousers back up and re-zipping my fly. With a smug, sated smile on her face, Jasmine rose up beside me, tipping her head in the direction of the master bedroom in silent invitation. But the thought of spending the night in her arms after the way I'd just betrayed her made me hesitate.

'What's wrong?' she said, her eyes immediately narrowing with suspicion.

'Nothing, it's just, it's late and it's been a crazy week for me so far – I'm absolutely shattered. I might just –' I was stroking her upper arms in an instinctive, placatory gesture but it did nothing to prevent the hard look that entered her eyes.

'You selfish prick! Do you think you're the only one in this relationship? You're hardly ever here and when you are you barely even notice me! Would you rather just be alone? Because I can leave and then, trust me, you would be utterly alone – no one else would put up with all your shit as long as I have!'

She was right – I knew she was right – I'd never be able to give Jasmine the love and attention she deserved. The only reason I was still with her was because I didn't want to be on my own – didn't want to have to find another girlfriend and go through the same cycle of brief relationship and break-up over and over again. It was totally unfair to Jasmine. Was now the right moment for me to be honest and break up with her?

The words lodged like bullets in my throat and, though I opened my mouth, no sound came out. Unable to bear the pain and anger in her expression I closed my eyes.

With an exasperated sigh she shoved me hard in the chest and stomped off to the master bedroom, slamming the door behind her with an almighty bang.

Chapter Eleven

Little paper sachets of sugar went everywhere, skidding and scattering across the floor as if in competition to see which could go further: the brown or the white. They disappeared under tables, between people's shoes and shopping bags, soaking up damp footprints and congealing on the lino. I swore under my breath, muttered a general apology and hastily started sweeping them up with a dustpan and brush. Such an idiot! Vic was going to be furious.

I'd been on tenterhooks all morning, all week if I was honest; restless with anticipation and a peculiar sort of hope that the handsome stranger would return. Not that I had any intention of trying to engage him in any way if he did turn up. I just wanted to see him again; he had brightened up my day. I couldn't really understand why; we'd barely spoken and we had nothing in common. He wasn't local – he was well spoken, refined, and exceptionally good-looking and made me strangely conscious of my own voice, clothes and lack of finesse – but the mere idea of him made me smile.

Sighing in irritation I tipped the wasted sugar into the bin. At least Vic didn't take sugar in his coffee. Everyone else would just have to manage without until his next trip to the cash and carry. The second breakfast rush was just about over now and the market outside was filling up with shoppers despite the cold and dreary weather, a complete contrast to last Thursday's sunshine. As I cleared the tables by the door I noted that Gary had sold out of all the planted containers in just a week. Tomorrow was the start of the school Easter holidays. Surely the mystery man would be back today to deliver more stock in time for the weekend?

Mags came in and ordered a round of teas and coffees to take out to her fellow stallholders. She was busy relaying all the details of her daughter's honeymoon – those details that were fit for public consumption anyway: the temperature in Tenerife, the size of the hotel swimming pool and the price of the cocktails – when mystery man pulled up outside, making my stomach tighten. He emerged from his van in a forest-green sweatshirt and combat trousers and gave a heart-melting smile. I fought to keep my eyes trained on Mags's face, listening without hearing a word, excitement mounting in my body, as he gently unloaded his wares in my peripheral vision. Would he come into the cafe today?

At last he locked his van, turned and headed straight towards me and my pulse leapt into my throat. He held the door for Mags as she departed and as he approached the counter he held out a small terracotta pot filled with dainty yellow, lilac and purple flowers. I could not have been more surprised if he had held out a bomb.

'I thought you might like this,' he said. 'I thought maybe it could sit on the counter.'

At first I could only stare.

'It's just a marketing ploy really,' he shrugged, the pot dipping as his arms began to sag with doubt. 'Hopefully people will like it and want to buy one for themselves?'

'Oh, OK,' I said, my voice returning.

'I promise they don't bite,' he said, humour dancing provocatively around his mouth, 'if they were snapdragons it might be different.'

I smiled impulsively. 'They're lovely, thanks.' I reached out and took the plant pot, carefully, so as not to touch his fingers with my own. Making some space I set it down on a saucer beside the till for everyone to enjoy. 'Are these daffodils? They're tiny.'

'Yes, miniature daffodils – narcissus – and these with the cheerful little faces are violas, miniature pansies that they grow from seed at the nursery.'

'But not you?' My curiosity was piqued by the distinction.

'I don't really work there. It was my dad's place; it's out in the countryside – I'm trying to sell it. I'm James by the way,' he added with a crooked grin.

'Rina,' I said, still smiling involuntarily.

'That's unusual. Is it short for something?'

'Just Rina,' I said with a shrug. The lie was an automatic reflex – I'd never liked the name I'd been given when I first went into care; had never wanted to be that little lost girl. At thirteen I started going by Rina instead – in the vain hope that a new name would make me a new person. He held my gaze for longer than I was expecting, almost as if he knew I was hiding something, but I felt unable, unwilling, to look away. James had the warmest cocoa-brown eyes I had ever seen. I'd heard the phrase 'come to bed eyes' before but had never understood it until now. There were tiny droplets of rain shining in his hair and yet I fancied I could taste the sunshine of his honeyed skin as if he had just arrived from another world entirely. 'Why are you selling it – your dad's nursery? Why don't you run it yourself?'

'What?' James looked confused and I wondered if I'd said something stupid.

'Sorry, none of my business; just ignore me,' I said flushing.

'No it's fine, it's just, I already have a career. I work in insurance.'

'Oh, OK.' This surprised me. With his bright eyes, windswept hair and muscular physique he didn't strike me as the sort of person who'd be content stuck in an office. But then what did I know? 'What can I get you today?'

He finally released my gaze and, as he perused the menu board above my head, I ran my eyes down over the contours of his chest. A logo was printed on the fabric across his left pectoral: the words 'University of Nottingham' in faded white lettering. He hummed thoughtfully deep in his chest and absently tugged his sleeves up to his elbows, revealing beautifully sculpted forearms, peppered with fine hair, bleached by the sun.

'Scrambled egg on toast sounds good.' I focused on the till, aware of his eyes on me and determined to appear normal, 'and a coffee, please.'

'No problem.'

Having loaded brown bread into the toaster, I poured him some coffee, broke some eggs into a small bowl and started whisking. James added milk to his mug and stirred it with a teaspoon as he glanced around, smiling pleasantly at the other customers – an elderly couple deep in conversation in the corner and a woman with a large bag and a small dog. As I surreptitiously eyed him I

66

decided James wasn't as young as I'd first thought; he was less baby-faced than he had been a week ago, with an attractive shadow of stubble at his jaw that I longed to touch. Maybe he was in his late twenties or early thirties?

'Do you run this place on your own?' he said, suddenly returning his attention to me.

'Yeah, more or less. It's my husband's really – we live in the flat upstairs.' I was conscious of a note of regret in my voice and focused on rescuing the toast and buttering it.

'It's great,' James said. 'I bet you get all sorts of interesting people coming in.'

'Yeah, sometimes. We cater to the stallholders mainly; they need a hot breakfast between six and seven in the morning but they're a friendly bunch.' The contents of the bowl sizzled when I tipped them out into the frying pan.

'Six? So you must have to get up at what?'

'Five-thirty, every day. The market's closed on Sundays but we get all the anglers coming in.'

'Anglers? In London?'

'They fish the canals.'

'Oh, right.'

'And they like to start early.'

'Of course,' he grinned. 'Still, five-thirty even on Sundays – that's a bit rough on you.'

'I'm used to it.' I shrugged, stirring the eggs with a spatula while James quietly watched. 'And then there's the second breakfast rush.' I was aware I was rambling. 'The regulars in a hurry on their way to work, college or school between eight and ten; the builders who come in to use the loo and grab a breakfast bap – it's all good business, y'know.' I scooped the scrambled mix onto the toast before it could turn rubbery or burn.

'But?' James prompted.

I looked up and our eyes met. He smiled as if he was seeing right inside me. The way I felt around this man was so unexpected, so compelling, like nothing I'd ever experienced. 'But,' I said, 'every day here is the same. I mean – if I had the chance to go somewhere else, anywhere else…' My words faltered as I became aware of what I was saying – confessing – without even realising I was doing it. James's eyes were filled with an unnerving compassion.

Jumping suddenly, I dropped his breakfast and cursed as pain seared through my hand. I'd inadvertently rested the side of it on the hotplate. Embarrassed I apologised and crouched to the floor, out of sight, to clear up the mess.

But then James was beside me, easing the broken plate out of my hand and tenderly turning my palm to look at it, his warm skin making my whole body tingle disconcertingly. Gently pulling me to my feet he guided me over to the sink where he turned on the cold-water tap, letting it run before holding my inflamed skin beneath it. Usually just the idea of someone being this close, invading my personal space – touching me – would make me deeply uncomfortable, anxious even. But somehow the situation felt soothingly unreal – as if I was dreaming, as if it wasn't really happening. As he cradled my hand in his, all the tension leached out of my body until I was resting my weight into the reassuring solidity of his side.

We must have stayed like that for several long minutes, without saying a word, until I came to my senses

68

and remembered that I had other customers.

'I think it's OK now, thanks,' I said quietly, avoiding James's gaze.

Releasing my hand he turned off the tap while I gingerly dabbed my hands on a tea towel and glanced around the cafe. Everybody else seemed to be minding their own business, oblivious to the riot of sensations battling it out in my body. How had I let him get so close? God I hope he doesn't think I stink of fried sausages. He smells wonderful.

'Sit down, I'll make you some more breakfast,' I muttered, nudging him with my elbow and still avoiding his eye.

He re-seated himself at the counter without a word, while I re-made his toast and eggs. By the time it was ready, more customers had come in and I was working on three requests for a full English. From that point on I worked hard and outwardly ignored James completely, though my body was fully aware of, and electrified by, his presence.

Eventually he paid his bill but seemed reluctant to leave. I saw him glance at the box of KitKats on the counter, the hole ripped in the cardboard at one end just large enough to dispense one biscuit at a time. Seeing them always took me back to my childhood – they were Jamie's favourites and I used to steal them from the local newsagents simply for the pleasure of sharing them with him. I wondered if Jamie, wherever he was, still liked KitKats? James took one out, as if on impulse, and stared at it for a moment before getting to his feet and placing a handful of change on the counter.

'See you next week, Rina.' He said it casually, perhaps

for the benefit of the customers stood next to him, but his eyes glowed as if he wished to communicate something more. He was gone before I could properly react or decipher his look but it stayed with me, bothering me, for days.

Chapter Twelve

'Trouble in the city?' Liam said over the rim of his glass before taking a large gulp of orange juice. It felt good to be back in the White Bear – the pub had a cosy, traditional country feel and, with it being just a short walk from Southwood's, it had always been my dad's local. The place was packed, since it was a Saturday night, but Liam and I had been offered two seats at the end of an otherwise occupied table because a regular had recognised me as being Reg Southwood's son.

Liam Hunt, at six-and-a-half feet tall with a tank-like physique and a prominent, often-furrowed brow, was someone people instinctively found intimidating, something that his quiet demeanour did little to dispel. But he was a good man – a teetotaller – and an old friend. An unexpected bonus to all my recent visits to Wildham was that we'd had the chance to become close again; Liam ran a garden maintenance business with his older brother Lester (another member of the rugby team) and was a regular customer at Southwood's Garden Centre. There were few people in the world I felt I could rely on but Liam was one of them.

'Ha. Sort of,' I said picking up my pint of beer. 'Jasmine's dumped me.'

Liam raised one eyebrow.

'Cheers,' I added, clinking my glass against his, before imparting the grizzly details while Liam listened in his usual patient way, without judgement.

The night before Jasmine had finally done what I could not and put an end to our ailing relationship – resolutely kicking me out of my own London flat. In all fairness she had been provoked: Jasmine had wanted to book the hotel and flights for a two-week holiday abroad and I'd been forced to admit that I'd already used up my paid leave on trips to Wildham.

'What – *all* of it?' Jasmine's initial stunned expression verged on comical but I didn't dare laugh.

'Most of it, yes.'

'What about our holiday? You said you'd take me to the Maldives this year.'

'Well, that was just a suggestion. It was never set in stone and –'

'I've just bought a two-hundred-pound bikini with diamante detailing!'

'Already? Why?'

'It was limited edition.'

'But diamante? Isn't that a bit impractical for swimming in the sea?'

Her eyes narrowed and nostrils flared.

'Look it's only temporary, until the business is sold, and in another few months I'll have accrued more paid time off and we can go wherever you want.'

She crossed her arms. 'When?'

'I can't say exactly. It all depends when a decent buyer turns up.'

To her credit Jasmine had made a brief, token attempt at staying calm before her full-blown fury won out. She had resorted to flinging things at me: books, CDs, the TV remote … anything she could get her hands on, screaming at me in staccato to 'Get out!' with the force of each painful impact (her aim was surprisingly good). Loud enough for all the neighbours to hear, she shouted that I was 'A selfish bastard and that she never wanted to see me again!' She almost sounded triumphant, as if auditioning for a role. But she was right; I was selfish; I had opted out of our holiday without consulting her, knowing full well that it might end our, already doomed, relationship. I had chosen a small, insignificant business in the country over my proud, glamorous girlfriend. I deserved her rage.

'Maybe she'll come around once the place has sold,' Liam said.

I shook my head. 'No, we're done. I should have ended it weeks ago.'

Liam gave me a sympathetic look but didn't make any attempt to contradict me.

'What's the secret?' I said.

Liam raised both eyebrows.

'You and Cally have been together, what, five years now?'

'Almost six.'

'So what is the secret to an enduring romance?' Outwardly Liam and Cally's relationship wasn't the most amorous I'd encountered – they didn't seem to go in for overt displays of affection, passionate outbursts or grand, romantic gestures – but there was a steadiness there, a sense of solid stability that I envied.

Liam shrugged. 'We were friends for quite a while before we got together – I think that helps – but otherwise, I couldn't say. Maybe you just haven't found the right woman yet?'

I snorted. 'It's not for want of looking.'

'You'll find her, one day.'

'Yeah, maybe,' I sighed. 'Trouble is, even if I do find her, chances are I won't be able to hang on to her.'

'Now you're just being defeatist,' Liam said. 'Another pint?'

A glance at my glass proved it was nearly empty and I nodded.

As Liam got up to go to the bar, I rubbed my face in my hands, wishing I'd thought to remove my contacts before coming out – my eyes felt gritty. A vision of Rina passed through my mind and I mulishly pushed it away. Whoever the right woman for me might be it was almost certainly not Rina.

Chapter Thirteen

I had made up my mind to play it cool by the time James returned the following Thursday morning. Chatting to customers was a perfectly normal thing for me to do, especially when someone was sitting at the counter where I could talk to them while I worked. In that sense James was no different to any other patron. Except that, privately, I looked forward to his particular visits all week, with an anticipation bordering on obsession. I was conscious that I must not let that show. Aside from the fact my enthusiasm was embarrassing, the regulars loved to gossip and the last thing I needed was for Vic to hear about James.

Just two days into April the month was already living up to its reputation, with a sporadic mix of sunshine and showers that made the world outside the window look clean and sparkly but which caught out any shoppers without umbrellas. The latest sudden downpour, just after ten o'clock, had created a mini-rush in the cafe, unusual for mid-morning on a Thursday. I was so busy serving customers that I didn't see James's van pull up and the first I knew of his arrival was at ten thirty, when he pushed open the cafe door and walked in with his arm wrapped around an attractive young woman.

For a horrible moment I thought they were a couple – that James had brought a significant other with him – but she was very smartly dressed in high heels and a stylish raincoat not the attire of someone who'd arrived in a van from a garden centre. These thoughts were pushed aside by the realisation that something was wrong. James's gaze was anxious as it sought mine and I was aware of a buzz of interest among the customers who followed him in, hovering near the woman with equally concerned expressions. At a second glance I saw that she looked limp and pale and that James was partly supporting her weight.

'What happened?' I said, moving round the counter as James helped her to sit in an empty seat near the door.

'She just fainted outside in the market,' said an elderly man who had come in with them. I recognised him as being one of my regulars. 'Luckily this young man managed to catch her just before she hit her head or it could have been nasty.'

The woman was bent forward with her head close to her knees as she took deep breaths. I crouched down before her but couldn't see much of her face other than to tell her skin was still pasty. 'Are you hurt?' I said.

She shook her head.

'Can I get you anything? Some water?'

She hesitated and then nodded.

'I'll get it,' James said, turning and disappearing from my peripheral vision.

'She suddenly went – just like that,' the elderly man was saying. 'One minute she was choosing flowers and the next minute her eyes were rolling back and –'

His account was cut off by James's return and the woman carefully straightened up to accept the proffered glass of water before tentatively sipping at it.

'Are you in pain? Do you want us to call an

ambulance?' I said. 'I don't have a phone but I'm sure someone else –' As I spoke James produced a mobile phone from his back pocket but she shook her head again.

'No, no, I'm fine thank you – just horribly embarrassed to have caused such a fuss.'

'Don't worry about that. Are you sure though? You still look a bit peaky; maybe you should get checked out just to be on the safe side,' I added.

She grimaced. 'No, really – I'm just pregnant,' she said, automatically placing a hand on her stomach. She wasn't obviously showing but it was hard to tell with the coat she was wearing. 'I sometimes get light-headed – it's my own fault. I should have eaten more breakfast but I felt too queasy at the time.'

'Ah, I see,' I said, relieved that there was a straightforward explanation. 'Do you think you could eat something now? Can I make you some toast?'

She smiled gratefully at me. 'That sounds lovely, thank you.'

The woman thanked James and the other good Samaritans who had come to her assistance and, with the excitement over and the sun shining outside once again, people returned their noses to their own business. By the time I'd prepared two slices of buttered toast and a cup of tea for the pregnant woman, James had returned to Gary's stall to finish unloading his planters and the cafe was all but devoid of customers.

I cleared the other tables while she ate and refused payment, especially since tea and toast were not things that Vic would easily miss. The colour had returned to the woman's face and she thanked me several times before leaving – exiting with a confident stride and not pausing to buy flowers after all.

'Do you think she'll be OK?' James asked me when he returned to the cafe for his breakfast several minutes later.

'I'm sure she'll be fine – thanks to you.'

James shrugged as I poured him a coffee. 'Is that experience talking?'

'Sorry?'

'Do you have kids?'

I felt the muscles in my throat tighten but kept my expression neutral and my voice light. 'No I don't. Do you?'

'No.'

This was a natural opportunity to ask James if he had a partner. He didn't wear a ring but that didn't necessarily mean he wasn't married and a man with *those* eyes and *that* perfect smile could not be short of female attention – so I assumed he had someone: a girlfriend or a lover. But I didn't ask. As innocent as our acquaintance was, his relationship status shouldn't matter to me either way but as long as my assumption went unconfirmed I could pretend to myself that those smiles and the disconcerting way he looked at me – as if I was suddenly no longer invisible – were just for me and me alone.

I was aware these thoughts were pure fantasy but what harm could they do, locked safely inside my head?

'Scrambled egg on toast?'

'Yes please.' He watched as I popped brown bread into the toaster and cracked, whisked, and stirred the eggs.

'How's work?' I said, forestalling any personal questions he might be about to ask.

James frowned, sighed and rubbed his jaw thoughtfully. 'It's OK. I'm lucky that I have a very understanding boss, and that the company has a flexitime policy in place, so I'm still able to go back and forth to Wildham to keep an eye on things at the garden centre.'

'What's a flexitime policy?' I said, plating up his breakfast.

'Basically, as long as I keep my clients happy, reach my monthly targets and clock up a minimum of thirty-five hours a week on my timesheet, the company aren't too fussy about how and when I go about it. I've been able to use some holiday leave and take some extra time off here and there by making up the time working from home in the evenings.'

'Oh, that sounds –'

'Exhausting?'

'Yes.'

'It is.'

I smiled in sympathy, setting his breakfast on the counter before him.

'This looks delicious, thanks.' Reaching for a set of cutlery he unwrapped the knife and fork from their paper napkin and immediately tucked in to his eggs.

'How are things at the garden centre? Have you found a buyer yet?' I said, as I tidied up the kitchen.

'No. No buyer.' He paused chewing and swallowing another mouthful. 'I've got Leah helping me manage things while I'm not there but it's only a short-term solution. She usually runs the outdoor plant area and she's got a great head for business but she's a single mum with other commitments so I can't rely on her help indefinitely.'

'Do you have any idea how long it might take to find a suitable buyer?'

'No,' he said, fork poised in mid-air. 'The trouble is, spring, and Easter weekend in particular, is the busiest, most profitable time of year for any gardening business. It's prime planting season and a popular time for homeowners to get out in their gardens and do some DIY. From a practical point of view it would be crazy not to take advantage of it, so the staff and I have been pulling out all the stops to get the place ready. You should see it, Rina – the shop is a blaze of colour: full of flowering scented bulbs in yellow, pink and blue. The perfume of the hyacinths is sweet enough to make your head swim. And outside the benches are crammed with new plant stock: herbaceous perennials sprouting fresh, feathery, green foliage and shrubs – glossy-leaved and fat with buds – ready to put on a vibrant summer display.' I stopped tidying and smiled, enthralled by the light in his eyes as much as by his description. 'And down on the tree line the cherry trees are all in full blossom, like a line of frilly, sugar-pink ballerinas, shimmying with every breath of wind.'

'You make it sound like paradise.'

James snorted. 'It's not all idyllic – last weekend a customer's dog peed on my leg, Frank threatened to go on strike because Max had adjusted the position of the seat in the forklift, and Lil found an infestation of vine weevil grubs in one of the polytunnels and unceremoniously dropped them on my desk in front of me.'

I laughed out loud and James grinned back at me, one eyebrow raised.

'Have you ever seen a vine weevil grub?'

I shook my head.

'Ugly little things – up to a centimetre long and fat, with no legs and a penchant for eating all the roots of a containerised plant.'

'Ugh.'

'Indeed. We've caught the problem early though and treated every plant on the nursery so hopefully it will be OK.' James shoved another forkful of scrambled egg into his mouth and I wondered how he could after visualising grubs.

'You know, dog pee and vine weevil grubs aside, it sounds like you really like the place – like being there.'

He swallowed. 'I do. The staff are wonderful, the customers are friendly and it's a great little business, with so much potential.'

'So, why are you selling again?'

'Because I already have a job, here, in the city.'

'In insurance?'

'Yes – mostly life insurance.' He picked up his coffee and took several gulps and I considered letting the topic drop – with anyone else I probably would have …

'What made you want to get into that?' I said.

He sighed. 'It's difficult to explain the appeal to someone outside the industry but I guess originally I was drawn to the security of it. I liked the idea of weighing up potential dangers and helping people prepare for the worst – providing people with some reassurance; some protection; something to fall back on.'

I smiled. 'I think I can understand that.' James was staring at his cleared plate and now set his knife and fork down neatly side by side. 'Do you still feel that way?'

He looked up at me and there was such sadness in his eyes that I had an impulse to reach out and touch him. 'The trouble is it's often the people who need the insurance most who can't afford to pay for it. And anyway, when you lose someone –' He swallowed, his Adam's apple bobbing in his throat, and I gave into instinct gently placing my hand over his. 'When someone dies, money is *something* – some help – but it's not really compensation. It doesn't bring that person back; nothing does that.'

I guessed that he was referring to the recent death of his father but I didn't ask. I'd never had parents of my own, to love and lose and grieve for, but I had lost someone and James was right: money couldn't bring them back. 'Maybe it's time to change career,' I said. 'Try something else?'

He smiled and turned his hand over so that my palm lay warm and tingling in his but I drew my hand back. 'Sounds terrifying.'

'Why? Haven't you been running your dad's garden centre for several months now – and enjoying it – and you said yourself how much potential there is in the business.'

'Yes, but it would still be a risk and it's taken me years of hard work to get where I am as a broker – build a life for myself in the capital. If I give it all up now, and go back to Wildham, it's going to feel like I've failed.'

I bit my lip. I was tempted to scold him and tell him he was being ridiculous but it wasn't my place. 'Well, it's your choice, obviously, but I have to say if I had the chance to leave London for somewhere like that I would jump at it.'

I could feel him watching me as I cleared away his plate and cutlery and greeted two customers coming in the door but James didn't say anything else. He still looked lost in thought ten minutes later as he paid his bill, waved goodbye and left.

Chapter Fourteen

Ten seconds before my alarm clock went off, I was chased awake by dreams of Rina and a stubborn hard-on. The structure of the dreams was already lost to me as I switched off the insistent beeping, stretched and yawned, but I was left with some tantalising impressions: the magnetic pull of her eyes; the soft translucence of her skin; the warm throb of her pulse against mine ... The more I saw of Rina, the more I wanted to see. Her bewitching beauty and poise, so understated and convincing, would have been enough but it was more than that. It was immensely satisfying making Rina smile and her laughter, when it came, was worth the wait, erupting like music from deep inside her with a raw pleasure that was entirely natural. She didn't giggle for effect, to attract men, or to put people at their ease and her amusement was never calculated, cruel or forced. She simply laughed when she found something funny. It was my new favourite sound.

Another huge draw was that I could talk to Rina – about things I hadn't even realised I needed to talk about. She was a mysterious woman with a carefully concealed fragility and a contrasting strength and passion, just craving release. Yesterday morning she hadn't just listened – she'd somehow held up a mirror: showing me the truth, pride and fear behind my own words before offering me her own honest, heartfelt opinion. If it wasn't for her I would never have had the balls to go straight back to my boss and hand in my notice that very afternoon.

He had been disappointed by my abrupt resignation but not surprised. When I discussed my situation with him he was amazingly supportive, almost envious, and I got the impression he was looking forward to his own retirement in just three years' time. Through careful negotiation – whereby I relinquished some pay and certain benefits and agreed to help train up my successor – we reduced the standard three-month-notice period I would have to work down to just one month. An hour later, with the termination of my contract finalised, I'd returned to my office, with its hard-earned view of brick and concrete, and called Leah. Squealing with excitement at my news she'd agreed to keep managing the garden centre for another four weeks until I could take over full time. With another call to the estate agent instructing them to take Southwood's off the market I suddenly had a whole new future lined up. It had been an incredible, adrenalin-rush of an afternoon and it would not be easy running the garden centre – I still had a huge amount to learn – but I *wanted* to do it. I wanted to make Southwood's a place to be proud of.

As I swung my legs out of bed and planted my bare feet on the carpet I was relieved to discover that I was still confident that I'd made the right decision. I was already starting to feel at home here in Dad's cottage, more optimistic than I had in months, and a downward glance at my crotch confirmed that my libido was back with a vengeance.

But it wasn't just a change in vocation that had me

excited. In the shower I sought relief while picturing a pair of sage green eyes, lit with a hint of a smile, and long, lean, naked female legs emerging from beneath a crisp, clean, white apron. I came quickly, taken aback by how much I wanted a woman I barely knew – a woman who wasn't mine – even as the water washed away all evidence of my inappropriate desire. With the immediate urge assuaged, I eyed my reflection critically as I dressed. Today was Good Friday and it would be six whole, long, days until I saw Rina again. The best thing I could do was to keep myself busy and try not to think about her at all. And in the meantime, to stave off any loneliness, I would ring Liam and arrange to meet him for a drink.

As the sun rose, chasing away yesterday's showers, I made a circuit of the grounds, mug of coffee in hand. Mentally I prioritised a list of the jobs which needed doing first: removing the protective fleeces from the tender shrubs and summer plug plants; moving any remaining saleable stock from the growing tunnels to the retail benches; dead-heading the polyanthus; labelling the new ceramic pots – and decided those jobs which could be suspended until later in the week, when there would be fewer customers to serve.

At eight fifteen I unlocked the main entrance, the side gate, the shop, the staff room and the tills. As the staff filtered in, laughing and teasing one another, I was pleased to see that even the newbies were joining in. For the Easter holidays I'd taken on some extra temporary staff – kids from the local horticultural college – to help out in the shop and provide a carry-to-car service for those in need of assistance. It was peak season – a bank holiday weekend with a near-perfect weather forecast – and I was determined to make the most of it.

By lunchtime the garden centre was heaving. The car park was full to capacity, with drivers forced to park on the grass verges along the road, where the local ice-cream van was cashing in, and we had a near constant flow of people through the checkouts. A variety of customers of all ages loaded up baskets and trolleys with plants, compost and sundries while children played tag, chasing each other up and down the pathways, giggling in the sunshine. For many customers a trip to the garden centre was a family day out and this reaffirmed the plans for expansion I had in mind. Of course in order to implement those plans – replace the old storage sheds with sturdy, metal, fireproof ones; re-surface and expand the car park and loading area; and extend the main building to create a coffee shop – I needed to sell my London flat.

Jasmine would accuse me of completely losing my mind once she discovered I'd jacked in my steady city job with its pension scheme, private health insurance and company car. She was no longer my girlfriend, so in theory I shouldn't have to worry what she thought of me anymore, but unfortunately she was still stubbornly inhabiting my flat and resolutely refusing to answer my calls, texts and emails. Past experience told me that if I was going to get her to move out, without kicking up an almighty fuss, I needed to tread lightly. Extricating myself from a failed relationship was never easy.

As the kids careered about around me, I mentally added an adventure playground to the growing list of things to build. After all, with the kids happily safely occupied the parents could afford to spend more time shopping. Perhaps I should ask the bank for a short-term loan.

Beside me a young girl with curly brown hair and spectacles stopped and bent down to carefully pluck a dandelion seed head from where it emerged through a crack in the path. As the girl cradled the delicate globe in her hand I was struck by a vivid memory of Kitkat. She used to pick dandelion clocks on our way to school, insisting I make a wish, before letting me blow the fluffy seeds into the air. Every single time I'd made the exact same wish: for the two of us to be jointly adopted, by the same parents, so that we would be brother and sister. But when the Southwoods had turned up and offered me a better life I hadn't asked them to take Kitkat too – I hadn't even mentioned her – I was too afraid to, and I'd regretted it ever since. With hindsight I'd realised that Reg and Ellen probably didn't have the financial means to raise two children anyway but at the time I'd been convinced that, had our roles been reversed and it had been Kitkat who was being adopted, she would have taken me with her. All these years later I still felt guilty about letting down my best friend, for betraying her, for leaving her behind. That profound sense of remorse had only intensified on the death of my mother and now Dad was gone too. Where are you Kitkat?

At the close of business, while Jenny and Priya cashed up the tills, I treated my frazzled staff to ice creams and thanked them for their sterling work.

'No worries mate; it was kinda fun,' Max said as he headed out the door with a wave and a slightly sticky grin.

'See you bright and early tomorrow,' I called after him.

He laughed. 'Yeah, yeah.'

'Yes, it was a great day,' Barb added. 'Almost felt like summer!'

'Too bloody hot by half,' Frank muttered under his breath as he passed by, compulsively swinging his keys around one finger.

'No I thought it went really well,' Lil said throwing her handbag over her shoulder and crossing her arms. 'Everyone I spoke to was really impressed by how smart everything looks –'

'And by the quality of the plants,' Leah chipped in with a smile.

'Yes indeed.' Lil replied, turning back to me. 'I think your parents would be proud, James.'

'Thank you,' I said, swallowing down a lump in my throat. 'I couldn't have done it without you, any of you. Now go home and get some rest; we're doing it all again tomorrow.' The others half-laughed, half-groaned as they said their goodbyes and left.

As I retired to the office at the back of the shop, it occurred to me that Liam had not returned any of my calls. It wasn't like him. Liam was nothing if not reliable and I was starting to worry that something might be wrong. Resolving to chase him up as soon as I was home, I settled at the desk and pulled the company spreadsheets up on the computer. Today's takings had exceeded my expectations; they were nearly double those of Good Friday the previous year. The unseasonably warm weather had played a large part in drawing customers out but, even so, the figures were encouraging – they should help with securing a bank loan – and I couldn't help feeling a little elated. Lil was right; my parents would have been pleased.

Before shutting down my desktop I noticed an email that had been routed through one of the online adoption forums. The subject heading was an intriguing eleven digit phone number but I mentally prepared myself for disappointment before opening it up:

Alright mate, sorry I dunno anyone called Kat but I lived with Alan and Josie Plumley a few years back when they were still fostering. They retired after that and moved into a smaller place. I don't have the address but I have this number for them. I dunno if it's still right because I haven't kept in touch, but maybe give it a try see?

Best of luck mate.

The hairs on the back of my neck prickled with anticipation as I re-read the anonymous message, reached for the office phone and dialled the number.

After three rings a generic recorded message kicked in and I left a stilted voicemail explaining who I was, who I was looking for and asking them to call me back. Having recited both my landlines and a mobile number, I hung up. But it was several minutes before the adrenalin had drained from my legs enough for me to walk back to the cottage.

Chapter Fifteen

Abruptly I was ripped away from my dreams with a jolt, disorientated, the muscles in my back and neck jarring painfully. I must have fallen asleep on the cramped two-seater couch, with the TV still on, and now Vic was home and waking me with a callous kick to the legs.

'Who the fuck is Jamie?'

My blood turned cold, my discomfort forgotten, at the sneered sound of *that* name on Vic's lips. 'W– what?' Squinting in the glare of the overhead light I drew my thin dressing gown tighter around me and lifted one hand up – partly to shade my eyes and partly to protect my face should my husband lash out again. How could he know about Jamie? He couldn't – I was always so careful – no one knew about Jamie but me.

'Are you deaf? I said – who the fuck's Jamie?'

His name was a knife in my heart – my own secret talisman being wielded like a weapon against me – and I had to fight to keep the hurt from my face. A furtive glance towards the kitchen reassured me that the freezer was closed and there was no sign of the fish-finger box. 'I don't know – I don't know what you're talking about; what time is it?'

'You said his fucking name in your sleep,' Vic slurred. 'Who the fuck is he, eh?'

Oh so that was all. I'd been watching a documentary on gifted children before I dozed off and wondering if Jamie was still good at maths – it was no surprise I'd

91

dreamt about him. 'I don't know, Vic – no one – I was asleep.' Vic was looming over me with his fists clenched but his eyes were bloodshot and he was unsteady on his feet – weighed down with drink and weariness. The breakfast news was not on the TV yet but I thought it must be close to dawn. Carefully I edged away from him, tensing my leg muscles ready for flight.

'I find out you've been fucking about,' he warned, jabbing a finger in my direction.

'Oh don't be stupid,' I snapped.

My retort surprised him but then his eyes narrowed in an exaggerated attempt at intimidation and I was struck by how pathetic he looked standing there, swaying, accusing me of things he knew nothing about. 'What? It's not enough that you control where I go and who I see – you want to control my dreams now too?'

He lunged at me with a snarl but was too slow and I leapt sideways on the balls of my feet, beyond his reach.

'I'm telling you, Vic, I don't know anyone by that name. It was just a random dream – probably something I saw on TV.'

He stared at me hard but his general lack of energy was sapping his anger.

'Look, the sun's almost up; why don't you go lie down – get some rest.'

I could tell this idea appealed – despite himself – and he glanced towards the bedroom before turning back to me. 'If I find out you're lying to me, I'll slit your fucking throat.'

Pressing my lips tight together I nodded in understanding and, with a final glare, he staggered into

92

the bedroom, slamming the door shut behind him.

Belatedly I realised it was Thursday today – James's day for coming to the market. I'd picked the wrong day to incite Vic's temper but thankfully he had not done anything to keep me from opening the cafe as usual. The sun was not yet visible above the roof tops but enough light filtered in through the bathroom window for me to see myself in the cracked mirror above the sink. At first glimpse I looked the same as ever – plain and drawn, as the strain of yet another fight receded from my features. But at a second look I noticed a strange glint in my eyes – a hint of the girl I once was and hadn't seen in my reflection for years.

It was rare for me to talk back to Vic like that – it was a risky thing to do when he was riled up and looking to inflict pain. So what had made me do it this time? Was it Jamie's name that had activated an old instinctive reflex to protect him – to keep him safe; keep him hidden – or was it more than that? It could so easily have been James's name I'd said in my sleep and the thought of Vic hearing that scared me to death – made me defensive. James's visits were special to me; they made me happy but they also made me more conscious of the life I was missing. He made me wish I was younger, prettier, single and carefree – things I couldn't be – but he also made me want to be bolder and braver. Was that why I'd recklessly provoked Vic? If so just knowing James was getting dangerous.

It was a beautiful, warm, bright, sunny day outside but to my dismay there were still three customers in the cafe when James turned up soon after 10 a.m. as usual. Worse still, Cherry was one of them.

James was clean-shaven but had dark shadows under

his eyes and a hunch to his shoulders as if carrying the weight of the world. I knew that he had quit his insurance job a fortnight ago and that he was currently working out his notice while also part-managing his dad's garden centre in the country – effectively working two jobs – but he had been doing that for weeks. Today he looked more tired than usual and I worried that something in particular was bothering him but, of course, I couldn't enquire in front of Cherry without arousing her curiosity.

'Morning Rina,' James said, his smile temporarily erasing any trace of trouble from his face.

'Morning. Just the usual?'

'Just some toast and coffee today, thanks.'

The fact that he had less appetite than usual only made me more concerned, and I was tempted to whip him up some eggs regardless, but I nodded and entered his order into the till while he seated himself at the counter, two places along from Cherry.

'I haven't seen you in here before have I?' she said.

'I don't know, have you?' James replied with a polite smile. 'I come by every Thursday morning.'

'Ah yeah, no, Wednesday nights are normally busy for me so I don't usually come in till the afternoon. Anyway, I'm sure you'd remember me if we'd met,' Cherry added with a wink and a smile.

James grinned at her. 'You're right, I would.'

Cherry regarded every man as a prospective client – old, young, single or married – only overtly homosexual males evaded her attention. For the most part she was fairly discreet – letting the men come to her – but good-

94

looking, potentially wealthy and successful men were by far her preferred clientele. As she proceeded to flirt with James all the goodwill and gratitude I usually reserved for her was quickly replaced with loathing.

'So what brings you to this part of town on Thursdays,' she said, shuffling to the edge of her stool and leaning closer to James, offering up a good eyeful of her cleavage.

James kept his eyes trained on the coffee cup I was filling in front of him and cleared his throat. 'I just deliver goods to the market, that's all.' With a lazy shrug he raised the cup to his lips and took a scolding sip, without having added any milk. The briefness of his answer surprised me. He didn't look embarrassed and I'd have expected him to take the opportunity to promote his wares. But he didn't describe to Cherry the planted pots and hanging baskets that were so lovingly prepared by his staff at the garden centre, or refer to the blazing red pot of dwarf tulips on the counter, which he'd set there the week before. And it made me glad. I didn't want everyone knowing James the way I did – a childish part of me wanted to keep him all to myself.

Cherry opened her mouth to say something else but I cut her off by addressing her directly. 'Cherry, if you're here to see Vic you're in for a long wait. He won't be down before midday – at the earliest.'

'I know – he never is – lazy bugger. I'm only here 'cause I've got an appointment at the clinic in fifteen minutes. I'll be back later.' I could feel James watching me as Cherry and I carried out this exchange but I avoided his eye.

For the next ten minutes I kept Cherry talking while I buttered toast for James, accepted payment from the other two customers and cleared the used crockery and cutlery from their table. It was a huge relief when she finally sashayed out the door and into the sunshine on her stiletto heels, leaving James and I alone.

'So that's why I never see your husband – because he's asleep upstairs?'

'Yes.'

'What does he do?'

'Oh, various things – minicabs, nightclub security. He works late hours so –'

'So you're left to open up the cafe.'

'Yes.'

James refrained from asking about Cherry's acquaintance with my husband and there was no judgement in his eyes when he looked at me, only sympathy, but seeing that was almost worse. I knew my marriage was not a happy one – everyone around here must at least suspect that by now – but I still didn't want James to feel sorry for me. Moving along the counter I started tidying the boxes of confectionery and straightening the lines of canned and bottled drinks. 'Are you OK? You look tired,' I said.

James stretched out his arms and then rubbed his face with both hands. 'Yeah, I'm OK.'

'Busy at work?' I prompted.

'Yeah but I'm coping – there's less and less for me to do at the office now that everyone knows I'm leaving – and Leah seems to have a good handle on things at the garden centre; sales are up.'

'That's great.'

'Yeah.'

'So what is it?' I said, fixing him with a gaze across the counter.

A strange, half-bemused smile spread across his face. 'I can't fool you, can I?'

I shook my head, returning his smile.

'It's not me – it's my mate Liam.'

'Go on.'

'We've been best friends since school days – we hang out, play rugby together. He's a great bloke – really down-to-earth and kind and sensible, y'know?'

Nodding, I refilled James's coffee cup.

'He's had this girlfriend, Cally, for years. I don't know her that well but she's always seemed nice – quiet and a bit shy but friendly enough. They always seemed great together – well-suited; happy; settled, I guess – and I always assumed they would end up married eventually. Anyway two weeks ago Cally just walked out on Liam and disappeared.'

I raised my eyebrows. 'Did she leave a note?'

'Yes, but no indication of where she was going or why. It has completely knocked Liam for six, as you might imagine, and I've been spending what little free time I have trying to help him track her down. With no success whatsoever I should add.'

I felt sorry for James's friend Liam – it sounded as though he hadn't deserved to be dumped so callously – but there was a part of me that admired this girl, Cally, for doing exactly as she pleased – for walking out of her life and simply leaving it all behind. I envied her freedom. Was she happy wherever she was now? Was she safe? 'I'm sorry,' I said. 'Maybe she'll just turn up when she's ready.'

'Yeah, maybe. The thing is they're such good people and seemed so content together. I can't help wondering – if they can't make it – what hope is there for the rest of us sinners?'

'Is that what you are? A sinner?'

James snorted and I was pleased to see his smile return. 'Almost certainly.'

'Are you Catholic?'

'No. My mum was Church of England – my dad too – but after she died he stopped going to church altogether. I don't know if that was because he only ever went to keep her company or because, after her death, his faith was shaken.'

'I'm sorry,' I said, saddened to discover that both his parents were dead.

He shrugged. 'Are you a believer?'

'No.'

'No, me neither, but I was once given a book of Bible stories when I was a child and it left me with a healthy fear of Hell.'

His wry smile was soothing despite the heavy topic of conversation and I found myself shaking my head and smiling back.

'Oh shit, no way!' James was gawping at me with his mouth open and pointing at the radio, which was on low in the background as usual.

'What?' As I listened I caught some of the lyrics from

the song that was playing and realised the vocalist was, in fact, singing about Hell.

'Turn it up, turn it up!' James said. Impelled by his sudden enthusiasm I automatically reached out and turned the volume dial and James burst into song – shouting out the chorus to 'Highway to Hell' loudly, repeatedly, and horribly out of tune. My hand to my mouth I doubled up with laughter, clutching at the counter with my other hand for support. Thankfully the song was already nearing the end and I was able to pull myself together and turn the radio down again, wiping tears from my eyes.

'What were the bloody chances of that? Do you think it was a sign?' James said, still grinning.

Before I could reply the door opened and one of my regulars sauntered in, head bent in concentration over the mobile phone in his hand. The sight brought me back to reality with a bump and I reflexively checked the time, silently hoping that Vic was still unconscious and had not heard James singing.

While I served my new customer, James – checking his own wristwatch and realising our moment was over – quietly finished his coffee, paid and then said goodbye and left. But I was pleased to note, as he stepped out into the blazing sunshine, that he looked less hunched and far happier than when he had arrived.

Chapter Sixteen

On the first Thursday following the May Day bank holiday I was late getting to market. A large delivery of specimen topiary plants I'd ordered from Belgium needed signing off at the garden centre, delaying my departure for London by an hour. I apologised to Gary for my tardiness, as I unloaded the van in the pouring rain and helped him display the dripping-wet planted containers on his stall, but he didn't seem too put out. The person I really regretted being late for was Rina.

Max had offered to do the weekly trips to market for me – he was our official delivery driver after all – and now that I had finished working out my notice and left the insurance industry for good, I had no other reason to be in London on a regular basis, especially while Jasmine was monopolising the flat. But seeing Rina was the highlight of my week. She was so easy to talk to; so wise and honest and reassuring. Despite spending less than an hour in her company a week our conversations felt more real to me than those I'd had with any of my girlfriends over the years. Somehow Rina, with her understated beauty and enigmatic eyes, gave me more confidence in myself, while also distracting me from my ongoing battle with Jasmine and vain searches for Kitkat and Cally. Rina was the one person in London I was reluctant to leave behind. I had to keep seeing her; I wasn't ready to give her up yet, no matter how married she might be.

Today I was keen to run my coffee shop ideas past her, and get her unique perspective on the plans I'd roughed out, but when I got to the cafe it was busy with customers sheltering from the rain and every stool at the counter was taken.

Having placed my breakfast order, I took a seat at a table in the corner and watched Rina from afar, as she dexterously served and chatted to the other customers with only the occasional, sympathetic smile thrown in my direction. The greasy spoon was damp with condensation today; the front windows completely steamed up and the worn lino floor treacherously slippery under foot. The fluorescent strip lighting overhead struggled to combat the cloud-dark day; the radio was completely drowned out by the sound of people talking over each other to be heard, and the air hung heavy with the stink of fried food. Looking at it properly for the first time, I realised the place was depressingly low-budget, shabby and unappealing and yet, right there, floating amongst it all, was Rina, moving with the practical grace and benevolence of an angel and appreciated by her customers, even if they didn't show it. I had come seeking her help and guidance with my plans but, now that I was here, I only wished there was some way in which *I* could help *her*.

Half an hour later the rain stopped and, although there was no sunshine peaking out from behind the clouds yet, the cafe finally emptied, leaving me free to approach the counter and pay for my breakfast. I collected up a few other dirty cups and plates along the way and Rina looked surprised.

'Thank you, that was delicious, as always,' I said, setting down the crockery and passing her a twenty pound note. 'Keep the change.'

She raised an eyebrow at me before extracting the correct change from the till and placing it neatly on the counter top. With a swipe of my hand I swept up the cash and stubbornly dropped it into the tips dish. Her lips tightened but she didn't comment.

'It's brightening up outside now; why don't you take a break? We could go for a walk and get some fresh air?'

'No I – I can't do that.'

'Why not? I won't come with you if you'd rather be alone but you deserve a break.'

'I've got too much to do here.'

'You could close up for just a few minutes, surely.'

'Maybe later,' she said turning away to load the dishwasher.

I was torn between wanting to get Rina out of the place and not wishing to offend her. 'Can I assist with the clearing up then? I could –'

'No, of course not!' she said turning back to me, looking appalled at the idea. 'Shouldn't you be going anyway – it's getting late?'

'Actually, now that I've worked out my notice, I don't have to rush back.' In truth I had a massive to-do list, waiting for me back at the garden centre, but I was my own boss now and nothing appealed more at this moment than spending time with Rina.

'But people will talk if you stay too long.'

'Which people?' I said, glancing over my shoulder. 'There's no one else here?'

102

'You know what I mean – another customer will be in any minute and people round here just love to make up gossip and spread it around.'

I did know what she meant and the last thing I wanted was to make life difficult for Rina but it still hurt that she was pushing me away. 'OK. I'll go,' I said.

'But I'll see you next week?'

I smiled and she smiled back, her whole face softening with warmth and light. 'Yes. Oh, I almost forgot – I brought you some books. They're in the van – I'll go and get them.'

'Books? What books?'

'Last week you said you liked reading fiction so I brought you some of my favourite books to borrow –'

'I can't accept them,' she said, cutting me off.

'Why not? You haven't even seen them yet.'

'Please – I don't want Vic to get the wrong idea.' Her voice had lowered to a whisper, as if she were confessing – admitting to something unspoken between us; something that she didn't want her husband to know about.

Her eyes held mine and I couldn't look away. 'He doesn't have to know they're from me.'

'He still wouldn't like it.'

'Why not?'

With a sigh she tore her gaze away and looked down at her wedding band. 'Our marriage is complicated.'

I left after that but only because she'd asked me to. I spent the whole drive back to Wildham trying to recall every reference to Vic I'd heard and turning them all over in my mind. He seemed popular among the locals but

Rina never looked happy when she talked about him; she was overly cautious about sparking rumours among her regulars and nervous about upsetting him – not signs of a woman secure in her marriage. So was Vic a particularly jealous man? Was Rina just trying to protect her marriage or was it worse than that? Was Rina actually afraid of her own husband?

Chapter Seventeen

It was Thursday and, as I stacked towers of dirty plates on autopilot, I looked forward to James's weekly arrival. I was keen to find out how the bank holiday weekend had gone at the garden centre. Was it as busy as the one at the start of May? Or had the rain affected sales as James had predicted? Over the course of his last two visits I'd learned a great deal about Southwood's and James's plans for the business. I loved to listen to him talk; to watch the animation in his face and picture the place he described. I'd never been anywhere like it, never left London in fact, and it was exhilarating imagining myself there with him: pure escapism.

Leaving the kitchen area, I started wiping down the nearest table, my mind still on James. What about the informal meeting with the planning officer? Were they likely to OK James's expansion plans? Last week James had told me about the new coffee shop he was creating. It sounded entirely different from Vic's Cafe – all afternoon tea, cake and scones rather than smelly, greasy fry-ups. He had asked for my input, or as he phrased it 'the benefit of my years of experience in the food service industry', which made my job sound ridiculously grand. I'd assumed he was taking the piss at first but he seemed genuinely interested.

James listened when I suggested that the tables needed to be easier to clean than the fancy ones he proposed and that the chairs and tables should be moveable (not bolted to the floor like ours) so that they would have the flexibility of accommodating larger parties of people. He made notes as I wondered aloud whether some simple soft furnishings – curtains, seat cushions, maybe a wall hanging or too – might help soak up the noisy clatter of crockery and cutlery. And when I asked him if he would have space for some outdoor seating, perhaps with parasols or a retractable awning for cover, he had gazed at me over his coffee mug, his eyes alight with humour, as he shook his head and said, 'I can't believe I didn't think of that.' To my surprise he took my advice seriously – all of it – and altered his plans accordingly, a fact which privately made me giddy with delight.

Of course I was under no illusions; I'd never get to see the coffee shop I'd helped design, not unless he brought me pictures. Nothing could ever happen between James and me. He was way out of my league and I was trapped in my life as surely as if Vic were standing directly behind me with a knife at my throat. But there was no harm in daydreaming a little was there?

As I moved aside a newspaper I did a double take. It was today's edition of the local rag, left behind by a customer and folded open at the entertainment section. The page covered all the usual things: a rundown of the weekly TV listings, cinema showings and live gigs but it was an image halfway down the page that had caught my eye. I stared at the picture in disbelief and sank slowly into a plastic seat as I read the accompanying text. The short piece was promoting the opening of a new West End show starring a local actress and minor celebrity, Jasmine Reed. I vaguely recognised her from a catchy toothpaste commercial on TV, pretty and petite with perfect white teeth. In this photo she looked every inch the glamorous film star as she posed for the paparazzi at a glitzy party. But it wasn't her image which had caught my eye. Stood beside her, with his arm around her waist, clad in a well-tailored tuxedo and flashing his now familiar, breathtaking, smile was, according to the caption, 'Jasmine's partner, James Southwood.'

Jealousy and disappointment surged up inside me, more potent than I could have thought possible, making me nauseated. But I had no one to blame but myself. I'd let myself get carried away, caught up in James's smile; his stories; his worries, hopes and dreams – even the small pots of flowers he brought into the cafe meant far more to me than they should. It was ridiculous – *I* was ridiculous. James Southwood was a customer, an acquaintance, a casual friend at best, but he would never be anything more than that. And who was I to him? Nothing but a bored, sad, old waitress stuck in a bad marriage. What man in his right mind would want me when he could go home to a glamorous girl like Jasmine Reed? No, I had conjured up this foolish fantasy out of nothing and now it had to stop, before I embarrassed myself.

Rising to my feet, I glanced out of the window to see James's van slowly reversing into its usual spot. Flustered I hurried back behind the counter, discarding the paper in the recycling box on my way.

'Sorry to keep you waiting,' I muttered to the customer hovering by the till. I'd been so distracted by my own thoughts that I hadn't noticed he'd finished. 'Can I get you anything else or do you just want the bill?'

As James walked in I was grateful to have other people to serve. I found myself completely unable to look at him, despite being fully aware of his every move. He had brought yet another freshly planted pot of flowers to replace the one that had started to wilt in the heat of the kitchen. Out of the corner of my eye I saw him nonchalantly swap them over without any encouragement or acknowledgement from me. But I felt absurdly angry and defensive and couldn't get my smile to work properly on my face. He waited patiently, watching as I worked until there was no one else to serve.

'Morning, Rina, everything OK?' His lovely warm voice was threaded with concern.

'Hi, yes fine, just busy. What can I get you?' I barely glanced in his direction.

He paused before replying and I knew he was waiting for me to look at him but I stubbornly held out, focusing on rearranging the serviette-wrapped pairs of cutlery instead.

'Just a coffee, thanks,' he said at last.

'OK.'

Once I'd tapped his order into the till, I served his drink and then quickly turned away before he had a chance to speak. I was fuelled by irritable self-disgust as I crashed about in the kitchen scouring pans that were already clean, all the while fighting the heavy pull of his eyes on my body.

By the time I'd finished noisily loading the dishwasher I'd run out of things to keep me occupied. The only other customer left in the place was a pensioner who was sitting in his favourite spot in the window and eating beans on toast at a leisurely pace. In desperation I decided to empty the waste bin, even though the bag was only half full.

'Have I done something wrong?' James said quietly, as I stalked towards the back door. I pretended I hadn't heard. It was stupid but I felt too confused to think straight. As I reached the relative privacy of the dimly lit passageway I was close to tears and fled out the back door, horrified.

A sob escaped as the heavy bin lid slammed shut and I pressed the back of my hand to my mouth in a lame attempt to hold the rest of my emotions in. I didn't cry often – but especially not over something as silly as this. Get a grip. As I took some deep breaths, despite the stench of blocked drains and cat piss, I started to feel calmer and more in control of myself. Stepping back inside I firmly closed the door behind me and as I passed the customer toilet I checked myself in the mirror, wiping a rogue tear from my cheek. I was about to re-enter the cafe when I recognised Jo's voice,

''Scuse me, this is you ain't it? In the paper? With Jasmine Reed?'

Shit. Now he'd realise I'd seen the picture too. Straining my ears I tried to catch James's response but his low voice was lost in the DJ chatter coming from the radio. How could I face him now?

Hoping I could wait him out, I turned on my heel and headed back the way I'd come. But as I reached the back door he caught up with me.

'Rina?' He touched my elbow and I flinched to a stop. 'Please look at me.' I turned and his tender dark eyes locked on to mine. 'Is this why you're not speaking to me?' He held the paper up in his other hand and then let his arm drop.

What could I say? I didn't want to lie to him but I couldn't bear to admit the truth either. 'No – I don't know – you never said. Why didn't you tell me?' I heard the hurt in my own voice as I fought to ignore the conflicting feelings his proximity provoked in the confined space of the passageway.

James stared into my eyes as if he was trying to read my mind, his fingers slipping down from my elbow and casually interlacing with mine, his touch both painful and exquisite. 'That picture was taken last year. We broke up a couple of months ago, after Dad died, and I moved out. But it was over between Jasmine and I long before that.' I tried to hide the relief I felt at his words but he was standing too close; he could read me too clearly. 'Rina I didn't tell you because I didn't think you'd care. I mean, you're married, and –'

'I know, sorry,' I said, interrupting him. 'Please don't say anything else.' My eyes stung with humiliation and regret, blurring my view of his face.

'Rina.' Reaching up he tenderly hooked a strand of my hair behind my ear, the simple stroke searing me with pleasure. 'Please don't cry.'

For a moment it was as if time itself held its breath – the air between us hummed with anticipation and I could hear nothing but the thumping beat of my own heart. And then, gently, as if it was the most natural thing in the world, James kissed me, his mouth firm and warm, his arms drawing me closer. I sank into his embrace as if I'd been waiting, yearning, for this

110

moment all my life, his touch both comforting and reviving at the same time. As his kiss deepened, his tongue tenderly caressing and tasting me, a strange rushing sensation coursed through my body, accelerating my pulse, heating my skin and stealing my breath. He felt, smelled and tasted divine and I was sure I must be dreaming. With a curious thrill I registered that he was hard against my hip and the knowledge made me ache inside. My god, I wanted him. I never wanted anyone – but I *really* wanted him.

Then there was a vague creak overhead.

It was a subtle shifting sound that would have meant nothing to anyone else but I knew that it was Vic stirring in the flat upstairs. My husband didn't usually get up this early but there was always the risk he might. As my brain registered the full implications of what I was doing, fear shot through my veins like iced water making me gasp and pull away.

'We can't do this. You have to leave,' I whispered in alarm.

James regarded me, his eyes darkly dilated. 'All right but meet me somewhere when you've finished for the day?'

'No, I can't.'

'Tomorrow then – I'll come back tomorrow.'

'No, I mean I can't meet you anywhere – ever – I can't leave here.'

James stared at me a moment, his expression shifting from bewilderment into disbelief and making me feel uncomfortable. 'What do you mean you –?'

'Please, James.' I tried to push him back towards the

cafe but his feet were firmly planted, his body as solid and immovable as concrete. 'You don't know me – you don't know anything about my life; please just go.'

'Is that really what you want?'

'Yes.' I moved past him. 'I'm sorry – this was a stupid mistake. Please go and please don't come back.'

Fear and adrenalin pounded in my ears as I returned to the cafe.

'Hi, Jo, sorry to keep you waiting,' I said, scrubbing my hands with soap in the sink. 'I was just dealing with the bins out the back. What can I get you?'

'Ah no worries, I'll just get a Coke if that's OK; I need the extra caffeine today.' I nodded, dried my hands and turned away to fetch one. 'Hey, Rina,' Jo added in a hushed voice, leaning forward over the counter, 'I think one of your regulars dates someone famous. He's using your lav right now! He denied it but –'

My cheeks heated but I avoided looking in James's direction as he re-emerged from the passageway, glanced at me, and then departed, his cup of coffee untouched.

I let him go. No doubt I would miss James and the transient joy he had brought into my life but my immediate feeling was one of relief. I'd had a lucky escape. It had been unbelievably stupid and reckless of me to risk my husband's rage and my own security – for the sake of a kiss.

But what a kiss…

Chapter Eighteen

When I signalled the barman for another beer he hesitated, silently assessing me and raising a dubious eyebrow. He thought I'd had enough. But I didn't. Two days ago I'd done something stupid; selfishly crossed the line with Rina, potentially destroying our friendship and I'd been trying not to think about it ever since. Staring calmly back without speaking, I made an effort to convey more sobriety than I felt and it worked. Opening another bottle the barman set it before me without comment, while I muttered my thanks. I was aware it would be my last, at this establishment anyway. It was Saturday night in the capital or, rather, early Sunday morning and, although the bar had been busy, the crowds were now thinning as revellers moved on to clubs or simply retired for the evening.

I'd come in to London seeking distraction but my friends, a group of people I'd met at university and loosely stayed in touch with, had not stayed long past dinner. Mostly they were couples with four-bed households to run and babysitters to relieve so I'd been left to continue drinking on my own. It was only just sinking in that I no longer lived in the city; I'd missed the last train back to Wildham and a cab from here would be as expensive as a hotel room. Technically I still owned a flat in London but I wasn't about to go round there and give Jasmine the opportunity to lay into me. I wasn't sure at what point I'd let my ex-girlfriend become a squatter but I needed to persuade her to leave before she started claiming rights. My turning up unannounced in the middle of the night would not only start an argument but might well induce her to change the locks on me. No, I was stuck here until the trains started running again.

A scruffy-looking guy with tattoos and piercings detached himself from a group of people across the room and leaned on the bar next to me. How he'd been allowed in, given the strict dress code, was beyond me.

'Ready to settle your tab, Bay?' the barman said.

Bay chucked a credit card down on the bar, without bothering to check the bill, and eyed me as I took a swig of my fresh beer.

'A woman is it?' I could tell from his voice that he was a smoker.

'I'm sorry?'

'That look on your face – either someone just ran over your dog or it's woman trouble.'

I sighed. 'I don't have a dog.'

'Yeah, I figured,' he said with a smirk, entering his pin into a card machine and handing it back to the barman. 'She's probably not worth it man. I'd steer clear if I were you.'

'Yeah, but, I don't know; there's something about her.'

He narrowed his eyes and stared at me for a moment and I got the feeling he understood exactly what I was talking about, though I barely did myself. 'Sounds like you need distracting,' he said, slapping a hand on my back. 'A few people are coming back to my place for a party if you fancy it?'

I glanced over his shoulder at his rabble of friends.

114

They looked interesting: one guy had a Mohican, while another reminded me of a young Andy Warhol and the girls were pretty, even the one with quirky, surfer-style dreadlocks. Bay was probably right – I needed distracting but right now I was drunk and morose and reluctant to socialise with a load of new people. 'Thanks mate, but I think I'll pass.'

Bay shrugged and left soon afterwards, his card receipt discarded along with a generous tip on the bar. Considering the way he'd been dressed I was surprised to note that the guy had spent over five hundred quid on drinks for his friends. Never judge a book by its cover.

At the far end of the bar a petite blonde in her twenties caught my eye. Or rather she kept staring at me and I inadvertently glanced in her direction. I took another swig of beer as she made her way towards me on cheap stiletto heels. Maybe that was what I needed – a mindless one-night stand to get my head straightened out.

'Hey, handsome, you wanna buy me a drink?' she said hopefully, flicking her hair back from her shoulders. My eyes automatically dropped to the ample cleavage she had on display. Surely her dress was too tight to be comfortable? Why did some women feel the need to reveal so much flesh? Were men really that shallow? Actually, yes – they probably were.

'Sure, what can I get you?' I said, returning my attention to her face.

She ordered an expensive cocktail of some description and the barman added it to my tab as she settled herself on the barstool beside me. 'Thanks, I'm Brooke.' She had a transatlantic accent.

'James,' I said, making sure to flash a smile.

'Do you often drink alone on a Saturday night, James?'

'No, not often – my friends left early.'

She nodded, seemingly satisfied with my answer. 'Mine too.'

'Is that an American accent I hear?'

Her face lit up in delight, her teeth a perfect row of tiny white pearls. 'Too right! I'm from LA, here on business; how about you?'

'British, born and bred, I'm afraid.'

'Mmmm, I just love the British accent; it's so yummy. Do you live in London?'

I sighed. 'No, not any more.'

'Aw, that's too bad.' The barman set a bright orange cocktail before her and she wrapped her lips around the straw before taking a long pull on it. 'Ahh that's good,' she said, her eyes temporarily closing. She smiled seductively at me as she licked her lips and I refrained from rolling my eyes at her obviousness. After all, obvious was good. Simple, uncomplicated, no strings and offered to me on a plate – I could work with that.

An hour later we were shut inside her hotel room and I was reaching down to unzip Brooke's dress while she fumbled with the buttons of my shirt. She was even shorter than I'd thought with her heels kicked off and I started to wonder if we were going to be compatible – I didn't want to hurt her. In between kisses she giggled repeatedly like a schoolgirl, the sound becoming irritating. I eased her backwards onto the bed and then struggled to maintain my balance as I bent to remove my shoes, socks

116

and trousers. My head was foggy with alcohol and part of me just wanted to crash out and sleep but I made sure I found a condom before tossing my wallet aside.

'Mmm, you're really cute,' Brooke purred, writhing on the bed as I straddled her and returned my mouth to hers.

I didn't reply but instead focused on working kisses down from her face to her chest.

'Eeek that tickles!' she squealed, before lapsing into more giggles. Her breasts were silicone-enhanced, perfectly shaped, unnaturally pert, and immobile as I rubbed my hands over them and I found myself wondering how much they had cost to create. Mentally shaking my head, I told myself to focus on the task in hand – I wasn't even hard yet.

Sitting back on my haunches I eased her thong down and she raised a petite leg so that I could remove it completely.

'Say something English,' she said.

'I'm sorry?'

'Y'know, with your sexy accent; say something really posh.'

I gazed at her for a moment as her request sank in and then closed my eyes, sighing in defeat. Who was I kidding? This wasn't going to work; this just wasn't what I wanted. 'I'm sorry, Brooke; I can't do this,' I said, getting to my feet and reaching for my clothes.

She gaped at me. 'What's wrong?'

'I'm too drunk, sorry. I'm just going to go.'

She propped herself up on her elbows and stared at me from the bed as I pulled my clothes back on and shrugged into my jacket, jamming my wallet into my trouser pocket and my feet into my socks and shoes. 'Are you serious?'

'Sorry,' I said again, 'You're a lovely girl and I never meant to –' I stopped speaking when I registered the hostile look on her face. 'Bye,' I muttered slipping out of the door and hurrying away down the corridor.

It was entirely fitting that it was pouring with rain when I stumbled out on to the pavement – I was a complete arsehole and deserved nothing less. Turning my collar up around my neck, I thrust my hands in my pockets, hunching against the deluge, as I set off down the road without any destination in mind. As I walked I tried to shrug off the shame and discomfort of what had just happened. In the grand scheme of things it was nothing; I'd never see Brooke again, I'd made no promises and she'd get over the rejection soon enough. But it still bothered me.

My feet squelched in my shoes as I kept walking, cold rainwater battering down relentlessly and soaking into my suit which now hung heavily from my bones. With every step I felt myself sobering up, restless with some unnamed emotion. What had got into me? Sure, Brooke wasn't perfect, but she was attractive, lively, friendly enough – and I needed to get laid, dammit; the last time I'd had sex must have been with Jasmine, back in March, more than two months ago. What was wrong with me?

The rain had begun to ease by the time I finally stopped under a street lamp and lifted my gaze. By coming here I'd answered my own question. The skeleton market stalls stood empty and exposed and Vic's Cafe sat in darkness. I shifted my eyes to the flat above, searching the barred windows for signs of life but, although there was a gap in the curtains, there was no internal light on,

118

no movement detectable in the shadows. This was what was wrong with me – Rina: a married, older woman that I barely knew, living in a city I'd just moved out of.

I must have slept with more than fifty young women over the years – most of them while I was at uni – but I had always been faithful, always tried to treat them with respect, and they had all been single – unattached and available – each and every one; a fact I was proud of. So why was I even entertaining the idea of sex with Rina?

Because of that kiss.

God, the memory of that kiss kept me awake at night. Nothing had ever felt so right: the heat of her lips, the soapy scent of her smooth skin, and the warm weight of her body as it softened effortlessly into mine: as if we were two halves of something, reunited and made whole again. And it wasn't just the physical chemistry between us, though Lord knows that was powerful enough. Rina had infected my mind too – I'd never experienced anything like it. I thought about her all the time, wherever I was, whatever I was doing. I'd always assumed that attraction as powerful as that was a myth; a fairy tale; an elaborate lie designed to sell perfume, lingerie and condoms, one which ultimately made most people feel inadequate. But now that I'd met Rina I wasn't so sure. For some reason that I couldn't explain I felt compelled to be near her, as if she was somehow fundamental, essential, to my well-being. It was deeply disturbing.

Chapter Nineteen

Vic stumbled into our bedroom, drunk as usual, temporarily blinding me as he switched on the bright fluorescent overhead light and cursing as he stubbed a toe. I stayed still and kept my head down, breathing through my mouth to avoid the sour stench that now permeated the air. It was raining heavily outside and the moisture looked clammy on his sallow skin. Through slitted eyes I watched him getting undressed, the sight of my husband's stringy, anaemic-looking body leaving me cold as usual. Time, along with Vic's rash lifestyle, was not being kind to him. Dispassionately I eyed his scrawny arms and legs and the spreading bloat of his gut, all the while alert to any subtle shifts in his mood. As he turned he tripped slightly, his arm swinging out towards me, and I sprang up and away, out of reach, on primed reflexes.

He glanced at me in surprise and chuckled darkly as I hovered by the bed. 'Relax you stupid cow – I ain't interested in you. Wouldn't fuck you even if you begged me, you miserable bitch.' Lifting the duvet he clambered underneath. 'Not that I ain't entitled to of course but you ain't worth the bother.' He settled comfortably on his side of the bed, his tattooed arms folded across his chest and his eyes closed. 'Turn out the fucking light,' he muttered on a sigh.

Keeping my back to the wall and my eyes trained on him, I felt for the light switch, listening to his breathing slow and lengthen as the room filled with street light and

120

shadows. As his breath morphed into snoring, I relaxed, wrapping my arms around my middle to keep myself warm. According to the glowing digits of the bedside clock it was 3 a.m. Now that I was awake I took the opportunity to use the bathroom, quietly relieving my bladder in the dark. The rain outside was easing, the hammering on the roof lessening and the splashing overflow of the blocked gutters subsiding, to leave behind the steady drip, drip, dripping of water from the vacant market stalls below.

Standing in shadow in the living room I gazed out through a gap in the curtains at the street below. A tall, lone, dark male rounded the corner, head down, shoulders hunched and hands thrust in pockets. He was well built and wore a smart-looking suit, his polished shoes slapping the wet pavement as he strode. But something about his long-legged gait was familiar. As he reached the lamp post directly opposite he stopped and glanced upwards and I stopped breathing. *James*.

His dark eyes searched the building, sweeping over me without seeing me, as I stood rooted to the spot, drinking in the unexpected sight of him. He looked cold, soaked to the skin, moisture dripping from his hair, the clean-shaven planes of his face and his cuffs. He had turned up the collar of his jacket, which reinforced the strong angle of his jaw line, but his shirt was casually unbuttoned at the neck, revealing a dark, tantalising smudge of exposed chest hair. He looked serious, sultry and sexy as hell – as if he'd just stepped out of the pages of a high-end fashion magazine – and I felt like I was dreaming.

But what was he doing here in the middle of the night?

Surely he wasn't here because of me – because of the kiss we'd shared two days ago? What was he going to do? As panic and confusion swept through me I started to tremble all over. He wouldn't try anything stupid would he? Not with Vic lying in the bedroom like a sleeping grenade? Wide-eyed I stared at the man across the street as he stood quietly gazing up through me, lost in thought. He shivered slightly and a wave of longing broke through me. I wanted to go to him, to comfort and warm him, to dry him with a towel and feel his mouth on mine. But I couldn't. He was only across the road and yet he was a million miles away, in a separate life, in another world, across a line I could not cross.

At last he withdrew his hands from his pockets, rubbed his face and shoved his fingers through his wet hair. Straightening his back, and with one last lingering look up at my window, he strode away out of sight. For a long time I stood staring after him, disappointed and relieved and burning with unanswered questions.

Chapter Twenty

My irritation grew as I sat impotently in a tailback on the A1, the June sunshine beating down on the van's windscreen, the engine idling and approximately five hundred quid's worth of plants wilting in the back. I needed to see Rina. It was wrong of me to kiss her last week and she was right to ask me to leave but – even if she'd meant it when she'd told me not to return – I had to. I needed to know that she was safe, that I'd got the wrong idea about her husband, and that I hadn't made things worse for her. But what then? She was still married – she still could not be mine.

With my fist I thumped the edge of the steering wheel in frustration, inadvertently beeping the horn. The woman in the car in front glared at me in her rear-view mirror and I mouthed an apology but she just rolled her eyes, unforgivingly.

Last night I'd finally managed to speak to Jasmine on the phone and her high-pitched outrage still rang in my ears. I was tempted to stick the flat on the market while she was still living there – except that Jasmine would probably retaliate by sabotaging the property, or the viewings, or both. At least a bank loan had been approved to tide me over in the meantime and I'd been able to give the builders, friends of Liam's, the go ahead on the new extension – they were scheduled to start in July.

Unfortunately Liam and I still hadn't managed to track down his girlfriend, Cally. I found it hard to believe that

Liam could have done anything to hurt her but, whatever her reasons, and whatever she was up to, Cally didn't want to be found. And Liam had finally admitted defeat.

Retreating into himself he now spoke even less than usual. I felt useless in the face of his rejection and pain – somehow moral support just didn't seem enough.

My search for Kitkat had hit a wall too. It was two months since I'd left my first message for the Plumleys. I'd left three more since then and nobody had called me back, not even to let me know I'd got the wrong number. I was at a loss as to what else to try. I wanted to talk to Rina about it – sometimes it felt like I could tell her anything – but after what had happened between us last week would she want to listen? And anyway Kitkat ... I never spoke of her, never – some things were just too personal; too painful; too deeply embedded in my soul.

It was later than usual by the time I'd reached the market and unloaded the van. I barely heard a word Gary said to me. As I entered the cafe through the open door I took a deep breath. For once there were absolutely no other customers and I took it as a good sign, as if the world was granting us some space to talk. She stood at the sink with her back to me, her shoulders stiff with tension as she brusquely dried a mug with a tea towel.

'Rina?'

She set down the mug and bowed her head. 'You shouldn't have come.' Her voice was heavy with emotion.

She turned towards me and, encouraged, I moved around the counter and approached her but she backed away. By the time I'd caught up with her we were in the

124

larder out of sight of any passers-by. I wanted to tell her that everything was OK, that I wouldn't hurt her but, before I could speak, she was kissing me. Her eyes were dark with anger and her skin flushed, as if she longed for me the way I did for her and resented it. I revelled in the sweet, eager taste of her mouth, her lips scorching mine, her fingers raking through my hair and holding me close. As the blood throbbed in my veins, my hands roamed across the contours of her back, her tiny waist, the curve of her hip bones, and the swell of her bottom – just savouring the feel of her.

Loosening the ties on her apron I edged my hand up under the hem of her shirt. As my fingers made contact with the smooth, warm skin of her back, my whole body buzzed as if charged with electric current and she gasped and tipped her head back to look at me, her eyes wide and lips swollen.

'Oh God,' she moaned.

I kissed her again, muting her raw words with my mouth before moving on down to taste her jaw, her ear lobe, her neck, all the while caressing her skin from her shoulder blades down to the soft hollow above the waistband of her jeans.

'No,' she panted. 'Just stop.'

We stared at each other for a moment as I tried to steady my breathing. She was so beautiful, so compelling. 'Leave him,' I said. She shook her head, her eyes fixed on mine. 'Yes. Leave him and come and be with me.'

'I can't.'

'You can. People do it all the time –'

'No, you don't understand.'

'Explain it to me,' I said, stroking the delicately flushed pink of her cheek with my fingers.

'I can't.' She pulled away from me.

As she re-tied the strings of her apron it occurred to me that, despite the warm weather, despite the heat of working in a kitchen frying things all day, Rina wore long-sleeved shirts with the sleeves rolled down. In fact I'd never seen her bare forearms. On instinct I reached out, took her hand in mine and eased her sleeve back with my other hand, unsure what I might find. She yanked her arm away from me, quickly drawing her sleeve back into place, but not before I'd clocked the faded yellow bruises where someone had grabbed her with brutish force.

A surge of rage swelled up inside me. Suddenly I wanted nothing more than to find this husband of hers and make him suffer. 'Where is he?' I bit out as I turned towards the passageway. 'Upstairs?'

'No, please, James, don't.' Rina clutched my arm.

I tried to shrug her off, trembling with fury.

'Just stop and listen to me.' I turned back to her stalled by the steady steel of her voice. 'You don't know me; you don't know the life I've led, the things I've done. I'm not some innocent little maiden that needs rescuing.' Her eyes blazed at me, determined.

'Tell me then; you won't change my mind. I can't just let him keep hurting you.' I meant it but at the same time I wondered why I wasn't just walking away. Did I really want to get involved in someone else's marriage?

Her eyes softened and she reached up and cupped my cheek, a fragile smile on her face. 'OK, I'll tell you.' Reining in my anger and confusion, I leaned into her palm

126

and released a heavy breath. 'Sit down; I'll make you a coffee.'

Doing as instructed, I left the kitchen area and took up my usual stool on the other side of the counter, my body already missing and craving her touch. As she poured my drink two men from the market wandered in and ordered some breakfast. I tried not to think about the bastard in the flat above my head while Rina calmly chatted to her customers and served their food. Eventually the men moved away to sit in the window and Rina began wrapping pairs of cutlery neatly inside paper napkins. I focused on the fluid movement of her long fingers in an attempt to keep my emotions in check as she spoke in a low voice.

'I didn't have a very happy childhood,' she began. 'I don't want to go into it but I'm sure it was completely different from yours. I didn't have any family to rely on.'

My chest tightened. Should I set her straight? Admit to my own unhappy start in life? As a rule I didn't divulge it to anyone, not even to my closest friends. Not Jasmine, not even Liam, knew that I'd been abandoned as a toddler. In fact, now that Dad was dead, no one left in my life was privy to the shameful truth. Should I confide in Rina? Could I? The idea made me feel sick and yet I wanted to know everything there was to know about *her*.

'By the time I was seventeen I was living on the streets,' she murmured. 'I had nothing; I was nothing.'

'No.' I searched her face but she wouldn't look at me and just continued as if she hadn't heard.

'I got a bad kidney infection and almost died. I ended up in the hospital. They removed one kidney completely;

it was too badly damaged.'

Overwhelmed with sympathy I had to refrain from vaulting over the counter and crushing her to my chest. Instead I reached out to touch her hand but she pulled away, her eyes darting nervously to the other customers.

'Vic was the only person to visit me while I was in the hospital,' she said. 'He was the nearest thing I had to a friend. He offered me a way out – marriage, a home and a job. For someone like me it was too good an offer to refuse.'

I shook my head. 'But if he won't let you go out, if he *hurts* you –'

'He isn't always violent. He's been good to me; he saved my life. I owe him some loyalty if nothing else.'

'But, Rina, surely you've more than repaid him by staying with him this long. No one deserves to be treated like a, a slave.'

'He'd find me,' she said quietly.

'How? He doesn't know me and –'

'He'd ask around, he'd work it out and come after me.'

'You could change your name –'

'He'd kill us.' Her voice was barely a whisper.

'We'll go to the police and –'

Floorboards creaked overhead and Rina glanced at the time in alarm – it was almost midday. 'It's late, you have to go.'

Sighing in frustration, I fished out my wallet and deposited cash on the counter. 'My offer still stands.' I reached out to take her hand again but again she moved away. 'Please think about it?' She looked at me and her stoic mask of control slipped, exposing a silent tumult of hope and well-worn despair. 'I'll come back next week, and the week after that, and the week after that and I'll keep coming back until you agree to come with me,' I said softly.

Blinking back tears she turned away and disappeared into the larder without a word. I gazed after her for a moment, my head aching with worry and frustration, and then I walked out, putting one reluctant foot in front of another, and climbing into my van. My fingers clenched tightly around the steering wheel as I drove away, my teeth grinding.

Chapter Twenty-one

My fingers brushed my stomach as I put on my nightshirt and my skin tingled. It was incredible how sensitive my body had become since meeting James – and unnerving. I felt as though I was coming round from a heavy dose of anaesthetic, as if I'd been numb up until now and was just starting to sense things properly for the first time. Sounds, scents, colours, flavours, and touches all had more meaning, more relevance, more power to hurt me. Mostly I felt angry – exasperated with myself for allowing my usual common sense to be compromised and mad at James for strolling into my miserable existence, like Prince Charming himself, showing me what I was missing and then refusing to leave again. There was no way I was going anywhere with him. Why couldn't he just bugger off back to his idyllic life in the country and leave me in peace?

But in the evenings, when I was alone and trying to sleep and there was nothing else to distract me, it was impossible to deny the effect he had on my body. Despite my frustration with him, I was finding myself hopelessly consumed with desire.

Until now I'd always been completely averse to anything even vaguely sexual, even as a teenager, perhaps unsurprisingly, given the abusive nature of my experience. Of course when I accepted Vic's offer of marriage I knew I'd have to sleep with him – it was part of the deal – so I'd taught myself to tolerate him, to be numb, to hold my body still and let my mind escape somewhere else entirely while he did his thing. Fortunately for me, Vic had never found our couplings satisfactory; he complained about my lack of enthusiasm and repeatedly told me I was lazy and frigid until, eventually, he lost all interest completely. Thankfully for the past sixteen years, with Cherry's help of course, I'd been comfortably celibate.

But now, since meeting James, it was as if some strange new sense of physical awareness, a hunger, had been switched on inside me. I'd tasted something new and exciting and now I craved more. My body ached for some kind of relief. As I climbed into bed, my mind and body flooded with teasing recollections – his mouth at my ear, his hands caressing my back, the hard heat of his erection straining against the damp ache between my legs. Closing my eyes, I lifted my nightshirt and let my fingers drift across my stomach, skating past my ugly scars, as I tried to imagine his hand in place of my own.

I started to visualise how James might look naked – all golden hair-sprinkled skin, firm rounded muscle and latent sexual power. Usually I couldn't stand the thought of someone touching me but with James – his touch was so different – so welcome. I pinched my nipples with my right hand as my left sank down between my legs, all the while picturing his hands in place of mine. I was surprised at how moist I was, how good it felt and how carnal. It was so new to me – fantasising about someone, touching myself and turning myself on. Exhilarated I conjured up his mouth on my neck, my breasts, my thighs …

Abruptly the back door slammed shut downstairs and I

scrambled up into a seated position, mortified at the thought of being caught. The clock read 21:52, far too early for my husband to be back but it must be Vic; no one in their right mind would be stupid enough to break into his cafe, surely? Barefoot I hurried quietly across the floorboards to the front door of the flat, carefully turned the latch and eased the door open a crack, listening all the while to the muted sounds of movement from below. There was a knock at the back door of the property and I heard the familiar sound of Vic cursing as he went to answer it.

'What the fuck are you doing here?' he growled. 'Someone might see you.'

'You'd better hurry up and let me in then,' replied a steady male voice I didn't recognise.

Vic swore repeatedly as he ushered the guy in and closed the door behind him. 'What the fuck?'

'Relax, Vic, no one saw me.'

'You'd better fucking hope not. You might've changed your clothes but folk round here can still smell a fucking pig a fucking mile away.'

'Oh yeah? Can they smell a rat too?' Vic didn't reply but I could picture only too well the fury in his eyes, the ticking in his jaw, the bunching of his fists. 'If you'd answered my messages I wouldn't have had to come down here, Vic. You know how this works; you keep us informed and we don't –'

'Yeah, yeah and I was gonna meet you tomorrow as usual – in the usual place where no one fucking knows me; not here on my fucking door step!'

'Tomorrow might be too late, Vic. We've got wind of

132

a job going down, south of the river, a warehouse in Croydon; you know the job I mean don't you?'

Vic hesitated. 'Maybe, what of it?'

'Hoping to get a piece of it for yourself were you?'

Vic sighed. 'What do you wanna know?'

'The usual – names, times, locations.'

'You'd better come through.'

The two men moved into the cafe out of earshot and I quietly closed the door and tiptoed, obsessively carefully, back to bed. Lying in the cold sheets I ran the conversation over and over in my mind, barely able to believe it. But I knew what I'd heard and I knew what it meant. There was definitely no question of my leaving Vic now. He was even better connected than I'd feared and not just connected – protected – by the law.

Chapter Twenty-two

The moment I stepped inside the cafe, I knew something was wrong. The astringent smell of burnt food hung in the smoky air, untidy piles of used plates and cups occupied every table, and gangster rap music blared out of the radio. The woman behind the counter was not Rina. I recognised her as someone I'd met briefly once before – a customer at the cafe and acquaintance of Vic's who was possibly a sex-worker. Her straw-like black hair was damp from the heat, she had a lipstick-orange mouth, purple talons for fingernails, and a faded string of hearts tattooed up one arm. I couldn't recall her name but thought it might be something sugary like Candy.

'I ain't doing any more breakfasts so if you want anything more than coffee you'll have to go elsewhere,' she said, jabbing at the till in consternation. The kitchen was in complete disarray with food spilt on every surface and dirty crockery and utensils heaped in and around the sink.

'Where's Rina?' I asked lightly, masking the worry that gnawed at my stomach.

She looked up at me, her eyes narrowing and her jaw flexing as she worked on a piece of gum, and tried to place me. 'Who wants to know?'

I fought the urge to bite her head off; Rina wouldn't want me to draw unnecessary attention to myself. As lightly as I could I said, 'I'm just a regular. I deliver to the market, remember? We met a couple of months back.'

The cash register bleeped and she returned her attention to it. I thought she wasn't going to tell me anything but then she muttered, 'She had an accident – she's in hospital. I'm just covering till she gets back.'

'Oh. Is she OK?' I forced a casual tone into my words.

'Yeah, she'll be fine. Clumsy that one – fell down the stairs.'

I struggled to remain calm as an image of Rina, lying in a heap on the floor, seared through my mind. There was nothing clumsy about Rina whatsoever – if she *had* fallen she'd been pushed. 'Oh right, OK,' I said through gritted teeth. So much for female solidarity – this woman's nonchalance made my blood boil. Someone like her must recognise signs of abuse surely? Was she in complete denial about what I suspected had been happening to Rina? Or just too afraid to intervene? I backed out of the door. 'Well if you're not doing breakfast I'll just find somewhere else.'

She nodded absently as she continued her battle with the till and I tried not to run as I made my way back to the van, trembling with adrenalin. St Mary's was the nearest hospital; I could be there in ten minutes if I was lucky with the traffic.

By the time I'd parked, discovered which ward she was on, found it, and begged the nurses to let me see her, it was almost noon. Rina looked fragile, curled up on the bed on her side like a child, with her eyes closed. She was on a large ward with several other women but the curtain drawn on one side of her bed gave some small measure of privacy. A fresh bruise was blooming on her forehead at the hairline, her left wrist was encased in a sleeve of white plaster and a clear plastic drip was feeding into her right hand. Any other damage was hidden from view.

I sat down quietly on the chair beside the bed, unsure if she was asleep and unwilling to wake her if she was. But she opened her big beautiful eyes, and saw me and smiled and something expanded painfully in my chest. Reaching out I carefully took the slender fingers of her right hand in my own.

'I'll be OK,' she said, her voice husky. I couldn't speak but I shook my head at her calm acceptance – it wasn't OK. 'They're just keeping me in as a precaution – make sure my kidney's healthy. I can probably go home tomorrow.'

'With Vic?' I said, through the lump in my throat.'

'No. He won't come here.'

'How do you know?'

She shrugged one shoulder, wincing slightly. 'He never does.'

'You can't go back there,' I said.

'I have to.' I clenched my teeth, furious with her for being so stubborn. 'How's Cherry doing?'

'The woman with the tattoos? She's fine.' Rina raised a dubious eyebrow. 'OK, the place is a mess but I'm sure she'll manage.'

Rina sighed. 'That woman will do just about anything to impress Vic.' She looked weary and closed her eyes and my anger receded.

'Rina,' I breathed, leaning closer and kissing her hand. 'What can I do? Tell me what you want me to do, please?'

'Just talk to me,' she said. 'Tell me about your week. I like listening to you.'

136

A voice in the back of my head warned me that Rina was a lost cause – not my problem – that you couldn't help someone who was not prepared to help themselves and I should turn around and walk away, leaving this mess behind. But I stayed all afternoon.

I began by telling her how the builders would be starting on the new extension in a month's time – laying concrete foundations before going on to erect a timber frame. I described how Frank, Max and I had fenced off that part of the garden centre to keep customers safe. Then I spoke about how I'd joined the Wildham Warriors, the local rugby club, about our practice sessions and our preparations for match season in September. I even recounted how my fellow teammates had given me an initiation of sorts on Tuesday night:

'They got me drunk at the White Bear and forced me to strip right down to my boxers.'

Rina's mouth gaped open. 'How did they force you to do that?'

I cringed. 'Well, they didn't actually physically force me – it's like a dare; I had to do it or they wouldn't have let me join the team.'

The look of incredulity was plain in Rina's eyes as she struggled to keep a straight face. 'So what happened next?'

'Well once they'd confiscated my clothes, phone, wallet and keys they marched me outside and sent me home alone.'

'What, barefoot? In your boxers?'

'Yep.'

Every smile I raised felt like a victory of sorts and

Rina was grinning at me now. 'That must have been a bit chilly.'

'It wasn't too bad actually,' I said, trying to sound nonchalant. 'It wasn't a particularly cold night and I think the alcohol in my bloodstream helped keep me warm.'

She'd started to vibrate with barely restrained laughter. 'Did anyone see you?'

'Oh, only all the locals; every person at the pub; two neighbours walking their dog; and everyone who happened to be driving along the road that night. There was a lot of beeping.' Rina was laughing out loud now, her face pressed into her pillow and her free hand clutching at the bed sheet. 'You might think it's funny but most of them are probably customers of mine – and now they've seen me in my underwear.'

'Stop, please stop,' Rina breathed, 'it hurts my ribs.'

'Sorry.' I passed her a tissue and she wiped the tears from her eyes and blew her nose. Making Rina laugh was a definite upside to my teammates' embarrassingly immature behaviour but I didn't want to cause her pain.

'Where did you sleep if they had your keys?'

'Oh, I wasn't as inebriated as they thought I was and I managed to find a spare key for the back door – didn't even have to break in. It wasn't a very imaginative initiation really.'

Rina shook her head, still smiling at me, and I wished I could keep her smiling for ever.

A file of her medical notes hung from the end of the bed with her full name, Mrs Katerina Leech, printed on the front. She had never told me that Rina was short for Katerina and I wondered why, since it was so pretty.

138

Leech, on the other hand, was a fitting name for Rina's husband but not nearly good enough for her. I was tempted to take a peek at her notes to reassure myself that she really was OK but, respectful of her privacy, I refrained.

The nurses came and went, carrying out various checks, proffering pain relief and casting disapproving looks in my direction. From time to time they urged me to go home and let Rina rest but Rina was adamant that she wanted me to stay. When I asked her if there was anything she needed, whether I could bring her anything, she seemed surprised by the question, as if it had never occurred to her.

Come three o'clock they had disconnected Rina's IV but she was so tired she could barely keep her eyes open.

'I must go,' I murmured, 'but I can come back first thing in the morning.' She gazed at me, her eyes begging me to stay. 'Try not to worry. Everything's going to be fine. He can't get to you here. I've told the nurses I'm your brother and I've asked them not to let him in. I've given them my mobile number and they've agreed to call me if Vic turns up.' I leaned in and kissed her temple, briefly savouring the softness of her hair. 'Now you must sleep.'

'I won't be able to.'

'I think you will if you try.'

She looked uncharacteristically vulnerable and I desperately wanted to hold her close to me. 'Here, let me try something,' I said, getting to my feet and releasing her hand. 'This used to work for me when I was little and I couldn't sleep. Just stay as you are.' I moved around to the other side of the bed. 'I'm going to spell out words on your back; see if you can understand them.'

Rina went very still as I perched sideways on the edge of the bed and began gently tracing letters on her back with my finger. I spelt out Y-O-U and when I paused she whispered the word. Satisfied that she had the hang of the game I continued to lightly scribe the rest of my sentence

A-R-E S-A-F-E W-I-T-H...

As I started on the last word her shoulders began to shake.

'Rina?' She turned to me, great big tears rolling down her face and soaking into the pillow. 'What is it?'

She stared at me, eyes wide. '*Jamie*?'

I gaped at her, stunned, as the world shifted and pieces of my life dropped, firmly, unexpectedly, into place. 'Kitkat?'

Chapter Twenty-three

He stared at me in shock, my childhood nickname whispered from his lips like a secret password temporarily transporting us back into the past we once shared. He touched his fingertips to my damp cheek as if checking that I was real.

'I've been looking for you everywhere,' he said in wonder.

'Have you? Why?'

'You were like a sister to me – you didn't think I'd forgotten you?'

His words made me cry harder. It was as if a dam had burst inside me; years of suppressed misery, disappointment and regret forcing its way up into my throat and choking me with every sob.

'Oh God, don't cry, please don't cry,' he implored as he cradled my face with one hand and squeezed my fingers with the other. I fought to regain control of myself, aware that I was upsetting him and causing a scene. The ward sister suddenly appeared, sweeping aside the curtain, fist on hip.

'What's going on? You shouldn't still be here,' she hissed at James – *Jamie, my Jamie*. 'Visiting hours are over. Go home. She needs rest.'

Taking some deep steadying breaths, I wiped my eyes and nodded reassuringly at Jamie and he released me and straightened up, reluctant to leave. 'I'll be back tomorrow,' he said gravely, his eyes still wide. I nodded and smiled tightly as I held my emotion in. The nurse was waiting, watching us impatiently. He turned to leave and just as he was about to disappear out of sight he turned back to me. 'Kat, I'm never leaving you behind again.'

'Out, out, out,' the sister barked, chasing him off. My face crumpled as I allowed my tears to take over once more.

I was calmer by the morning. I still felt tired, emotional and sore but I was able to think more clearly. I knew from the nurses that Jamie had arrived early but that he was being kept from seeing me until I'd been discharged. I was thrilled to have him back in my life, of course I was; I'd missed him for so long. But the way I felt about Jamie, the little lost boy I once knew, was so entirely different to the way I felt about the strapping great man James that I was having trouble getting my head around the fact they were the same person. Jamie had always been family, like a sibling to me, and now I felt unnerved, almost guilty, that I found him unbearably sexy. And how did he feel about me now? He'd said he wouldn't let me go back to Vic – as if it was simple. But it wasn't.

Vic would never let me go. Not because he loved me or anything sentimental like that; if my husband had *ever* loved me it had been short-lived. But he liked wielding his power over me, having me at his beck and call, reliant on him and running his cafe so that he didn't have to. And Vic was a proud man. His tough guy persona and the respect of his peers was everything to him. If I embarrassed him by trying to leave he would take it out on me with violence.

142

The events of the night before last were a prime example of Vic's vicious nature – after his 'covert' meeting he had vented his frustration by sweeping the contents of the cafe counter top onto the floor. Unable to stop his rage there he had hauled me out of bed and commanded me to tidy up, pushing me down the stairs when I moved too slowly, despite the fact that his dissatisfaction was nothing to do with me. No, if I tried to leave Vic, if I gave him a real excuse to hurt me, I had no doubt he was capable of murder.

So was I brave enough to do it anyway?

That night I'd lain at the bottom of the stairs pretending to be unconscious until Vic had gone and only then had I dared to move. On autopilot I'd awkwardly cleaned up the mess one-handed, while deliberating about going to the hospital. I suspected my wrist was fractured and I knew there was a chance I could be bleeding internally. I'd made the journey to St Mary's a few times before and I had the short bus route memorised. But I was still hesitant about breaching the invisible boundaries of my daily life and not just because of Vic – it was my own anxiety holding me back. The outside world was alien, unpredictable in its multitude of variables and overwhelming on the senses. Quite simply the thought of venturing beyond the market filled me with dread and it was easier to stay within the familiar confines of my prison, where there were fewer unknowns.

Despite my trepidation and my pathetic excuse for a life, my impulse to survive rose up from somewhere inside me like a silent roar, forcing my limbs to override my fear. I wish I could say that it was self-respect or even defiance that gave me the courage but in all honesty I just wanted to be well enough to see James again.

Decision made, I'd pulled on a pair of jogging bottoms, shrugged into a cardigan and stuffed my fish-finger box into a rarely used handbag. Having dropped the cafe key and an accompanying note through Cherry's door, I stumbled on to a double-decker bus and into a seat at the back. By focusing intently on the seat in front of me I could ignore the strangers around me and the bewildering intensity of London as it passed me by. I had never felt so alone. As the pain and nausea grew steadily worse I'd concentrated on thoughts of James to distract me and somehow, at last, I'd made it to A&E before collapsing.

I'd made it this far; could I go further?

Jamie wanted to take me away and, in spite of everything, I desperately wanted to leave with him, if only for a little while. Vic tended to disappear whenever I ended up in hospital, lying low to avoid any difficult questions. Maybe I could take advantage of his absence, just for a few days – go with Jamie and see his home, meet his friends; enjoy a temporary escape from my own life. I could get back before Vic even noticed I was gone. One thing I knew for sure; I absolutely did not want the two men to confront each other.

Jamie was physically bigger, younger and almost certainly stronger than my husband but he was also a nice guy, whereas Vic always fought dirty. And besides my husband had an army of jacked-up, steroid-enhanced bouncers at his fingertips. He was fully capable of having Jamie killed without risking a single scratch to himself. Shivering I folded my arms around myself. It just didn't bear thinking about.

In anticipation of being discharged I'd changed out of the hospital gown and back into the scruffy, mismatched outfit I'd arrived in. The nurse had drawn back the curtains from the end of my bed to let the daylight in and I kept an eager eye on the entrance to the ward. As soon as the doctor had signed the relevant sheet of paper Jamie's tall, distinctive form appeared in the doorway. All broad shoulders, sun-kissed skin and long athletic legs, he drew interested glances from the other patients and nurses alike, as he strolled towards me across the room. Would I ever get used to the sight of him? Would he always set my pulse racing? Was it right that he still did, knowing who he was to me?

'Hey, how are you feeling?' Jamie smiled but there was a shyness about him that hadn't been there yesterday.

'Much better, thanks.'

'Did you manage to get any sleep?'

'Yeah, some.'

He nodded. 'That's good.' He sat down in the chair without taking my hand and I tried not to notice, tried not to think about it, tried not to read any meaning into the slight distance between us. The irony was not lost on me that, after years of avoiding physical contact at all costs, I now craved even the slightest of touches from Jamie. 'Has Vic tried to visit?'

'No. He usually disappears when something like this happens – goes on a bender: drinking, gambling, that kind of thing. He probably won't be around for at least a week.'

Jamie shook his head in disgust, his stubbled jaw

145

flexing with tension. He braced his hands on his knees and sighed. 'You can't go back to him, Kat.'

I didn't reply – couldn't decide what to say – and Jamie didn't push it but changed the subject instead. 'Do you mind if I call you Kat?'

The way he said my childhood name did strange things to me but I liked it. 'Not if I can call you Jamie,' I said.

Smiling he held up a plastic carrier bag. 'I've brought some things for you. I didn't know what you'd want but I've brought some toiletries, a hairbrush, a change of clothes. I'm not sure if they'll fit but hopefully they'll do for now.'

'Thank you,' I said, moved by his thoughtfulness. He put the bag on the bed beside me but I felt too self-conscious to look inside.

'Do you want me to fetch any of your things from the flat?'

'No.'

'Are you sure? If Vic's not around then –'

'There's nothing I want.'

He held my gaze in that way of his, as if reading my mind with his large chocolate eyes. 'OK. I'll leave you to get changed and then we can get out of here.'

In the bathroom I washed and re-dressed myself in the clothes Jamie had provided. The outfit – plain white long-sleeved T-shirt, blue floor-length skirt and flip-flops – was not flashy or conspicuous but it was brand new. I couldn't remember ever being given brand new clothes before. They were well fitting, comfortable and chosen with me (and my bruises) in mind – a complete contrast to the second-hand cast-offs that I'd always worn. Even the underwear Jamie had bought for me – a white bra with matching knickers – though simple and functional, fitted me beautifully, gently hugging me as if tailored to my measurements. I felt like a new woman, dressed to rejoin the human race.

My wedding ring had been cut away from my swollen left hand when I first arrived. Turning the ugly piece of twisted metal over in my fingers it looked small and insignificant and yet as heavy as an iron shackle. Taking a deep breath I dropped it into the bottom of my handbag out of sight.

As I attempted to hide the bruise on my forehead under my hair, manoeuvred my sling into place, and eyed myself in the mirror it occurred to me that I must have some small sense of pride left. I regretted that, after all this time, Jamie had discovered me living in such a state – hidden away in a greasy spoon, afraid to go out and letting life pass me by. I was nothing like the gutsy girl he once knew – I'd bowed to Vic's will for too long, suppressed my own instincts and emotions for the sake of an easier life, and become a ghost of my former self in the process. What must Jamie think?

I had no idea how much time I would get with my not-so-little brother but I wanted to try and make the most of it. He was risking a lot for me, whether he realised it or not, and I didn't want to let him down. Jamie's opinion of me was the only one I cared about.

He was talking on his mobile phone in the corridor as I left the ward with my handbag on one shoulder, and the carrier bag, which now contained pain medication, clutched in my right hand. He ended the call when he saw me.

'OK?'

I nodded and smiled, determined to act normally.

'You look lovely.'

'Thanks,' I said.

'So ... will you come back to Wildham with me?'

I took a deep breath. 'I will, thank you.' His expression brightened with relief. 'Thank you for everything.' I could feel my own face heating and I turned away but he pulled me into a clumsy hug, my cheek against the firm curve of his shoulder, my bruised ribs complaining, my plaster cast sandwiched awkwardly between us.

'We have so much catching up to do, Kat.'

But we didn't talk straight away. Jamie took my bag and led me along several corridors, down two floors in a lift, through a lobby and into a car park, where he helped me into the passenger seat of a battered old maroon-coloured estate that he said had belonged to his dad. As we set off Jamie turned the radio down to a murmur to allow conversation. I was sure he had plenty of questions for me, as I did for him, but he seemed to sense that I needed some more time. It was certainly disorientating being outside in the world again after so long. It was a vividly bright June day and I tried to suppress my impulse to panic as I stared out at an infinite assortment of strange faces and unknown places. Jamie steadily navigated our way through the traffic and out of London and I repeatedly reminded myself that the world was not necessarily a big scary place, filled with pain and danger – not if you had someone to trust, someone to look out for you, someone to care. And as ridiculous as it may seem, given that we'd spent most of our lives apart, I did feel like I could rely on this person beside me. Jamie was the only person I had ever trusted.

As the roads grew wider the terraced shops and houses gave way to larger ones, outlets the size of warehouses and homes with front lawns and driveways. These in turn fell away to be replaced by grassy banks, lines of tall trees, and open blue sky. I tried to appear unaffected as we hit the motorway and vast verdant green fields rolled out around us, the likes of which I'd only ever seen on TV and in other people's magazines.

Eventually we turned down a long narrow road lined with lush green hedges and swathes of frothy white wild flowers. Beyond a large entrance sign for Southwood's Nursery & Garden Centre, and a modest car park, lay a small gravel driveway almost concealed by bushes. Jamie pulled the car in and we stopped outside a pretty stone cottage, complete with roses scrambling up around the door. Switching off the engine he looked at me and it was only as the engine cooled and the silence grew that I realised how tightly I was gripping the edge of my seat with my uninjured hand. Easing my fingers open, I took a breath and turned to meet his gaze.

'This is my home, Kat,' he said softly. 'It's your home too now, for as long as you want it to be. You're safe here.' The warmth in his eyes and his words made my heart ache. Smiling back at me, he released his seatbelt. 'Come on in. I'll show you around.'

Beyond the quaint timber porch and the cheery glossy-red front door was a tiled entrance hall with a narrow staircase leading off it. As Jamie squeezed past a heavily

149

laden coat stand and disappeared through a doorway, I avoided the mirror on the wall and glanced down at the narrow table below it. An old-fashioned telephone and answering machine were perched atop a pile of directories, which had slithered awry with their own weight. But my eyes snagged on the framed photograph almost concealed at the back; a formal studio shot of Mr and Mrs Southwood posing proudly with their young son. I recognised all three faces from a lifetime ago but also registered the unfamiliar details – the ruler-straight edge of Jamie's haircut, the crisply ironed planes of the shirt he wore, the bright optimism in his smile – before forcing myself onwards into the house.

The interior of the cottage was warm, bright and cosy with flowery comfortable-looking furniture, curtains around the windows and paintings on the walls. The fireplace in the living room harboured a stack of real logs along with a coal scuttle and a stand of old-fashioned-looking metal implements. On the stone slab mantelpiece above an ornate clock was ticking unnervingly loudly, as if emphasising the steady march of time.

Jamie hovered uncertainly in my peripheral vision.

'So many books!' I murmured enviously under my breath, spotting the overloaded bookcases in the corner.

'Yeah, help yourself. The books on these shelves are mine and the rest belonged to my parents – actually I guess they all belong to me now – but just help yourself to anything that takes your fancy; there are lots of reference books, fictional classics, thrillers, sci-fi. My mum liked romance novels but I imagine they'll be a little dated now.'

The kitchen was what I'd once seen referred to in a magazine as 'country farmhouse' in style, with warm wooden units and surfaces, a white Belfast sink and a solid-looking, iron cooking range. Jamie hastily tidied piles of books and papers on a worn timber table by the window and then proceeded to open various cupboards pointing out the locations of coffee, teabags, mugs, tumblers, biscuits, boxed cereals, and numerous other items while I tried to take it all in. Jamie's home was welcoming and disorientatingly familiar. It was as if I had just stepped on to the set of a fictional TV show where happy families lived and loved and regularly ate meals together. Except that this was real. I was really here and Jamie's adoptive parents, sadly, were not.

The bedroom he showed me to had a sloping ceiling, uneven white-washed walls and a pretty bed piled high with cushions as soft and inviting as clouds. But it was the view out of the window, sparkling with verdant life, which really captured my attention.

Below and to the right, beyond a tall fence, were long benches crowned with colourful signs and laden with row upon row of potted plants, many of them in full bloom. The stock was made accessible by a bisecting network of paths where a middle-aged couple was pushing a trolley and slowly making their wandering way between neat lines of rose bushes, oblivious to my attention. Over to the left were yet more rows of plants but these were less formally arranged, without retail signage or labels, and situated against a backdrop of plastic-covered growing tunnels and a jumble of small outbuildings. This was the growing area – the nursery side of the business – the

'Staff Only' sign on the gate leading to it confirmed as much.

All of this would have been enthralling enough but beyond the nursery and the garden centre an immense expanse of grass stretched out like a carpet – lush green fields that gently unfurled uphill, rising to where a ridge of leafy trees met the vast blue sky. Shaggy, brown, contented-looking cows punctuated the open space, while a lightly trampled footpath, over on the far side, followed the fence line up to a rustic-looking stile in the distant top corner. The overwhelming and unfamiliar sense of freedom I felt, as I took in the idyllic view before me, gripped me with light-headed hope and fear.

Joining me at the window Jamie talked about one or two aspects of the business while I quietly fought to subdue the panic rising inside me. My heart thudding in my chest, I listened intently, focusing on the calm, soothing sound of his voice. I had never experienced such seemingly unconditional kindness, never been anywhere so beautiful, and never been so close to living a life I'd hardly dared dream about. I was aware that I should be enjoying this moment and delighting in my new surroundings, the way anyone else lucky enough to be in my position would. But instead I felt desolate, dizzy with emotion, swamped with a sense of impending dread. How was this lovely dream going to end?

Chapter Twenty-four

I woke early, despite not having slept for very long. Just knowing that Kat, *Kitkat*, was asleep in the room next door, kept me awake for hours. I could still barely believe it – that I'd found her, that Kitkat and Rina were the same person. Of course, it went some way towards explaining the strange connection between us, the way I'd felt drawn to her at first sight – maybe on some subconscious level I'd recognised her. Either way, she was even more important to me now; the urge to look after and protect her was stronger than ever.

But the physical attraction between us had me confused. Kitkat had always been a big sister to me. Was it wrong to lust after her the way I did? She wasn't technically my sister – not biologically or legally – and we were different people now: adults. I'd spent the last thirty-six hours or so trying not to think about Kat sexually but it was impossible – I wanted her more than I'd ever wanted anyone and I was worried my body would give me away. How did Kat feel about me now?

She had been subdued the day before, quiet on the drive back from the hospital and watchful as I showed her around the cottage. Kat didn't openly display her emotions on her face, not the way Jasmine did, and I was curious to know what she was thinking. But I hadn't dared ask. I was afraid of what she might say. Instead I'd pointed out those parts of the nursery and garden centre that were visible from my parents' freshly decorated

153

bedroom – it was her bedroom now. I could tell she was struck by the place, maybe even impressed, but her body remained tight with tension, her uninjured arm defensively wrapped around her middle and her face set in a mask of neutrality. She'd declined to come with me when I went to check in with the staff and I'd figured she needed more time.

We'd had lunch together; I'd made sandwiches and asked Kat once again if there was anything she wanted or needed – anything I could do for her to make her more comfortable – but she had only said no. I'd suggested that I could take her shopping in Wildham the next day to buy her more clothes and things. I suspected she didn't have any money, and was unlikely to accept any, but she couldn't live in one set of clothes indefinitely. Having listened to my carefully worded proposal she eventually agreed, on the proviso that I would let her pay me back one day.

Later I had run her a bath, hot and deep and filled with bubbles. I'd waited downstairs at the kitchen table, my hands clutching invoices but my eyes seeing only her. I held my breath, listening to every splash and sigh, thoughts of her naked body making me uncomfortably hard. Afterwards she had retired to bed early, sweetly scented and hidden from neck to toe inside a set of my winter pyjamas.

Now daylight seeped in around the curtains and my eyes followed the cracks in the ceiling, still familiar from my childhood. My feelings unnerved and confused me and I had no idea how Kat felt. Did she still want me the way she had when she'd kissed me or did she now just see the small boy she once knew? She had made no physical contact with me since we'd left the hospital so I suspected the latter. We were sleeping in separate bedrooms like siblings and it was right that Kat should have her own space. But every night would now be torture for me, secretly wanting her and knowing she was so close by.

Kat's bedroom door opened and I strained to hear as she quietly made her way barefoot into the bathroom across the landing. I wanted nothing more than to get up and go to her, see if she looked all mussed up from sleep and take her in my arms. But I couldn't. I had a raging hard-on again. I'd have to wait until she was safely back in her own room.

Over breakfast Kat and I talked. I reiterated that she was welcome to stay as long as she wanted, while a private part of me, the part that preferred an easy life, wondered if it was sensible having her to stay at all.

'Maybe, once you're feeling better, if you fancy it, you could explore the nursery?' Kat just looked at me. 'It's up to you though – you're free to do whatever you want.'

'Thank you, but I can't stay long.'

'Why not?'

'He'll find me,' she said, her un-bandaged hand clasped tightly around the mug of coffee I'd just poured. 'As soon as Vic finds out I've gone, he'll hunt me down. I have to go back to the hospital in two weeks for a check-up and then again in six weeks to get this taken off,' she said, raising her plaster cast. 'He could just have someone waiting for me there.'

Concerned she was burning herself, I had a fierce urge

to reach across the table, gently loosen her fingers from the mug and take her hand in my own but I refrained, unsure of myself and of her. 'Listen I've already thought about this. We can get your arm checked at the local hospital here – get your records transferred across. You don't have to go back to London for that. Vic has no reason to suspect you're with me – I'm just one of many customers at the cafe. On Thursday I'll go to the market, as usual, and go into the cafe afterwards like I usually do and have breakfast.' Kat stared at me. 'I'll ask after you in a casual way, as if I don't know anything, and I'll see how Cherry reacts – see if she says anything about Vic.'

'And what if Vic's there?'

I shrugged. 'Then I'll talk to him too. He can tie me to a chair and interrogate me for all I care – I won't admit to knowing a thing.' Kat scowled at me and her hands trembled. I desperately wanted to pull her into my arms and hold her tight but I no longer trusted my body enough to get close to her.

She swallowed heavily, her eyes still trained on mine. 'What if he follows you?'

'I'll lose him.'

'And when he does turn up here? Because he will, eventually.'

'I'll call the police, Kat; I'll have him arrested for trespassing.'

'You really think that'll help? They're on his side!'

'What do you mean?'

'I think Vic is an informer for the police.'

At this revelation a new, improved plan formed in my mind. I didn't verbalise it – I didn't want Kat to worry any

156

more than she was already. Instead I vowed to protect her and keep her safe and I asked her to trust me, to try to relax and to enjoy her new home. Of course Kat was sceptical and stubborn and wouldn't make me any promises. As she left the room, the defiant lift of her chin and the glint in her eyes sent blood rushing to my groin with desire and I stifled a groan, fervently hoping she would stay.

'I reckon these hebes will be ready to go on sale next week,' Lil said, lifting one up and tipping it so that I could see the fine white roots that were sprouting from the drainage holes in the bottom of the pot.

'They look great,' I agreed. 'What sort of –'

An eruption of deep-throated male laughter stopped me mid-sentence and Lil and I turned in unison to where Frank Bridger was sat in his forklift with Kat stood beside him. His evident amusement at whatever Kat had just said was subsiding into a chuckle.

'Well, well,' Lil observed. 'Anyone who can make our Frank laugh must be pretty special.'

I nodded, captivated by the sight of Kat smiling in the sunshine, but I didn't reply. It was Lil's gentle way of fishing for more information but all anyone needed to know for now was that Kat was a friend who was staying for a while.

I'd spent all morning showing her around the nursery and introducing her to the staff. She'd showed genuine interest in everything and everyone and, despite seeming distinctly uncomfortable with any form of physical contact – handshakes included, she'd made friends easily.

157

Frank was a case in point.

Originally a farmer by trade, Frank had been unhappy ever since his wife had died and his land had been repossessed back in the seventies. My parents had offered him a job when he needed one and he had been fiercely loyal to them in return; he was well into his retirement years and still worked a full five-day week. But he had never remarried and working for someone else had never sat comfortably with him. Keeping himself to himself, he avoided contact with the other staff and customers as far as possible and preferred to eat his lunch alone. Over the years Frank had grown stubborn and cantankerous. This was the first time I recalled hearing him laugh and I wondered what Kat had said to him.

'She seems lovely,' Lil said.

Aware that I was staring, I turned back to the hebe in Lil's hands, avoiding the knowing look in her eyes. 'Yes, she is. We're going into town this afternoon to do some shopping. I don't think it will be massively busy here and everyone seems to think they'll manage without me but I'll be on my mobile if anything crops up.'

'Just go and enjoy yourselves.' Lil grinned.

Chapter Twenty-five

Jamie jogged over to a pay-and-display machine to buy a ticket, while I stood next to his car and took some deep calming breaths. It wasn't the dull throbbing pain in my arm that bothered me, or even the aching of my bruised ribs – I was used to feeling bruised and the painkillers took the edge off, making the discomfort relatively easy to endure. It was anticipation of the task ahead that had me feeling tense. Feigning nonchalance for prolonged stretches of time was hard work but I was determined to keep it up, to act normally for Jamie's sake, despite the fear and dread I felt inside. Wildham, the local town he'd brought me to, was a tiny fraction of the size of London but with recognisable shops, amenities and features, all slightly smaller in scale. Thankfully it wasn't as crowded as a typical Saturday at the market but the pavements were still nerve-wrackingly busy with shoppers, all in close proximity to one another and moving about unpredictably in all directions.

Jamie returned, his eyes searching my face. 'OK?'

'Yep.'

He leaned in through the door and placed a ticket on the dashboard before locking the car. 'I thought we could try over there.' He indicated a row of clothes shops beyond the car park.

I clutched my handbag tight. 'Sounds good.'

The first two shops we entered we spent little time in. They were beautifully furnished and the staff were unexpectedly attentive, with welcoming smiles and polite offers of assistance. But it was exhausting repeatedly stepping out of people's way and automatically cringing when they brushed by me accidentally and I was shocked and appalled at the eye-watering cost of things. How could one simple T-shirt cost nearly my entire rainy day fund? Admittedly it was many years since I'd ventured into a proper clothes shop and back then, when I was a teenager, it was purely out of curiosity since I didn't have the money to pay for anything. Whenever my various foster carers had run out of hand-me-downs they had re-stocked my wardrobe in charity shops and I'd always done the same, though I wasn't about to let Jamie know. But even the brand-new clothes sold on the market were never as expensive as those displayed before me now. Each immaculate garment was available in a range of sizes and arranged within colour co-ordinated groups. They hung in perfect lines from shiny chrome rails, sat neatly folded and stacked on glass shelves, and adorned haughty-looking mannequins. A sense of panic built up inside me and I began to despair.

Thankfully the third shop Jamie took me into was some sort of discount store and, by carefully rooting about in bargain bins, I was able to find the items I wanted without sending him bankrupt.

As I shopped, Jamie stood back and watched me from afar, something I was grateful for. I'd worried he might try and help, or make suggestions, but he instinctively knew not to crowd me. Still I found it reassuring that he stayed within sight and kept his eyes on me, even when other people stopped to greet him and talk business.

160

Jamie stationed himself outside the entrance to the fitting rooms, leaning casually against a pillar and idly flicking through his phone, while I went to try on a few pairs of jeans. Hidden safely within the privacy of my own cubicle I removed my sling and awkwardly wrestled denim garments up and down my legs as quickly and modestly as I could manage – unlike the blonde in the cubicle next to me. Through a gap in the curtains I could see her parading about in front of the mirrors by the doorway, as if on a catwalk. She had clearly taken a shine to Jamie and with each change of outfit her clothes grew tighter and more revealing. Privately I was pleased that he ignored her completely. When I reappeared he seemed relieved and insisted on carrying everything to the till for me like a gentleman.

Finally, laden with bags and a frighteningly long till receipt, we exited the shop. I felt weirdly exhilarated and conspicuous – as if I was getting away with something naughty, or acting out a scene from a movie, but I tried not to let it show. At Jamie's suggestion we stopped in a small coffee shop in the square for refreshments and sat at a table in the window gazing out. He told me a little about the town, pointing out the sweetshop he'd visited as a boy and the Rose and Crown – a pub he'd frequented as a teenager. His description of himself as a pimply seventeen-year-old trying to charm Wendy, the middle-aged landlady, into serving him beer made me smile.

It surprised me how quickly I'd got used to being around him – and frightened me how much I liked it. After all it couldn't last could it? And it was hardly fair to pin all my hopes on Jamie just because a long time ago

161

we'd known each other as kids. We didn't really *know* each other, not really. I felt strangely compelled to trust him – all my instincts told me I could – and yet it was illogical to do so, stupid, reckless even. I never normally trusted anyone. It was a rule with me, one that had kept me alive until now. But something inside me wanted to believe in Jamie, to believe in the promises he made and the life he offered. I had never wanted anything so much. I had to try. I owed it to myself to attempt to relax and embrace this new life with Jamie, even if it couldn't last.

So I sat in the busy coffee shop on a Saturday afternoon, surrounded by shopping, listening to him talk and calmly sipping tea – happy – *normal*. But still, every now and then, someone with bleached hair and a denim jacket would catch my eye and my blood would freeze.

Realistically it was unlikely that my husband had noticed my disappearance yet, let alone found me, but he'd been my keeper for so long, and his rules and threats were so ingrained in my mind, it was hard to believe that Vic wasn't lurking around every corner.

Chapter Twenty-six

I thoroughly enjoyed treating Kat to a hot beverage in a cafe and having her sit beside me instead of serving me across a counter. We talked a bit about Wildham, the town outside the window that I had grown up in, and then discussed the layout and design of the establishment in which we sat – comparing it to our own plans for a cafe at the garden centre. I thought of it as *our* project – our exciting new coffee shop – because she was so much a part of it in my mind and yet I could not be sure that Kat would stick around long enough to see it finished. I hoped she would.

'Are we going to get some food while we're in town?'

'What did you have in mind?'

'Well, we ate the last of the pasta last night and your kitchen cupboards are almost bare so unless you intend to have cereal for dinner…'

'Oh – we could just get a takeaway tonight and do an online shop for tomorrow,' I trailed off at the look on Kat's face – my throwaway suggestion seemed to floor her.

Back in the city I'd regularly eaten out and ordered takeaways; Jasmine didn't cook and I only knew how to heat things up – ready prepared meals from the freezer, a tin can, or a microwaveable dish – bad habits I'd picked up from Dad. He had never been domestically minded; he couldn't even be trusted not to let the kettle boil dry on the stove and used an electric one instead. For the last few years a lady who lived nearby had done all his food shopping for him, dropping it off at his door once a week. Similarly I'd always done my grocery shopping online and had it conveniently delivered to my doorstep. I took it for granted. The shocking realisation that Kat may not have had access to the World Wide Web, at all, made my mind boggle. But before I could decide how to ask without insulting her, she spoke.

'It costs extra to shop online doesn't it?'

'You pay for delivery but it's not much.'

'Is the supermarket far from here? Is it out of our way?'

'No, not at all; we can stop in on our way back if you prefer?'

'OK, good, if you don't mind?'

'Of course not. But you don't have to cook y'know.'

'We have to eat.'

'Yes, but we can go out for dinner – or order in.'

She shook her head. 'I'd rather cook. What sort of things do you like?'

'I like most things.'

'But?'

'I've been a vegetarian since university.'

Kat's eyebrows rose in alarm, her cheeks flushing pink. 'Vegetarian! You never said!'

'Well, I –'

'All those times you came into the cafe and I cooked smelly meat right under your nose. I'm so sorry, Jamie.' She hid her face in her hands.

I laughed and reached out, prying her hands away and enjoying the fleeting feel of her fingers in mine. 'Don't be

164

silly; it's fine; it never bothered me. I'm not particularly strict or fussy.'

'You still should have said something,' she admonished with a scowl and I couldn't stop smiling. 'Vegetarian,' she mused, 'how about vegetable lasagne, mushroom risotto, pasta salad, saag aloo?'

My mouth watered in anticipation. 'That all sounds amazing, Kat.'

'It won't be anything fancy – they're just recipes I've picked up from TV and magazines.'

'I'm sure anything you cook will be delicious.' She didn't look convinced but she was all business as she set about compiling a shopping list.

While Kat shopped, I steered the trolley up and down the supermarket aisles behind her. I hadn't set foot inside a supermarket since I was a student on a last minute, late night beer run. Today it was chock-full of the bad-tempered and the harassed: those on a mission and armed with lists, re-usable bags and family-sized trolleys. But, weirdly, I found I enjoyed following Kat around; it brought back vivid memories of doing the same thing for my mother. She was the last person who had cooked for me with any regularity and she had shopped for real ingredients too. Unfortunately she was never a very successful cook – she tended to burn things – but she tried hard and that had meant everything to me at the time.

Kat was a sight to behold. She glided quickly and efficiently along the aisles, her eyes scanning the shelves as she swerved smoothly around the other customers, without appearing hasty, causing offence, or breaking her long, graceful stride. Her lips moved silently in concentration as she crouched to compare big-name brands against those on the lowest shelves before swiftly rising again in a lithe motion, a budget alternative held aloft in one hand.

Though mesmerised by Kat, I kept a subtle but constant eye out for anyone looking suspicious. I only had a vague description of Vic to go on but anyone who took more notice of Kat than they should drew my attention. Just a few hours ago, while she was choosing a pair of pyjamas in a clothes shop so that she wouldn't have to keep wearing mine, I'd caught a guy staring at her. I could tell he was just a stranger, charmed by her beauty rather than a threat, but I was still relieved when he caught my protective glare and slunk away looking sheepish.

As Kat carefully deposited an armful of items into the trolley she clocked the extra little luxuries I'd slipped in while her back was turned: a selection of Danish pastries, a packet of smoked salmon, a boxed Camembert for baking, fresh strawberries, four bottles of wine (two red and two white), a tub of ice cream and a large box of chocolates. The sneakiness of my actions made me feel good – like a kid again. I wanted to spoil Kat; to treat her to everything she might have missed; to make it up to her. I had only refrained from adding lobster, champagne and caviar because I was worried she might take it the wrong way. But she made no comment.

'I've finished. Is there anything else you want?' she said, her face unreadable.

'No, I'm good; let's go to the checkout.'

As we stood in the queue, Kat's gaze snagged on a women's magazine in the rack beside us.

'Get that if you want it.'

'No thanks.' A fleeting look of discomfort crossed her face as she turned away. Reaching over I added the magazine to our trolley. 'I don't want it!' Kat's indignant eyes met mine.

'I know but I want to have a look at it myself – maybe it'll give me a better understanding of women.' As she shook her head, her eyes softened and her mouth edged into a reluctant smile, which made me want to hug her. I was debating doing just that when a loud voice interrupted.

'James! I thought that was you!' I turned to find Rosalie Saunders, a girl I'd been to school with, standing beside me. She had a big toothy grin on her face and a trolley loaded with groceries and small children.

'Rose! How are you?' I said, limply returning her over-enthusiastic hug and wishing it was Kat's.

'Wonderful! We're properly settled in Richmond now and Andrew has just been made vice-president of his firm so things couldn't be better!'

'Congratulations,' I said. 'That's great.'

'We're just up here visiting Granny and Grandpa aren't we?' she said, addressing her offspring. There was a baby asleep in a carrier in the front of the trolley, a chubby toddler in a pink dress strapped in next to her, and a small boy with chocolate around his mouth standing in the back, surrounded by bumper packs of nappies and baby wipes. Rosalie spat into a tissue and wiped at the boy's face before turning back to me.

'What about you? I heard about your Dad, I am *so* sorry.' Stepping too close she scrutinised me, presumably searching for signs of grief.

'Yeah, thank you, but I'm OK.' I took half a step back.

'But are you just visiting or – Mum said you might be back for good? That you'd taken over the garden centre?' She sounded incredulous, her expression the same picture of confused concern that I'd seen on the faces of the friends I'd left behind in London.

'Yes, that's right. Just fancied a change. Rose, this is Kat,' I said, turning to where Kat had started unloading goods onto the conveyor belt. 'Kat, this is Rosalie – we went to the same school.'

Rose took in Kat with a dismissive glance, guffawed and hit me on the arm. 'It's a bit more than that!' she exclaimed, before turning to address Kat. 'James and I were high school sweethearts. You can ask anyone around here. Everyone thought we'd end up married – until I cruelly broke his heart, that is. I think I must be the one that got away,' she added in a stage whisper.

'Oh right, well, it's lovely to meet you,' Kat said smiling. 'But just so you know Jamie was sleeping in my bed before you even met him.'

Rosalie laughed abruptly in surprise, unaware of the joke, while Kat calmly carried on unloading our shopping without further elaboration. The rush of affection I felt for Kat in that moment almost winded me, as I fought to keep the grin off my face.

'Good to see you again, Rosalie,' I said, turning to help Kat with our groceries.

'Yes,' Rosalie said, distracted. 'Take care, James.' Eyeing Kat uneasily over her shoulder, she wheeled her children away.

'Sorry,' Kat said as she thumped down cans of tinned tomatoes.

'Don't be. I never liked her half as much as she thought I did.'

Chapter Twenty-seven

In the shadows, on the threshold of Jamie's bedroom, I hesitated, listening intently to his slow measured breaths. I had to be sure he was asleep before I ventured closer to his bed.

I'd been here five days – five days in Jamie's world – and it was everything I'd imagined and more. I didn't want to leave.

I loved working down on the nursery, tucked safely away from public view with the sun, wind and rain on my face and storybook hills and trees in every direction. Or in the polytunnels with Lil working the dark, rich compost between my fingers, learning to cultivate and nurture living plants and witnessing their growth and development day by day. My plaster cast was an annoyance I could have done without – restricting me to the lighter work – but at least my wrist didn't hurt too much and by occasionally slipping off the sling I could still use the fingers of that hand. It wasn't the only thing that had taken a little getting used to – there was the dizzyingly vast expanse of open space and sky; the strange, sweet stench of manure when the wind blew in a certain direction; the way my skin began to tingle and burn after less than half an hour in the sun; not to mention the assortment of peculiar-looking, but apparently harmless, insects that I'd encountered. But I relished each new day.

And then there were the evenings Jamie and I spent

alone together in the cottage, just talking and eating, reading books or watching TV. I savoured every new detail I learned about him – his borderline addiction to geeky science-fiction series, the lamer the better; or the way he consciously wore mismatched socks in memory of his mum, who used to pair them incorrectly by mistake; or the fact that he was slightly short-sighted. Jamie wore disposable contact lenses during the day but, in the evenings, when his eyes grew tired, he would swap them for a nerdy pair of black-rimmed spectacles. Rather than making him look more grown up and serious, they somehow highlighted his boyishness and only contributed to his inadvertent sex appeal. Life with Jamie was unexpectedly easy to settle into and yet, at the end of each day, no matter how weary I felt and as comfortable as my bed was, I was incapable of sleeping there.

I wasn't afraid of the dark the way Jamie used to be. It was the silence – the eerie absence of sound. There was no chronic wheezing to signify Vic's slumber, no traffic noise, no rumble of trains, no buzzing street lights, no TVs blaring, no stray music, no people talking too loud, no babies crying, no dogs barking, no alarms going off … The hush pressed in on me, surging up into my ears until it almost hurt.

And when I did sleep I invariably dreamt of Vic. His familiar words grating through my head on repeat until his voice became my own, 'You fucking well wind me up, you know that? You and your smart mouth – I should just kick you out, see how you like that – no one else'd take you on, that's for sure. I mean, what have you got to offer anyone? You're useless; spoiled goods, for fuck's sake!

You're so lucky I married you, so fucking lucky – I didn't have to, wish I hadn't. I felt sorry for you, you ungrateful cow. And what do I get in return? Nothing, that's what! Fucking nothing! I should teach you a fucking lesson.'

On my first night in the cottage panic had propelled me into Jamie's bedroom in the early hours of the morning. I was instinctively drawn to him, to his warm, reassuring scent and the comfort he exuded. Of course I was careful not to rouse him; I didn't want him to wake and find me in his bed – that would be awkward and difficult to explain – but by curling up on one side of his mattress and listening to his steady, restful breathing I could finally sleep in peace. I was confident that I'd be up early enough to return to my room before Jamie caught me out, because my body clock automatically woke me at dawn. And so it had – not to the squabble and flap of urban pigeons as before but to a light trilling, twittering mix of musical melodies, as a whole host of small songbirds welcomed the new day.

Sleeping in Jamie's bed had become a bad habit. Carefully I lay on my side, under the duvet beside him, my plaster-clad wrist tucked in the sling across my chest. Tonight there was a clear sky and moonlight was filtering through the thin curtains, softly illuminating Jamie's peaceful form. He lay on his back, one arm flung up on the pillow beside his head, the other resting across his bare chest, his fingers splayed over his heart. I lay still beside him, my eyes travelling over every beautiful contour, starting with the dark tousled hair on his pillow, the smooth planes of his face, the fan of his eyelashes, the soft swell of his mouth, the stubble at his jaw … and on down across the sheer breadth and solidity of his form, the sinuous ridges, dips and bulges of muscle in his shoulders, chest, arms and stomach – his skin flawless and sculpted to perfection. I marvelled at how a small abandoned boy had transformed into the impressive physical specimen of manhood before me. Of course he concealed his raw underlying strength beneath easy charm and a gentle, loving nature, just as he hid his sexy body beneath clothes, but I knew the real Jamie and it aroused a hunger in me like nothing else I'd ever known.

As my eyelids drooped with drowsiness, he made a low sound deep in his chest and the covered area below his stomach twitched and swelled beneath the duvet. I longed to reach out and touch him, my fingers physically tingled with the urge, so I pressed them safely between my own legs, squeezing my thighs together and quietly sighing at the near-constant ache there. I longed to know what Jamie was dreaming about and almost wished I was still Rina – the woman who had once turned him on – but I was Kat again. He had found his long-lost sister and I would not let him down.

Chapter Twenty-eight

My head was full of Kat as I made her a cup of tea. I'd set my alarm to ensure I would reach the market at the usual time. I'd showered, dressed, eaten some breakfast and done all the washing up from last night's delicious home-cooked meal but sensual images of Kat still lingered in my mind. My dreams of her were so vivid nowadays that I fancied I could smell the subtle fragrance of her skin when I woke.

In the past having to spend prolonged stretches of time with another person had made me uncomfortable. For reasons I didn't understand I'd always struggled to lower my guard and really be myself in front of anyone else and it was exhausting maintaining a pretence. But Kat had been here almost a week now and spending time alone with her (provided we were not in physical contact) was remarkably easy – I found myself relaxing without realising it. When I didn't have too much paperwork to do, we spent whole evenings just chatting or watching TV. She seemed happy to sit through some of my favourite shows, while simultaneously reading a book or completing a sudoku puzzle in the local paper. She clearly had a head for numbers and even the grids labelled 'difficult' were soon solved, once Kat was focused and chewing the end of a biro in concentration. Today would be our first time apart since I'd brought her home six days ago and I was oddly anxious about leaving her. But I had to go; I had important things to achieve in London.

I would start by surreptitiously convincing Cherry, Gary and any other curious locals that I was entirely clueless about Rina. Then I would pay a visit to Brian, my old college buddy who was now a private investigator based in nearby Fulham and owed me a favour. With Brian's help I could make sure that the right person or people would be enlightened about Vic's snitch status before the day was out. I was in no doubt that 'they' would make certain that Vic never snitched again but I didn't dwell on how that might be achieved. From what little Kat had told me, Vic had enslaved, bullied and abused her for years – as far as I was concerned he deserved everything he got. All I wanted in return was to remain anonymous to be free to keep Kat happy and safe for the rest of her life. The thought of anything happening to her was too unbearable to contemplate.

I was halfway up the stairs with Kat's cup of tea when she unexpectedly emerged from the bathroom wrapped only in a very small towel. We both stopped in surprise and scalding hot tea spilled over my fingers as my stunned gaze swept the full length of her – from her perfect toes, up impossibly long graceful legs and on to where her wet hair dripped onto the soft mounds of her breasts, rivulets of water disappearing into her cleavage. It was only a momentary glance, a few seconds nothing more, but it was long enough for me to clock the faded multicoloured array of bruises which spread out from under the towel in every direction – long enough for my initial shock to morph into horror at the pain she must have endured.

And then she was gone. She bolted back into the

bathroom like a startled gazelle, locking the door firmly behind her.

'Shit, Kat?' Setting down the tea and gingerly wiping my sore fingers on my trouser leg, I moved quickly to the door, resting my forehead against it. 'Kat, I'm sorry, I didn't mean to surprise you, are you OK?'

'Piss off, Jamie.' She was angry and I wasn't sure why – I hadn't deliberately caught sight of her half-naked, though lord knows I'd wanted to for long enough.

'Please, Kat, I just want to help.'

'I know I'm a mess; I don't need your pity,' she snapped.

'What? You're not a mess and I don't pity you Kat, I -' I what? How did I feel about her? I cared about her, deeply, perhaps more than I'd ever cared about anyone but that knowledge unsettled me and I couldn't tell her, not now, maybe not ever. 'It's the opposite of pity, Kat, I admire you – you've been through so much and yet you're so strong! You never complain about anything, never ask for help.' The temptation to force open the door was almost overwhelming. 'I want to kill your husband for the way he's treated you – hell, I wish him dead just for knowing you all those years when I didn't. I just want to help.'

'Thanks, but I'm fine,' she said evenly.

I sighed, relieved that she sounded calmer and disappointed that I wasn't brave enough to tell her how I really felt. 'OK. Look I have to go – I'm driving down to London and then I'm going to meet with some suppliers.' I omitted to mention Brian. 'I'm not sure when I'll be back; it might be quite late.'

176

'OK.'

'But you can call me on my mobile any time, Kat.'

'Yeah, OK.'

'And there's half a cup of tea out here if you want it.'

She snorted. 'Thanks.' I could hear the smile in her voice.

'I'll see you later,' I said, backing away down the stairs.

'Be careful,' she said softly.

Chapter Twenty-nine

I was reading a book and half-watching the nine o'clock evening news when a car pulled up on the drive. I assumed it was Jamie returning from London but when I peeked through a gap in the curtains it was not the van parked there; it was a sleek expensive-looking sports car. Convinced that Vic or one of his friends had tracked me down adrenalin spiked through my system. But just as I was preparing to run and hide the driver's door swung open and a delicate high-heeled foot protruded, followed by another. By the time she had fully emerged from the car, like a butterfly stretching its wings, I'd recognised Jasmine Reed.

As she crunched her way across the gravel towards the front door I hovered in indecision. Should I let her in? Should I call Jamie? Could I just hide and pretend there was no one home? I only realised it wasn't up to me when she inserted a key – how come she still had a set? – opened the door and walked in as if she owned the place.

'Well hello, what have we here?' she said, looking me up and down and shrugging out of a sequinned wrap. 'Who are you?'

'Kat,' I said, in shock.

'Cat!' She gave a little trilling laugh. 'Oh, how wonderful! Are you James's little pet?'

Caught off guard, I flushed with humiliation. 'No. I'm a friend; I work here.'

She nodded, seemingly satisfied that I was no threat.

'How lovely.' Wafting past me in a cloud of perfume, she headed through the living room towards the kitchen. 'Where is he? I need to talk to him.'

'He's in town; he's not back yet.'

Jamie had mentioned that Jasmine was still living in his London flat while she arranged somewhere else to move to – it was typically generous of him to allow such a thing – but I thought he'd said that they'd broken up back in March – that she was his *ex*-girlfriend. And yet here she was, acting like she owned him. Had I misunderstood? Jamie wouldn't lie to me would he?

In a daze I watched as Jasmine opened the fridge door and bent over. Her silky red dress rode up to reveal the tops of lacy black stockings, as she helped herself to a chilled bottle of Pinot Grigio. Collecting two huge wine glasses from a cupboard she set them on the table with a flourish, before filling them both to the top.

'There you go,' she said, holding one out to me and flashing her pearly white smile.

I wasn't much of a drinker but impelled by her self-assurance, confused, and not wishing to offend, I accepted the drink.

'Cheers, Cat!' Chinking her glass against mine she took a large swig, while I stole a tentative sip. 'Oh that's good,' she groaned, closing her eyes momentarily before glancing around and then pinning me with them. 'So, Cat.' She sashayed over to me and hooked her arm through mine, ignoring my cringe. 'Let's get comfortable and you can tell me all about yourself.'

I gulped down more Dutch courage as she led me into the lounge and pulled me down onto the couch with her.

Jasmine sank back against the cushions, her immaculately made-up face tipped up towards the ceiling and glossy blonde, corkscrew curls spilling out decorously around her head. I prepared myself for some sort of interrogation but soon realised she was far more interested in talking about herself. I watched, transfixed, as she drank and talked, occasionally gesturing with great sweeps of her arms, giggling prettily or wrinkling her neat little nose in distaste. She told me about the party she had just come from – the champagne, the canapés and the celebrities she had met. She spoke as candidly as if she had known me for years.

As she relaxed further she kicked off her heels, throwing one petite, stockinged leg across my lap and making me flinch. I drank self-consciously while her fragrant body heat seeped into the fabric of my new pyjamas. The low neckline of her dress splayed open revealing her small breasts – they jiggled each time she laughed, her nipples barely concealed by the fine lace of her bra. And she touched me frequently – the manicured tips of her fingers fleetingly applying pressure with a tap, a pat, or a stroke on my shoulder, forearm, knee and thigh – each contact making me jolt at the unexpectedness of it.

I had never met anyone famous before. I was enthralled by her perfect looks, her confidence, her charm, and fascinated by the people and the places she described. But more than anything I was utterly absorbed by the idea of her and Jamie as a couple. I began to picture them together – his eyes, his hands and his mouth on her skin; his arms around her as she spoke, slept, and fucked him... And I found myself viewing her as he might – the sexy red pout of her lips, the glitter of her eyes, the flawlessness of her bronzed complexion.

By the time she leant forward and kissed me I barely knew who I was. My mouth fell open in surprise and her lips were soft and coaxing, her tongue gently teasing mine as she took my hand in hers and pressed it to her own breast. As if in a trance my fingers spread out cupping the delicate lacy mound in my palm. *Like Jamie*, I thought. Has he touched her like this? Kissed her like this? Does he miss it? Jasmine pressed her hand between my legs and a shudder of nausea swept through my body. I couldn't breathe properly, her perfume was clogging my nostrils, my head was spinning and my vision swam.

What was I doing and more to the point what the hell was she playing at? Pulling away from her in alarm I glanced at the coffee table. We had polished off two whole bottles of wine – way more alcohol than I was used to.

'Aw c'mon now. I saw the way you were looking at me,' Jasmine purred.

'No, I –' With the back of my hand I wiped her waxy lipstick from my mouth. Was she deliberately trying to intimidate me? Humiliate me? 'What about Jamie?'

'*Jamie*?'

'James, I mean, James. Don't you? Won't he –?'

Jasmine sighed and collapsed back against the couch rolling her eyes. 'I don't think James cares what I do any more. I thought you might be worth a try – see how he reacted. He's never caught me with a woman before but it probably wouldn't have made any difference.'

'I don't understand.'

'No, of course you don't.' Jasmine sighed again.

Standing up, and swaying slightly, I made my way to the kitchen where I filled two pint glasses with water and awkwardly carried them back to the lounge. I set one in front of Jasmine before sitting carefully at the other end of the couch, out of reach. She had lit up a cigarette and appeared to be considering something as I sipped my water.

'What has James told you about me? About our relationship?'

'Not much,' I said, honestly. 'He said you broke up after his dad died and he moved back here.'

Jasmine nodded and tapped ash into her empty wine glass and I took a cautious breath of relief. I hadn't really doubted Jamie's word. 'It's not as if *I* could come and live *here* is it?' she said, indicating her distaste with a sweep of her hand. 'But I didn't think we were really finished – not for good. I thought he'd come to his senses and come back.'

I didn't comment; I was curious to know what had gone wrong between them but it was none of my business.

'He doesn't seem to realise how lucky he was to have me, that's what I can't understand! I'm beautiful, sexy, talented – people are starting to recognise me now; everywhere I go men are falling over each other to date me. I'm number 64 on this year's Up-and-Coming Actresses list for God's sake!'

Suddenly amused I pursed my lips, trying not to laugh. Was she for real?

'Not that he was ever any good for me,' she said, angrily stubbing out her cigarette. 'He's never really loved me – not the way he should; he doesn't hang on my every word like other guys do. He's so damn laid-back! He just doesn't adore me the way I deserve to be adored.' Crossing her arms like a spoilt child she looked at me, as if expecting me to respond.

'Maybe he's just not as – expressive – as you?'

Jasmine threw her head back and let out a high-pitched squeal of a laugh. 'Now there's an understatement! He's dead inside, that's what he is! Maybe it's because he grew up without a mother, I don't know; he was never very close to his dad either –'

'What happened to his mother?' I'd wanted to find out long before now but it was a sensitive question and I'd been waiting for the right time to ask Jamie about her.

'She died when he was about ten, I think. I don't know; he never talked about her – that's what I mean! He never once told me how he was feeling, not really. Never showed real emotion, never let me in.'

I couldn't speak. Inside my heart was breaking for a ten-year-old Jamie. To have lost his mum just three years after she adopted him, after everything he had already endured.

'Between you and me, I cheated on him all the time,' Jasmine said, with satisfaction. I stared at her, incredulous, anger boiling up inside me. 'I was careful at first and he had no idea but then I got annoyed and I started deliberately leaving clues. I wanted him to find out; I wanted him to do something! Get jealous; get angry; shout at me; fight for me; something! But he wouldn't – he didn't.'

Taking a deep breath, I attempted to rein in my

183

growing fury. 'If he's so wrong for you why are you here, Jasmine? Why do you want him back?'

'Because he was *good* to me – not in a passionate way – but he always looked after me; called when he said he would; made sure I had enough cash for a taxi; gave me nice things –'

'You want him for his money?'

'Ha!' she snorted. 'What money? He's blown it all on this bloody dump.'

'I'm not judging you; I'm just trying to understand.' I, of all people, was in no position to judge anyone – hadn't I effectively married Vic for his money, for the security he offered? But then I'd been desperate; I'd had no other choice. Jasmine Reed was, in her own words, 'up-and-coming' – a rising star with a career and a bright future ahead of her. It couldn't just be about the money. Suddenly I realised – recognised – what Jasmine was trying so hard to hide. 'You still love him,' I said.

With a roll of her eyes she pulled a face and shook her head in disgust but her acting skills fell short and I could see I'd hit the mark.

'Jasmine, you know he's not right for you; you *know* he doesn't love you and yet you've come all the way out here –'

'Fuck you,' she said, her eyes flashing. 'Who are you anyway? Some tramp he picked up off the street?'

Her words, startlingly close to the truth, effectively sobered me up and stamped out any pity I might have felt for her. 'Get out,' I said, standing up.

She laughed. 'Don't worry; you're welcome to him.' Scooping up her handbag she staggered to her feet. 'He's

184

messed up. Maybe you are too – you probably deserve each other. I mean just look at this place, he's a fucked-up loser and –'

Lashing out, I flung the contents of the glass in my hand into Jasmine's face, the cold water stopping her mid-sentence with a gasp. For a second I couldn't even register what I'd done; my own rage rang in my ears as she stared at me, wide-eyed and dripping.

'Kat?' a shocked voice said from the doorway.

Jasmine burst into tears and ran past me, past Jamie and out into the night, slamming the front door shut behind her. Jamie just stood motionless, staring at me, his keys in his hand.

Chapter Thirty

There she was – the Kitkat I once knew – wildly beautiful, shoulders back, chin held high, passion radiating from every pore. And she was defending me again; like a lioness, dressed only in pyjamas and a sling, yet breathtakingly magnificent. I had never witnessed anything so sexy.

'Shit. Sorry,' she said, the fire in her eyes cooling. 'I needed to shut her up.'

'Right,' I said, unable to prevent amusement from spreading across my face. 'Mission accomplished.' Outside Jasmine's car roared off down the road.

Kat looked down at the splashes of water on the carpet. 'I'll clean this up.' With one arm she awkwardly gathered glasses and headed for the kitchen.

'Just leave it; it doesn't matter,' I said, following her. 'Are you OK?' Reaching out I lightly touched her elbow.

She stopped and turned towards me but wouldn't look me in the eye. 'I'm fine.'

'Why was she here anyway? What did she say to you?'

She glanced up. 'You didn't hear?'

'Only the last part; what else did she say?'

'Nothing – just a whole load of bullshit. I can see why you broke up with her.'

Her eyes were darkly dilated, glowing with a greenish light that captivated my soul. I desperately wanted to kiss her and my gaze lingered on her lips but I hesitated, the force of my feelings paralysing me.

She swallowed. 'Are you going after her?'

I shook my head.

'She's had a lot to drink.'

'I know,' I sighed. 'But if I chase after her I'm likely to make things worse. I'll call her in an hour or so; make sure she made it home all right.'

Kat nodded, turned away and began rinsing out glasses in the sink one-handed. 'Did you see Vic?' Her shoulders were stiff with tension.

'No, he wasn't there; the cafe was all closed up. I think Cherry must have given up trying to run it.'

'He'll go mental when he finds out.'

'Kat, I don't want you to worry. I don't think Vic will be a problem for you anymore.'

'Why?' Her eyes met mine, briefly betraying her anxiety.

'I – I went to meet an old friend of mine, someone I've known a long time. I was very careful; it won't come back to you.' Taking a deep breath, I braced myself for her reaction. 'Look, the people Vic informed on – they'll know now; they'll know it was him.'

Kat's eyes widened in alarm. 'What?'

'I had to, Kat. I had to do something to keep you safe.' Her face paled as she stared at me, the silence stretching out.

'They'll kill him.'

'I – maybe, I don't know.' I wasn't sure what I'd expected her response to be – anger? distress? grief? I was hoping for some kind of relief but she expressed none of that. She simply dried her fingers on a tea towel lost in thought. 'I'll keep going back to the market each

187

Thursday and deliver stock to Gary as usual. Hopefully that way I can avoid suspicion and keep an eye on things but, Kat, are you OK?'

'I'm fine.'

'Are you angry with me?'

'No. I understand.'

'Really?'

'Yes. But I'm tired. I'm going to bed,' she said, stepping around me.

'Kat, wait.' As I caught her right hand, heat zinged up my arm and I quickly released it again. 'I just wanted to say I'm sorry you had to deal with Jasmine; she can be pretty unpleasant sometimes. But thank you for sticking up for me; it means a great deal.'

She glanced at me, her expression unreadable, nodded and then walked away.

While Kat was upstairs in the bathroom I opened my post and checked my emails to distract myself from my own thoughts. When I estimated that Jasmine had had enough time to reach the flat in London I called her mobile. She ignored my first call but picked up on the second, just as I was about to leave a message.

'What?' She sounded miserable rather than hostile and, though I was still angry about the way she'd spoken to Kat, I tried to soften my tone.

'I'm just checking that you made it back alive.'

She sighed and I could picture her rolling her eyes. 'I'm alive. That it?'

'We still need to talk about the flat, Jas.'

'Oh for heavens sake, you're like a broken record. Come round on Sunday evening.'

'Sunday? Really?' Her sudden capitulation was a surprise. 'What time?'

'After six.'

Jasmine hung up before I could agree and I stared at my phone wondering what had caused her to give in. Was it something Kat had said?

Locking the front and back doors and turning off the lights, I went upstairs, brushed my teeth and retired to my own bed. But with no more distractions my mind returned to my earlier meeting with Brian. Had I done the right thing about Vic? My hope had been that giving Vic bigger problems to deal with would keep him from coming after Kat. I'd given little thought to what might actually happen to him and hadn't really considered they might kill him. Still, knowing how badly Vic had treated Kat over the years I had no sympathy to spare for him. Keeping Kat safe was all that mattered.

A sound woke me in the middle of the night. Outside it was raining, gently tapping on the roof and windows and the room was pitch dark. I listened and then I heard it again. A soft whimper of distress in the bed beside me. Stretching out my fingers I recognised Kat's long silky hair and intoxicating scent immediately. She was here? In my bed? Was I dreaming?

'Kat?' I whispered. 'Kat, is everything OK?'

She moaned, as if she was in pain. 'No. No don't –'

Her words made my skin prickle but I realised she was asleep, probably having a nightmare, and instinctively moved closer, gently stroking her shoulder soothingly.

'It's OK, Kat,' I whispered. 'Wake up; you're just

having a bad dream; wake up.' She jolted and gasped, her hand clutching at my chest in the darkness. 'It's OK, Kat, it was just a dream, you're OK; you're safe with me.'

'Jamie?'

'Yes, you're OK. I've got you. Shall I put the light on?' I felt her shake her head as she began to cry and I held her close and kissed the top of her head, her hair, her forehead, her cheek... 'Don't cry, Kat,' I murmured. 'Everything's OK.'

Turning her head she pressed her mouth to mine, her lips soft and warm as they parted and as eager as my own. In the darkness her hot tongue stroked along mine – licking, sucking, tasting me – and I groaned in the back of my throat, overwhelmed with wanting her. As her fingers roamed across my chest the intensity of her touch almost burned, the coarse edge of her plaster cast tickling my skin.

Should we be doing this? Kat was like a big sister to me, emotionally stronger than me, out of my league and a married woman besides – surely she was forbidden fruit. But I desperately wanted to soothe her, erase her fears and nightmares and feel her warm body against mine. Was that so wrong?

Emboldened by the dark I slowly began to unbutton her shirt, aware that she might stop me at any moment, but her fingers fisted in my hair urging me on. At last I peeled her top open, sensing the heat radiating from her skin, savouring her scent and wishing I could see her. Sightlessly I planted kisses along her jaw, down her throat, across her breasts, until I found the erect peaks of her nipples, drawing them into my mouth and sucking

190

them tenderly in turn, our breathing loud in the damp hush of the night.

Easing her pyjama bottoms and knickers down from her hips, I steadily, carefully, moved my lips down her ribs, her belly, and her hips – gently tracing her softly sculpted curves and hollows, while she shivered, panted and squirmed beneath my touch. Her right hand slipped inside my boxer shorts and I groaned again as she gripped me firmly in her lean fingers. I was close to coming already but this was not supposed to be about me and my selfish needs.

Drawing myself away out of her grasp I shifted my mouth to the soft apex of her thighs. She was liquid with heat and I used my tongue to explore and tease her. Soon the muscles of her whole body tightened, her breathing sped up and she braced her legs against the bed, moaning my name in warning. Cupping her bottom in my hands, as if drinking from her, I licked her rhythmically over and over, absorbed in her delectable taste, until she cried out in climax – her body arching off the bed and shuddering in one wave after another – before collapsing back onto the mattress, breathless.

The feel and sound of Kat's orgasm had me dangerously close to the edge – my balls aching and tightly primed, my cock rigid and twitching with need. But I couldn't allow myself to enter her. I'd idolised her for too long and, anyway, she wasn't mine to take. Kat's pleasure was enough – a gift in itself. Returning my face to hers I kissed her but she reached for me in the darkness again, squeezing my length in her palm, and her touch was everything – too much. With a groan I spilled my seed across her thigh, light-headed with the sheer force of my release.

Kat intercepted my mumbled apology with another lingering kiss but I was grateful that she hadn't actually witnessed my helpless undoing. There were no words for what had just happened between us. Cocooned in darkness and wrapped in each other's arms, we listened instead to the soft patter of the rain above, sinking, wordlessly, into a sated slumber.

When I woke in the morning the sun was bright and Kat was gone. I could hear the kettle boiling in the kitchen below and the springy rattle of the toaster offering up its load – the reassuring early-morning sounds of Kat making herself breakfast as usual. But as I recalled the night before – the very best night of my whole existence in potent detail in my mind – I knew that I'd fucked up. Big time. This was *Kat*, not just some girl that I could afford to lose like all the others. She was everything to me – my last remaining family; what the hell was I thinking? How could I have done that – ravaged her body and come all over her while she was feeling vulnerable as if I was some randy teenager; as if she didn't have enough to deal with? My alarm clock started beeping and I slammed it hard with my fist, the plastic shattering and splintering into pieces.

Distractedly sucking blood off the side of my hand I fought to calm myself. Would she forgive me? I sincerely hoped so. I didn't want her to hate me or to leave – I'd just got used to having her around. But why was she in my bed in the first place? The thought brought me up short. She must have been feeling anxious – that was the only conclusion I could come to. She felt safer near me than in a room by herself, in much the same way I used to feel safer in her bed as a child. Regret washed over me afresh. She had trusted in me and I'd abused that trust – let her down.

As Kat finished up in the kitchen and quietly let herself out the back door on her way to the nursery, I resolved to find a way to make it up to her – to provide the reassurance she needed while keeping my selfish hands to myself. After all she deserved so much better.

Chapter Thirty-one

Staring unflinchingly into my own eyes in the mirror, I systematically brushed my teeth. I'd managed it – survived the whole day without making a fool of myself, without cracking up or launching myself at Jamie.

Amazing Jamie.

I'd worked all day on the nursery with Frank and Lil, sweeping and weeding the paths, watering the beds, and planting up pairs of large terracotta pots with palms, phormiums and bay trees. With only one good arm I couldn't do any heavy lifting – and with the sling on I had do things entirely one-handed – but watering only required one hand and there was always plenty of that to do in the polytunnels now that the weather was getting hotter and sunnier. All day I acted as though nothing had happened between Jamie and me in the middle of the night and so did he. I still couldn't quite believe it *had* happened; one minute I'd thought Vic was about to hit me and the next I was safely wrapped up in Jamie's arms – his bare chest, hot and deliciously musky, at my fingertips. Tantalising remembered echoes of his touch had been seeping into my thoughts all day – unnerving me with their clarity and their ability to make me flush and smile with pleasure. I'd never experienced anything like it: so sensual, so intense, so out of this world; words could not do it justice. Jamie wasn't just devastatingly good-looking; he was tender, passionate, loving and toe-curlingly skilful. He had made me feel special. He had made me forget myself, if only for a short while.

But why? Why had Jamie pleasured me like that, without taking anything in return? Why me, when he could have any pretty young girl he liked? Did he feel sorry for me? Was it just out of pity? Thank God it was too dark for him to see all my ugly scars and bruises. Whatever his reasons, and as wonderful as it had been, it wouldn't happen again. Jamie had clearly come to his senses this morning and I didn't want him to feel uncomfortable about it. I owed him so much; he'd gone to extraordinary lengths to help me escape Vic and he didn't need me lusting after him like some old 'tramp off the street'. A fresh flush of shame crept into my face as I recalled Jasmine Reed's words. She had me pegged right away. I'd endured far worse insults from Vic for years but somehow it had sounded worse coming from Jasmine's pretty mouth – harsh but no less true. Shit, did I really let that bitch kiss me? I spat out a mouthful of toothpaste in disgust.

Jamie was standing in the doorway of his bedroom when I emerged from the bathroom. He was wearing just boxers and a T-shirt, his arms and legs bare, tanned and softly hairy. He leaned one solid shoulder into the door frame as his eyes swept up over me and I was grateful for the ample coverage of my pyjamas, despite being too warm.

'Did you speak to Jasmine last night?' I said.

'Yes, I called her before I went to bed.'

'She made it home all right?'

'Yes. I don't know what you said to her but she's finally agreed to have a proper discussion about the flat.

Hopefully she's coming round to the idea of moving out. I'm going to go and see her on Sunday.'

'That's good.'

'Yes.'

I couldn't think of anything else to say and as the silence became awkward I started towards my bedroom.

'You can sleep in my room if you like?'

I stopped and stared at him confused, my heart pounding in my chest.

'I promise I won't touch you. I know last night was – wrong, but my bed's plenty big enough for two and, well, the offer's there if you want it.'

Ordering my thoughts I tried to read between the lines. Had Jamie guessed why I was there in his bed? Was I really so pathetic and transparent? The idea that he might pity me was a sour taste in my mouth. 'Why?'

Jamie shrugged and picked at the paintwork at his elbow. 'It feels good having you around – just like old times.' He looked so young, his voice so soft and uncertain, and yet his words resonated somewhere deep inside me. The truth was I wanted to be near him more than ever and I couldn't sleep properly on my own anyway.

'If you're still afraid of the dark you should just say so,' I said.

Jamie laughed, a genuine boyish smile spreading out across his handsome face. 'OK, fair enough – you got me. Does that mean you'll stay?'

'OK,' I said, feigning nonchalance.

'Thank you,' he breathed, as I stepped past him and made my way to his bed.

We stayed awake for hours, side by side in the dark, not touching, just talking; reminiscing about our shared past. It was such a short period from our childhood, just four years that we'd shared, compared to the long twenty-three years we'd been apart, and yet Jamie recalled more from that time than I would have thought possible.

'Do you remember the back garden?' he said.

'What that fenced in area of mud and weeds masquerading as lawn?'

'Yeah – it was like a meadow in the summer and we spent almost all our time out there. I used to go around gathering daisies and buttercups for you so that you could make them into long chains.'

'Why? You didn't have to.'

I sensed his shrug. 'I don't know; it was something to do, I guess, but it was nice, peaceful – until the other kids took the piss out of me for picking flowers.'

'Little shits.'

Jamie chuckled. 'I think you said something similar at the time – you descended like some angry, avenging flower fairy, wreathed in petals and inflicting Chinese burns without mercy.'

Jamie went on to reminisce about Mungo, the Plumleys' arthritic mongrel, who habitually growled at passing motorbikes, farted when he sneezed, and slept at the end of Jamie's bed. I smiled at his memories as he talked. It was a novelty being able to discuss some of my childhood at all, let alone with someone who was actually there. I was also reminded about Martin, an unpleasant, chubby child with beady little eyes and an unfortunate stutter. But he held a lot of sway over the other kids

197

simply because he was bossy and quick to use his fists. Apparently on one occasion – when Martin and friends had Jamie surrounded and were laughing and barking at him like animals – I'd appeared out of nowhere, slipped Mungo's lead around Martin's neck, dragged him off, and forced him to eat dog food from Mungo's bowl while the others looked on silently in awe.

'That sounds like me,' I said, grimacing. 'I was a troublemaker back then.'

'You were fantastic, Kat. Martin left me alone for weeks after that.'

'I bet I got punished for it though.'

Jamie sighed. 'Yeah, I think they took all your books away.' His voice was heavy, the humour gone.

'Is that all? It could have been worse.'

'Yeah, I guess the Plumleys weren't too bad really.'

I didn't reply. The Plumleys, though emotionally detached and financially overstretched, with as many as eight kids in their care at a time, were still the most benign foster parents I'd ever had. Those I'd had since were significantly worse – neglectful, abusive or downright violent. But I wasn't about to burden Jamie with that knowledge.

The next morning I showed Jamie my old photograph and the scrap of handwriting I'd treasured for so long. Sitting heavily on the edge of the bed he stared at them, silent with emotion.

'Why did you change your name to James?'

He shrugged. 'That's the name they put on my adoption certificate. I think my Mum preferred it. To be honest I'd forgotten I used to be called Jamie until you suddenly said it at the hospital. Why did you change yours?'

'I was thirteen – I wanted to be someone else – I thought changing my name might help make that happen.'

I left to take a bath, allowing Jamie some privacy while he contemplated the small fragments of personal history that would seem insignificant to anyone else but which trembled in his hands. The childhood thread that connected us was tenuous and insubstantial and yet it had always felt like a solid bond to me. Now, as we got to know each other again, I was starting to wonder if Jamie might feel the same.

Chapter Thirty-two

On Sunday evening I rang the doorbell rather than using my key to get into my London flat. My goal was to get Jasmine to agree to move out so that I could get the place sold; to that end I would make it as easy as possible for her, despite the bitchy things I'd overheard her saying to Kat two nights previously. While I was here I'd also collect the spare keys to Southwood Cottage so Jasmine couldn't turn up there unannounced again.

Answering the door, my ex was as immaculately turned out as ever and calmly composed, as she invited me to sit down and offered me a drink.

'A cup of tea would be lovely, thank you.'

'You'd better make it – you never did like my tea,' she said, sitting down and inspecting a long fingernail.

'That's not true.' With a sigh I moved into the kitchen and filled the kettle. 'You want one?' She nodded. Neither of us spoke again until I'd returned with our drinks and settled at the opposite end of the settee.

'So, you're here to kick me out,' she said, ever the drama queen.

'That's not fair, Jasmine. You know I need the money tied up in this place. I've already given you nearly three months to find somewhere else to go.'

'That was good of you,' she muttered. I picked up my mug of tea to distract myself from my growing irritation. 'If you're really going to sell my home out from underneath me then there's something you ought to know.'

'Yeah?'

'I'm pregnant.'

I'd just taken a mouthful of tea and, rather than spit it out, I swallowed heavily. It burned all the way down. 'What?'

'You heard.'

'But you're on the pill, aren't you?'

She folded her arms and shrugged. 'These things happen.'

'But it can't be mine?'

Her steely blue eyes narrowed. 'What's that supposed to mean?'

'I mean, we're not together anymore; we haven't slept together since –' I tried to think back but something resembling blind panic was brewing inside me, making it hard to concentrate.

'I'm three months along. Don't tell me you don't remember; it happened right here on this sofa!' Her voice rose in pitch along with her anger.

'No, of course I remember –' *Jesus*, did I really make a baby with Jasmine while thinking about Kat? I was going straight to Hell. 'But – I thought you were seeing someone else, maybe –?'

'A woman knows these things, James.' She said it dismissively and it sounded like a line from one of her plays.

'Hang on; you're three months gone? So you've decided to keep it?'

She shrugged again. 'No, but it's too late to terminate.'

'But, you've been drinking – and smoking.' My eyes

swivelled to the overflowing ashtray on the coffee table as a new kind of horror spread through me.

'I only just found out, OK.' Swiping the ashtray off the table she stalked into the kitchen where she dumped the contents in the bin.

'Jesus, fuck, Jasmine.'

Huffily she returned to her seat. 'That's really helpful, James, thanks.' Picking up her tea she blew on it, a scowl on her face.

'What are we going to do?'

She laughed, one of her fake laughs which didn't reach her eyes. 'We? I thought there was no "we" any more.'

My hands had begun to shake so I set my tea down on a coaster on the table. 'OK, what do *you* intend to do?'

'I suppose I'll put it up for adoption as soon as it's born.'

'Just like that.'

'Yes, James; just like that. It's not like I asked for this to happen and I have a career to get on with. If you still *wanted* me it might be different but clearly –' Tears had welled up in her big blue eyes and as her lip wobbled a surge of guilt impelled me to move over and hug her.

'I'm sorry,' I said, absently rubbing her back. 'It's just such a shock and I – please don't just give it away.'

'I can't keep it, James; I'm not cut out to be a single mum!'

'I know, I'm sorry; don't worry; we'll work something out, together, OK?'

I felt her nod and relax slightly in my arms, while my anxiety quietly mounted and I fought the urge to hit something.

203

Chapter Thirty-three

I was glad I'd waited up for Jamie when he stepped through the front door after midnight. Something was badly wrong.

'What is it? What happened?' His gaze found me as I hovered in the living room in the glow of a side lamp. His eyes, usually so warm, seemed hollow as he reached out wordlessly and pulled me into a hug. The sudden bodily contact was alarming, partly because of what had happened between us just three nights ago but mainly because Jamie was usually so careful to maintain a distance between us. Whatever had occurred this evening had upset him, badly.

'I'm so glad you're here, Kat,' he said into my hair. I wanted to comfort him, to ease his pain and relish the feel of his arms around me, but he smelled of Jasmine's perfume and cigarettes and fear made it impossible for me to relax.

'Tell me.' I could feel the steady hammering of Jamie's heartbeat against my chest and my own heart rate had picked up in anticipation.

'She's pregnant.'

No! Not that! I closed my eyes and my body tensed all over as if to shield me from hearing more. His arms banded tighter around me in response. 'She says she's three months gone. She says it's mine,' he added, his voice heavy with despair.

In my head I did some quick calculations. Jamie

first walked into Vic's Cafe three months ago – that was when we met each other, as adults, for the first time – and he was still sleeping with Jasmine then? Of course he was; just because she was a complete bitch and cheating on him, didn't mean ... 'Do you believe her?'

'I have no idea, Kat; she seems so sure.'

'But three days ago she was here smoking, drinking, drink-driving –' *and trying to seduce me.*

'I know. She says she's only just found out, but Kat –' He pulled back and looked at me, his face taut with pain. 'She wants to give it up; she wants to give the baby away – it's like history repeating itself all over again; I can't stand it.'

I pulled him back into a hug, unable to bear the look in his eyes, and he buried his face in my hair, holding me close, as if that might save him. 'It will be OK,' I said, wishing I believed it.

After a few moments we climbed the stairs together and got into bed. I lay close behind Jamie as we stretched out on our sides in the dark, almost spooning. He took my uninjured arm and wrapped it round his waist as if he needed the extra reassurance – just like when we were children. It was cosy and comforting but his pain was my pain.

'Tell me what I should do, Kat.'

'How did you leave things with her?'

'I said she could stay in the flat as long as she needed to and that we'd work something out.'

'She wants you to go back to her, doesn't she?'

'She didn't say that but she's adamant she won't keep the baby while she's on her own.'

'Do you want to go back to her?' I said, more calmly than I felt.

'No. You know I don't.'

His reply gave me some small relief. 'Do you think she'll let you have the baby when it's born?'

'I don't know – I wasn't brave enough to ask her. I doubt it and anyway I don't know the first thing about babies.'

'You'd make a much better parent than she would.'

Jamie was silent for a while. 'How do you know?' he said at last.

'Because I know you – you're kind and patient and generous and caring –'

'But not loving,' he said, cutting me off.

'What do you mean?'

'You know what I mean, Kat; I'm not like other people.'

I wanted to hit him – to stop him being down on himself and release my own frustration at the situation – but I grabbed his jaw instead and turned his head to face me. In the low light I could just make out the resignation in his expression and it made me even angrier. 'You have as much capacity to love a child as anyone else; more, in fact, because you know what it's like to have to go without. Don't you dare talk like that again.'

Jamie looked slightly bewildered but nodded. 'OK.' His gaze dropped to my mouth and altered, his breathing deepening, his lips parting slightly. The heat of my anger began to stir into a different kind of fire inside me. Releasing his jaw, I wrenched back my hand and turned away, settling on the far side of the bed with my back to him.

'Go to sleep.'

'Night Kat,' he sighed.

Chapter Thirty-four

'Right, hold it there,' our coach bellowed, clapping his hands together.

The rest of us slowed to a stop, sweaty and breathless from twenty minutes of concentrated attack and defence drills in twenty-four-degree heat. Wiping my forehead on my sleeve I reached for a bottle of water and took a long thirsty gulp. The sun was strong in the sky and there was barely a breath of wind. Summer was asserting itself with unseemly haste this year – drying out the last of the spring-flowering bulbs and pushing the summer bloomers into a veritable orgy of lush growth and colour. The heat was good for business and sales were up but it was still only June and I couldn't help worrying the season might burn itself out too quickly.

'Time to warm down, guys,' Coach said. 'One last lap of the pitch and then back here for stretches. Off you go.' A few of the guys rolled their eyes and groaned as we set off but Adam and I exchanged a grin. We'd known each other since school and although Adam wasn't as close a mate as Liam he was far chattier. He was a winger and I was an outside centre – we both liked to run.

As the team settled into a comfortable pace, I glanced over my shoulder to where Kat sat in the dappled shade of a birch tree. I'd warned her our training sessions were boring to watch but she'd insisted on coming along anyway. And I liked having her here; it was strangely reassuring. An old book, *The Brinkworth Guide to Ancient*

Myths and Legends, lay on the grass beside her but she hadn't picked it up once – every time I looked over and smiled at her she was gazing in my direction. The skinny jeans she wore showcased her improbably long legs and she had bravely pushed her shirtsleeves up above her elbows, revealing smooth porcelain skin as pale as the cast on her wrist. It was almost two weeks since Vic had pushed her down the stairs and Kat never gave the impression she was in any pain or discomfort but I worried that she was using her arm too much. Tomorrow I would take her to the local hospital to make sure her wrist was healing properly.

With private longing I wondered if the bruises had finally faded from the rest of her body too because, despite the climbing temperatures, she still wore a full set of pyjamas in my bed each night. Not that that prevented me from waking with a fierce erection every morning but if Kat had noticed she was too polite to mention it. Nowadays all my showers were cold ones, for all the good it did.

'She's hot, man,' Adam said between breaths. 'Nothing like Jasmine but still –'

'We're just friends,' I said.

'Yeah, right.'

'No, really, we're old friends.'

'OK, so you won't mind if I hit on her then?' I glared at Adam and he laughed, his hands up in mock surrender. 'Joke! I'm just joking, jeez!'

We kept jogging, our studded boots thudding out a rhythm, while behind us our fellow Warriors grumbled, keen to have a shower, a burger and a pint. I'd thoroughly enjoyed today's session – it always felt good to be part of a team and expending physical energy with a fully focused mind. But it was also an invaluable distraction. The possibility of impending fatherhood scared me witless. Most of the time I tried not to think about it – the baby still might turn out not to be mine and I was clinging to that hope with near desperation. But if I did turn out to be the father I wasn't sure what would be worse: a child of mine being abandoned to strangers or brought up by me alone. Maybe not entirely alone of course – I hoped Kat might stay and help me.

Kat – for five days now I'd been haunted by memories of pleasuring her. The whole encounter was just so extraordinary: the thrill of finding her in my bed, the sublime feel of her body as she fell apart in my mouth, the sound as she moaned my name… The quiet darkness had heightened the overall sense of illicit excitement but it was more than just a physical release – I'd felt something else; something visceral; something deeper; something I'd never experienced before with anyone else and it had blown my mind completely.

I was still convinced that any kind of romantic relationship with Kat wasn't an option, especially now. And anyway, she deserved better than me. My track record with women proved that I would fuck up and lose her, possibly hurting her in the process. So where did that leave us?

'You're not getting back with Jasmine then?' Adam interrupted my thoughts. I hadn't told anyone except Kat about the baby yet.

I shook my head. 'No.'

'Good,' Liam grunted on the other side of me.

Adam and I squinted up at him in surprise but Liam just kept moving, his breathing laboured.

'Where did that come from?' I said.

Liam glanced at me impassively and shrugged his enormous shoulders. 'I don't like her,' he said, returning his gaze to the ground.

His comment surprised me. They had only met a couple of times and certainly Jasmine had had no time for Liam, Adam or even my city work colleagues and had rarely made any effort to socialise with them. Regardless of this most of my friends were captivated by Jasmine Reed. In fact, Liam's missing ex-girlfriend, Cally, had been particularly star-struck when she and Jasmine met. Liam had always conveyed the same affable respect towards Jasmine as he did towards anyone else. 'Why not?'

Liam scratched his burly chest with one hand. 'She wasn't good for you.'

My best mate's words were oddly moving. I'd gradually come to the same conclusion about my ex myself but I was impressed that Liam hadn't been blinded by her popular façade like everyone else.

'In what way?' Adam interjected. 'You never said anything to me?'

Liam shrugged. 'I like Kat though,' he said, avoiding Adam's question and glancing in her direction. 'She seems nice.'

I couldn't help smiling. 'Thanks man.' I slapped him on the back as we neared the end of our lap. 'Good to know.'

211

The White Bear held a long-standing Tuesday-night reservation for the Wildham Warriors: three pushed-together picnic benches in the beer garden, complete with parasols. The sun had grown hazy as cloud gathered high up in the sky but the air was still sticky with heat.

I left Kat chatting to Liam's brother Lester and his wife, Maire, while Adam and I went to the bar to order a round. By the time we'd returned with drinks everyone was seated, with Kat at one end entirely surrounded by large, freshly showered, hungry-looking men. I took the only available space at the opposite end of the table with the girls.

Even from a distance I could tell Kat was out of her comfort zone – she sat very still, head held high and her posture perfect; given a choice she preferred to sit with her back to a wall. But she smiled often, her cheeks flushed and her eyes bright, as she sipped a single Archers and lemonade and soaked up the banter around her. It hurt to think that this was all new to Kat – that she'd never experienced the simple pleasure of a drink in a pub with friends before; she'd admitted as much this afternoon. And that wasn't all she'd missed out on: dinner in restaurants, trips to the theatre, days at the seaside, college, concerts, parties, festivals, driving lessons, learning to swim – so many things. But it was thoughts of the ugly things she'd experienced instead, the things she wouldn't talk about, that really worried me.

I still only knew the basics – that she'd gone straight from school to poorly paid menial labour, to living on the street, to an abusive marriage. We'd both been abandoned as children and my subsequent life had not been perfect

212

but it was a holiday camp compared to hers. I desperately wanted to help her, make it up to her, and shoulder her pain. And not just because I felt guilty for leaving her behind all those years ago but because she was important to me, and becoming more so by the day. If I was honest that realisation made me uneasy.

Turning away from Kat, I swallowed a third of my pint and focused instead on the person sat beside me. Poppy, Adam's younger sister, was here to chauffeur her brother home and usually only allowed him one drink before leaving but it was his birthday so tonight she'd stayed to socialise. As a child she was chatty and excitable, like Adam, with cute freckles across her nose and curly red hair – always wanting to tag along. It'd been a long time since we'd seen each other and in the intervening years she had blossomed into a bubbly young woman: her freckles concealed under make-up, hair tamed straight, and new curves in all the right places.

As Poppy babbled on, enthusing about her new job as an events planner, relaying tales of various disasters and making me laugh, I became aware that she was flirting. All the signs were there – the way she kept blushing; stroking her hair; touching my arm; glancing at my mouth while I was talking. I didn't mind; it was harmless; nothing would ever come of it and I was grateful for the distraction. It helped keep my mind off the enigmatic and bewildering woman seated at the other end of the table. I was on my third pint by the time Poppy tried to foist her number on me.

I raised an eyebrow at her. 'What for?'

'Just in case you need an event organising,' she said,

colour rising to her face.

'Don't you have a business card you can give me?'

'I'm just getting some new ones printed.'

'I'm sure I could get your number from Adam if –'

'Look, just put my number in your phone and then you've got it if you need it, OK?' Poppy said, exasperated.

'OK, OK.' Amused I stretched out my leg and reached in my pocket while Maire grinned at us from across the table. 'Shit, I've left my phone at the club.'

'Oh shut up!' Poppy laughed. 'Stop teasing.'

'No I'm serious,' I said getting to my feet and grabbing my jacket. 'I'll be back in a bit.'

My gut tightened as I moved over to where Liam and Kat sat together in conversation. I explained I'd left my mobile in the club changing room and Liam passed me the keys so that I could go and retrieve it.

'Will you be OK? I'll be as quick as I can,' I said to Kat, feeling strangely anxious, as ever, about leaving her alone. She nodded and smiled and, as I left under a steadily darkening sky, a voice in my mind pointed out that she wasn't alone this time.

214

Chapter Thirty-five

Liam was describing the landscaping commission he'd recently landed. It sounded impressive – a rambling old estate of some kind – but he seemed reluctant to go into detail about the project and, in all honesty, I was too distracted to fully concentrate on our faltering conversation.

Rugby practice had been quite the experience. I'd never taken much interest in sport before but seeing Jamie and his equally full-bodied teammates interact was enthralling and undeniably sexy. It was the camaraderie and respect between the men; the way they controlled their physical strength and power with focus and determination, not to mention the visual feast of meaty thighs, broad shoulders and tight bums. The heady fug of testosterone that now surrounded me in the pub garden was almost too much for my newly awakened body to endure.

If I was really honest with myself it was Jamie himself that was the main attraction. No matter how much I tried to fight it, I was unbearably, uncomfortably, achingly aroused by him in a way my body would not let me deny. But I didn't want to think of him that way; it wasn't helpful, especially if he was about to have a child with another woman. Observing a pretty redhead fawning all over him was not helping either.

Jamie suddenly stood up and I concentrated on masking my thoughts behind a smile as he approached.

'Liam, do you still have the key for the clubhouse? I've left my phone behind.'

'Yeah sure.' Standing Liam retrieved a bunch of keys from the pocket of his jeans and handed it to Jamie.

He thanked him before turning to me. 'Will you be OK? I'll be as quick as I can.'

I just nodded, not trusting myself to speak, and followed him with my eyes as he walked away, wishing I was going with him.

As I struggled to focus on the conversation around me, the storm that had been brewing all day finally broke above our heads. As the thunder clapped and rain poured out of the sky, I was jostled indoors along with everyone else, clutching my drink and hoping Jamie had made it back to the rugby club in time to stay dry.

The White Bear was old-fashioned and modestly sized with a low ceiling and even lower exposed beams. The air was stuffy with stale heat and the windows fogged with condensation as we piled in, dripping moisture onto the floorboards. Adam, the birthday boy, who was drunk and speaking too loud, ushered me onto a velvet-covered bench along the back wall. I intended to shuffle along to the far end of the seat but before I had a chance another rugby player, whose name I couldn't remember, sat down on the other side of me with a wink. As the rest of our ramshackle group dragged tables closer together, pulled up more chairs and stools and settled themselves noisily around me, I began to feel trapped, hemmed in on all sides. They chatted and joked with one another, drowning out the background music with their voices, filling up the air so that I couldn't breathe.

With Adam too close beside me I tried to keep a smile on my face and concentrated on inhaling and exhaling. I'd assumed I'd be perfectly fine without Jamie for a few minutes but now I felt lost, out of my depth, and anxious without him. How much longer would he be? I needed to see his eyes, feel his calm, protective gaze on my skin. Without him I didn't belong here – these were his people; his friends, not mine – I was an imposter.

Lester's wife, Maire, was seated across the table from me and, like her brother-in-law, seemed to favour orange juice over alcohol. She seemed kind and sensible, her soft Irish accent hypnotic, and although she was clearly curious to know more about me, so far, she had refrained from bombarding me with personal questions. But right now Maire was deep in conversation with the pretty girl who had been flirting with Jamie all evening. I gathered her name was Poppy and although we hadn't been properly introduced, and I knew it was irrational, I already resented her – the way she was with Jamie made me sick with jealousy.

Both women looked relaxed and stylish; their natural-looking make-up perfectly applied, matching designer sunglasses perched on their heads and expensive-looking wristwatches glinting. I couldn't hear what they were saying but they laughed often, occasionally glancing in my direction as they sipped their drinks. I tried to convince myself to speak to them but I couldn't think of anything to say so I anxiously scanned the crowd for Jamie's best mate Liam instead. His stooped head and shoulders stood out above the crowd at the bar, where he was chatting with his brother, but he was several feet away with his back to me. Why did Jamie want me here? What made him think I would fit in? The other night when he'd found out he might be a dad he'd been worried he wasn't up to it; that there was something wrong with him. But that wasn't true. Jamie had escaped foster care; he'd been adopted; grown up with these people – he was one of them. I was the black sheep here.

Adam suddenly threw a heavy arm around me, making me jolt. 'Kat, lovely Kat, how are you doing? You're as quiet as a mouse this evening.' His wet mouth was close to my ear and his armpit clammy at my shoulder.

As nausea surged up in my stomach I smiled tightly; his slurred voice triggered memories and emotions that I had worked hard to forget. I was cornered, vulnerable; there was nowhere to go. Alarm pulsed in my chest and ears as I tried to suppress the urge to vomit in my lap. Briefly I considered slipping down off my seat and crawling away under the table like a child but that would be ridiculous.

'Where'd you come from eh? I can tell you're not from around here.'

'Leave her be, Adam,' Maire said.

'What? I'm just being friendly.' He laughed, his breath hot and beery on my cheek.

'Please don't.' My nails dug into my flesh as my panic levels rose.

'What was that?' Adam said, leaning his face closer into mine to hear. And that was when something snapped inside me. Abruptly I launched myself out of my seat and on to my feet, taking the edge of the table with me. There was an almighty crash and the dramatic sound of glasses

218

smashing as the table upended and people gasped as I pushed through a sea of shocked faces and fought my way to the door without looking back. Outside I didn't stop moving until I found myself on the far side of the pub garden, gasping for breath, trembling with adrenalin, and alone in the wet, encroaching night. As reality hit me, I collapsed with weary shame inside the shelter of a covered bench, covering my eyes with my hand. Fuck. I groaned as the horrified facial expressions of Jamie's friends burned into my mind. Even if my husband's 'friends' did silence him for ever, there was no way I could stay here now – I was an embarrassment, a liability, a freak show. Maybe it was for the best.

A low gentle voice interrupted my mounting despair. 'Do you mind if I sit down?'

Liam stood a few feet away from me, his hands in his pockets and his shoulders hunched against the rain. I liked Liam and couldn't let him stand there getting soaked so I shifted over to one side of the seat. Wordlessly he came over, folded up his large body and sat down beside me, far enough away that we weren't touching.

For a while we just sat in silence, staring out at the rain. I picked absently at the frayed edge of my plaster cast and listened to the thunder as it rumbled across the sky. Eventually Liam spoke without facing me.

'Anything I can do to help?'

His compassion was unexpected and I didn't know what to say.

'Look, I don't know exactly what happened in there – from what I gather Adam was being a twat – but I just wanted to say not to worry about it. It doesn't matter, no one got hurt and no one's bothered. You can come back inside if you want – no one's going to hold it against you.'

'But, I –' my voice sounded shaky and I cleared my throat. 'I freaked out completely.'

'Hey, like I said, no real harm done. We all lose it from time to time and, anyway, it livened up an otherwise dull evening.'

I couldn't help smiling. 'That's kind of you to say but I doubt anyone else sees it that way.'

'You're wrong – they're a friendly bunch and you're here with James; that makes you one of us, part of the family.' His words pierced me. I'd never had a family before.

'I don't think he'll want me to stick around; not after the way I've behaved – it's probably best if I just go.'

Liam shook his head. 'Don't do that.'

Belatedly I remembered that Liam's ex-girlfriend Cally had run out on him three months previously and felt a pang of sympathy for him.

'Kat, I don't know what the history is between you two but –'

'What do you mean, history?' I interrupted. Jamie had promised not to tell anyone about my past.

'Well, no offence, but you just turned up out of the blue one day and moved in with him. I figure there must be some kind of history. Besides you only have to look at the way you two are around each other to know you're not exactly strangers.'

Curiosity got the better of me. 'How do you mean?'

Liam shrugged. 'The way you're always so aware of each other, even across a rugby pitch; the way you sometimes look at one another, kinda solemn and tender at the same time; the way he lights up when you call him Jamie instead of James... Like I say, I don't know your history. I don't need to know – I can tell that James cares about you way more than any of the girlfriends he's introduced to me in the past. He's happier than I've ever known him and I can't see him giving you up over some minor understanding. I would hope he's smarter than that anyway.'

At some point the rain had stopped. Liam's insight was comforting and made me cautiously hopeful that I might not have wrecked everything after all. As I tried to find the words to thank him, Jamie emerged from the back door of the White Bear. My heart rate picked up pace as he jogged across the wet grass and through the gloom towards us.

Chapter Thirty-six

I held my jacket up over my head to fend off the worst of the rain as I returned to the White Bear. Assuming that our party must have relocated inside I turned towards the front entrance but a movement in the garden caught my eye, stopping me in my tracks. As the rain eased I could just make out two people sitting side by side in an arbour in the gathering dusk. A bitter pain pierced my chest as I recognised Kat and my so-called best mate, Liam, sitting alone together in the dark.

I'd never experienced jealousy before; in fact it was a complaint common among my previous girlfriends that I was devoid of that particular emotion. Many of them assumed it was arrogance that prevented me from behaving like a possessive jerk but it wasn't arrogance. The truth was I'd never had a girlfriend that I wasn't prepared to lose. Kat wasn't my girlfriend; she was a friend; a sort of sister – maybe; either way it made no sense to feel jealous at all. Knocked for six, I ducked around the side of the pub and out of sight before they saw me. In all honesty Liam was just about the only guy I might consider good enough for Kat. He was a better choice for her: strong, well adjusted, reliable, and I could trust him to look after her. But Kat and I had only just found each other again – she was important to me. If nothing else I needed her help with the whole Jasmine situation. I just didn't feel ready to share Kat yet.

A quiet voice of reason struggled to be heard in the

emotional chaos of my mind. What had I actually witnessed? What if they were just being friendly? Lately I had got the impression that Liam was finally getting over Cally; that he was moving on and focusing on work. But he wouldn't go after Kat would he? Shaking my head I let out a deep breath. It was unlike me to jump to conclusions. With a fresh resolution to keep my head and give my friends the benefit of the doubt, I walked over to the front door and stepped into the bright and clingy heat of the pub.

'Is Kat OK?' Maire said, immediately addressing me with concerned eyes. My stomach tightened.

'What do you mean? What's happened?'

'Adam was acting like an eejit. I don't know what he said to her but Kat stormed out.' My gaze flicked over to where Adam was standing at the bar, my jaw tightening. He caught my look and cringed visibly, with an apologetic shrug of his shoulders. 'Liam went after her to see if she was all right but they haven't come back yet,' Maire added.

A strange mixture of worry and relief churned in my gut as I headed out the back door and made a beeline for Kat across the wet grass.

'Kat? Are you all right?' Her face was taut and her fists clenched tightly in her lap as I approached. 'What happened?'

'They didn't tell you? I freaked out, trashed the place, spilled everyone's drinks – I'm a freak.'

'Don't say that, Kat, it's not true.' She stared at me defiantly and every fibre in my body begged to reach out and hold her, to reassure her that I wouldn't give up on her that easily, but the general effect Kat had on me, the

223

way she made me feel, was disconcerting. As a compromise, I reached forward and draped my jacket around her shoulders to keep her warm.

'You find your phone?' Liam asked, getting to his feet.

'Yeah, thanks,' I said, handing him back the keys to the clubhouse.

'I'll head back inside – give you two some privacy.'

'Thank you, Liam; you're much nicer to me than I deserve,' Kat said.

'No worries,' Liam shrugged, as he walked away.

I sat down heavily in the space he'd vacated. 'Do you want to tell me what Adam said to upset you?'

Kat laughed bitterly. 'He didn't say anything. It was too hot – crowded – I felt kind of trapped. Adam was just being friendly and I completely lost it – I'm sorry.'

'Don't apologise. I shouldn't have left you on your own like that.'

She glared at me. 'I wasn't on my own and I'm a grown woman – I don't need babysitting.'

'That wasn't what I meant, Kat. I'm just glad you're OK. You are, aren't you?'

'Yeah,' she said with a sigh. 'But I should probably leave Wildham.'

'No. Why?'

'I don't fit in here, Jamie.'

'That's bollocks. Everyone who's met you loves you – you just need to give yourself more time to adjust.'

She shook her head. 'I'm never gonna be a Jasmine, or a Rose, or a Poppy. I'm just a weed, Jamie – a sodding dandelion or something.'

I laughed. 'If you're a weed then so am I, Kat. We

224

came from the same place; had the exact same start in life. But you're right. You're not some fancy, ornamental garden plant – you're a wildflower: rare, resilient and naturally beautiful.'

She snorted. 'Could you get any cheesier?' Her face was averted and hidden in shadow while her fingers worried at the edge of her plaster cast. 'We may have had the same start but you got away – you made something of yourself.'

'Kat, look at me.' She lifted her eyes to mine and the dark directness of her gaze almost made me lose my train of thought. 'You do like it here, don't you?'

'Yes.'

'And you like my friends? Some of them, anyway?'

'Yes.' The air around us felt heavy with tension, despite the recent storm, and I had to summon up every last drop of willpower to keep from kissing her.

'So stay – give it more time, please.' She moistened her lip with the tip of her tongue and I thought I might lose my mind.

'OK,' she said, a smile touching her eyes.

'OK, good.' I cleared my throat. 'Are you ready to go back inside?'

She grimaced. 'Do we have to? I'm ashamed.'

'Don't be; people only want to know that you're all right and you'll have to face my friends eventually – but if you'd rather just go home we can.'

'No, you're right,' she said, sighing. 'Anyway, I should apologise to Adam; it's his birthday after all.' Kat stood up, unconsciously smoothing a hand down over her lean denim-clad thigh.

'Knowing Adam, he was probably downright obnoxious and doesn't deserve an apology,' I said, rising to my feet beside her.

On our return to the pub my friends greeted Kat with casual warmth, as if nothing had happened. She made a general apology, offering to pay for any damage and a whole round of drinks, and her efforts were waved off and dismissed with good humour. Refusing a seat, Kat remained standing close to me at the bar, head held high, and by the time we left for home she had begun to relax again.

The night air was considerably cooler and fresher now that the storm had passed.

'Are you sure you don't mind walking? We can stay and get a lift with the others or I can call a cab?' I said.

'No, I'm happy to walk.' As we strolled Kat casually slipped her arm through mine and I secretly thrilled at the simple act – so innocuous but so welcome. 'Your friends are lovely,' she said.

'I'm relieved you think so.'

'They don't curse as much as the people I'm used to.'

'That may be a middle-class thing,' I cringed, 'I'm not sure.'

Kat shrugged. 'I don't understand half of what they talk about but they are kind. Especially Liam – he's not nearly as fierce as he looks, more like a gentle giant.'

'Yeah. He's been a good friend to me over the years.'

My sentence tailed off as it dawned on me that, for the first time ever, I had an urge to talk; to tell Kat things that I had never told anyone. I wanted her to know that my life had not been as idyllic as she might think – to reassure her that we were not so different. The impulse to volunteer personal information was alien and unnerving but then I reminded myself that my stubborn inability to share had been reason enough for women to leave me in the past, permanently.

'You probably don't remember Ellen, my mum?' I began.

She hesitated, seemingly surprised by my question. 'I do actually. I only met her once but I remember.'

'Really? What did she say?'

'It wasn't so much what she said that stayed with me … It was the day they came to take you away. We'd already said goodbye to each other and your dad had taken you out to the car. I was sitting on the stairs while your case worker talked to your mum.' Kat paused and my pulse thumped in my ears as I waited for her to continue. 'She was softly spoken and pretty, with pale wispy blonde hair. I remember staring at her scarf. It was pale blue with little pink roses on it and I remember thinking that she looked gentle and kind – just like a mother from a fairy tale. I didn't think she had noticed me but as she left she took off her scarf, draped it round my neck and said goodbye, as if we were friends. I wore that scarf everywhere for weeks – it was the prettiest thing anyone had ever given me – until somebody stole it.'

I swallowed. 'I'm glad you met, even if it was only brief. She was a great mum, unreservedly kind and generous. She never got angry, never raised her hand or her voice, and never had a bad word to say about anyone. If anything she was too soft on me, let me get away with too much. And she was a terrible cook,' I added with a smile. 'She tried hard – she was always trying to fatten me up – but every new recipe she attempted went wrong in one way or another.' I paused, unsettled by the influx of memories I'd evoked. I could almost hear my mum's voice, smell her perfume, and taste her burnt tomato soup.

'Do you mind me asking how she died?' Kat said quietly.

I braced myself. Saying the words aloud made it more real but for once I wanted to say them. 'It was sudden – a brain aneurysm. I was supposed to be doing my homework and Dad was finishing up for the day on the nursery. Mum called for me to come and lay the table for dinner but I was watching something silly on TV. I was slow to respond and when I got there she was lying on the floor, already dead.'

Kat sucked in a breath, her arm tightening in mine. 'Fuck. I'm so sorry.'

The starlit sky was steadily clouding over again and the sweeping headlights of cars passing on the road were growing more intermittent. I kept my eyes on the dimly lit path ahead as we walked. 'It was a shock – obviously – but, weirdly, a part of me wasn't surprised at all. Things were going too well for me; I had great new parents and I was happy. I think deep down I'd known it couldn't last. I assumed it was my fault that she'd died. Other people tried to tell me otherwise but I wouldn't believe them. They just couldn't understand.'

'I understand,' Kat said softly.

I stopped. The lump of emotion in my throat threatened to choke me and I swallowed hard. 'You're probably the only person I know who can,' I said, turning to meet her gaze. Her cheeks were streaked with silent silver tears. It was time to confess. 'I went back for you, you know. After Mum's funeral I made Dad take me back to the Plumleys' to look for you. I needed you. I needed to know that you were all right, that you still cared.'

'I'm so sorry that I wasn't there,' Kat whispered.

'No, *I'm* sorry – I waited too long Kat. I should never have left without you in the first place.' We stood shaking our heads at each other at the side of the road and then Kat reached up and kissed me, her mouth softly pressed to mine and salty with tears. It was unlike any previous kiss: solemn, drawn-out and saturated with long-held compassion. Just as I was tempted to deepen it she pulled away, wiping beneath her eyes with her fingertips.

'We were just kids,' she said firmly. She was right but I couldn't speak yet so I just nodded. 'How about this – I'll forgive you, if you'll forgive me?'

'Done,' I said gruffly.

Kat released a shaky sigh as she hooked her arm back through mine and we started to walk again. 'You still had your Dad and Liam though, right?'

'Yeah,' I said, still recovering from Kat's soul-wrenching kiss. 'He was a good man, Reg Southwood: proud, hardworking, capable – but we weren't close. He never once offered me a hug; he wasn't that sort of man. With Mum gone he quietly accepted his responsibility as my sole parent without complaint. He fed me, clothed me and made sure I did my homework but without ever really embracing the role. I think the only person he ever truly loved was my mother. He cared for me out of love for her rather than for any other reason I could discover.'

I'd always felt aggrieved that my dad was not openly

affectionate towards me – always assumed it was a reflection on me; that I was unworthy of such attention, unloveable. But now, as I heard myself describing Dad aloud, I realised I was being unfair.

'Then again, I didn't make life easy for him. I was so angry, furious with everyone and everything but mostly with myself. I lashed out, picked fights; I wasn't a nice person to know. I'm ashamed to say my dad bore the brunt of it, even though he had his own grief to deal with. In desperation he enrolled me in the after-school rugby club to tire me out and give me something to focus on – and I'm so glad he did.' I smiled at the memory, relieved to be back on safer ground.

'It was before my growth spurt though; I was still small for my age and I didn't know the first thing about playing rugby. Luckily Liam stepped in to help me out. He was two years above me at school and his dad ran the classes. It was Liam who taught me how to throw, catch and pass, expose the space and be elusive while running at speed. By twelve I was already faster than him and as I grew in size he helped me develop my strength and endurance. He was like a big brother to me really. Without him I would never have got a scholarship to play rugby at university – I owe him a great deal.'

Kat squeezed my arm with her fingers. 'Then I do too,' she said, smiling.

Talking aloud about my parents was difficult and unsettling but I felt better having done so at last. I just hoped that Kat was the right person to open up to. First I'd allowed myself to care about her and now I was trusting her with my feelings – I'd never been this close to anyone before, never felt so optimistic, nor so dangerously exposed.

Chapter Thirty-seven

Jamie had opened up and confided in me – just like that!

Lying on my back I stared at the shadows cast by the tree outside the window as they slowly crept across the ceiling. It was the middle of the night and Jamie was fast asleep beside me – his breathing slow and steady – but I just couldn't switch my thoughts off. I tried to focus on the time I'd spent working on the nursery the day before. The twenty-four-degree heat had made my cast itch like mad but it was a fresh, summery, scented heat – not like the inescapable, stinking, suffocation of meat frying in an airless kitchen – and I found the simple routine of tidying, feeding, and labelling plants for sale incredibly soothing. I'd even made a new friend – a collarless, scrawny, black cat with white paws and a ripped ear. I'd fed her cheese from my sandwiches. The stray feline was stand-offish at first, wary of strangers and too proud to beg, something I could easily relate to, but with patience I had gained her grudging trust. If the cat turned up again tomorrow I would have to get some proper food for it – Jamie's Quorn burgers were not going to cut it. Jamie. It was no good – my thoughts always returned to him.

He had spent most of the day preparing for the planting workshop he had planned for the weekend. The free promotional event, in which Lil would show people how to plant up their own pots, was designed to lure more customers into the garden centre but if it was a success Jamie would be able to sell tickets to more workshops like it in future. It was a great idea and Jamie was giving it his all but I could tell he was distracted – the possibility of impending fatherhood never far from his mind. Rugby practice had seemed to help – enabling him to burn off some physical energy and spend time with his friends – but I could still see Jamie's fears behind his eyes.

Though I didn't trust Jasmine Reed further than I could throw her I did believe what she'd implied about Jamie finding it difficult to talk about his past. It wasn't unusual for people with a start in life like ours – being rejected as a child made it harder to trust. And yet, despite that, Jamie had invited me into his home, introduced me to his friends, involved me in his business and in his plans for the future and, now, confided in me about his parents. It was awesome, awe-inspiring, all too much.

Jamie's faith in me affected me deeply. For one thing I could no longer keep lying to myself. I didn't just care about Jamie and privately lust after him; I loved him – I had fallen in love with him.

The feeling was new to me; I'd never been in love before and it was some strange kind of agony. Right now, being a part of Jamie's life, being his friend and sharing his home, should be enough; I should just enjoy this brief, happy interlude in an otherwise trying existence, while it lasted. But if I was really, uncompromisingly, honest with myself, now that I'd had a taste, I wanted more; I wanted Jamie for myself.

Of course that was impossible. Even if Jamie didn't go back to Jasmine Reed and her baby, even if my husband didn't turn up and kill us both, I would never be worthy of a man like Jamie. If Jamie didn't already know that he would work it out eventually. There was no question of me spilling my guts and confiding in him the way he had in me. I risked losing him entirely if I did. I had no doubt he'd want nothing more to do with me if he ever knew the ugly truth – the real me. So here I was, greedy and ungrateful, knowing I couldn't stay and deeply reluctant to leave.

Wincing I released the tender flesh at the top of my arm. I'd barely registered that I was pinching myself, beneath my sling where the bruise would not be seen, but the pain was a welcome distraction. As the sensation began to ebb I deliberately repeated the action in the same place with greater intensity, forcing my anger and frustration into my thumb and fingertip, squeezing them together, and twisting the skin for good measure. As I increased the pressure I bit my lip to prevent myself from crying out and then, when I finally released my grip, I sighed in relief. The pain and heat subsided into a gentle reassuring throb, coaxing me towards sleep at last.

234

Chapter Thirty-eight

The little girl carefully deposited a wriggly earthworm in my open palm, her tiny hand dwarfed by my own, and looked up at me expectantly.

'Wow, thanks, you found a worm! Is it for me?'

She shook her head vehemently, her pigtails swinging alarmingly, and then stuck out an arm, pointing a mucky finger in the direction of a nearby bird table.

'Ah I see; it's for the birds; my mistake.' Dutifully I went over and placed the worm on the feeder, exchanging a smile with her mum as I returned to the welcome shade of the awning. Within seconds a blue tit had hopped down from a nearby tree, collected the worm and flown off out of sight. I glanced down at the little girl in mock amazement and she giggled in delight.

'Come on then, sweetie,' her mum said, directing her attention back to the task in hand. 'You've still got half this pot left to fill; which plant are you going to put in next?'

I left them to it. It briefly crossed my mind that Jasmine might be having a little girl – that I might have a daughter – but I pushed the thought away. She had stopped returning my calls again. Jasmine only wanted to hear from me if I was prepared to give up my new life in Wildham and move back in with her and, as much as I didn't want her to give up our baby, I wasn't convinced that our getting back together was the right solution. So nothing had been decided. We'd reached a stalemate and I was unsure what, if anything, to do next.

Continuing my way around the long trestle table, I chatted to the other customers, making sure everyone was enjoying themselves, and salvaging the occasional wayward plant or trowel from the floor. At least the planting workshop was a success. Lil was directing proceedings with a physical demonstration at one end of the table and additional staff were on hand offering encouragement and advice. This enabled the participating customers, who varied widely in age and horticultural ability, to arrange plants in pots of compost at their own pace. The Saturday afternoon event was even drawing a crowd, as other customers stopped to gain inspiration to take back and apply to their own gardens.

'Do we need more plants, Lil? I can pop down to the nursery and get some?' I said.

'No you're all right; Frank's already bringing some up for me.'

'Oh, OK; great.' I tried to hide my disappointment at an opportunity missed. Even as busy as I was, I still found myself thinking about Kat a hundred times a day.

On Wednesday I'd taken her to the local hospital and, despite a two-hour wait to get her arm x-rayed, the results had been good – it seemed Kat's wrist was healing nicely and she was on course to have the cast removed in a month's time. While she was getting a fresh sling put on though I'd caught sight of a nasty-looking bruise on her upper arm. She'd dismissed it as nothing and waved me away but I sometimes worried that she might be in pain and keeping it from me. In many ways Kat was still a closed book and I used all kinds of dubious excuses to go down to the nursery and see her every chance I got.

'You could always just go down to say hello,' Lil said gently.

'What do you mean?' Feeling foolish, I glanced guiltily at those customers within earshot but they were seemingly engrossed in their floral creations.

Lil pursed her lips and threw me a knowing look over her reading glasses as she eased a root ball into a tight corner with her gloved hands. She still managed to make me feel like a school boy rather than the person in charge.

'No, I'd better stay here for now; we'll be finishing up soon,' I said, moving away to rescue a bellis plug-plant that a small boy had dropped into a watering can full of water. 'Hey there, are you giving that plant a good drink?'

'No, I'm seeing if it floats or sinks,' he said solemnly.

'Ah, fair enough.'

In companionable silence we watched and waited as the compact root ball gradually darkened, slowly absorbing water like a sponge. The patient look of concentration on the boy's face reminded me of Kat the evening before. I'd spent half an hour or so after dinner teaching her how to use my laptop computer. She'd been taught the basics of computer literacy at school – how to compose a Word document, create an Excel spreadsheet and send an email – but she'd had virtually no access to a computer since then and the Internet had changed dramatically in the intervening years. Nevertheless Kat picked things up quickly, apparently learning and committing new information to memory without even the need to make notes. At first she asked me to explain things like social media, blogging, apps, and terms such as 'cookies' but before long Kat was simply googling the answers to her own questions as if she'd been doing it all her life. While I half-watched a movie and half-watched Kat from across the room, she browsed the Internet for hours. Finally just before midnight I'd shut the computer down and insisted she go to bed, saving her from herself.

The bellis plug sank below the water line, dragged down by the weight of the soil at its roots, and the little boy looked up at me. 'Will it die in there?'

'It will if we leave it in there, yes – most plants need air and sunlight to survive.'

'Like people?'

'Yes, people need those things too.'

He turned back to the watering can and peered thoughtfully into the murky depths.

'We should be able to save this plant if we get it out now, give it a good home and let it grow – shall we try that?'

The boy nodded and together we eased the bedraggled bellis back out and planted it safely into his pot with the others. He was pleased with what he'd accomplished, proudly pointing out the dripping daisies to his older sister, while she rolled her eyes.

As I rinsed out the watering can and refilled it with clean water I wondered when Kat would start to feel confident enough to venture further than Wildham. Two weeks had passed since she'd left her husband but we'd seen no sign of him and she couldn't live in fear of Vic for ever. There were so many places I wanted to show her; so many things we could see and do. The garden centre had been unusually busy recently but in just over a fortnight the schools would be breaking up for the summer and I fully expected trade to slow down while local families jetted off on their holidays. I could afford to take Mondays and Tuesdays off then, leave the business in the capable hands of my staff and take Kat out exploring. The question was where to start? Perhaps something simple like a walk in the woods, followed by a pub lunch? Or perhaps she would prefer something more interesting – some place further afield; a drive out to the sculpture park in the neighbouring county maybe?

Checking my watch, I moved back to the head of the

table and clapped my hands to claim everyone's attention. I thanked the customers for their attendance, Lil for passing on her skills and experience, and the other members of staff for helping make the afternoon such a success. Finally I closed the workshop with a parting offer of free ice cream for all the kids, which was greeted by a cheer of enthusiasm.

By the time we had cleared up and packed everything away the car park was deserted, the last customers having left, and it was six o'clock – closing time. It had been a perfect summer day but now the staff looked as worn out and sweaty as I felt. Priya and Jenny stayed to help me cash up and then I sent them home with my thanks, locking the gates behind them.

On my return to the cottage I found a post-it note, with my name on it, stuck to the kitchen table beside a small pile of money. Sighing to myself I traced the sweep of Kat's handwriting with my fingertips. I'd started paying Kat a weekly wage as soon as it became apparent that she enjoyed spending all her time working on the nursery. She didn't have a bank account or any current means of acquiring one, and she was reluctant to do anything that might reveal her whereabouts to her estranged husband, so I was simply paying her in cash for the time being. But she kept trying to give it back to me, to cover the clothes and other minor bits and pieces I'd bought for her.

It was frustrating. I wanted to give her everything but I understood the impulse and I wanted Kat to know that it was her money to dispose of in any way she wished (even if that meant it came straight back to me). Scooping the cash off the table I deposited it in a tin in the drawer which held cling film and tea towels – effectively accepting her repayment but leaving it where she would still have easy access to it.

I was showered and changed by the time Kat came in through the back door, smiling. 'How did it go?' She kicked off her boots and then bent to line them up neatly by the door.

'Great. The workshop was a big success. We'll definitely do something like it again.' Kat's clothes clung provocatively to her body in places, damp with perspiration, and a small leaf was caught in her hair. Stepping closer to her I carefully removed it with my fingertips. She went very still, as if holding her breath, until she saw the wayward foliage in my hand. 'I've started the bath running for you upstairs; I thought I could make dinner tonight?'

Raising her brows she smiled. 'Oh yeah?'

'I was only going to reheat yesterday's leftovers. Maybe make a salad to go with it?'

'Sounds great, thanks.' As I gazed at her she smoothed her hand down over her trousers self-consciously and I wanted nothing more than to kiss her, as if we were a couple, as if she was mine. 'I'll go get cleaned up,' she said, disappearing through the doorway.

By the time Kat re-emerged and stepped out into the garden I had our dinner, her home-made vegetable lasagne, all ready and waiting on the patio table.

'We're eating outside?'

'Yeah, I thought we might as well – it's still so warm, even here in the shade.'

'It's lovely,' she said, taking a seat and glancing around while I poured a little wine. She was wearing the long skirt that I'd bought for her when she was in the hospital but this time she'd teamed it with a short-sleeved T-shirt and, aside from the cast and sling on her arm, she radiated good health.

As we ate I asked Kat to tell me about her day down

on the nursery and she enthused about the feral cat which had taken up residence under a bench in the shady depths of the potting shed. She'd named it 'Socks' and had started feeding it specially bought cat food, twice a day from a tin. I suspected Socks was only a fair-weather friend and riddled with fleas but I didn't have the heart to say so when Kat was so obviously smitten. Instead I filled her in on the planting workshop and she smiled as I described Lil's ill-disguised disapproval of the clashing colour combinations some of the customers had produced.

'Maybe you could help out with the next workshop?'

Kat stilled, her eyes locked on mine. 'I don't think that's a good idea.'

'Why not?'

'You know why not.'

'Because of Vic?' Kat blinked and I took her silence as confirmation. 'But you've already been into town, to the supermarket, the rugby club, the pub.'

'Yeah, but only 'cause I didn't think he'd look for me there. I've been lucky so far – I don't want to make it too easy for him to find me.'

'You don't even know that he's searching for you; he's probably too busy looking over his own shoulder – if his enemies haven't got to him already.'

A flash of infuriation flared in her eyes, temporarily eclipsing the fear. The conversation was not going as I'd hoped; rather than being encouraging and supportive the words out of my mouth sounded dismissive and judgemental. 'I'm sorry. I'm not trying to push you – I know it's not been three weeks yet. I just don't want you to feel trapped that's all.'

Calmly collecting my empty plate, Kat placed it on her own, neatly lined up the cutlery on top and set the pile carefully to one side. But she didn't speak. The delicate hollow above her right collarbone was visible above the line of her T-shirt and I had an aching urge to trace it with my lips, to dip my tongue inside and taste her there. Beneath the table my cock twitched and I subtly adjusted my trousers and cleared my throat.

'The thing is I was thinking of taking some time off work once the summer holidays start, just a few days here and there, but I thought maybe we could go out somewhere, do something – it's just something to think about.' Sparrows chirped at each other in the hedgerow as the sun sank lower in the sky and the shadows lengthened.

'OK,' she said at last, taking a sip of wine. 'I'll think about it, thank you.'

I shook my head. 'You don't have to thank me, Kat.' She looked down at her lap and I wondered what was going through her mind but I knew better than to ask.

'Now,' I said, wondering if I could safely get to my feet without Kat seeing how much I wanted her. 'Can I interest you in some strawberries for dessert?'

Chapter Thirty-nine

Stepping into the polytunnels I liked to pretend I was entering a foreign country: not that I'd ever been abroad, but the cloying fragrance of heliotrope, nemesia and scented geraniums hung in the humid heat above an underlying musty, earthy smell and I liked to imagine I was inside a tropical jungle. Humming to myself I knelt down to deadhead another tray of osteospermums. It was gratifying being right down in among the plants and knee-pads enabled me to work in comfort. I'd even started to catch a bit of sun – plaster cast aside, my arms looked healthier than I'd ever known them, like they belonged to someone else.

It was early July, the sun was shining and with each passing day I felt myself grow a little braver, a little stronger, and a little more normal. But then how could I not when the work I was doing was so satisfying, the place around me so beautiful, and the people so kind? And there was Jamie of course: generous, patient, trusting Jamie.

But as optimistic as I tried to be a dark sense of dread lingered like a malignant shadow at the back of my mind; fear of my past, coiled tightly in the pit of my stomach like a viper, poised to strike. Sweat trickled down between by breasts and I shivered despite the heat. Resolutely pushing thoughts of my husband away, I pulled my mismatched gloves back on. I'd ditched the sling for good because it was too restrictive but a man's-sized glove fitted over my bulky cast. Gathering a tray of purple osteos in one arm and a tray of pink nemesia in the other I retreated to the cool shade of the potting shed. Once there I slid the trays onto the workbench with the others, crept into the back corner and crouched down to check on Socks and her two new kittens: 'Right' and 'Left'.

I was aware I spent far too much time fussing over them but Socks didn't seem to mind and the little one-week-old, blue-eyed, bundles of fluff were too cute to resist. I marvelled as they fed from their mother; snuggled up to each other; or staggered about on their tiny paws, squeaking meows with their ears flattened and their heads bobbing. The night before, in the White Bear, Lester and his wife Maire had announced that they were expecting a baby in six months. Jamie, who was sitting across the table from me at the time, had made a convincing job of looking happy for his friends, congratulating them along with everyone else, and buying another round of drinks in celebration, but I sensed his anguish as if it was mine. Would he have to make a similar announcement of his own at some point in the next few months?

Tearing myself away from the kittens and returning to my workbench I scooped some fresh compost into a decorative terracotta pot and set about planting it. The peace and quiet of the afternoon was perfect; the silence only broken by birdsong, the occasional rustle of a breeze in the trees and the distant sound of customers wandering around the garden centre. As much as I appreciated Lil's company, and the background chatter of her small wind-up radio, having the place to myself on her day off was even better.

Standing back to assess the finished planter, I turned it to view it from different angles, as Lil had taught me. The tall white geranium in the middle was complemented by the mix of plants around it and the sides of the pot softened by those which trailed over. It was oddly satisfying picturing Gary on his stall at the market unknowingly flogging the planters *I* had created to the well-to-do residents of London, possibly right under Vic's nose. Jamie was still delivering to the market like he'd said he would and Vic's Cafe remained closed so maybe Jamie's plan was working. I decided the planted pot was good enough for sale so I gave it a long drink with the watering can before moving on to the next one.

As I worked a robin alighted on the edge of the wheelbarrow just inside the door, his head twitching as he considered me and then belted out a pretty tune. Digging around beneath a few pots I found something he might like and flicked it in his direction. Startled by the action he nearly fled but he was plucky enough to stay – the juicy slug his reward.

I was on my way back to the polytunnels to gather more plants when I heard the gate to the nursery clanging open and shut and voices drawing near. Raising my gloved plaster cast to shield my eyes from the sun, I saw Jamie walking towards me followed by two other men. The sight of him made my heart beat faster as usual. He wore his customary garden centre uniform – a dark green, close-fitting polo shirt with the logo printed in one corner and khaki combat trousers that hugged his thighs and bum. His gaze swept up over me in return and I felt conscious of my muddy knee pads and scruffy boots. But

245

even as I registered the warm look in his eyes, I saw it was replaced with one of concern and unease. Instantly on my guard I assessed the two men with him.

The older of the two was tall, slim and crumpled with greying hair, while the younger was shorter and rounder with smooth dark skin and tightly cropped hair. Both wore suits, which, although not unheard of, was unusual in a garden centre. There was a chance they were company reps promoting the latest lines in gardening tools, pest-control products or bird food but if that was the case they wouldn't need to come down to the nursery and see me. No, something about these two men set alarm bells ringing in my head – in my gut I knew they were police.

Standing my ground, I told myself to relax and stay calm as the men reached me. Jamie took my hand, immediately reassuring, his eyes steady and fixed on mine.

'Mrs Katerina Leech?' the older man said, 'I'm Detective Inspector Lambert and this is Detective Sergeant Benton. Do you mind if we ask you a few questions?'

'What about?' I said.

'Your husband – Victor Leech.'

'What about him?'

'When did you last see him?'

'Four weeks ago, just before I went into hospital.'

DS Benton started taking notes in a small book. 'Why were you in hospital?'

'I fell down the stairs,' I said, lying automatically before realising that I didn't need to keep covering for Vic any more, that maybe I shouldn't.

DI Lambert was watching me closely. 'You fell?'

I hesitated, absently noticing his yellowed teeth and the sprinkling of dandruff at his jacket collar. 'Vic pushed me,' I admitted, my voice barely more than a whisper and Jamie squeezed my hand. The inspector nodded sympathetically as if he'd already known. I cleared my throat. 'How did you find me?'

'The hospital – they had a record of Mr Southwood's name and CCTV showing you leaving together.' I nodded, desperately hoping that Vic wouldn't be able to find me with such apparent ease. 'Your husband didn't visit you while you were in St Mary's?'

'No.'

'Has he contacted you since then? By phone? Email?'

'No.'

'You're sure?'

'Yes.'

'Is that unusual would you say?'

'I, I don't know – our relationship wasn't *usual*. I've left him,' I said. It felt amazingly good – liberating – to say the words out loud for the first time – now I just had to believe them. 'I don't want him to know where I am. What is this? Why are you here?'

DI Lambert sighed. 'Your husband has been reported missing, Mrs Leech.'

'Missing? Who says he's missing?'

'Carol Yates.'

I stared at him confused.

'You probably know her as Cherry?'

'Oh.'

'It seems you may have been the last person to see

247

him. Do you know where we might find him?'

I shook my head.

'He didn't give you any indication of his plans? Mention he was going away? Anything like that?'

'No, but then, he never told me anything.'

DI Lambert nodded wearily and glanced around at the polytunnels. 'It's nice here,' he said glumly. 'I can see why you prefer it to where you were.'

'Look,' Jamie interrupted. 'Can I ask why you're here? I mean, you obviously know what sort of man Vic Leech is; he's probably off on a bender or something so why go to all this trouble?'

DI Lambert shifted his gaze from Jamie to me and then back again, his face impassive. 'It's our duty to investigate when a missing person's report is filed, regardless of who is missing, and in Mr Leech's case an extended absence from all his known businesses is highly unusual. Add to that the fact he hasn't used his mobile phone, his passport, his credit cards or withdrawn any money for three weeks and his disappearance looks suspicious.'

'So what do you think has happened to him?' Jamie's voice was reassuringly calm and steady, like that of a man with nothing to hide.

'It's hard to say but he was mixed up with some unpleasant people. I can't go into details but I wouldn't be surprised if you never see him again.'

'You think he might be dead,' Jamie said, a statement rather than a question.

DI Lambert's attention temporarily flicked to me in concern, as if Jamie's blunt words might have upset me, but he'd find no hint of grief in *my* face.

'It's possible he's gone into hiding, fled the country under a false name, but I don't think it's likely,' the inspector admitted. Scratching the back of his head he surveyed the surrounding countryside, his shrewd eyes taking everything in, while Jamie, DS Benton and I remained silent. 'Mrs Leech, I'll be honest with you,' he said, settling his gaze on me. 'In all probability he is already dead and we'll never find his body. If I were you I'd just forget about him and move on.'

I kept my expression neutral as our meeting was brought to an end but I barely registered the rest of what was said. Something about keeping informed, further enquiries and an inquest. DS Benton tucked his notebook away and Jamie released my hand as he offered to show them out. Dumbstruck I stared after the three men as they walked away. They thought he was dead. Vic was dead. Could it really be true?

On autopilot I moved back into the shade of the potting shed, sitting down on a wooden crate as my legs gave way beneath me. Was I really free? Pulling off my gloves I sat staring mutely at the cobwebs in the rafters for several minutes as I considered the chance, the extraordinary possibility, of real freedom.

'Hey, are you OK?' Jamie had returned and was crouched in front of me, his handsome face creased with concern.

'They think he's dead,' I said.

'Yes.'

'Do you know what that means?' I raised my fingers to Jamie's brow to wipe away the anxiety there. 'Do you

249

realise what that could mean for me?' I whispered.

'I think so,' Jamie said, his eyes searching mine. Elation finally bubbled up inside me, a smile breaking out across my face. The tension in Jamie's expression faded to be replaced by a corresponding grin, laughter lines extending into his dark stubble, eyes glowing.

'I don't have to go back,' I breathed.

'No. You can stay here with me.'

'You still want me to?'

'Yes, of course,' he said firmly.

On impulse I reached out, grabbed a handful of his shirt and kissed him on the mouth, our smiles colliding. He laughed deep down in his chest, the sound reverberating against my lips, and I laughed too, suddenly giddy with relief. 'Thank you,' I said.

'You're welcome,' he replied, his voice low, his face just inches away from mine. My lips tingled from where we'd connected and as I looked at him I was shocked to see my own desire reflected in his dilating eyes. Releasing his shirt, I straightened up and looked away, flustered by the sudden heat between us.

He cleared his throat. 'Hey, you know, if Vic really is gone, you don't have to hide down here anymore.'

I took a deep breath. 'No, I guess not.'

Reaching out Jamie tenderly hooked my hair back behind my ear. 'You're free to go anywhere you want, Kat – beyond the White Bear, beyond Wildham; anywhere you want.' I gazed back into his now serious chestnut eyes. 'So, would you like to do that? There are so many places I want to take you to, so many things I want to show you – we could start off small, maybe go out for dinner? Or maybe we could just go for a walk, take a picnic or something? What do you think?'

All my familiar insecurities screamed inside my head, my doubts and fears churning in my stomach. But ignoring them I focused instead on the hope and enthusiasm in Jamie's face, the gentle reassurance in his words and my own fledgling optimism. 'Sure, why not.'

'Thank you, Kat.' Jamie grabbed my hands in his. 'I'm going to make you happy, you'll see.'

'You already do,' I murmured under my breath.

Chapter Forty

Two beakers of beer held aloft in her hands, Kat glided through the crowd towards me. Three days ago I'd taken her back to hospital to have the cast removed from her wrist. Her forearm looked pale and delicate where it had been deprived of sunlight for six weeks, but a doctor assured us that the fracture had healed well and a physiotherapist had given Kat some basic strengthening exercises to improve her wrist's flexibility.

Kat no longer resembled the downtrodden woman I'd met in London. Nowadays she was as beautiful on the outside as on the inside. Even when her pretty summer dress was teamed with muddy wellies she looked like a goddess, bare willowy limbs to rival Kate Moss and hair dancing in the breeze like ribbons of maple syrup. She still moved with the same hypnotic, long-legged grace, shoulders back, head held high and pale eyes bewitching but she looked younger and more carefree every day. And her smile! Sometimes it was subtle, a light gleaming in her eyes, and sometimes, like now as she approached me, it was wide and highly contagious. It was the reason people were always smiling back at her, or stopping to talk, compelled by the delight she now radiated from every pore. Knowing I'd helped bring about her happiness gave me satisfaction beyond all belief.

'Here you go,' Kat said, raising her voice to be heard above the music and handing me a pint with flourish. Another first. She'd deliberately braved the beer tent alone, a crowded place jostling with unpredictable strangers, to challenge herself but she had accomplished it with decorum and finesse. I was in awe of her determination and proud of how much she had achieved in such a short space of time.

'Cheers!' I said, knocking my cup against hers and enjoying her grin as I took a swig of lager. The festival was much smaller and more compact than Glastonbury but still atmospheric and alive with positive vibes, providing an experience which I hoped Kat would enjoy.

Since the police had said we no longer had to worry about Vic each week we had spent a couple of days away from the garden centre doing something fun together. It was almost August and business was slow. It was too hot and dry to plant anything and most people were away on holiday, only dropping in on their return to replace the hanging baskets that had wilted in their absence. Kat and I made the most of the glorious weather by going for drives and walks and picnics, taking day trips to the seaside and eating ice cream. Yesterday I'd spent the evening teaching Kat to drive, in Dad's old car. She had good coordination and quickly got the hang of it, despite the sticky gearbox. She drove round and round the car park with a smile on her face until I suggested she should venture on to the road. She didn't like that idea. I had no doubt she would do so before long, but only in her own time.

Introducing Kat to new things, new people and new places, was, I'd discovered, one of life's greatest pleasures. So far I'd been careful not to take her anywhere she might feel uncomfortable, avoiding those places with formal etiquettes and dress codes until her confidence had

had time to grow, but in my mind there was an infinite list of activities and destinations that I was eager to experience through Kat's eyes.

Right now she was staring off in the direction of the Main Stage. 'I can't believe how rammed it is! I've never seen so many people in one place.'

'Yeah, there'll be even more by the time the headline act comes on.' Her eyes widened fractionally. 'You OK?'

'Yeah, course, this is amazing.'

I reached for her hand and gave her fingers a gentle squeeze. 'We can go back to our tent, or leave, any time you want.' She nodded and sipped her drink and I changed the subject. 'What do you think of this band?'

'They're all right. But if I'm honest I prefer something with a bit more beat, something you can dance to – not that I dance – but something cheerful.'

'OK, so are we talking pop music?'

Kat shrugged. 'I guess so – I don't know that much about music. I've only heard whatever the local radio station used to play.'

'Fair enough. Do you know any artists or songs you like?'

Kat scrunched her nose. 'I'll only tell you if you promise not to judge – my tastes are probably not cool.'

I laughed. 'Kat, it won't matter to me if you like Engelbert Humperdinck.'

'Who?' She laughed.

I squeezed her fingers again, enjoying the subtle electric current that flowed between us. 'C'mon, tell me what you like.'

'Why are you so interested?'

I laughed. 'I'm interested in everything about you, Kat, you must know that by now.'

She shook her head in mock disapproval, her eyes shining. 'OK, you asked for it, let's see: Rihanna, Taylor Swift especially that "Shake It Off" song – that stayed in my head for weeks. Oh, and there's this "Gravity" song by DJ Fresh which I'm completely addicted to, and a song called "Real Love".' Kat blushed. 'I don't know who sings it but there are all these classical instruments in the background.'

'Clean Bandit.'

'If you say so,' she said, bemused. 'Oh and, I think there's a band called Chasing Status?'

'Chase & Status. Wow, you like Drum'n'bass?'

'Is that another band?'

'No, it's a type of music,' I said, tucking a silken strand of hair back behind her ear. 'I would never have guessed that about you, Kat – it's very cool.'

She grinned at me and I ached with the urge to kiss her. How did she manage to be both formidable and sweetly innocent at the same time?

'Do you know Pendulum?' Kat shook her head. 'They're headlining tonight on the Main Stage; I think you're going to like them.'

'OK. So are you going to tell me what music *you* like?'

'Well I like most of the stuff you just mentioned but I like guitar-based stuff too. Have you heard of Bleeding Trees?'

She shook her head.

'I'll have to introduce you to my iPod some time.'

'I'd like that.'

'Hey are you hungry?'

'Yes, the smells coming from that noodle bar are making my stomach rumble.'

'Let's go check it out,' I said.

We perched on a pair of oak barrels, drinking beer and eating vegetable stir-fry as the sun began to set behind the hills. Many of the other festivalgoers wore fancy dress – a spectacular array of colourful costumes ranging from the subtle to the extreme. Kat liked the wackiest ones best – people dressed as traffic cones, a group of human-sized, walking bananas and a poor man sweating inside a lobster outfit – the claws severely hampering his attempts to drink beer. I had to explain things like Stormtroopers and the Super Mario Brothers to Kat, as she'd never seen Star Wars or played a computer game, but it was fun seeing her reactions and laughing along with her at the, often absurd, nature of popular culture.

Once night fell and the festival ground was sparkling with multicoloured lights we disposed of our rubbish and made our way back towards the Main Stage, lured by the music and the excited hum of the crowd. Dancing with Kat was magical. She loved Pendulum so much that she was physically impelled to move. And though, by her own admission, she had never been taught and had no real experience of dancing, she was a natural – instinctively moving her body sinuously to the rhythm as if she was born to do it. And whenever, wherever, Kat danced those nearby joined in. We stayed a fair distance back from the stage, where we could still see all the action on huge electronic screens, but where the crowd was thinner and

256

Kat had space to move without having her personal space invaded – only I was occasionally afforded that privilege. And when I grew tired of dancing (long before Kat) I stood back, my mind foggy with alcohol, and took hundreds of photos of her on my phone – she was the sexiest woman alive.

When Pendulum finished their encore and departed the stage for the last time we ducked into the shadow of a nearby tree to wait for the mass exodus to pass us by. Kat leaned back against the trunk, breathless with exhilaration, excitement glinting in her eyes. She was completely unlike any other girl I'd ever known. Obviously her confidence had been badly undermined by abuse so social situations, that other people took for granted, frightened her. But despite all that, underneath it all, there was something of the rebel about her. She shunned most material possessions, spoke her mind with well-thought-out intelligence to the point of bluntness, and danced like no one was watching. Kat enthralled me like no one else.

The temperature had dropped and as we picked our way back to our tent in the semi-darkness our conversation gradually petered out. Exchanging toothpasty smiles we brushed our teeth with bottled water and then, shivering, wriggled down inside our separate sleeping bags still clothed. Once we were settled side by side and I'd turned off the torch, I lay there listening to the distant music and the muffled voices, laughter, and snoring from the hundreds of people camped around us. But I soon became aware of a tension in the air. Kat was lying unnaturally still and silent.

257

'Kat? Everything OK?' I murmured.

'Fine.' The strain was obvious in her voice from just one word. Raising myself up on an elbow, I fumbled for the torch and switched it back on, squinting in the light bouncing off the canvas. Kat lay still on her back, her face impassive, eyes closed.

'Talk to me.'

'No.'

'Kat?'

She tutted in irritation. 'Fuck it – I'm not doing this.' Sitting up, she unzipped her sleeping bag and shook it off.

'What? What's wrong?'

'Nothing. Just go to sleep.' Unzipping the door flap she tugged her wellies back on and I began to struggle out of my own bedding.

'Wait, where are you going?'

Kat launched herself out of the tent into the wet grass and I crawled out after her, my legs still tangled, in time to see her striding away between the other tents. Once free I raced after her, barefoot, tripping over guide ropes, folding chairs, beer bottles and various bodies, cursing and mumbling general apologies as I blundered through the shadows. By the time I caught up with her, Kat was climbing a dimly lit path that wound up through the woodland at the edge of the festival campsite.

'Stop, Kat please – tell me what's going on.'

'You wouldn't understand,' she muttered without looking at me.

Her cool dismissal annoyed me and as she began to move away I reached for her arm. 'How would you know? You haven't given me a chance – you never tell me what you're thinking!'

'OK fine!' she said, rounding on me with an angry glare. 'I think this is disgusting!'

'What? Camping?'

'If that's what you want to call it. I can't believe your lot do this sort of thing for fun.' she said, her voice heavy with condemnation.

'*Your* lot? What's that supposed to mean?'

She pressed her lips together in a hard line, as if trying to hold back her own words. 'Nothing, forget it,' she said, turning away again. 'Just leave me alone.'

But I was too angry now to let her walk away. Stepping around her I positioned myself in the space between two large trees, blocking her escape. 'No, Kat, you've obviously got something to say so come on – what did you mean?' With a raise of her chin, her beautiful eyes locked with mine, dark with angry determination. I fleetingly wondered if she might hit me but I wasn't about to back down. 'You think I'm too rich? Too privileged? You think I've had life too easy or what?' She frowned and gave an almost imperceptible shake of her head and I exhaled with relief. 'So why are you fighting me, Kat? All I want is to help you be happy. Why won't you let me?'

I saw a brief flicker of regret in her eyes before she hid it away. 'Because it's fucking stupid. I don't *need* help.'

'Fine. What *do* you need?'

'Just fuck off, Jamie,' she said, trying to push past me.

'Come on, tell me!' I said, blocking her way again. I could almost taste the delicious fragrance of her skin; feel the heat of her body radiating out to mine; sense the fire raging inside her.

259

'Nothing! I don't need anything!' she shouted in my face. 'I never have and I never will!' Then Kat kissed me. She dragged my face down to hers with unapologetic force, her wild distress and fury morphing into savage hunger as she bit my lip. And I could no longer hold back. Five long weeks of sexual frustration – thirty-six nights of sharing a bed and trying not to want her – had me about ready to explode. As thousands of strangers slumbered in the field just metres away, I pushed her back against the smooth trunk of a beech tree and took her sweet mouth with my tongue, savouring her unique flavour and revelling in the low sounds she made.

Splaying one long leg out to the side, and hitching it up on my hip, Kat forced me closer into her with a booted foot. Without breaking our kiss, I cupped the lean muscle of her thigh, squeezing her supple flesh, her soft skin burning me. She clung to me as if she couldn't get near enough, as if she wanted to be inside my body as much as I longed to be in hers. Even through our clothes I could tell she was aroused, her nipples taut with anticipation against my chest. Overwhelmed with need, I leaned into her, grinding my barely constrained erection into her damp crotch like a horny teenager. Dragging and bucking her hips up against me, she met me thrust for thrust. And we gloried in the delicious friction as our muscles tightened and our rhythm increased to a frantic pace.

'Oh God, Jamie,' she gasped, her head falling back to expose her elegant long neck. 'Don't stop. I can't – oh God – I'm going to –' As I supported her weight she climaxed, the look of euphoria on her face and the ease with which she came apart triggering my own urgent release.

I'd never come in my pants before; it wasn't something a grown man should do. But then no one had ever had such an overwhelming effect on me; in that moment I felt no hint of shame. I simply loved what Kat did to me.

We stayed where we were for several minutes and I relished the feel of her in my arms, as our heart rates slowed and our breathing returned to normal.

'I didn't mean what I said,' she said, her face hidden against my chest. 'I know camping's supposed to be fun; I honestly thought I'd enjoy it.'

'But?'

She released a heavy breath. 'Lying there on the ground, in the dark – I kept thinking – it felt like, like I was back on the street.'

'Oh, Kat,' I said, squeezing her closer and pressing a kiss to the top of her head.

'It's just knowing there's no walls between me and everyone else – it's stupid.'

'It's not stupid; it's completely understandable. I'm so sorry, Kat, I should have thought. We can go home, right now.'

Amusement danced in her eyes as she looked up at me. 'It's nearly three in the morning.'

'So?'

'And you're over the limit,' she said, gently stroking her fingertips down through the stubble at my cheek. Closing my eyes I leaned in to her touch. 'Don't you need to take your lenses out; your eyes must be tired?'

'I took them out a few hours ago.'

'Oh, can you see all right?'

261

I laughed. 'I can see you, Kat, that's enough for me.'

A blush crept into her cheeks and she smiled. 'If you want to go back to the tent and get some sleep, I'll be OK on my own.'

'No, if you're staying up, I'll stay up with you – I'd like to see the sun rise anyway,' I said, reluctant to be parted from her. Smiling she shook her head but didn't argue as I straightened up and took her hand in mine.

We stopped at a bank of plastic Portaloos to clean ourselves up, the cloying chemical smell transporting me back to my student days. Neither of us made any mention of what had happened between us, maybe because it had felt like a fitting conclusion to an alcohol-fuelled night of live music, dancing and confrontation. Despite our quarrel it had been a welcome encounter for me – a rare glimpse into Kat's true feelings and a brief respite from the almost constant hunger that she aroused in me. But it was not enough. I still knew very little about Kat's past, I'd still not seen her naked, and it still felt like she might leave at any moment.

In another field we found a small, brightly lit marquee where a DJ was smoothly churning out Motown classics on a simple sound system for the night owls. One middle-aged couple danced barefoot on a chintz rug in the centre, while everyone else sat or lay around on cushions in various states of intoxication. Taking possession of two corduroy-covered beanbags, Kat and I settled in a corner where I rested one arm around her shoulders and she leaned contentedly into my side.

'Did you say Frank was going to open up tomorrow?' Kat said.

'Yes. I left him with the spare set of keys. But if we get back in time I'll do it myself.'

'Or you could just let Frank do it and get some sleep?'

'Yeah, but Sundays can still be really busy in the shop if the weather's nice.'

Kat grinned at me. 'You love it there don't you?'

'Yes. More than I ever expected to actually. Thank you for convincing me to keep it.'

She shrugged. 'You would have come to your senses eventually.'

'Maybe, I'm not so sure.'

'You're not moving back in with Jasmine then?'

'I really don't want to – I can't see how it would ever work. And anyway, I'll need to sell my flat if I'm going to support her and a baby financially.'

'Doesn't she have any family?'

'She does – both parents, grandparents, two older brothers and a sister, and she's close to them, but if I've got her pregnant then the responsibility is mine not theirs.'

'Do you think she'd ever agree to move to Wildham?'

'No. She won't speak to me so I don't know what she's planning. But I think I need to see a solicitor. If the baby is mine I need to know what my rights and options are.'

Kat nodded. 'That sounds sensible.'

As Smokey Robinson sang about his tears, the couple swaying in the middle of the floor were joined by two more pairs of dancers and we watched them for a while in silence. I couldn't imagine Jasmine living at Southwood's any more than I could now imagine living there *without* Kat. I had to keep reminding myself that our current situation might only be temporary; that I might lose her again; that with enough confidence built up inside her,

Kat should have the freedom to move on.

'Hey, Kat, you do know you don't have to work at Southwood's forever, don't you?' She looked up at me in surprise and I hastily continued, 'I mean, you are welcome to, of course – on the nursery, in the garden centre, in the coffee shop when it's built – anywhere you like, for as long as you like; you'll always have a job as far as I'm concerned. What I'm trying to say is – don't ever feel you *have* to work there.' Kat's eyes were fixed on mine but unreadable, as if she was reserving judgement until she could be sure of what I was saying so I tried a different tack. 'What were your favourite subjects at school?'

'I hated school,' she said evenly.

'I'm sorry, I remember. But were there any subjects that interested you? Any topics that you enjoyed just a little?' She turned away and was quiet for so long that I wondered if I'd offended her.

'Science and Geography,' she said at last.

'Wow, really?'

She nodded. 'The teachers weren't so shitty – and I liked hearing about faraway places and knowing how things worked.' I waited to see if she would volunteer more but, as ever, talking about herself did not come naturally to Kat.

'The thing is you could do almost anything you wanted to. There are loads of courses available nowadays, everything from full-time degrees right down to part-time courses and evening or weekend classes. There's a college just a twenty-minute bus ride away and you can even do courses online, remotely.' Kat eyed me with her penetrating gaze. 'I'm not saying you *have* to study anything; I'm just pointing out that you *could*. All the colleges have online prospectuses – just have a look sometime; see if anything takes your fancy. Because whatever you decide you want to do with your life, Kat, we can make it happen.'

I could tell a whole host of thoughts and feelings were hidden behind Kat's carefully composed expression. 'Thank you,' she said. As she returned her eyes to the DJ I couldn't help hoping that one day, with time and reassurance, she would share them with me.

Chapter Forty-one

At a table for two we sat in the dappled shade of an apple tree that had been grown in a vast round oil drum and underplanted with lavender bushes. The lavender had finished flowering, and the grey-green foliage had been pruned back into cloud-like forms, but every time Jamie's arm brushed against it an aromatic scent was released into the air.

'This place is amazing,' I murmured as I gazed around the rooftop garden full of flowers and out across the River Thames below. Despite the sunglasses Jamie wore I could feel the warmth of his attention on me, rather than on the spectacular view before us. I smiled at him before picking up a menu in my right hand and slowly scanning the prices while gently flexing my left wrist. It was still occasionally stiff after weeks of Vic-induced incarceration and I hated that my pale forearm drew attention to the various little burns there, evidence of a life spent serving hot food. A past life.

I'd been apprehensive about Jamie's suggestion of a day trip to London. Not just because I was still afraid Vic might be alive and out there somewhere looking for me, but because Jamie wanted to make an occasion of my birthday. I'd never seen a reason to celebrate my birthday before – August the third was the made-up date recorded on my medical notes when I was found abandoned, aged roughly two years old. It was some doctor's best guess at the time and had always seemed rather arbitrary to me – I would never know the real date of my birth any more than Jamie would discover his. But in the brief three-year period when Jamie had had a mother she had made a big fuss of his birthdays and now, for some reason, he was keen to do the same for me.

Many aspects of the city were all too familiar – the traffic, the smells, the drifts of litter and the sadly ignored individuals who slept wherever they could. I simply couldn't pass a homeless person without stopping to acknowledge them and offer them something – it was small consolation but at least I now had some money to give. London had always been my home and yet I'd never been happy there and felt no great compulsion to return.

Despite all that, experiencing London with Jamie was a complete revelation – so far the day had been far more enjoyable than I'd imagined. We'd journeyed into the capital on a surprisingly comfortable and efficient overland train and crossed town by Tube before emerging at the iconic, vast and beautiful Natural History Museum. With its high ceilings, cathedral-like architecture and Victorian detailing it was even more impressive than I'd been prepared for. At Jamie's suggestion we avoided the dinosaur galleries, crowded with children, in favour of the undeniably spectacular Wildlife Photographer of the Year exhibition.

The breathtaking backlit images transported me around the globe with their luminous clarity, each story more compelling than the last. I'd unconsciously taken Jamie's arm for support, as if I might be swept away by the sheer magic the pictures contained. Jamie was quiet for the most

267

part, just allowing me to take my time and offering simple explanations when I came across things I didn't understand. He was much more knowledgeable about the world than me but never made me feel stupid or inferior in any way. Quite the opposite in fact. Jamie had this way of glancing at me but then being unable to look away again – as if the mere sight of me was somehow remarkable or diverting. I loved the way he centred his attention on me and yet I wished he wouldn't – any hint of false hope for a future together nagged painfully at my vulnerable heart.

Jamie had suggested the Southbank for lunch and, a gentle stroll along the river later, here we were about to eat al fresco, surrounded by flowers.

'Rina! I thought it was you.'

I jumped at the name I no longer used and Jamie tensed opposite me as I looked up at the young waiter standing beside our table.

'Andy!' I said, my mind working furiously to determine whether I was in immediate danger. But I quickly recalled he was a college student who used to order coffee and a bacon bap at Vic's Cafe on his way to nine o'clock lectures. He was not, I decided with tentative relief, a friend of Vic's. 'What are you doing here?'

'I work here,' he said, with a downward glance at his apron. 'Summer job. What about you? I've not seen you in ages. What happened to the market cafe? It always looks shut when I walk past?'

'Oh, yeah, I, er, left.' I forced a smile.

There was an awkward pause as Andy took in my non-answer. 'Oh right, OK. Good for you; you look well anyway.'

'Thank you, so do you. How's college going?'

'Really good, yeah; finals next year though.' He grimaced. 'Can I get you something to eat or drink?' Raising his eyebrows expectantly, he lifted a notepad, pencil poised. Jamie and I ordered drinks and sandwiches and Andy collected our menus and gave a funny little salute as he departed.

'Are you OK? Do you want to go?' Jamie said, leaning forward across the table and taking my hand.

'No I'm fine. I don't think he ever met Vic and, anyway, the police think Vic's dead now, so –' I squeezed his fingers. 'It's fine, really.'

Studying my face for covert signs of something, he nodded as if satisfied. 'Small world,' he muttered.

Once we'd eaten Jamie produced a small gift-wrapped object from his pocket and placed it on the table in front of me. 'Happy birthday, Kat.'

I looked from him to it and back again, wishing I could read his eyes, but I only saw my own pensive expression reflected back at me in his shades. As if reading my mind he suddenly removed them and I was bathed in the reassuring warmth of his expression. 'It's nothing much OK? There are so many things I could have got for you, there's so much I want to give you, but I know you won't let me. So this is just one small, practical gift that I hope you will accept, for me.'

'What is it?' I said, my mouth dry.

'You have to open it to find out – that's how presents work,' he said, with a teasing smile.

269

Unwrapping it carefully I stared at the mobile phone in my hand. I'd never had one before, never needed or wanted one before. After all who would I call?

'Kat?' I looked back at Jamie's earnest face. 'It's just a pay-as-you-go but we can get you a contract if you decide you want one. It just means that if – when – you want to go places without me, you can call me.' Taking it from my hand, he switched it on, dabbed at the screen and then turned it to show me. 'See? I've programmed it with my mobile number, the house landline, the number for the garden centre. I've even put the number of a local taxi firm in there just in case you get stranded.'

'Wow, thank you,' I said, floored by the extent of Jamie's thoughtfulness. My words were all the encouragement he needed and with a childlike enthusiasm he went on to show me how to use it to make calls, send emails, browse the Internet and locate myself with satellites. It was lovely that Jamie considered me worth locating but it was too much.

As Jamie was paying our bill his own mobile rang. He didn't recognise the caller but answered with his usual cheery greeting and I watched with growing apprehension as the colour drained from his face.

'How bad? OK, yes, of course. I'm on my way,' he added, before hanging up.

'Jamie?'

'Jasmine's been in an accident – she's in hospital.'

'What sort of accident?'

'I don't know – they didn't say.'

'OK, try not to worry. Are you going to go and see her?'

'Yes. But you'll come with me, won't you?'

'I –' I didn't want to. I hated hospitals and if she, if *they*, had lost the baby I didn't want to witness their grief. 'I'm not sure she'd want me there, Jamie –'

'But I need you there. Please, Kat, come with me.' His appeal was raw and powerful in his eyes.

'OK, let's go.'

Chapter Forty-two

While I paced the small, half-empty waiting area, Kat, perched on a hard chair, followed me with her eyes. I felt bad for bringing her here; it was selfish. Hospitals were no fun and Jasmine was not Kat's problem. But I needed her here. Kat had only been back in my life a few short months and yet I'd come to rely on her and the inner strength she exuded.

All the nurse had been able to tell us so far was that Jasmine had been in a car accident on a dual carriageway and that no other vehicles had been involved. She wasn't in intensive care – which was a good sign – but the doctor was in with her and we would only know more once a proper assessment had been made. Right now all I could think was that the baby, possibly my baby, might be in trouble. Despite the less-than-ideal circumstances, I wanted the child to live – and if he or she did I could not, would not, let any child of mine be brought up by strangers. If I had ever believed in any kind of god I would have prayed. As it was, I just kept pacing.

At last a blonde woman wearing glasses, a white coat and a stethoscope approached me and I stopped. Kat moved to my side and slipped her hand into mine but I kept my eyes on the doctor.

'Mr Southwood?'

'Yes.'

'I'm Dr Riley; I've just been assessing Miss Reed's condition.'

'Yes?'

'She's been very lucky; aside from a mild concussion and a few bumps and bruises, she doesn't seem to have sustained any serious injuries.' I wanted to tell her to go on but my mouth had completely dried up with fear. After a pause she continued anyway, 'I'm afraid the police will want to talk to her because her blood alcohol level is three times over the legal limit but you can go in and see her now if you like.'

'Alcohol?' I croaked, hoping I'd misheard. Kat's hand tightened in mine and I turned to her, unable to organise a coherent thought. Kat sensed I was struggling.

'What about the baby?' she said, calmly turning to Dr Riley.

'Baby? Sorry – you are?'

'I'm family,' Kat said dismissively. 'What about Jasmine's baby?'

'I'm sorry, I –' Dr Riley looked confused, 'as far as I'm aware there was no baby in the car.' I wanted to grab her by the shoulders and shake her for prolonging the agony.

'Jasmine's four and a half months pregnant,' Kat said, impatiently.

'No.' She looked at me, then back at Kat, then back to me again, her expression serious, 'not according to her notes or her blood work.'

'What?' My shock came out as a whisper.

'There is no baby?' Kat said, her voice hard. 'Was there ever a baby? Did she abort it?' I flinched at her harsh tone as I tried to comprehend what was being said.

'I'm sorry. I can't discuss a patient's history. You'll

273

have to talk to her yourself. Are you all right?' she said, peering up at me through her spectacles. 'Do you need to sit down?' I let the doctor steer me towards a seat and I sat down heavily. 'Let me get you some water,' she said, moving away.

As the full weight of understanding spread through me I groaned, leaning forwards, bracing my elbows on my knees and taking my head in my hands. It was then that I realised Kat was no longer with me.

'Kat?' Looking up I scanned the waiting area. Dr Riley had filled a small plastic cup with water from a cooler and was making her way back towards me but Kat was not with her. I couldn't see her anywhere. 'Oh, shit,' I muttered, rising quickly to my feet.

Chapter Forty-three

Pushing open the door to the private room I marched over to the bed. Jasmine lay on her back with her eyes closed, her hands folded neatly across her flat stomach, and her golden curls fanned out on the pillow around her head. She looked as peaceful and virtuous as an angel.

'You selfish bitch!' Her eyes flew open and she stared at me in surprise. 'Do you have any idea what you've put him through?' She looked fearful and confused as she tried to place me, which only made me angrier. 'Was there ever a baby?'

Finally recognition dawned in her expression and her features hardened. 'What are *you* doing here? Who do you think you are?'

'I'm family, Jamie's family, that's who, and I care more about him than you ever will.'

'Get out,' she snapped. The door opened and I sensed Jamie entering the room behind me but I was too riled up to stop now.

'No, not until you admit you're a lying, manipulative bitch.'

Jasmine gasped dramatically for Jamie's benefit and he gently placed his hands on my upper arms. 'Kat, she's just been in an accident.' His touch and his voice were soothing but I knew he was ready to restrain me if necessary.

I snorted. 'She's fine, look; there's barely a scratch on her – she's just attention seeking.'

'How dare you,' she said.

'I dare because it's true – come on where's this baby of yours?'

'That's none of your business,' she said, flushing. 'James, get her out of here or I'll call security and have her dragged out.'

'Answer the question first,' he said quietly.

Jasmine spontaneously burst into tears, her voice changing to a pitiful mewl. 'I can't believe you're doing this to me – I'm recovering from a head injury you know.'

'A hangover more like,' I muttered.

Jamie sighed. 'Just tell us, Jasmine, and we'll leave you in peace.'

'I just wanted you to want me,' she whimpered. Neither Jamie nor I spoke and she swiped her cheeks with her fingers, wiped her nose on the back of her hand and sighed heavily. 'OK, I didn't get pregnant,' she admitted.

Fresh anger swept through me making my fists tremble at my sides and my newly healed wrist ache. Jamie's grip tightened on my arms. 'Let's go,' he said in a low voice at my ear.

'But I could have been pregnant. I mean, it could have happened.' I glared at her and allowed Jamie to manoeuvre me towards the door. 'Wait, James, I know I've made mistakes but *she's* not perfect either. Did she tell you that she kissed me?' I froze, mid-step, shocked at Jasmine's audacity and instantly shamed by the memory. 'I bet she never mentioned that, did she?' Jasmine taunted.

Jamie had gone ominously still and quiet behind me but I couldn't turn around; I knew he'd see the truth of it in my face and I didn't want to give Jasmine the satisfaction of a response.

'I've called your parents. They're on their way.' Jamie said evenly, releasing his grip on my arms and holding the door open for me while resolutely not looking at her. 'I suggest you change your medical records, Jasmine. I'm not your next of kin.'

Jamie ushered me through the door then turned back. 'And you'd better arrange for somewhere else to stay when you leave here. The flat is going on the market today and I'm having the locks changed. Text me an address and I'll forward your stuff on to you.'

She started to cry again as the door closed behind us and I almost pitied her. Almost. As we left I surreptitiously glanced up at Jamie; his expression was impassive but he took my hand as we walked away.

I hated Jasmine Reed for everything she'd put Jamie through and was glad he'd finally stood up to her but wondered what her parting shot might mean for us. He was tense and distracted and kept a firm grip of my hand but he didn't mention Jasmine's accusation – didn't ask me if it was true that I'd kissed her or why it had happened – and I worried in silence about what might be going on in his head, too afraid to ask.

True to his word Jamie called an emergency locksmith and we travelled straight from the hospital to his flat in Willesden Green, still not talking.

The two-bed flat, the converted first floor of a Victorian terrace, was tastefully decorated, with high ceilings and large windows, but very messy indeed. As the locksmith set about replacing the locks on the front door, Jamie stalked about the flat unceremoniously stuffing Jasmine's strewn belongings into black bin bags, while making phone calls to estate agents – discussing valuations, marketing strategy and viewing arrangements. At a loss for anything better to do I set about clearing up the kitchen – disposing of the array of fast food containers and tackling a pile of washing up. Jamie told me not to – that it was the last thing I should be doing on my birthday – but I insisted since I couldn't leave without him and needed to keep busy. By the time we returned to Wildham, late in the evening, everything was organised and the London property was ready for sale, if not yet devoid of contents.

Now I lay beside Jamie in bed listening to his even breathing but unable to sleep. What Jasmine had told Jamie about me still rankled. It wasn't even a proper kiss; just Jasmine's evil attempt at manipulating Jamie through me – and I had far worse secrets – but I wished Jamie had said something about it. The longer Jamie and I spent together, the more he lavished me with kindness and attention, the greater my own inadequacies seemed. I would never be the person he wanted me to be. Nothing he said or did would change my past and tonight the pain, as I pinched the underside of my arm with my fingernails, was doing nothing to alleviate my anxiety.

Quietly slipping out of bed, I crept down to the kitchen and poured myself a glass of red wine. I wasn't a big drinker as a rule; tonight I simply needed something to help me sleep. Downing half the glass in one go I topped it back up again and sat down at the kitchen table, my head in my hands. Why was Jamie so bloody good to me all the time? Taking me to all these amazing places, teaching me stuff, encouraging me to try new things. What did he hope to get in return? My friendship? Sex? Despite my body's extraordinary yearning for his, I still didn't want him to see me naked; I didn't want to have to explain my past to him. And that was wrong. If nothing else Jamie deserved some honesty. He'd put his trust in me time and time again and I was completely unwilling, incapable, of returning the compliment.

The wine wasn't strong enough to prevent a familiar and deeply rooted sense of self-loathing from unfurling inside me. Almost without thinking I went upstairs to the bathroom and retrieved my old hospital bracelet from its hiding place, along with a disposable plastic razor, before bringing them back to the kitchen table.

Gently I stroked my thumb over my name and the date printed on the admissions bracelet. The flimsy bit of plastic was physical, tangible proof of a life that was never meant to be. My baby was never born; I never knew its gender and it never had a name. But it was not an imaginary baby like Jasmine's; it was real enough to leave me with an acute sense of grief. Grief based on little more than an idea, a notion; my chance at a family dismissed – but it was grief nonetheless. I reminded myself, for what felt like the millionth time, that it was for the best. Vic and I would not have made good parents – the life we shared was not conducive to a happy childhood and it would have been selfish to imagine otherwise. But that knowledge didn't lessen the pain.

Setting the bracelet aside I picked up the razor. With practised ease I snapped the casing apart, carefully extracted the blade and placed it on the surface before me. Staring at it I took another sip of wine while calculating how many years it had been since the last time I'd needed to do this. Seventeen. It had been seventeen long years since I'd lost the baby I hadn't known I was carrying. Where had the time gone? Back then it was grief that had eaten away my insides until I felt so numb that I wasn't sure if I was alive or dead. And now it was shame and guilt gnawing away at me. I would never be safe from my past. How could I go on hiding from, and lying to, the only person I'd ever loved? Just one small cut was usually enough to get me through, to release some pain and make me feel better for a while. And Jamie would never have to know...

'Kat?' I woke with a jolt, my neck stiff and cheek sore from the grain of the table top and my eyes squinting against the glare of the overhead light. I must have fallen asleep.

'What time is it?' I croaked.

Jamie was crouched beside me in boxers and a T-shirt, his eyes unnaturally wide with fear. 'It's one in the morning. What are you doing?'

As I glanced in horror at the items on the table before me I was fleetingly relieved that I'd not gone through with it. 'It's not what you think,' I said, the hackneyed phrase grating as I pushed back my chair, snatched up the blade and deposited it in the pedal bin. Jamie took my arm and turned me to face him with none of his usual hesitation.

'Explain, Kat, please – you're scaring me.'

'Fuck, I'm sorry –' I wrenched my body away from

280

him just in time to throw up in the sink; wine the colour of dried blood splashed dramatically against the white ceramic. Quickly turning the cold tap on, I washed away the mess and gulped down water from the cupped palm of my hand. I could sense Jamie standing beside me, radiating tension. How could I have been so stupid? So careless? Worry Jamie when he had already been through so much? I felt utterly disgusted with myself. 'I'm sorry,' I started again, 'I didn't mean to; I wasn't –'

'Tell me you weren't going to; surely you wouldn't even consider – not *that* – you wouldn't leave me like *that*; not after everything we've –'

'No! No! Of course not!' Throwing my arms around him, I pressed my face to his warm chest, squeezing him tight. He remained heartbreakingly frozen and unyielding in my arms. 'I wasn't; I wouldn't; I promise.'

Shrugging out of my embrace Jamie stepped back away from me, his jaw taut with emotion. 'Is this about Jasmine – is there something between you two?'

'God, no! That – what she said – it was *her* that kissed *me*, Jamie; she was trying to get back at you or something and I – no this is nothing to do with Jasmine, honestly.'

'Then what, Kat? I thought you were happy or at least happi*er* – I thought things were getting easier.'

'I am; they are. It's just that you, you're so good to me, so generous and honest and I – I owe you some honesty in return. And I want to tell you, I want to tell you everything,' pathetic, self-pitying tears threatened to spill down my face, 'but I can't, Jamie, I just can't do it – I'm a fucking coward, I'm sorry.'

281

'Then don't, for God's sake!' he said with exasperation. 'It doesn't matter! You're not a coward; you're just not ready. There's no rush. You don't *ever* have to tell me if you don't want to – I'll still be here for you; I still need you in my life, Kat.'

'I need you too,' I admitted, the words heavy on my tongue.

Jamie exhaled and crushed me to him in a vice-like hug. 'Promise me you won't do anything like this *ever* again.'

'I promise,' I said over the thunderous racing of his heart. Pressed close together we just stood there, the heat of his body seeping into mine and warming me as his heart rate and blood pressure gradually evened out.

Eventually Jamie released me. 'It's late; will you come back to bed?' he said, rubbing his eyes.

'Yes.'

Without another word he wearily motioned for me to go before him. As I passed the table I subtly palmed my hospital bracelet and he followed me out, in silence, switching off the light.

Chapter Forty-four

At five thirty I left the stuffy confines of my office to walk the shop floor. It had been a weird day; the sky dark and oppressive with cloud that refused to release any rain and only a handful of customers through the door – the type who spent a long time browsing but purchased little. Some brought their elderly relatives to the garden centre and wheeled them round the plant area at a leisurely pace so that they could savour the flowers and fragrances. Others brought their kids and let them loose to race up and down the aisles, burning off surplus energy. One regular, an unobtrusive Eastern European-looking fellow in his forties or fifties, visited at least a couple of times a week but bought random token items such as carrot seeds, protective fleece or the odd marigold. Perhaps he was lonely and simply used a visit to Southwood's as an excuse to leave his house. Either way all our customers were welcome and we did our best to keep them happy, regardless of how much, or how little, cash they parted with.

I'd spent most of the day cooped up inside, researching alternative plant suppliers and weighing up the pros and cons of importing more stock from abroad, but I would much rather have been doing something physically active. There was always plenty to do: whether it was re-stocking, watering or simply keeping the place tidy. The land behind the garden centre also belonged to the business and, although a local farmer rented the fields for grazing his cows, it was down to me to maintain the boundaries. Up near the tree line a section of fence was in need of replacing and I was keen to tackle the job myself rather than pay someone else to do it. But it was difficult finding the time.

In the outdoor pot area someone had been searching through a selection of glazed blue planters and had left them blocking the path. As I lifted them back into position I idly wondered if I would find Kat working in among the herbaceous perennials. She'd taken well to working in the public areas – the customers enjoyed chatting to her and she was fast becoming an expert on the plants she tended. Manoeuvring the last pot into place I yawned widely. Despite a day spent sat at my desk, I was shattered; I was having trouble sleeping.

I'd grown used to Kat sharing my bed each night; it was comforting. Even when I'd lain awake worrying about a baby who never existed I'd been reassured by Kat's presence at my side. But since the early hours of Tuesday morning, since discovering her slumped over the kitchen table with an empty wine glass and a razor blade at her elbow, I could no longer relax at all. I woke in the middle of the night with panic chasing through my chest like a scared animal. I'd been afraid of losing Kat since the moment I'd found her and the more time we spent together, the closer we became, the bigger that fear had grown. But it had never crossed my mind that she might leave me like *that* – kill herself. Now the nightmarish thought tormented me relentlessly.

Every time I'd woken up since Tuesday, Kat had been right there beside me. She'd promised that she wouldn't do anything stupid, and I wanted to believe her, but it wasn't enough to dispel my worries.

The fact was I had no idea how to best help Kat. She had an old hospital tag with her name on it, which clearly held significance for her, but was it from when she had had her kidney operation or from something else? I wanted her to share her story with me, as much as she wanted to be able to. Obviously I was apprehensive about what she might tell me but I couldn't imagine her saying anything that would make me care about her any less. The not knowing was worse.

Despite her general aversion to physical contact, Kat didn't seem to mind me touching her and in the dead of the night, while she was unconscious, I couldn't help reaching out and holding her hand. Lately it was the only way I could sleep at all.

'James?' Barb was hurrying breathlessly towards me. 'Is Frank burning rubbish or something down on the nursery?'

As soon as she spoke I could smell smoke. 'No – he's unloading a delivery with the forklift isn't he? I was already turning in the direction of the nursery and my scalp prickled as I spotted the plume of grey smoke, almost camouflaged against the leaden sky. 'Where's Kat?' I said, leaving Barb behind and starting to run towards the plant area. Stay calm; it's probably nothing – just a bonfire or something, I told myself, not Kat, not Kat – anything but that.

My stride faltered with relief the moment I spotted her standing chatting to Lil and Max. Kat's gaze connected with mine immediately, her face paling as she took an automatic step towards me in alarm.

I pointed. 'Does anyone know what that's about?' I shouted to the trio as I started to sprint towards the nursery gate. By the time I'd yanked it open and reached the source of the smoke, Kat and Max were close behind me. The fire was coming from the potting shed.

'I don't understand,' Kat said, 'no one's been working down here today. I left it all locked up.'

'Max, call the fire brigade,' I said over my shoulder,

'and then get Frank and help me get some hoses over here quickly.' Max nodded, turned on his heel and ran off. I was about to run to the nearest polytunnel to retrieve a hose when Kat's anguish stopped me.

'Jamie! The kittens!' The raw pain in her expression almost stopped my heart. Flames were licking up the timber of the locked gable doors and flickering out through the small cat-flap Kat had installed to enable Socks to come and go. Even at a distance of several metres the heat from the fire was intense. Behind me Lil, Barb and Leah were dragging a heavy water hose out of a polytunnel and across the gravel towards us, but the length of rubber was cumbersome and awkward to manoeuvre and would not reach us immediately. Kat took a panicked step closer to the inferno and I seized her arm.

'Stop! Don't even think about it,' I said. 'I'll get them – just stay here.'

Without pausing I grabbed an axe from where Frank had been chopping wood, moved around to the side of the shed and pulled the hem of my shirt up over my mouth and nose. The heat was too fierce for me to get anywhere near the front doors so I waded into the thick tangle of undergrowth that surrounded the other three walls.

'Wait, don't!' Kat cried out behind me.

'Just stay back,' I shouted over my shoulder.

The twisted mass of hawthorn saplings was threaded with brambles, creating a vicious, almost impenetrable mass of barbs and thorns that reached up to my shoulders. Ignoring the smarting as my skin was snagged, scratched and punctured, I wrestled to get close enough to the rear of the building, the smoke stinging my eyes. With some indiscriminate hacking I was able to get close enough to thrust the blade of the axe through a window but, as the glass smashed, the flames swelled and a billow of black smoke engulfed me making me choke. Pressing my face into my sleeve I coughed and wiped my eyes in an effort to regain my vision.

But now, at last, the others had brought water and I gasped in relief as it rained down on my skin, blissfully cool. By training one jet of water on the front doors and the other over my head and through the broken window before me, my staff provided me with space to breathe. Without further hesitation, I forced my way closer to the window, leaning in and calling to Socks in a rasping voice. To my surprise she appeared on the bench top right in front of me, her fur damp and bristling, her eyes wide with fear, and one of her kittens dangling from her mouth. I stretched a cupped palm out towards her and after only a few seconds hesitation she relinquished the kitten to my care. Quickly I passed the kitten backwards into Kat's waiting hands while Socks disappeared to retrieve her other offspring. The fire was still burning, the water pressure of our hoses too weak to combat the flames and as the seconds ticked by I started to worry that Socks wasn't coming back. But then she reappeared, the second kitten in her jaws. Without ceremony, I snatched them up, mother and baby both, and beat a hasty retreat. As I finally staggered free of the heat, smoke and undergrowth, and handed the animals to safety, it was to the wailing approach of sirens and a round of cheers and applause from the small crowd of customers who had gathered at the gate to watch.

Within ten minutes of the fire brigade's arrival the fire had been put out. Kat, her face streaked with soot and tears, would not leave my side as two paramedics checked me over. My clothes were ripped to shreds and I was covered in bloody gouges and scratches but it was my

287

level of smoke inhalation that had them concerned. It was embarrassing being the focus of so much attention and after repeatedly insisting that I'd only had limited exposure they eventually agreed to let me go, on the strict proviso that I check myself into hospital should any untoward symptoms arise.

By the time we'd closed for the day and everyone, including the emergency services, had departed, the adrenalin in my system had well and truly drained away. I got as far as the living room before collapsing onto the settee with an almighty sigh, my head back and my eyes shut.

'Can I run you a bath?' Kat said quietly.

I reopened my eyes to find her hovering in the doorway as if preparing for flight, her eyes wide. 'That would be great, thank you, but sit down first; take a load off,' I said hoarsely, patting the space beside me. Her gaze darted from my face to my hand and back again before she slipped fluidly into the room and perched gingerly on the armchair opposite. 'Are you all right? Are the kittens OK?' As she returned my look I noticed she was trembling. 'Kat?'

'They're fine – they're settled in a box in the corner of the kitchen with Socks,' she said, disregarding the first part of my question. 'What did that fireman say to you? Does he know what caused the fire?'

'Oh, yeah.' I sighed. 'He thought it was probably just an accident; a stray fag butt – though who'd been smoking down there I couldn't say. Max and Leah are regular smokers but they don't do it down on the nursery.' The intent look in Kat's expression surprised me and I leaned forward towards her. 'What? What is it, Kat?'

'It's my fault. He's found me – he knows I'm here.'

For a moment I had no clue what she was talking about. 'He must know I work in that potting shed and he obviously tried to –'

'No, Kat, that's crazy!' I said, cutting her off, shocked. Standing up I moved over to her but she sprang up and stepped away from me. 'It was an accident, Kat. Nothing to do with Vic – you weren't even in the shed today, thank God –'

'It might've been a warning – a threat.'

'No, Kat,' I said, reaching out for her hand. 'You're being paranoid – it was just a silly accident.'

Shrugging away from me and avoiding my touch, she shook her head. Weary frustration spiked inside me. She was the most unbelievably stubborn woman I'd ever known; I loved that about her but right now it was maddening. Heavily I sank into the seat she'd vacated.

'Please don't let this worry you. The Fire Crew Manager I spoke to knows his stuff and he's confident it wasn't arson.'

'Why?'

'Well for one thing there was only one point of origin; just outside the door – usually when someone starts a fire deliberately they do it in several places to make sure the flames take. And there were no signs of chemical accelerant, no petrol or anything. If someone had really wanted to cause some damage they would have set fire to the chemical store surely? God knows there are all kinds of flammable liquids in there!'

Kat sighed and bowed her head, gazing down at her hands. I could tell she wanted to believe me and I hoped I'd said enough to convince her. Even in our filthy, sweaty, bedraggled state I wanted to hold her.

'Please, Kat, just forget about it,' I said gently.

'I'll go run your bath.' Straightening up she disappeared out of the door.

Chapter Forty-five

Despite the sultry weather and the intense heat of the fire I'd just experienced, I now felt chilled to the bone. My hands shook with delayed shock as I set the bath taps running, returned to the kitchen and plundered the fridge for leftovers. As cold as I was I didn't feel much like cooking. Having found half a goat's cheese and red pepper quiche, some vegetarian sausage rolls, potato salad, cherry tomatoes, houmous, breadsticks and olives I set them all out on the table so that Jamie could help himself. Now that the adrenalin was wearing off, a whole host of disturbing implications were elbowing their way into my mind. Was the fire really just an accident like Jamie had said? Vic's cold eyes and mocking smile sliced through my mind and I fought the urge to vomit.

As soon as Jamie had finished in the bathroom I nipped in, re-filled the bath halfway, stripped off and washed myself briskly. He could have died! Jamie could have been burnt to death and it would have been all my fault – why the hell had I let him go after those kittens?

Everything had happened so quickly and once he'd made his mind up to rescue them there'd been no stopping him; he was so damn calm and fearless, intently focused on getting those animals out alive. And, yes, they were adorable but not worth Jamie's life! Another shiver raked through me and I bit my lip. Thank God he wasn't badly hurt; I'd never have forgiven myself.

Socks and her two kittens were still in their box,

291

sleeping soundly, when I came back downstairs but Jamie was not in the kitchen and the food lay on the table untouched. Stepping through the open back door on to the terrace I scanned the plant area but couldn't see him. Over to the west, the dense clouds were finally breaking up and dazzling chinks of light burst dramatically through the gaps as the sun sank towards the hills. With a pang of unease I wondered if Jamie had gone back down to the nursery to survey the damaged remains of the potting shed. I hoped not.

'Jamie?' I called out.

'Over here, Kat.' His voice came from beyond the temporary fence that closed off the new coffee shop extension. 'Come round and have a look; I'd value your opinion.'

Beyond the fence lay a large, smooth, rectangular concrete foundation, which glowed apricot in the fiery evening light. A new, sturdy, timber frame had recently been erected above it, outlining the new room, but, without walls or a roof, it currently lay open, exposed to the elements. In the centre of the space solid stacks of paving slabs had been bridged with a section of vinyl-covered worktop, providing a makeshift table. Jamie was standing perusing the architectural plans and drawings spread out across its surface. We were both familiar with the design but it was different – amazing – actually seeing the place taking shape in situ.

'These walls will be mostly glass,' he explained, pointing through the gaps in the timber frame to the view of the plant area and the countryside beyond. Then he paced back and forth to show me where the kitchen would go; where the counter would be positioned; and how the tables and chairs would allow for flexible seating arrangements, as per my suggestion. Jamie's face was animated with enthusiasm as he talked, the sunlight glinting off his glasses, and yet I could tell he was exhausted. Even before his firefighting heroics he had been sleep deprived. Four nights of broken sleep was taking its toll on both of us and that was my fault too. One stupid moment of weakness – one innocuous little razor blade – had got Jamie worrying unnecessarily and frustratingly it was within my power to soothe away his concerns – if only I could explain it to him; if only.

While Jamie spoke I handled the laminated plans, ostensibly to re-acquaint myself with them but mainly to give myself more time to think. Jamie's optimism, his hopes and dreams for me, for us, were intoxicating. And I loved him. The bittersweet knowledge of that fact taunted my every waking moment, making it hard to think of anything else. But mine was a selfish and secretive love – I was concealing my past to protect myself.

Jamie stepped away to the outer edge of the concrete floor, surveying the view with his back to me, his solid, athletic silhouette outlined in orange sunlight. 'And over here, through the doors, this will be the outdoor seating area,' he said.

I didn't go over to him, didn't comment on the extension; I held back. I thought of the countless times I'd stood in the shade of a sycamore tree and observed Jamie from afar as he mingled effortlessly with his customers and put them at their ease. Even from a distance it was obvious just how popular he was with the staff and customers: adults, teenagers and children alike. He genuinely enjoyed motivating people, making them laugh. With a pang of intense sorrow I reminded myself that Jamie would make a wonderful father. We hadn't discussed Jasmine since leaving her behind at the hospital. Clearly Jamie was relieved that she was not about to have his child but he had been mentally preparing himself for fatherhood. A part of him had been looking forward to being a dad and that same part of him was now sad to have had that opportunity taken away.

He turned back to me, his face in shadow. 'You OK, Kat?'

I didn't reply. Once Jamie knew everything I would lose him. But he could have been *killed* today. I hated myself – I was sick of feeling like an imposter and a fraud and tired of being held hostage by my own secrets. The other night when he'd caught me with that razor he'd said that he needed me – and that was bad. I could not be relied upon. I couldn't go on hurting him any more – I had to set him free.

'Kat?'

It was now or never. 'You've been so honest with me,' I began. 'And I – you deserve to know the truth about me: who I am, what I am, so that you can tell me to leave.'

'I'll never want you to leave, Kat,' he said, moving towards me.

'No, stop.' I held a hand up to stay him, my determination sounding desperate. 'Don't say that; you can't know that.'

Jamie shook his head but stayed where he was.

'I just need to get this out, OK?'

'OK, I won't say another word.'

Closing my eyes I braced myself, resolving to keep my voice steady. 'A few months after you left the Plumleys a boy called Daniel moved in to take your place. He was thirteen, a year older than me. He tried to rape me in the middle of the night so I broke his nose with my forehead and kneed him in the balls. It was enough to stop him. In the morning he told the Plumleys I'd beaten him up without provocation and they believed him; he was very convincing. My case worker transferred me to a different foster home but, before I left, Daniel cornered me, held me down, and gave me this to remember him by.' Opening my eyes I tugged down the neckline of my T-shirt to reveal the round cigarette burn visible on my right breast, just inside the cup of my bra. I was grateful that I couldn't see Jamie's face and that he remained mercifully mute as promised.

'There were other people I didn't get on with over the years – sometimes it was another kid or a foster parents' own child. Occasionally it was the carers themselves – one woman resolutely refused to feed me and another guy kept walking in on me in the bathroom. He tried to touch me; it made me feel sick and I knew it was wrong. But whatever the situation I knew how to escape – to get myself evicted and moved on, usually by fighting, breaking something or stealing. Of course I was my own worst enemy; all my bad behaviour went on my record and I became completely ineligible for adoption.'

I pulled the neckline of my T-shirt to the side, but it wouldn't stretch far enough so I grabbed it by the hem and brazenly yanked it off over my head. Raising my arm high above my head, I turned the left side of my body towards Jamie and into the warm spotlight of the sun.

'This is where I used to cut myself,' I said evenly, indicating the neat row of parallel linear scars, like a barcode, on the underside of my upper arm. 'Not to kill myself but to release some pain. I'm not proud of it but it was something to do, something to focus on when things became too much. That's what I was considering doing the other night.' Jamie's legs had given way and he had sunk to his knees on the concrete floor but I knew he was still listening and I couldn't stop now; I was on a roll, stripping away the layers and baring my soul.

Lowering my arm, I let my T-shirt drop away, turning to expose the right side of my body and pointing to the long diagonal scar at the edge of my ribs. 'This is where the hospital removed my kidney. I've mentioned it before but I didn't mention that it was my own fault. I wasn't looking after myself properly. I got ill from sleeping in doorways, not washing, eating out of bins – and all because I was too proud to sell my body, beg for money or stay in hostels with strangers.'

Jamie radiated tension and I could tell he was shaking his head but ignoring him I turned so that he would have a clear view of my stomach. 'And Vic – marrying him was preferable to prostitution. He's only violent when he's drunk or upset. Most of the injuries he's given me over the years haven't left marks at all. He has broken this wrist before but it always heals again. I'm not making excuses for him; it's true. I could have fought back, maybe I should have, but it was easier not to.'

Glancing down, I traced the three scars on my belly

with my fingers. 'A year into our marriage I fell pregnant. I had no idea at the time, I didn't recognise the signs, but it was an ectopic pregnancy – the baby was growing in my fallopian tube – and one day I was rushed into hospital in agony. These two small, crescent-shaped scars are from the laparoscopy and this larger one is where they removed my tube with the dead foetus inside.' I swallowed, unwilling to crumble at this late stage. 'I, after that, they said I was unlikely to conceive again; they found scarring on both ovaries. I wanted you to know that – to know that I'm infertile – that I'll never be a mother. Not that you –' My throat finally seized up. My body had begun to shake and my eyes ached with unshed tears.

Wordlessly Jamie reached out, his upturned palms imploring. As my legs buckled he caught me, gently drawing me onto his lap and wrapping his arms around my body. The shock of ripping myself open at last was overwhelming and I curled into him, burying my face in his chest and crying like a child. While I fell apart the silent acceptance in Jamie's embrace was deafening. As the sun set below the horizon he sat and rocked me, pressing kisses to the top of my head.

Eventually I struggled to pull myself together, amazed that Jamie was still there; that he hadn't shrunk away from me or walked off in disgust. But then I should have known – Jamie was too polite; too kind, to react that way.

'I'm so proud of you, Kat,' he said into my hair, his warm voice rumbling deep inside his chest. 'You are the strongest, bravest, most beautiful woman I have ever known.'

Trying to calm my breathing I raised my head to look

297

at him. He was still backlit by fading pink light but I could tell that his face was damp with tears behind his glasses. Had he not heard a word I'd said? 'But I –'

'You're perfect to me, Kat.'

I shook my head.

'Yes. And none of it was your fault,' he added, his voice hard. 'Do you hear me? None of it. You were dealt a shitty hand but you survived; you kept going; you gave me time to find you again.' His large dark eyes were locked on to mine as he spoke, as I tried to listen, tried to comprehend. 'And now I have found you, Kat and I'm here for you. We are together and you will never have to suffer like that again, do you understand? You are safe with me.'

He repeated himself over and over, while I tried to believe him and grappled with a fragile, desperate, sense of hope.

'OK, OK,' I said at last, pressing a finger to his lips.

He smiled then, warmth slowly spreading out across his face until it glowed in his eyes. As the knot in my chest began to loosen I became hyper-aware of his powerful body around me, his arms against my bare skin, his warm breath on my lips…

Our mouths met, inexorably drawn together with magnetic force. Deep in his chest Jamie moaned, gently devouring me as if for the first time, one hand cradling my head, his stubble teasing my lips. He tasted mouth-wateringly, intoxicatingly good, making my whole body hum with warmth and I never wanted him to stop. But he broke away from me, searching my face with focused concern, so that I felt naked in the beam of his gaze.

'It's starting to get dark. Let's go inside,' he said softly. Jamie helped me up as he rose to his feet, his hands still touching me. But before he could move I kissed him again, compulsively, addicted to the reassuring heat I found in his lips and afraid to let him go. He returned my kiss chastely at first, as if holding back, but as I tentatively probed inside his mouth with the tip of my tongue, he responded passionately and I wanted more. Stepping backwards a couple of paces, I drew him along with me until I felt the edge of the makeshift table at my back. Still kissing him I perched on the edge and kicked off my flip-flops, wrapping my legs around his and lifting the hem of his T-shirt.

'Wait, we don't have to do this,' he said, breaking away.

'You don't want to?'

'Oh, Kat, I want to; believe me I've never wanted anything more. But you're upset and after everything you've been through –' I waited for him to continue, 'I don't want to hurt you: physically or emotionally. I'm not the right guy for you.'

I stared at him, confused, rejection threatening to surge up inside me, like water in a blocked drain.

'You're free now, Kat, free of your past. You can have any guy you want; you don't have to settle for me. I'll always be here for you but you could do so much better.'

'What are you talking about? What do you mean *better*?'

Pulling off his glasses and casting them aside, Jamie closed his eyes and pinched the bridge of his nose in frustration. And my own doubts and insecurities rushed

299

in. Was this Jamie's polite way of letting me down gently? Did he just want us to be friends? If that was the case I didn't want to embarrass myself, or him, any further.

'I understand if you don't want me,' I said evenly, steeling myself.

His eyes flew open and locked on to mine, black with desire. 'Kat, I want you so badly it's like physical pain – with every breath my whole body aches just to be near you. I can't sleep for craving even your slightest touch; can't eat without needing to taste you. I didn't even know it was possible to feel as utterly aroused as you make me feel.'

Jamie's words had me struggling for breath – they were more than I'd ever dared hope for. 'I feel the same way about you,' I said at last.

He looked doubtful. 'You do? Why?'

'Jamie, you're everything to me, why wouldn't I?' The tension in his expression began to ease and, as a cautious smile spread out across his face, he kissed me again.

'Just let me look at you,' he said, leaning back, his gaze sweeping down over my body, just visible in the fading light. My hands lifted reflexively to cover myself but he stayed them with his own. 'You don't have to hide from me any more, Kat.'

Dipping his head Jamie softly pressed his lips to the burn mark on my chest making me gasp. Before I could even process the sensation he was lifting my left arm and tenderly kissing the scars of my self-loathing, as if to heal the pain. The bittersweet intensity of his touch was almost too much to take and I trembled as he moved on to my

300

other disfigurements, kissing them softly, almost reverently, one by one. My limbs turned to jelly and I collapsed backwards onto my elbows as Jamie eased up my skirt exposing my bare legs, my skin tingling with awareness.

'Oh, Kat,' Jamie said, sinking to a crouch between my thighs and brushing his lips across my tremulous knee. 'You have the finest legs in the world.'

I laughed, unnerved by his sincerity and the hungry look on his face. As he began to trail soft kisses up the inside of my thigh, heat rushed through my bloodstream making me ache with desire. When he reached the top he pressed his hot mouth to my knickers. It felt deliciously indecent, transporting me back to the night he had pleasured me in the dark and I groaned, involuntarily pushing up against him.

With a sigh he returned his mouth to my thigh. 'I don't want to take advantage of you when you're feeling vulnerable, Kat, and anyway I haven't got a condom,' he muttered against my skin.

'We don't need one; I trust you. I know you won't hurt me. Please, I want you to show me what it can be like – I want you to make me forget everything else.'

Jamie stood, his gaze sliding over my body before returning to mine. I could tell he was deliberating and see the yearning in his eyes.

'Please – you're the only one I trust.'

Dragging his T-shirt up over his head, Jamie threw it aside and I watched, transfixed, as he proceeded to remove his shorts and boxers. There were numerous scratches across his skin marking his recent heroics but they did not lessen the masculine perfection of his body. His broad chest and solid shoulders tapered to a smooth, streamlined stomach above slim hips and sturdy, hair-sprinkled thighs. And his package, my god; I'd never seen a more provoking sight. His erection stood proudly to attention and there was no doubting that he wanted me. I marvelled that something so impressive could possibly fit inside my body while my inner muscles clenched shamelessly, eager with anticipation.

With a new sense of bravery I sat up, removed my bra and discarded it, shivering under Jamie's heated gaze. I reached out to him and he stepped into my embrace without hesitation, enveloping me protectively in his arms. The close contact made me breathless as he kissed me again, his mouth urgent against mine, his stubble exciting my skin and his tongue exploring. My nipples tightened with arousal as I pressed my breasts to his warm chest and with his fingers he eased my skirt and knickers down from my hips. As he bent to unhook them from my feet, he took my nipples in his mouth one after the other, licking, sucking and grazing them gently with his teeth, sending jolts of pleasure through my core and making me gasp.

The last of my clothing discarded, Jamie slowly, deliberately, sought out and circled the throbbing place between my legs with his fingers. At the same time he trailed kisses back up the sensitive skin of my neck, to my ear and along my jaw line. I could barely process so much blissful sensation all at once. As his mouth returned to mine I took him in my hand and guided him firmly between my thighs. The feel of him there sent a tremor of pleasure rolling right through my body from my toes to the tips of my hair. But he hesitated at my entrance, his face taut with tension. Jamie was giving me a chance to change my mind but I wanted him, more than life itself.

With a flex of my pelvis I drew him right up inside me, naked flesh to naked flesh, and he groaned in my mouth, his breathing deepening along with his kiss. Gripping my hips with his strong hands, he stilled deep within me and my internal muscles rippled and tightened possessively around him as if he were mine all along, a part of me, missing for too long. His dark eyes opened and searched my gaze as if he was staring into my very soul.

'Kat,' he whispered against my lips.

'Jamie,' I breathed in reply.

With a roll of his hips he made me arch backwards in an involuntary swoon and I gazed up at the now indigo sky in open surrender. As he began to move the pressure built quickly inside me, my body a willing slave to Jamie's rhythm. Tightening my legs around his waist, I urged him on, listening to the mounting desperation of our combined breathing.

Needing to see him, to reassure myself that this was all real, I drew myself up again, taking him deeper. But I had wanted him too much, for too long; the sight of the barely restrained power in his muscles, the determined set of his jaw and the intense look in his eyes was devastating. Finally losing control, a scream tore out of my throat with the unexpected violence of my release and Jamie lifted me up off the table, burying the seed of his own climax deep inside me. After weeks of tension our bodies shuddered, wracked with unleashed pleasure and flooded with sensation, while Jamie held me tight.

Resting my forehead against his, I smiled and he smiled back at me breathlessly. Right there, in that moment, naked in Jamie's arms, under a blanket of emerging stars, I felt liberated, weightless and carefree – as if I was exactly where I was meant to be.

'I'm taking you to bed now,' he said.

We gathered up our clothes and I laughed, hugging him tighter, as he lifted me up again and carried me away with him, back to his home.

Chapter Forty-six

The nagging sense that something wasn't right pulled me out of a deeply satisfying slumber. As my eyes registered the empty space where Kat should be my ears picked up the thrumming hum of a car engine somewhere outside. Stumbling out of bed in the early morning light, I slipped on my specs and pushed the curtains aside in time to see Kat emerge from the front porch below, a bag in hand, her footsteps crunching on the gravel. With a plunging sense of inevitability I watched as she climbed into the back of the waiting minicab and shut the door, without a backward glance. Quietly the car turned, indicated and moved away down the road and out of sight. And I just stood there, immobile as a statue, numbly staring after it.

Everything was fine when we went to sleep the night before, more than fine – fantastic. Kat had finally opened up to me; told me everything; literally laid herself bare. The sight of Kat's scars, the physical proof of the pain she'd endured, had ripped me apart inside. But the way she'd revealed them to me, the way she bore them on her body with such dignity, only made her that much more compelling and beautiful in my eyes. We'd had the most incredible sex; the emotional connection we'd shared, when she held me deep inside her, was stronger, deeper and more powerful than anything I'd ever known – I couldn't get enough of her. Before falling asleep I'd taken her all over again. I could still taste her, still smell her on my skin ... and now she was gone.

In the bathroom I took a shower, purging the residue of sex from my body and mind while trying to ignore the dearth of feminine toiletries. On autopilot I put in my lenses, dressed in my usual uniform of cargo pants and a polo shirt and shoved my wallet, keys and phone in to my pockets. Downstairs, as I filled the kettle, I noticed a yellow post-it note on the table which simply read: 'I'm sorry, I can't stay'. Snatching it up I crushed it in my fist before dropping it in the bin and making a cup of coffee.

Unable to keep still, I took the hot drink with me as I unlocked the front gates, opened the doors and started up the tills. A large kitchen knife was lying on the counter. I recognised it as being the carving knife from the chef's set at home – its presence in the garden centre was bizarre. Kat must have borrowed it for something the day before but what? And why use a kitchen knife when there were so many other garden tools she could have used? Stowing the knife safely in a drawer beneath the counter I stubbornly pushed all thoughts of Kat from my mind.

Making a sweep of the shop floor and the plant area, I straightened packets, signs, tools, plants and pots. I said hello to various members of the team as they filtered in, yawning, grumbling, and depositing their belongings in the staff room but I didn't stay to chat. Instead I went into my office and shut the door. I drew the blind against the glare of the sun. I sat down at my desk. I switched on my computer. I clicked on the sales figures spreadsheet. I stared at the screen...

There was a knock at the door and I was surprised to see Liam standing there, a hand shoved in his pocket. 'You all right mate?'

'What are you doing here?'

'I was just checking everything was all right.'

'Why?'

'Why? Because it's half ten at night, the place is deserted and you haven't locked up yet.'

'What?' Glancing around I blinked my gritty eyes as I registered for the first time that the room was completely dark but for the cool glow of the computer screen before me.

'The front gates are wide open – anyone could just walk in.'

'Fuck, I didn't realise,' I muttered.

Apparently Jenny and Priya had cashed up the tills without me and left the takings just inside my office, though I had no recollection of seeing them do it. Liam accompanied me as I went around closing up and then followed me back to the cottage where I pinched out my contact lenses, poured him some juice and grabbed a beer for myself. The cool liquid was a welcome relief to my dry throat and without thinking I drained the bottle in one. When had I last drunk something? Setting the empty down I reopened the fridge and cracked open a second beer.

'You wanna tell me what's going on?' Liam said.

'Nothing's going on.'

'Come on mate, you look like shit. Where's Kat?'

Her name made me wince with physical pain and I

took a pull on my new drink before replying. 'She left.'

'Left?'

'Yes, she got in a cab and left.'

'Why?'

'I don't know.'

'Well, didn't you go after her to find out?'

'No.'

'Why not?'

Liam's question was an obvious one but caught me entirely off guard. His expression was as nonchalant as ever, matching his calm tone, but I read the frustration in his eyes. Setting down my drink I sat heavily at the kitchen table, my head in my hands. 'I don't know.'

Liam pulled out a chair and seated himself opposite. I glanced up at him and he looked at me impassively.

'She had good reasons for going,' I said.

'I'm sure she did; Kat's a smart woman,' he said, 'but don't you want to know what those reasons are?'

I gulped down more beer. Did I want to know? I'd always known Kat would leave me – and she had. Since then I'd felt nothing; a whole working day had slipped by with relative ease because I'd refused to let myself think about her. Ignorance was working for me, even if it was not bliss. I was afraid to ask questions, afraid to acknowledge the indescribable pain and grief that lurked inside me like a monster in the dark; I wasn't sure I would survive it.

'Are you really just going to let her go?' Liam prompted.

His remark confused me and I shrugged. 'It's not up to me – she left.'

'Isn't Kat worth fighting for?'

I swallowed back a tight knot of emotion. 'She's everything.'

'Then what the hell are you doing just sitting here? She's not dead!' Liam's blunt words made me flinch but somewhere inside me they sparked a small flame of hope. 'Go find her and work it out.'

'I don't know where she's gone.'

Liam considered for a moment. 'You said she got a cab; was it one you recognised?'

'What?'

'The car – was it a local taxi firm?'

'Probably. I programmed Ken's number into her phone so it might have been him.'

'Great. I'll call him now and ask him.' Standing up, Liam pulled out his mobile and started making the call.

Unease unfurled inside my gut, spreading out until it felt heavy in my limbs. Could I do this? Go after her? Convince her to come back? Was there any point? She was bound to leave me eventually anyway – women always did – and she was strong enough to survive without me. Wouldn't it be better to cut my losses now? My mind reeled in agony. This was Kat – the only woman who'd ever really known me. My entire body hurt at the thought of life without her. I needed her to feel alive, to feel real, to feel whole. Liam was right, Kat was worth fighting for – I had nothing else to lose.

'Right, she hasn't gone far,' Liam said, hanging up. 'Ken thinks she's staying at the Rose and Crown in town. She was looking for somewhere to stay – that's where he recommended and that's where he dropped her off.'

'Right,' I muttered.

'Come on, I'm driving you there now,' he said firmly.

Liam insisted on stopping off at the petrol station so that I could pick up something to eat and then dropped me in Wildham town square. He offered to wait for me, in case Kat wasn't in the pub, but I told him to go home to bed. I was a grown man after all and should be able to look after myself, despite recent evidence to the contrary.

The interior of the Rose and Crown was just as I remembered it: the same row of booths down one side, same pictures on the wall, same sticky carpet – even the old guy hunched over a pint in the corner looked vaguely familiar.

'Hello, James!' Wendy greeted me with surprise from behind the bar – she looked older and her hair was a different colour but otherwise she seemed much the same. 'Haven't seen you in here for a while; how are you?'

'Good thanks, Wendy, you?'

'Same as ever – y'know; can't complain. I was sorry to hear about your dad. You've taken over the garden centre I hear?'

'Yes, that's right; haven't managed to run it into the ground so far but there's still time.'

Wendy laughed. 'Ah, speaking of time, you've missed last orders I'm afraid. I was just about to close up.'

'That's OK; I've actually come to see a friend who's staying here. Kat: tall, slim, long brown hair –'

Wendy was nodding. 'I know who you mean. If I'd known she was a friend of yours I mighta given her a discount. She expecting you?'

'Yeah, I'm just running late that's all.'

Wendy tipped her chin in the direction of the stairs. 'You'd better go on up.'

'Thanks. Hey,' I said, turning back to her, 'which room was it again?'

Wendy narrowed her eyes at me while she debated whether I was likely to be trouble and I held my breath; I'd certainly caused her plenty of bother in the past. 'Four,' she said at last with a clear warning tone in her voice.

'Great, thanks Wendy.' Quickly I ducked through the door and up the stairs before she could change her mind.

Chapter Forty-seven

A soft knock at the door made me jump.

'Kat? It's me.'

Despite being muffled, his low soothing voice rumbled right through me. Frozen in indecision I stared at the narrow strip of light beneath the door where it was interrupted by Jamie's shadow.

He'd found me. I wasn't sure if he would or if I'd wanted him to. When I'd left I'd been absolutely set on never seeing him again. It felt good at first – running away – as if I was taking control, leaving my rising sense of panic behind and moving on, just like when I was a kid. But I wasn't a kid any more and I hadn't got very far. I should have spent the day on the move, taken a train or a coach, clocked up the miles between us – but running away from Jamie was so much harder than I'd expected. It hurt so much that the pain was physical, debilitating, unbearable.

'Kat? Please, I just want to talk.'

Shifting my gaze back out of the window I tried to refocus on Wildham town square, now devoid of people and lit by tangerine street lamps, competing with the moonlight. From my place on the bed I'd been quietly observing the outside world – idly watching people go about their lives while I failed to decide what to do with mine.

I had finally told Jamie everything – confessed my ugly past: secrets, scars, the lot – and he hadn't kicked me out in disgust; on the contrary he had made sweet love to me. But it was overwhelming, too much. I was in too deep, too vulnerable – in love with a man I could never have. My feelings for Jamie scared me more than Vic ever had.

So I had run.

But I was starting to understand that I didn't want to be anywhere that Jamie wasn't. Even if he was never truly mine, he was the only home I'd ever known.

He knocked again. 'Please, Kat, I'm not leaving. I'll just stay here all night if I have to.'

Uncurling I stretched out my stiff limbs, my skin sore from lying rigidly still, in all my clothes, for too long. Barefoot I stepped through the shadows to the door. But when I got there, I paused, one hand on the latch, trembling with anticipation.

'Please,' he uttered once more, his voice barely more than a whisper, and I opened the door.

Just the sight of him almost knocked me over; I had missed him so much. Clenching my fists to stop myself from touching him, I turned on my heel and went straight back to sit in the patch of light on the bed. After a few seconds' hesitation he followed me inside and closed the door. I kept my eyes trained on the view out of the window but even in my peripheral vision his large body, his raw physical presence, filled the room and made my blood sing. He took a step closer towards me.

'Don't. Don't touch me, please.'

'OK, I won't.'

Holding his hands up he stopped. He had a plastic carrier bag dangling from one wrist and I wondered what it might contain. Had he brought the rest of my things? Was he here to say goodbye?

He glanced around the small room and then down at the floor. 'I'll just sit here,' he said, leaning back against the fitted wardrobe and sliding down until he was seated on the carpet, his legs bent in front of him, his feet just touching the base of the bed. With a sigh he rested his arms on his knees, removed his glasses and rubbed his eyes. I registered that he was effectively blocking my route to the door but I realised I didn't mind. I wasn't going to run again. I had no idea what I *was* going to do but it wasn't that.

'I can't do this. Us,' I said, looking down at my hands in my lap. 'I don't know how; it's not me; it's too much, I can't –' I was choking on my words and gasping for air.

'Just breathe, Kat,' Jamie said gently. 'Just take some deep, slow breaths.' I nodded and concentrated on my breathing and the panic slowly subsided again.

'I'm sorry,' I muttered, finally meeting his naked gaze.

'Don't be.'

'I thought it was time I moved on. That's what I do when things get difficult – I move on.' His deep, warm eyes steadily held mine but I could see pain there.

'And yet you stayed with Vic,' he said evenly. '*Vic* – of all people. You stayed with him but you can't stay with me?'

'It was easier to stay with Vic than to live on the street but I never cared about Vic, not the way I care about you. Being with you is too much, Jamie; it's all too much.'

'In what way? Tell me and we can –'

'No! Why? I mean, I'm really grateful for everything you've done for me – you've no idea how much – but maybe you should just focus on someone else now.'

He frowned, looked away and then down at his hands, apparently deep in thought. I hated seeing Jamie look so unhappy, hated that I was hurting him, but I had to try to put some distance between us for the sake of my own sanity – for both our sakes. For several minutes Jamie stayed quiet, as if considering what I'd said, and I started to worry that he might just agree with me. As the silence and the sound of my fear became unbearable, he started to talk.

'When we first met all those years ago, I was completely alone. I was small and weak; I was too afraid to speak half the time – I would never have survived foster care if it wasn't for you.' He returned his gaze to mine. 'You were there for me when I needed you and I want to be there for you in return. I don't want to focus on anyone else. Stay and let me look after you, please.'

'But that was years ago – you were just a kid and I was happy to look out for you. Really, you don't owe me anything.'

'No, I know that – but it's not just that.' Scowling, he rubbed his face with his hands. 'Shit, how can I expect you to understand when I'm so crap at explaining? I don't know why it's so hard for me to just say what I mean.' Jamie's eyes darkened. 'Last night, last night was so – it's like right now, Kat; don't you feel this thing between us? I'm sitting here just inches away from you and it's like some kind of agony not being able to reach out and touch you.' His words resonated with my feelings, making my chest tighten painfully and he held out his right hand, palm up towards me. 'Tell me you don't feel it, Kat?'

Closing my eyes against the naked hunger in his

expression I silently fought the urge to seize his hand and press it to every part of my body. 'I do feel it, of course I do, but that's just –' The very tip of Jamie's finger touched mine making me gasp but I kept my eyes tight shut and tried to concentrate on what I was saying. 'I can't keep sleeping with you, Jamie. I'm sorry, I –' Jamie slowly shifted closer in the semi-darkness, his large warm hand lightly caressing mine and circling my bare wrist. 'It's not as if I can be your girlfriend or anything.' His hand inched slowly up my bare forearm, his thumb skating softly back and forth across my skin and making my insides melt with longing. 'I mean, I'm still married and I know it's just sex, but –' His hand reached my elbow and edged on upwards, 'It confuses things; it confuses *me* and – when this doesn't work out – when it all ends' His grip tightened around my upper arm, 'I don't want to destroy our friendship.' Breathing hard, I opened my eyes.

Jamie was on his knees beside me; his head level with mine; one side of his face bathed in light from the window. 'You're far more important to me than any girlfriend, Kat.' I thought he might be about to kiss me and I desperately wanted him to. He leaned in, his breath smelled of peppermint and I closed my eyes, my heart racing, and my lips parting… But then the back of my neck prickled as Jamie put his mouth to my ear and, for the first time in twenty-three years, whispered in my ear. 'I love you, Kitkat.'

Goosebumps spread out across my skin and my breath caught in my throat at the sense of déjà vu and the sheer weight of his confession. Pulling back, he looked at me, his eyes burning with sincerity.

'It's hard to say it out loud, because it scares the hell out of me, but it's the truth and I need you to know.'

Struggling to believe him I stared at Jamie and swallowed hard. 'No – why?'

'You're everything to me, why wouldn't I?' he said, throwing my own words back at me.

'Well, for so many reasons; what about –'

'Will you just believe me, Kat?' he cut me off, exasperated. 'Please, I mean it and I need you to believe me.'

'I love you too,' I said.

He blinked. 'You don't have to say that. I'm not asking for –'

'But I do,' I interrupted. 'So much.'

'Really?' he murmured doubtfully.

I nodded, shaking all over and rendered speechless by the huge knot of emotion in my throat. Taking my face in his hands he kissed me at last – his lips warm, soft and steady against mine and I sobbed against his mouth, overwhelmed.

Releasing me, Jamie sat down on the bed beside me and took my hand in his. 'Listen, I don't want you to worry, Kat – nothing has to change between us. There's no pressure. This relationship is just between you and me – it can be anything we want it to be. If you need more time, more space, just say so. We can go back to how we were before if you want, take it slowly, one day at a time.'

Could he really love me the way I loved him? Could this beautiful man really be mine? The notion seemed too far-fetched to be true. He was waiting for me to speak.

'OK,' I said, staring into his eyes, afraid to blink in case I was dreaming.

Lifting my hand to his lips he kissed it, his stubble tickling my skin. 'Good. Now, have you eaten?' The question was unexpected but I was grateful for the subject change.

'No.'

'Are you hungry?' he asked with a tentative smile.

'I don't know. I suppose I must be.'

Bending down he scooped up the bag he'd brought with him. 'We stopped at the petrol station on the way here and I picked up a few things, just in case you needed feeding.'

'We?'

'Liam gave me a lift. It was him who tracked you down, actually.'

I cringed. 'He must think I'm such high maintenance.'

Jamie smiled and shook his head. 'Not at all – he made me realise I'd be mad not to come after you.'

'Oh god, his ex ran away and left him didn't she? I hope he doesn't think all women are this flaky and undependable.'

Jamie laughed. 'You are neither of those things, Kat, but, anyway, Liam's more of an optimist than a cynic.'

'Did he ever find out what happened to her?'

'It's still a bit of a mystery. We know she's living somewhere in London; she called him about a month ago to say she was OK, but other than that – I think Liam's moved on. He's landed a great job restoring the grounds of a grand old country estate.'

'Oh yes, he told me – it sounds intriguing.'

Jamie nodded, tipping the contents of the bag onto the bed cover between us.

Somehow, in his own easy-going way, Jamie had successfully managed to lighten the atmosphere between us. I couldn't help smiling as he showed me the random and unhealthy assortment of goodies he'd bought: cheese pasties, various packets of crisps, two cans of coke, a box of jam doughnuts, a bag of chocolate-covered raisins, a KitKat and a pack of mint-flavoured gum. 'Sorry it's a bit of an odd selection. I was in a hurry but there's enough for a bedroom picnic.'

I raised my eyebrows at him.

'What? Don't tell me you've never had a bedroom picnic before?'

'I don't think so,' I said, bemused.

'Midnight feast?'

'Once, when you were little, you ate Hula Hoops in my bed; you threaded them all on to your fingers and then crunched them one by one – got salt and crumbs everywhere. Does that count?' Jamie gazed at me his eyes bright with emotion and nodded slowly.

He loves me! The astonishing concept leapt into my mind with fresh intensity making me bite my lip. Could it really be true? Could we really make this work between us? Jamie picked up the KitKat from the bed and held it out to me. He watched as I eased the paper wrapper off sideways, set the foil-covered biscuit aside, took his hand and slid the band of paper over his fingers.

'My hand's too big now,' he murmured, his voice low.

'It doesn't matter – you're still mine.' The words were out of my mouth before I realised what I was saying.

319

Jamie's head snapped up, his eyes glowing and his Adam's apple rising and falling as he swallowed. 'Yes, I'm yours,' he said gruffly.

Stretching up I pressed my lips to his and he closed his eyes and sighed into my mouth. I could taste his simmering desire as tangibly as my own but again he held it in check, curtailing our kiss before I could deepen it. I sensed he was trying to keep things casual, put my mind at ease and I loved him all the more for it. 'Let's eat.'

Kicking off his shoes, Jamie picked up the remote and switched on the TV while I peeled back the covers. We climbed into the bed fully clothed to eat our picnic feast. Jamie ate one handed, with one arm wrapped protectively around my shoulders and I snuggled into his side as we watched an old Western in weary, but comfortable, silence. Gradually my eyelids grew heavier, lulled into closing by the steady rhythm of Jamie's breathing, his reassuring scent, and his strong fingers as they gently combed my hair. Every now and then he paused to plant a tender kiss on my head and, as I began to drift away, an incredulous voice in my head repeated over and over: 'Jamie loves me?'

Chapter Forty-eight

Waking to find Kat in my arms I felt the greatest rush of relief I'd ever experienced. She'd said she loved me and I desperately wanted to believe her but I'd still half-expected her to vanish in the night. Pins and needles tingled in one arm and I felt hot and stuffy from spending a night in my clothes pressed up against Kat's body, my nose buried in her hair, but it was all worth it. I'd never been in love before, the thought alone was utterly terrifying, but now that I'd told her, now that she'd said she felt the same, I was determined to make it work. I would do anything. Anything.

'I love you, Kat,' I whispered in her ear.

She stirred, making a soft sighing noise as she stretched out her limbs, her denim-clad bottom pushing up against my trapped morning wood. Shifting away I suppressed a groan of desire. I wanted nothing more than to be buried deep inside her but I had to be sure everything was OK first – make sure she hadn't changed her mind about us. I couldn't risk scaring her away.

Turning her head she smiled at me shyly, her cheeks flushed pink with uncertainty, completely un-Kat-like. 'What time is it?'

Raising my arm I glanced at my watch. '8 a.m.'

'Wow, really? We never lie in that late.'

I shrugged, brushing a strand of hair back from her face and hooking it behind her ear. 'It's Sunday and Frank will open up if we're not back in time.'

She was watching my face intently and then a wide smile forced its way out across her lips, lighting her eyes, and she turned away hiding her face in her pillow.

'What?' She shook her head. 'Tell me what you're thinking,' I pressed, encouraged by the fleeting look of joy I'd witnessed. Still shaking her head, she laughed and it was such a young, happy sound. 'I love you, Kat,' I repeated in her ear, the words becoming easier to say with each confession.

'I love you too,' she admitted without turning. Her muffled voice was music to my ears.

'Is everything OK?'

'Yep.'

'You sure?'

'Yep.'

'OK, good. Shall I leave you to get washed and dressed?'

At last she turned to face me, pinning me with her soft grey-green gaze. 'Actually,' she said hesitantly, 'I was going to take a shower and I, I wondered if you would join me?'

Her simple invitation made me happy out of all proportion. 'It would be my pleasure, Kat.'

We undressed in the modest en-suite bathroom before stepping into the shower cubicle together, a strange, shy sort of tension between us. I offered to wash Kat's hair for her and she stood with her back to me, her arms self-consciously wrapped around her own waist, but as I stood behind her lathering shampoo into her glorious long hair she relaxed against me with a sigh, her warm slippery body igniting my blood. I murmured an apology for my blatant arousal – it was impossible to hide in the confined space – but she didn't seem to mind. Once I'd rinsed the suds away I began massaging conditioner into her scalp and she moaned, making my balls ache.

'That good huh?' I said.

'You have no idea.'

'Up to salon standard?'

'I've never been to a salon.'

I faltered at this new nugget of information, so minor but so deeply affecting, before continuing my ministrations. I wanted Kat to feel cherished.

She shrugged. 'I just trim the ends of my hair myself when it gets too long. You remember how Mrs Plumley would make us take turns sitting on a chair in the middle of the kitchen while she went at us with the scissors?'

'No?'

'Yeah, she literally put a mixing bowl over your head once and cut round it! I was terrified she would slip and take your ear off.'

I laughed. 'I'm sure Mrs Plumley knew she'd have you to answer to if she did.' Angling the shower head I rinsed her silky tresses clean again.

Kat tipped her face up, her eyes closed. 'Yeah, she knew all right.'

With a cloth I gently soaped every inch of Kat's lovely lean body, fighting hard not to react as her skin flushed, her nipples puckered and her breathing quickened beneath my fingers. Once she was clean she quietly and methodically washed me in return, her eyes dark and thoughtful. I trembled with the strain of my own need for her, under her touch and her powerfully heated gaze, but I was determined not to make a move unless she asked me to.

At last I switched off the water and wrapped Kat up in a large towel before securing a smaller one around my waist. She remained mute and, as I carefully rub-dried her hair, I was conscious that I had lived thirty years without ever caring for another human being in this ordinary but, for me, intensely intimate way.

Taking her by the hand, I led Kat back into the bedroom. 'So, what do you want to wear?' I said.

Without replying she reached up and kissed me, her soft lips infusing me with intense gratitude and relief, whether it was hers or mine I couldn't be sure. Consumed with hunger I deepened the kiss, relishing her unique taste and aroma and pulling her body close into mine.

But seeing Kat walk away from me had shaken me more than I wanted to admit and, while I understood that it was the feelings between us that frightened her, rather than me personally, I couldn't risk giving her any excuse to leave me again. With great effort I dragged my mouth away from hers, took a step backwards and sat down on the bed. She needed time and space and I absolutely would not rush her for my own selfish reasons. 'Sorry,' I muttered.

Kat moved closer, cautiously, calmly taking control, loosening the towel at my waist and spreading it open to reveal the erection that mocked me. Without a word she hitched her own towel up to her waist and climbed onto my lap, straddling me. In such close proximity the delicate fragrance of her skin was intoxicating. Locking her big beautiful eyes on mine, she sank down, painstakingly, deliciously, slowly, drawing me deep inside her. We groaned in unison, luxuriating in the phenomenal sensation of our bodies combined. Being here inside Kat, being connected to her in the most profound and carnal of ways, I'd never felt so safe, so sound, so complete – it almost made me cry. As I rolled my hips she moaned.

'Oh, Jamie.'

The way she said my name gave me goosebumps. A small smile played across her face as she eased herself slowly up on her knees and then down again onto my length, clenching her muscles and delighting in the sheer pleasure she was conducting.

As she rode me I gripped the bed tightly with my fists: to refrain from ripping her towel away, to prevent myself from touching her, to stop myself from coming at once. I watched, hypnotised, marvelling again at her inner strength and beauty, as she tentatively experimented, adjusting the angle of her hips, the pressure, and the pace. I reminded myself that Kat had experienced little control in her life or over her life – indeed hardly any control over anything at all – and it felt good to be giving her some of that power back. As her muscles tightened, her rhythm increased and she raced to claim her orgasm, a tell-tale pink flush creeping up her neck to her face, while I fought harder to hold back my own.

When I could take no more, I grabbed her hips and confessed. 'Ah, Kat, I need you so much.'

'You're mine,' she said. We detonated together and I came hard and deep inside her, biting out her name.

Chapter Forty-nine

I hummed cheerfully to myself as I watered the herbaceous perennials, starting at the acanthus and working my way through the neat rows of pots towards the zantedeschias. There were no customers nearby to be disturbed by my singing and I was enjoying the steady routine of the task. Ever since Jamie had brought me back from the Rose and Crown just over a fortnight ago, I felt different – lighter somehow, as if I hadn't been breathing properly before and now it was easier. Last night he had made gentle love to me, late into the night, and I'd drifted to sleep in his arms in a pure state of what I can only describe as bliss. The knowledge that Jamie loved me seemed to change, brighten, everything. I still had bad days – mornings when I woke from nightmares with Vic's voice in my ear and my skin crawling with cold dread. On those days I depended on Jamie's patient reassurance and all my courage in order to leave the house. But Southwood's, with its green places, relaxed pace, and kind faces was a wonderful antidote to anxiety and was starting to feel like home – a comforting, if alien, concept.

I wasn't naive – I was aware that this precious new life could be snatched from me at any moment but right now I refused to give that fear any power over me – I was sick of the old, frightened me. This new person, hopelessly in love and loved in return, was far, far better company.

In an effort to strengthen my wrist, I swapped the water gun into my left hand, clumsily spraying myself with icy cold water in the process. It was late August and the temperature was edging up to a predicted high of 30°C so the shock of the cold was a welcome one but it still made me gasp. A muffled laugh caught my attention and I turned to find the five builders who were working on the coffee shop extension sat watching me from the shade of the fence.

'Cold is it?' one of the men asked, eliciting a snigger from his colleague.

The guy who'd spoken – I couldn't recall his name – was about my age with short, curly hair and sparkly blue eyes. It was clear what he was referring to from the way all five men were trying not to look at my chest and I rolled my eyes. 'Shouldn't you be working?'

'Tea break,' blue-eyes said, grinning and holding up his mug in illustration.

I'd chatted to the builders several times over the last few weeks – mainly because I was excited about the new coffee shop and liked hearing about their progress. Several of my cafe regulars had been construction workers, of one sort or another, so I was familiar with the cheeky, occasionally lewd, banter common among them. These guys were nice enough, ranging in age from eighteen up to forty-something and blue-eyes was a good friend of Liam's, which helped put me at ease. They generally worked hard, putting in long hours while the weather was fine and on the odd rainy day I had taken over a pot of hot, freshly brewed coffee and a packet of biscuits to keep their spirits up. Now that the roof was on, the glazing was in and the extension was watertight, rain was no longer an issue. Today they had all stripped off their shirts and, though they still wore fluorescent hi-vis safety vests, the tanned, bulging muscles of their arms were on display, all streaked with sweat, dust and grime. 'How's it all going?' I said.

'Getting there. First fix was completed last week and this one,' blue-eyes elbowed his co-worker, 'is busy wiring-in all the kitchen equipment.'

'You haven't electrocuted yourself yet then?' I said to the electrician.

'Not yet,' he said, hiding his smile behind a cup of tea.

'We should be able to start on the tiling soon,' blue-eyes added, reclaiming my attention, 'but we're still waiting for the big freezer cabinet to arrive.'

'So that you can take turns lying inside it, I suppose,' I said, wiping my forearm across my sweaty brow.

The men laughed. 'Yeah, it's all right for you,' blue-eyes said, 'swanning about out here in the fresh air, dousing things with water, but it's bloody boiling in there.'

'I'll douse you then, shall I?' Swinging the hose around, I aimed the gun and sprayed water at their feet. All five men yelped and leapt up, several of them spilling tea and laughing as they made for the other side of the fence. But blue-eyes stood his ground, chuckling, and I raised the water gun, aiming at his chest and narrowing my eyes in warning.

'Kat? Everything OK?' The perfect rumble of Jamie's voice almost made me shiver with pleasure as he strolled towards me.

Lowering the hose I turned towards him, like a plant leaning towards the sun. 'Yes, boss, everything's fine.

The builders have just been filling me in on their progress.'

Jamie glanced over at blue-eyes with an eyebrow raised in question and the builder nodded in confirmation. 'All going smoothly.'

'Great,' Jamie said, turning back to me. 'Kat, can I talk to you?'

'Yes, sure.' In my peripheral vision I registered the builder sidling back to the building site. 'What is it?'

'Shall we go back to the office?'

Immediately I worried that something was wrong, even though Jamie looked perfectly relaxed. 'OK,' I said, reaching to turn the water off at the tap.

We didn't attempt conversation as we made our way through the garden centre, though I could swear static crackled in the space between us. The shop was busy with customers and cluttered with trolleys and the recycling bins by the door were full to overflowing. Jamie stopped to clear some space and empty the bins, while I re-lined them with fresh plastic sacks. One of the escaped items Jamie retrieved from the ground was an empty vodka bottle and I shivered reflexively as I recognised Vic's favourite brand. Would he ever get out of my head? Would there ever come a day when I could look at bulldog tattoos, denim jackets and Embassy cigarette packets without automatically feeling nauseated? My stomach turned as I wondered if the police had ever identified the brand of cigarette which had started the potting-shed fire. I would have to try and find out somehow without worrying Jamie.

Before we could leave the shop floor Jamie was

330

intercepted by various customers and members of staff requiring his attention. Curbing my impatience, I lifted plants out of customer trolleys, making it easier for the till staff to scan the labels, while admiring Jamie in action. He politely dealt with each query with gentle proficiency, as if he was in no hurry and had been running the business for ever.

At last we entered his office and Jamie abruptly grabbed hold of me, kissing me and pinning me to the back of the door. His kiss was as welcome and intoxicating as ever, suffusing me with desire, but there was a desperate edge to it that had me concerned. With some regret I pushed him away from me so that I could speak.

'What is it? What's wrong?'

'It's nothing, not really. It's just – it's hard to explain.'

'Try.'

He took a deep breath, while I held mine. 'You make me feel amazing; stronger; braver; like I could do anything at all and yet there are these moments when I look at you and I feel the exact opposite – as helpless and needy as a child – terrified that I might lose you.'

'Oh, Jamie,' I whispered.

'In those moments the need to be with you; inside you; to feel you wrapped around me, is so intense that I can hardly breathe. Seeing you with those men –'

'The builders? We were just messing about.'

'I know, god, I know,' he said squeezing his eyes shut and resting his forehead against mine.

'You were jealous?'

He groaned. 'I know it's stupid.'

'I think I understand.'

He opened his eyes and I willingly lost myself in their deep, warm, brown depths. 'I hate how other women look at you sometimes; soaking up your smiles, lapping up your words and drinking in the sound of your voice, as if they have a right to those things. I know it's irrational but that's how I feel. And sometimes I want to tear my own eyes out, I want you so badly.'

He drew back. 'Please don't.'

'I'll try not to.'

He was silent for a moment. 'Is that just how it is then, between you and me?'

'I think it's going to take time to really trust in what we have – in love – to really believe in it and let our fears fade.'

'Time.'

'Yes.'

He took another deep breath and let it out slowly. 'OK.'

I planted a kiss on him. 'So, are you going to let me get back to work, boss?'

'It sounds so disrespectful when you call me boss,' he muttered against my lips.

'I don't know what you mean,' I said.

'Yes you do. If there's ever a staff revolt, I'll know who started it.'

I laughed and he released me, giving me a final kiss before opening the door.

Chapter Fifty

As Liam moved to take up his place in the scrum his gaze met mine. Breathing hard through his mouthguard and smeared in mud, he looked as knackered as I felt but his eyes were full of the satisfaction we both shared. September had arrived, kicking off rugby season and the promise of matches galore. Which was just as well since the heady days of summer seemed at an end, following two days of almost continuous rainfall. Today the wet weather was holding off but we were a man short because Lester had injured his leg and was unable to play. Despite this, with just three minutes of play remaining, and barring a catastrophe, we were going to win the match. It was only a friendly game against the neighbouring town, to raise money for a local charity, but it was my first match since joining the team back in June and it made for a great start to the season ahead.

As the referee said 'crouch', I took up my position, my boots firmly planted but leg muscles primed to take flight. I kept my eyes forward but I was aware of the people around me, like Adam over to my right bouncing on the balls of his feet in anticipation. Beyond him on the sidelines, Kat – a force of nature in her own right – had her arms raised, head high and hair streaming as she cheered us on. Throughout the match, much to everybody's amusement, she'd clapped, shouted and led the home crowd in singing various chants that she'd found on the Internet. But her unrestrained excitement was infectious – spurring my friends and me on to victory and ramping up the entertainment level for the spectators, regardless of which side they were on. Her enthusiastic support had surprised me at first and yet it was pure Kat – my wild Kat – always fighting my corner with unconditional spirit. Most of my life I'd walked around – half-man, half-zombie – with an emptiness inside me, a hollow space in my chest where love should be. For years I'd masked it with confidence and smiles, relying on other people's pleasure to shore up my own and feeling like a fraud. But now, with Kat in my heart, I felt human, whole, a complete person at last. My love burned fiercely through my veins more potent than adrenalin. I'd never experienced happiness like it.

But the match wasn't over yet. As the ref called 'bind' I took a deep, calming breath, returning my head to the game and eyeing my opposite number. With the word 'set' the two packs locked together with a grunt and Will, our scrum half, fed in the ball. Before long our forwards had pushed the other pack back and taken possession of the ball. As it was passed swiftly towards me I darted into position, my peripheral vision trained on the inbound tide of opposition, but as the ball slipped neatly into my waiting hands I was tackled to the ground and the end whistle was blown. We'd done it; we'd won the match – eighteen points to fifteen. Elated I shrugged out of the opposition's grasp, staggered to my feet and kicked the ball high into the sky above the pitch, while Adam punched the air and the crowd erupted in applause. My teammates and I grinned tiredly at each other while the losing side stood hands on hips, breathing hard, but gracious in their defeat. As if drawn by magnetic force I turned just in time to catch Kat as she propelled herself up into my arms.

'Kat, I'm all muddy!'

'I like you muddy,' she growled. I laughed, staggering slightly as she kissed me, her long legs wrapped tight around my waist, her beautiful butt cradled in my hands in place of the ball.

'Get a room you two,' Liam said, slapping me on the back while someone else wolf whistled.

'Easy, Kat,' I mumbled against her mouth. As she relaxed her legs with a sigh I set her back on her feet. She now had mud streaked across her skirt but she didn't seem to care.

'I'm so proud of you,' she breathed. I wiped a tear from her cheek with my thumb and kissed her again, unable to resist the sweet taste of her lips.

'It was just for fun,' I said.

'Yeah, I know, but when you scored that try I felt like I was right there with you – my heart nearly exploded out of my chest; you were so fast. I've never seen anything so sexy.' I laughed but her enthusiasm pleased me more than I would admit.

'I'm glad you enjoyed yourself.'

'I did, thank you.' Around us the pitch was emptying as players dispersed and headed for the changing rooms. 'You'd better go get showered and changed,' she said, taking a step back.

'In a minute,' I said, placing my hands on her hips to prevent her escape. She frowned slightly in question but then her eyes dropped down to the obvious swell of my

335

shorts before returning to mine with a knowing smirk. 'You're a menace, Kat.'

She laughed. 'You sure you're not just *really* happy to have won?'

'I don't like rugby *that* much. This is all your fault and now you're going to have to shield me from all the innocent men, women and children over there until I've calmed down.' She laughed again, stepping closer. 'Don't, Kat,' I warned, raising my chin so that she couldn't kiss me again.

'I want you so bad,' she said, huskily.

'Kat! I'm serious, cut it out or we're never gonna get out of here.'

Chapter Fifty-one

While the other players drifted back towards the changing rooms I helped Jamie collect up the red plastic cones marking the side of the pitch. But the sight of him in his shorts, combined with the scent of mud, sweat and cut grass, did nothing to subdue the steady ache of desire inside me. By the time Jamie had spoken to several friends and fans and we'd finally reached the clubhouse the other team had gone and the Warriors were leaving for the pub.

'I'll be as quick as I can,' he said, pecking me on the lips before ducking into the changing room out of sight. I stood with my back to the wall by the door, light-headed with thoughts of my nearby naked male. Two more players departed with nods goodbye and I bit my lip. Was that the last of them? Was Jamie alone now? Quietly I pushed open the door and poked my head inside. A masculine aroma of sweat and body wash, suspended in clouds of steam, billowed around me and I could hear a shower running in a cubicle at the back of the room. Scanning the benches that lined the walls I was reassured to discover only one gym bag with one set of clothes hanging from the peg above. Recognising them as Jamie's I boldly moved into the room, letting the door swing shut behind me. I was lifting his shirt to my nose and deeply inhaling my favourite scent when the water was abruptly turned off and bare footsteps rounded the corner. Suddenly unsure, I held my breath but released it again when Jamie appeared naked and dripping before me.

'Oh Jesus,' he muttered, his step faltering, his eyes

scanning the room to establish that we were alone. In two strides he'd closed in on me, pulling me into the firm, wet heat of his body with a groan. We kissed hard, as if our desire for each other had been pent up for days rather than hours. His hands moved up my skirt, dragging my knickers down over my knee-high boots, while I wrenched my shirt off over my head and unhooked my bra. 'Do you have any idea how beautiful you are, Kat? How much you mean to me?' he muttered, lifting me off my feet and effortlessly carrying me into the shower cubicle.

Wearing only a pair of boots I leaned back against the wall and he sank to his knees, kissing me between my legs. I moaned, dragging my fingers through his wet hair and gripping his broad shoulders for support. Here I was, a 'tramp off the street', with a handsome young god-of-a-man knelt before me, pleasuring my most private parts, in a place reserved for strong naked men. The idea of all that testosterone, combined with Jamie's reverent attention, made me feel like a goddess.

Drawing back, Jamie looked up to meet my gaze, his eyes darkly dilated with desire as he continued to stroke me with his fingers.

'I think I fell in love with you the first time I saw you in that cafe,' he said, his voice even but low and heavy with need. 'No, before that – the first time we met – the moment my parents abandoned me, Kat, I became yours.' Tears of emotion sprang to my eyes even as he stoked up the fire inside me, my muscles tightening, my fingers digging into his back. 'I'd do anything for you, Kat. *Anything.*' And with that I took off, my body splintering with release, my nerve endings jangling and my mind adrift.

As I returned to earth Jamie rose to his feet, pressing soft kisses up my neck to my ear and spreading goosebumps across my flushed skin. I hooked one booted leg up over his hip and he leaned his strong body into me. Taking a firm grip on my bottom he lifted me up off the ground, high enough that I could see right over the stall and across the empty changing room. Throwing my other leg around his waist, I locked my ankles together across his firm butt as he braced my back against the wall. Holding me still he looked into my eyes, into my soul, in the way that only he could – as if he really knew me, as if he'd always known me and always would. 'You are safe with me,' he said.

'Yes,' I breathed.

I clung to him as he made love to me, his hips thrusting, his eyes squeezed shut in concentration, and my core tensing in anticipation. And then the door to the changing room opened across the room.

'Oh, fuck,' I gasped as Liam's gaze met mine.

Jamie, oblivious to his best mate's presence, continued to drive us on, pounding out a perfect rhythm inside me. In the doorway, Liam raised an eyebrow with a wry grin and then held up a bunch of keys for me to see before placing them on a bench. Biting my lip, I desperately held back a second orgasm as Liam stepped backwards through the door. As it swung closed he winked at me before disappearing out of sight and I exploded, my release ripping through my body, as Jamie came with a yell of exultant relief.

* * *

Once we'd recovered and made ourselves decent, Jamie
locked up the rugby club and we walked over to the White
Bear. Jamie made no particular reference to the club keys,
when he returned them to his friend. And Liam, despite
my apprehension, behaved like a true gentleman,
betraying no hint of what he'd witnessed. The sun had
returned and we spent the rest of the evening in the pub
garden, surrounded by friends and enjoying the last of the
light. I sat comfortably on Jamie's lap to leave space for
other people to sit down while we drank, chatted and
laughed about the game. With Jamie's arms around me
and my new friend Maire to talk to, I felt supremely
blessed.

I even spent some time getting to know Poppy, the
redhead I'd seen flirting with Jamie. She turned out to be
Adam's younger sister and initiated a friendly
conversation with no hint of jealous rivalry. While Jamie
was away at the bar she told me she was glad we were
together because I obviously made him happy. I was
immensely grateful to her for her kindness, and slightly in
awe of her as she described how she'd set up her own
events planning business. Some of what she said got me
thinking about Southwood's Garden Centre and its
potential for holding more workshops but also book clubs,
painting classes, family fun days, barbecues – the
possibilities were almost endless.

As the sun set and the air cooled, Jamie wrapped me in
his jumper and we walked home together hand-in-hand.
Every few feet we stopped to kiss and smile and stare into

each other's eyes like lovesick teenagers, illuminated now and then by the occasional passing car. For once in my life I felt happy, confident, secure – and by seeing myself through Jamie's loving eyes I was even starting to like myself.

Back at the cottage I set about making coffee while Jamie checked the answerphone for messages. The first was from a neighbour, a friend of Jamie's dad, offering him free firewood if he would be prepared to go round and chop up the logs himself. As the kettle started to boil I moved into the living room to better hear the second message as it started to play. Jamie stood by the window, sifting through the pile of post in his hand, as a distantly familiar voice filled the room,

'Ah hello there, I'm sorry it's taken me so long to return your call. We've been out of the country you see – staying with family in Australia – and we've only just got back. It's Josie Plumley by the way.' Jamie's head snapped up, his eyes locking with mine in shared surprise, and as the kettle grew louder I stepped closer to the answering machine, anxious not to miss a word. 'Anyway I'm pleased you got in touch; I do remember you – and Kat, of course. I'm not sure I'll be much use to your search but I'd like to help if I can. I always thought you two might be blood relations; y'know brother and sister – the signs were all there – so I'd like to help you find Kat if I can.' Jamie's face paled, the post in his hand dropping to the carpet as he stared at me. 'Anyway, call me back, God bless.' The message ended with a prolonged beep, the roar of the boiling water merging with a high-pitched ringing in my head. And then the kettle clicked off and a profound

341

silence set in as Jamie and I stared at each other, dumbstruck, across the seemingly endless room.

Chapter Fifty-two

My limbs locked with incomprehension as Kat sank gracefully onto the settee behind her, her face white, her eyes glazed with shock.

'No,' I said, my voice hoarse. 'She's got it wrong; she's misunderstood. She must be quite old now – she must be thinking of someone else, not us.'

Kat didn't reply and the silence stretched out, heavy with potential pain.

I cleared my throat. 'This is ridiculous – it's a mistake. I'll call her back and sort it out,' I said, reaching for the phone and pressing the handset to my ear.

'No,' Kat said, her voice eerily calm, 'it's gone midnight.'

'So what? I'm not having this hang over us all night.'

'But what if it's true?'

The dialling tone buzzed impatiently in my ear as fear crawled through my mind. We don't even look alike, Kat and me; we have different-coloured eyes. Admittedly we don't look *vastly* different from each other but – 'It can't be true.' Exhausted I hung up the phone and collapsed into an armchair, a voice in my head screaming in horror. How could this be happening? We were so happy; it felt so right. We can't just go back. I need her. It has to be a mistake.

'What signs?' Kat muttered, a frown creasing her forehead.

'What?'

343

'She said, "the signs were all there" – what signs?'

I shook my head. 'I don't know, Kat, she's wrong.'

'What's your blood type?'

'What?'

'Your blood type – what is it?'

'A positive.'

Kat looked like she might throw up.

'That doesn't mean anything, Kat; it's one of the most common blood types there is!'

'Is that why we're so close? Is that why we feel such a connection?' Delayed panic was rising in her voice. 'Because we're –' Kat abruptly bolted from the room and projectile vomited into the kitchen sink, her whole body shaking. Following I reached out to gather her hair in my hands but she cringed away from me. 'Don't,' she spat.

I recoiled as if burned and a fresh sense of terror swept through me. 'Don't do this, Kat; it's not true, it's all a mistake – don't pull away from me, not again.'

She rinsed her mouth and splashed water on her face before hiding it in a tea towel. 'Didn't I warn you?'

'What?'

She looked up at me her eyes flashing with fury. 'I knew this could never work between us; that we could be together – I just knew it would end badly. You should have let me go! You should have let me leave!' Tears spilled from her eyes betraying her pain as I shook my head and automatically reached out to wrap her in my arms. But she stepped away, swiping angrily at her tears.

'We'll find a way, Kat. We'll work this out – even if it's true. I'm not giving you up, not now.'

'It might not be up to you,' she said.

'Don't just assume the worst, please; this will all be sorted out in the morning.'

We went up to bed and Kat insisted on sleeping alone in the spare room. All night I lay awake in agony, my mind reeling at a hundred different questions and possibilities, my ears pricked for any sign that Kat was trying to leave. When she emerged at dawn I was relieved to see her but upset by the dark shadows around her eyes and the bone-chilling resignation in her expression. We sipped coffee across the table from one another, in silence, while the clock on the wall ticked away the hours.

'It's eight o'clock; I can't wait any longer; I'm calling her,' I said, setting down my empty mug.

'What are you going to say?'

'I'm going to tell her I've found you and ask her if we can go and see her.' Kat's knuckles were white as she gripped her own empty cup. 'I won't ask her anything else, or tell her anything, until we are both there with her in person, OK?'

'OK.'

Mrs Plumley finally answered the phone the third time I rang her number. She was out of breath and irritated. Having apologised for the early hour, and exchanged pleasantries, I arranged for us to meet her later that afternoon on the London estate where she and her husband now lived. I felt physically sick as I hung up afterwards, the taste of coffee unusually bitter in my mouth. Kat was already out the door, clearly determined to work in the garden centre all morning as if it was a normal day – as if our life together didn't hang precariously in the balance.

Chapter Fifty-three

Mr and Mrs Plumley lived on the fourth floor of an ugly block of flats. The lift was out of order and the concrete stairwell we climbed reeked of skunk and piss. As I followed Jamie up the steps, prickling with cold sweat, I tried to focus on deciphering the multicoloured tags graffitied across the walls. Every now and then Jamie tried to take my hand out of habit but I wouldn't let him. I desperately wanted to feel his skin against mine, to allow the soothing warmth of his love to spread up through my arm, ignite my blood and arouse my soul. But I couldn't do it – I didn't want to acknowledge the intoxicating chemistry between us if it was about to be ripped away for good.

The last time I'd seen the Plumleys was when I was twelve years old and they were evicting me. I still remembered Josie Plumley standing with her arms crossed and her back to me as my case worker led me away. The prospect of seeing her again, a ghost from my past, would be unsettling enough without the weight of the bombshell she now held over us.

Since hearing that crackly recorded message everything had changed. All our recent happiness and everything I'd pinned my hopes on was tainted. Our love for one another, the time we'd spent together, the things we'd said and done to each other – it was all mired in shame, suspicion and, as yet untold, pain. When I was a child I used to wish with all my heart that Jamie was my brother, that he was my blood relative, my family, so that I wouldn't be alone. The phrase 'be careful what you wish for' now taunted my every step.

Josie Plumley opened the door before we'd even knocked, a sure sign she'd been watching our approach through the peephole. She'd always been a large lady, tall and muscular with wide hips and an ample, cardigan-swathed bosom, her sleeves stuffed full of tissues, her pockets loaded with lemon drops and fluff. Now she looked older and saggier, her shoulders rounder and her hair grey, but familiar – right down to the balled tissue in her hand and the sickly sweet lemon scent of her breath.

'Come in, come in,' she said, ushering us into the stuffy confines of a small sitting room decked out in lurid shades of pink and green. 'My, aren't you both tall! Sit down, sit down; Alan's out at the moment so there's plenty of room. What would you like to drink? Coffee? Tea? Fruit Juice? Pop?'

'Coffee would be lovely, thank you.' Jamie said, sounding his usual relaxed self as we lowered ourselves onto a tartan couch. He turned to me. 'Kat? Coffee?'

Josie was smiling expectantly as she waited for my answer and I nodded my head, not trusting myself to speak. 'Lovely! Two coffees coming up.' Blowing her nose she bustled into a tiny kitchenette and started to clatter about.

'You OK?' Jamie said, gently.

I nodded again but my skin was crawling under the blank stare of hundreds of pairs of eyes. An army of twee porcelain figurines filled almost every available surface, the little bodies crowded together on shelves and inside cabinets as if jostling to get a better look at me. One wall of the room was covered in framed portrait photographs of all shapes and sizes, a gallery of faces grinning down at us from above a seventies-style gas fire. There were no house plants or flowers in the room, not even artificial ones, and I wondered if that was something I would have noticed a year ago.

Mrs Plumley brought out five bourbon biscuits, neatly spaced on a plate, and set them on the glass table in front of us before returning with two cups of instant coffee and a mug of tea for herself. She spent some time nestling her bottom into an armchair with a sigh of satisfaction before smiling and blowing noisily on her tea.

'Are these all photographs of your family?' Jamie asked politely.

'Yes, more or less. My three are all grown up now. I think they were still teenagers when you came to us but they have kids themselves now. I have fourteen grandchildren would you believe! Terrors the lot of them!' She grinned, revealing pink lipstick smeared on her teeth. 'My eldest lives in Oz, hence our big trip out to visit them, and the rest are foster kids and their families; you know, the ones who kept in touch anyway.'

'That's amazing – quite a legacy,' Jamie said and Mrs Plumley flushed with pleasure.

'And what about you two? Have you got families of your own?' I took a large gulp of flavourless coffee and it burned its way down my throat, while Jamie shifted in his seat.

'Not yet, no,' he said. 'But maybe one day, y'know.' He shrugged and smiled.

348

'You're young; you've got time.' Her smile faltered almost imperceptibly as she shifted her gaze to mine and then back to Jamie again. 'So you two are doing all right for yourselves? And you clearly managed to track each other down, so, is this just a social call or is there a reason for your visit?'

Jamie cleared his throat and I stared hard at a patch of swirly carpet, swallowing back the bile trying to escape from my stomach. 'Well, first of all I think we'd both like to thank you,' he began. 'Kat and I have good memories of our stay with you and we're grateful to you for looking after us – we appreciate it can't have been easy.'

'Not at all, not at all,' she flapped, turning pink and dabbing at her nose again. 'You were good kids for the most part – especially you Jamie. It was a pleasure, really.' I clenched my teeth.

'The thing is,' Jamie said, his hand trembling slightly as he set his cup down, half empty. 'You said in your message that you thought that we, that Kat and I, might be blood relations –'

'Oh that!' she interrupted with enthusiasm, making me jump. 'Yes of course; I'd almost forgotten – have you looked into it? Was I right?' She leaned forwards in her seat.

'Well, I, we – what made you think that?' Jamie stammered.

'Oh your circumstances, of course. You were both abandoned at about the same age, around two years old if I remember correctly? Which is unusual you know, not unheard of, but unusual – most babies are abandoned as newborns before the mother has a chance to get too attached.' She reached for a biscuit. 'And you were both found in the same place – in that old community hall on Bridge Street. It's long gone now but you were both found there, in a box in the porch, just a few years apart.' Josie shrugged as she took a large bite and started crunching. 'Stands to reason that you might have been left there by the same person, come from the same place; maybe even shared a mother or father,' she mumbled with her mouth full. Absently she brushed crumbs from her bosom and swallowed. 'And then of course you took to each other immediately, struck up a friendship, became inseparable – are you all right dear?' she said, squinting at me.

I could taste blood where I'd bitten my cheek. I nodded and tried to smile, aware of Jamie's concerned eyes on my face but unable to meet his gaze. An awkward silence permeated the room while Mrs Plumley waited for us to offer some sort of verbal response. But we didn't.

'So, that's exciting isn't it?' she said. 'Are you going to get DNA tests done?'

'Um, maybe. I guess we'll have to think about it,' Jamie said. He stood up. 'Thank you again, Mrs Plumley.'

'Call me Josie, please.' Flustered, she scrambled to her feet. 'You're not going already?'

'Yes, sorry, we need to get going,' he said glancing down at me. My body felt like lead but I managed to stiffly push myself up into a standing position. 'It was lovely to see you again,' Jamie added, as we all moved towards the door.

I was barely aware of anything as we left. Mrs Plumley

may have given Jamie a hug and patted me awkwardly on the back but I wasn't able to reciprocate in any way. I was too busy dying inside.

Chapter Fifty-four

Once we'd left the city and the motorway behind I drove with the windows down, despite the autumnal chill in the air, my eyes on the road and Josie Plumley's words careering around in my head. It was strange seeing her again; her familiar mannerisms triggered all sorts of memories I'd long since forgotten or worked hard to forget. But I wasn't about to let them get to me – it was just the past. It was Kat's prolonged silence in the seat beside me that was really eating me alive.

On impulse I slowed down and turned into a side road. It was more of a farm track than a road and narrow, straggly tendrils of honeysuckle and wild clematis reached out from the hedgerows and caressed the car as I slowed to a halt. I expected Kat to ask me why I'd stopped but she didn't. I switched off the engine and the roar was replaced with the lazy hum of insects buzzing and a plane passing far overhead.

'Talk to me, Kat.'

She held her back straight, her body rigid, her eyes staring ahead down the lane. 'What do you want me to say?'

'That nothing's changed between us – that nothing has to change.'

'You want me to lie to you.' Her statement caused physical pain in my chest.

'No, Kat, don't you see? We can forget about this; leave it right here; forget we spoke to Josie; forget her half-baked theory – we can just carry on as we were.'

She was shaking her head. 'You don't really believe that.'

'I do, Kat.' I took her hand; she tried to pull away at first but I held on tight, lacing my fingers between hers, and she relented, her shoulders sagging, her arm going limp. Pressing the back of her hand to my mouth I savoured her warmth against my lips, her addictive scent, the taste of her skin.

She closed her eyes. 'How the fuck did we let this happen?'

'We weren't to know.'

'*I* should've known,' she said, her voice hard. 'I should've read the signs, just like she did. I wanted you to be my brother so badly back then. Why didn't she say anything? How could she keep something like that to herself?'

'She probably didn't want to get our hopes up – it would have been difficult to prove back then.'

'But if she'd just *said* something – why didn't I know?'

'Don't do this. Don't blame yourself; don't start regretting what we have.'

She sighed heavily and looked down at her lap. 'We need to get a DNA test.'

'No.'

'Yes.'

'No. Don't you understand, Kat, I can't lose you. I can't take that risk; I don't want a sibling, I want this – I want what we have.'

'But it's wrong,' she said, turning to me at last, her

eyes flashing. 'Could you really fuck me knowing I might be your sister?'

The force of her words caught me like a slap in the face. She wrenched her hand back as if I was hurting her, unclipped her seatbelt and climbed out, slamming the door behind her.

Deep down I knew she was right. I wouldn't be able to forget, not completely. Doubt would forever eat away at us, undermining our relationship and ruining what we had. But I still didn't want to accept it.

Her arms tightly folded, she leaned against the bonnet with her back to me. 'We need to know, Jamie, one way or the other.'

Dread brewed in my chest. 'And if we *are* related? What do we do then?'

She shrugged. 'I don't know.'

Climbing out I stalked around the car until I was stood right in front of her, looming over her, needing to be near her. But she wouldn't look at me. Her eyes rested on my chest, her gaze staring right through me.

'I can't just change how I feel about you, Kat. I love you; I'm *in* love with you; I can't be around you all the time and not –' My frustration morphed into irritation as she continued to avoid my gaze. 'Are you even going to try and fight this? You're going to leave me again aren't you?' I accused. 'You're just going to run away, like you always do.'

'No. I don't know. I have no idea,' she said, tears slipping down her cheeks.

'God, I'm sorry,' I whispered, wrapping my arms around her. 'I'm just so angry – this whole thing is so unfair.' She pressed her face into my chest, hot tears soaking through my shirt.

For several minutes we stood in that quiet leafy lane, in the middle of nowhere, away from everything and safe in each other's arms. I wished that time would stop altogether, that we could stay like that for ever, but there was no escaping my own thoughts. Our foster mother's speculations, the so-called 'signs' of our kinship, though flimsy, were nevertheless convincing. Not least because the connection, the bond, Kat and I shared felt so strong – completely unlike anything else. And now there was a simple explanation for it; one I didn't want. But at the same time I was equally convinced it couldn't be true. I couldn't possibly be so aroused by Kat if she was my sister, right? I mean that would just make me sick in the head.

Kat pulled away from me and, as she wiped her eyes, something caught her attention. Bending down she carefully collected up a dandelion clock in her hand – the delicate, spherical seed head perfectly intact.

'Do you remember making wishes on these as a child?' she said.

'Yes.'

She looked at me, her eyes rimmed pink from her tears. 'What did you use to wish for?'

I swallowed, almost choking on the bitter irony. Briefly I considering lying but I couldn't, not to her. 'I used to wish for us to be adopted together so that we could be brother and sister.'

She nodded sadly, quietly considering the spent flower as she slowly turned it in her fingers. At last she closed her eyes, made a wish and blew. The seeds dispersed on the air and Kat dropped the bare stem to the ground before climbing back in the car without another word.

Two days later I sat in my office staring at a small cardboard box on my desk. I had done my research, read up on DNA testing, found a reputable company and ordered a home testing kit. And here it was – a simple, discreet, brown box – no slogan, no branding, no return address: just sitting there like it was nothing.

Kat knew I'd ordered it, despite the fact we'd barely spoken in the past forty-eight hours. We'd worked long hours, kept ourselves busy and spent the nights lying awake in separate bedrooms. It was killing me. I missed the intimacy that we'd shared; that I'd begun to depend on. The exquisite landscape of her body had become more familiar to me than my own and I craved her like a drug. I was an addict and I was in withdrawal – it took all my strength to keep myself from falling apart completely.

But Kat was adamant that we do the test; she was fully expecting it to arrive any day now: today or tomorrow. It *could* have arrived tomorrow – the postal service was unreliable sometimes. Picking it up I opened a drawer, slipped the box inside and closed it again. Tomorrow then. I knew I was only delaying the inevitable but I just couldn't lose her, not yet; I needed more time.

Soon after seven o'clock I returned to the cottage through the back door, just as Kat was removing a vegetarian moussaka from the oven. It smelled divine. As I sat down to take off my boots I saw the DNA test kit, open on the

356

table before me, and froze. Kat said nothing as she collected two plates from the draining board and began serving up our meal.

Removing my boots I placed them neatly by the back door and returned to my seat, clearing my throat. 'I meant to tell you the kit had arrived.'

Kat raised an eyebrow at me as she set our dinner down and seated herself across from me. 'I already knew it had arrived; it was me who put it on your desk.'

'Oh, right.'

'When you didn't mention it to me at lunchtime I went back to your office to retrieve it.'

'Sorry,' I said, feeling foolish.

She shrugged. 'It's OK. I've done my swab but we can do yours after dinner.'

'Tonight?'

'Yes. It's very easy; you just follow the instructions.'

Sighing, I picked up my fork and shovelled food into my mouth, resigned. In my heart I knew that Kat loved me, the same way I did her, but she was much better at hiding it. I'd lost my appetite; I could hardly taste anything, barely swallow, at the painful thought of losing her.

'I'd like to get the samples back in the post tonight; it will be at least another week before we get the results.'

'I know, I know,' I mumbled with my mouth full. 'I'll do it tonight.'

She made no reply and we endured the rest of our meal without speaking. I felt like shit.

Chapter Fifty-five

With a sharp pair of secateurs I hacked back the prickly brown foliage of the Papaver orientale in my hand and then knocked it from its pot with my fist to inspect the roots. Jamie had had a job lot of five hundred, tatty, end-of-season perennials delivered to the nursery. He'd purchased them at a bargain price since they were unsellable in their current condition: withered, pot-bound and half-starved of nutrients. But with a little care and attention – re-potting, watering, feeding and over-wintering – most could be salvaged ready for re-sale in the spring. I was grateful for the task; Mondays were always quiet in the garden centre and now that the extension was finished and the builders had gone it was even quieter than usual. The coffee shop was still awaiting furniture and a few other finishing touches and would require the necessary food hygiene inspections and certificates before we could start serving the public. The plan was to have a grand opening in October but I'd lost all enthusiasm for the project in the past week. At least this re-potting was keeping me occupied, if not happy.

Would I ever feel happy again? My soul weighed heavy with exhaustion and my limbs ached with grief, as if mourning the loss of Jamie's touch. The long nights were the worst: alone in bed too restless to sleep, my thoughts chasing round in circles and a knot of tense frustration throbbing relentlessly between my legs. And when I did slip into unconsciousness, peace still eluded me. My thwarted desire saturated my dreams, conjuring up Jamie's mouth on my body, his lips soft and teasing, his tongue, firm and insistent. Sleep had become dangerous. I had never felt so wired and confused, so close to losing my mind.

From where I sat at a workbench I had a clear view across the fields and up the hill to the tree line where Jamie and Liam where replacing a section of boundary fence. The leaves on the trees had turned glorious shades of gold, fiery red, and sunset orange and the men looked focused as they toiled – working in partnership and taking turns with a pickaxe and a heavy post rammer. Jamie had predicted that the earth up there would be dry, stony, and riddled with roots, and from where I was sitting I could tell that progress was tough going. As the September sun had climbed higher in the sky, behind me both men had stripped off their T-shirts, casually tucking them into the back pockets of their jeans like labourers on a building site. Even from afar I could see their tanned muscles flexing, rippling and shining with sweat. They made for a fine sight and, despite my attempts to stop looking, my eyes were repeatedly drawn in that direction.

Finding myself staring at Jamie once again I transferred my attention to Liam. He wasn't as classically good-looking as Jamie and lacked boyish charm but his rugged features and burly physique conveyed a straightforward masculinity that appealed, despite the stern expression he wore by default. It occurred to me that I might have been attracted to Liam under different circumstances, if I'd never known the all-consuming intensity of loving Jamie – if I'd never discovered who we were together. But I had and now there would never be anyone else for me. Not even if Jamie turned out to be my brother.

In two more days we would learn the truth, and everything would change, for better or worse. I had done my best to mentally prepare for the worst, strived to make some sort of decision about what I was going to do, but it was proving impossible. We couldn't continue a sexual relationship if we were related; even if no one else knew we were siblings *we* would know and it would be horribly wrong. So either I ran away, cut myself off completely, and accepted a hollow existence without Jamie or I stuck around and struggled to love him chastely, as a sibling. I'd been attempting the latter, unsuccessfully, for days. I tried visualising myself living separately in town and only seeing Jamie occasionally but I could only envisage a protracted, miserable existence of longing and regret. Would the intensity of my feelings ease with time and distance? It was hard to believe.

Jamie glanced over and caught me looking at him and we both turned away. I had run out of slow-release fertiliser so picking up the empty tub I made my way behind the polytunnels to the chemical store. As I yanked open the door to the metal storage container the astringent chemical odour tickled my nostrils, the cold air escaping and making me shiver. To allow my eyes to adjust to the gloomy interior I paused before stepping inside the narrow galley-shaped space and scanning the shelves. Past the rows of pest and weed control solutions I was advancing on the fertiliser when someone stepped out of the shadows behind me, blocking the light from the door.

'Rina, babe.' I froze. The stale stench of cigarettes swamped all other smells and a familiar sense of despair spread through my veins like liquid nitrogen. 'You're my wife. Did you really think I wouldn't find you?'

'No.' As I said it I realised it was true.

He laughed, making me flinch, my shoulders hunching around my ears to block the sound, my body automatically cowering in well-practised defeat. 'No, I didn't think so – you're stupid but not that fucking stupid.' Grabbing my shoulder he yanked me round to face him.

Vic looked different: the denim jacket that he always wore had been replaced by an old army shirt, which didn't quite hide the ugly bulldog tattoo at his neck. His hair was dyed black and slick with grease, accentuating his sallow skin, and his eyeballs were threaded with red lines as they darted about my face. He looked twitchy and desperate.

'Been hiding out here, on and off, for weeks – keeping an eye on you – watching you make a fool of yerself. Torched that shed just to see the look on your face,' he added with a grin. Been working on a way to get us out of the country but maybe I should just kill you,' he sneered, raising a large knife in front of my face. It looked just like one of Jamie's kitchen knives.

'Go on then.'

His eyes flashed dangerously. 'Don't fucking tempt me. Just shut your mouth. I've got enough fucking problems without your lip. The Russians are after me – know anything about that do you?'

361

I shook my head.

'Well I ain't leaving you behind to cause trouble and spend all my money – either you come with me now or I gut you like a fucking pig right here.'

I could tell by the look in his eyes that it was not an idle threat.

'C'mon we're going.' Stepping around me he positioned the blade at my side and shoved me towards the door.

'Where?'

With his free hand Vic smacked my head so hard that it rebounded off the edge of a metal shelf, knocking several things to the floor and temporarily dazing me. 'What did I just say?' he snarled. 'Keep your fucking trap shut! You'll go wherever the fuck I tell you.'

Stumbling out into the light I instinctively raised my fingertips to my head, checking for blood as the pain unfurled. With jabs of the knife he goaded me along the path behind the polytunnels, towards the back exit, out of sight of the garden centre and the fields beyond.

'You really wanna stay in this shithole?' he sneered. 'I bet it ain't the job you wanna stay for; fancy yerself as lady of the fucking manor, I bet. Maybe I should slice up that pretty boy of yours, make you watch while I cut his balls off.'

No! To protect Jamie I ground my teeth together hard, determined not to say anything to provoke Vic further. Putting one foot in front of the other I kept walking, internally wrestling with the fear and shame Vic had instilled in me over the years. He had always been a poor excuse for a husband.

'This ain't your place, Rina – you'll never belong here.'

With sudden clarity I realised Vic was wrong. I did belong here; my place was with Jamie. Regardless of whether he was my brother or not, Jamie and I belonged together. We always had. Who was Vic Leech to dictate my life? And why was I letting him? Didn't I owe it to Jamie to stand up for myself and fight for the life I wanted? Didn't I owe it to myself?

With an impulsive surge of defiance that I'd not felt since my teens, I rounded on Vic, thrusting my knee firmly up into his groin and shoving him aside. At full pelt I ran back towards the open space of the nursery, towards the life I wanted, towards Jamie. As I cleared the end of the polytunnels the colourful expanse of hillside and trees sprang back into view. My eyes immediately pinpointed Jamie in the distance, swinging a pickaxe at the ground, and then flicked across to Liam, who was pulling his shirt back on and strolling down the hill towards me. I opened my mouth to shout but before I could make a sound I was thrown to the floor.

Vic's body weight pinned me to the ground with brutal force, crushing the air from my lungs. Unable to move or breathe, my face and hands stung as they pressed into the rubble path I'd painstakingly weeded, not two days before. In fighting for a breath I coughed and a sharp pain lanced through my torso, almost blinding me with its intensity.

'You stupid, ungrateful, fucking bitch,' Vic spat in my ear. 'I gave you everything – *everything!*' Wrenching my head up by my hair, he brought his knife up to my throat.

363

The blade was hot and sticky with blood. My blood?

In the distance Liam swam back into my vision and as he shouted something I couldn't hear, Jamie's head snapped up. My Jamie. His gaze zeroed in on me in an instant and he dropped the pickaxe as he launched into a run.

Vic's rant continued to rage in my ear but I was no longer listening. I knew he was going to kill me; I'd always known it; I was surprised it had taken him this long. But part of me no longer cared. I could only stare, mesmerised, as Jamie ran. I'd seen him sprint before and it was beautiful, the way his body moved with such power, agility and focus. And he was fast, so very fast; he'd already reached the fence that separated the fields halfway down the hill. He jumped the gate without slowing, swinging his long legs out to one side, high up and over like a gymnast, every taut muscle in his chest defined by sunshine and shadows, his gaze still fixed on mine. Even at this distance he looked determined, heroic, sexy. He was so quick that he was already gaining on Liam, who was also powering towards me. But they were still a long way off and, as Vic pressed the edge of the blade into my throat, I knew that they would not be fast enough.

Chapter Fifty-six

Liam's sudden shout startled me, making my neck prickle as I looked up. The sight of Kat – sprawled on the ground of the nursery with a man hunkered down over her, had my heart lurching out of my chest. Dropping the pickaxe, I was moving before I'd even decided to; my body propelled into a sprint by pure instinct. It must be Vic – that sadistic bastard was alive but not for much longer; I was going to kill him.

I kept my eyes trained on Kat as I ran, my mind a panic of questions I couldn't answer and fears I couldn't bear to contemplate. Was that a weapon in his hand? Was that blood? I was vaguely aware of people staring up at me from the garden centre, open-mouthed in surprise, but they were of no consequence. I had to get to Kat – that was all that mattered.

Halfway down the hill was a gate but I braced my hands on the top and vaulted over it without stopping. I'd promised I'd protect her; I'd *promised*. Willing myself to move faster, to fly, my heart rate hammered through my body like a runaway train. Don't do it, Vic, you bastard – don't you dare!

Suddenly another man stepped out from the burnt-out remains of the potting shed. He looked familiar; I recognised him as one of our regular customers – the Eastern European guy who never spent very much. But he had his arm raised towards Vic. Was that a gun? A loud crack rang out, Vic's whole body jerked sideways away from Kat and her head dropped to the floor as if she was dead. *No! No! No!*

Liam was unlatching the side access gate into the nursery and wrenching it open. I flew past him and re-established sight of Kat again in time to see the gunman kick Vic's limp body over on to its back, snap a picture on his mobile phone and stride away.

At last I skidded on to my knees beside Kat, shouting her name and lifting her face. Her eyes were closed, her skin streaked with blood and dirt. A large bloody knife lay beneath her neck and she had a cut there but thankfully it didn't look deep. I recognised the knife – it was the same one that had mysteriously shown up in the shop by the tills six weeks ago. Had Vic been here then? I shoved the blade away in disgust.

'Kat? Oh God, Kat, speak to me, please?' Her eyes fluttered and I almost sobbed at the small sign of life. 'Where are you hurt, Kat?' My eyes roamed blindly over her body before fixing on her lower back where her T-shirt was ripped open and soaked in a dark, spreading pool of blood. 'Fuck!' Yanking my own T-shirt out of my back pocket, I balled it up and pressed it to the wound to stem the flow. She cried out in agony and my stomach heaved in response. 'I'm sorry; I have to stop the blood.'

I was aware of Liam on his phone breathlessly requesting an ambulance and directing other members of staff somewhere behind me but I could only focus on Kat. Returning one trembling, bloodstained hand to her face, I stroked her hair back behind her ear.

'Kat? Can you hear me? Can you open your eyes?' Her eyelids flickered again.

'I've got this,' Liam said, crouching down on the other side of Kat's body and applying pressure over my wadded shirt. With both my hands free I gently cradled Kat's head, shifting my face down, nearer to hers.

'I love you, Kat, you hear me? Everything's going to be all right.'

Her mouth opened and I leaned in closer. 'You're so fast,' she whispered, 'thank you. I'm so glad I can say goodbye.'

'No, Kat! Not goodbye, you're all right! You're going to be OK. Don't leave me, Kat. I can't be alone again. Open your eyes, Kat, look at me!'

Her eyes struggled open, her pupils tiny points in her deathly pale face, but she met my gaze with determination, her voice steadying. 'You won't be alone – so many people love you, all your friends, even customers–'

'It's not the same, Kat. You are my foundation. You're my place in this world – without you I've got nothing. Stay with me, Kat, please.' Her eyes closed again, a frown creasing her brow.

'The ambulance is here,' Liam muttered, his voice almost drowned out by the approaching sirens.

'You hear that Kat? Help is coming; you're going to be OK. Kat? Look at me please.' But she didn't move her eyes again, her face had gone slack, her breathing shallow – she lay lifeless in my hands.

Various law enforcers – some of them armed police officers – spread out across the nursery rounding up witnesses and working to clear the area as they searched for the gunman. But I ignored them all.

'She only has one kidney,' I heard myself say, as the paramedics elbowed me out of the way and took over. Liam helped me back up on to my feet and I stood, swaying, my legs weak, staring impotently, choked with desolation, as Kat was carried away from me.

Chapter Fifty-seven

I woke sore, woozy and hooked up to machines, the hospital sounds and smells depressingly familiar as I struggled to open my eyes. I couldn't recall why I was in this time but I didn't care because for once I wasn't alone. Jamie Southwood was holding my hand. Nothing else mattered. He looked older and more haggard than I'd ever seen him but his eyes were warm and bright with emotion as they searched my face.

'Kat, you're awake; I should get someone,' he said, rising to his feet.

I couldn't speak but I concentrated my meagre energy into squeezing his hand and he sank back into his seat, his gaze never wavering. I just wanted to look at him, to enjoy the feel of his hand in mine – who knew how long this precious moment would last. Even as the thought drifted through my mind I could feel the darkness closing in again, reclaiming me, pulling me under and dragging my heavy eyelids closed.

'Keep fighting, Kat, please. Come back to me,' he said, as I floated away.

Some time later I came to again still halfway between sleep and consciousness. It took me a while to register that I could hear voices, male voices, and even longer to realise that one of them belonged to Jamie. I was reluctant to rouse myself – I felt numb, weightless, as if my head was disconnected from my body – and the low familiar rumble of Jamie's tone was more soothing than any lullaby. But once I'd identified his voice I tried to listen.

'You said that the operation went well but she's still not waking up?'

'It did go well; we managed to stop the bleeding and repair the puncture wound to her kidney but it has gone into shock. So far it hasn't recovered enough to function properly so the longer she rests the better.'

'What if her kidney doesn't recover?'

'We need to give it a few more days first; we'll keep a close eye on her —'

'But if her kidney fails? What then?'

'With regular dialysis a person can manage without kidneys but it's obviously not ideal. In that instance we would look to find a suitable replacement on the donor register.'

'And what are the odds of finding a match?'

'It may not come to that —'

'But if it does could she have mine? Can she have my kidney?'

'Mr Southwood I appreciate that you want to help Katerina, and of course we can get you tested, but the chances that you will be a compatible blood and tissue match are —'

'She might be my sister.'

'I'm sorry, I, I thought —'

'It's a long story. We were both adopted — or rather I was adopted and she wasn't — but someone recently suggested that we might be related. We were waiting for the DNA test results when this happened.'

'Oh. Right. I see.'

'So can you test me for donation? How long will it take?'

The doctor sighed. 'Even if you are blood relations it doesn't necessarily mean you'll –'

'I know but I want you to test me – I want to be the one to help her, if I can.'

'Very well we can start the ball rolling but, if you really want to help her, you should go home and get some rest –'

'I'm not leaving. I'll rest here but I'm not leaving.'

I'd forgotten that Jamie and I might be siblings. The memory was a bitter one and made me reluctant to remember anything more. I assumed it was Vic who'd put me in the hospital – it usually was – but I had no desire to recall the specifics. Of more immediate concern was Jamie's reckless offer to donate his organs! Was he crazy? Didn't he know the risks that surgery carried with it? Why hadn't the doctor pointed them out? But the more my worry and frustration grew, the less equipped I felt to do anything about it. My energy was leaking away again, my thoughts separating and floating off in different directions like dandelion seeds dispersing on the wind. Was that the heady of scent of roses I could smell? Had someone brought me flowers? With Jamie's voice no longer anchoring me in the room, I sank back into a welcome unconsciousness once more.

Chapter Fifty-eight

Kat let out a soft sigh and I lifted my head from the bed, searching her beautiful face for signs, silently willing her to wake. If she would only look at me, like she had before, I could live again. Every time I closed my eyes I saw her lying on the ground like a rag doll, limp and bloodied, or in the ambulance strapped to a gurney – her heart had stopped beating, her lips had turned blue and I'd thought she was dead; or being rushed straight into the operating theatre where the doors had swung closed behind her, shutting me out. I'd been sure I'd never see her again and that I would never forgive myself.

After all it was me that had let this happen. I'd dropped my guard; let that fucker find her. Had Vic deliberately stabbed her in the kidney or was it blind luck on his part? Not that it mattered. He was still a murderous bastard. He would have slit her throat too if he hadn't had his brains blown out. I almost wished he was still alive so that I could kill him with my own bare hands – at least then I'd be doing something useful rather than just sitting here in limbo, waiting, endlessly, anxiously – desperate for Kat to look at me.

She was fundamental to my existence – the only woman I would ever love. I needed to know that she would forgive me for not protecting her, for not being there when she needed me. I needed to know that, despite everything, she would come back to me.

Kat's eyes shifted behind her lids, her lashes fluttering against the smooth planes of her cheeks and filling me with hope. In my hand her fingers twitched and flexed and I squeezed them gently.

'Come back to me, Kat.' She went still as if she'd heard me and I held my breath. And then, just like that, she opened her eyes and pinned me with her soft green gaze.

'No,' she croaked.

'No?'

She frowned, closed her eyes, moistened her dry lips with the tip of her tongue and tried again. 'I don't want your kidney.'

I laughed, taking her argumentative tone as a good sign, and delirious with relief. 'You don't want my kidney? I'm offended.'

She scowled and she was so beautiful I wanted to cry.

'You don't need it, Kat; you're going to be OK; your own kidney is recovering – you're going to be OK,' I repeated, reassuring myself as much as her. The creases on her forehead smoothed out and she closed her eyes again. 'Wait, Kat, don't go back to sleep; let me call someone.'

I stood back while a male nurse checked Kat's vitals in a way that was familiar to me from TV shows, stopping to jot down notes on her chart as he went along. Kat refrained from wincing or crying out as he inspected the bandage on her back, but I could tell from the tension in her face that she was in severe pain. Thankfully the nurse noticed too and, without my having to mention it, he administered more narcotic relief. The wound would become yet another scar in Kat's collection but I solemnly made a vow to myself that it would be her last.

'Do you remember what happened?' the nurse said, gently.

'Yeah, it's coming back,' muttered Kat.

'We can arrange for some counselling, when you feel ready.'

Kat dismissed this idea with a shake of her head. 'What day is it?'

'Thursday,' the nurse said. Kat fixed her gaze on me, her face grave, eyes burning, and I knew exactly what she was thinking, what she wanted to know. 'We kept you sedated and let you rest for a while so that your body had a chance to heal,' the nurse continued, oblivious to the unspoken question, heavy in the air between us. As he tucked in Kat's covers, plumped up her pillow, and adjusted her drip we held our silence. 'The consultant will be along to see you shortly to answer any questions you might have but in the meantime if you need anything just press this red call button.'

'Well?' Kat said, as soon as we were alone.

I took her hand again. She looked exhausted, despite days of rest, but she was braced for bad news and intent on an answer. 'We're not siblings, Kat; not even half siblings: the index value was less than one, on both tests.'

She just stared at me at first, as the news sank in, and then her face crumpled, tears spilling from her cheeks. 'Are you sure?' she croaked.

I nodded.

'If you're lying to me, Jamie.'

374

'It's true, Kat, I promise. I wouldn't lie to you. You're going to be OK – *we* are going to be OK.'

I handed her a tissue and she wiped her nose, her head sinking back into the pillows and her eyes closing as her strength waned.

'Kat? Are you all right? Can I get you anything?' She didn't reply straight away and I wondered if she'd fallen asleep again.

'Kiss me,' she whispered.

Her gentle command warmed me from head to toe and as I leaned in she smiled, her eyes shimmering with a familiar green light. Pressing my mouth to hers was like coming home. The sweet taste of Kat's lips spread through my body like honey, soothing away ten long days and nights of tension and fear, healing the aching sense of loss, and bringing me back to life.

To catch my breath I drew back slightly and she sighed, a contented sound, her cheeks flushed, as she slipped back into sleep.

'Rest, Kat; we have all the time in the world.'

The End

The
Cornish
Hotel
by the Sea

Karen King

Escape to Cornwall with this
perfect summer read...

For more information about
Grace Lowrie

and other **Accent Press** titles

please visit

www.accentpress.co.uk